**"It's a risk, and it might be hard for you, but you are the only person I trust there. If they hurt you, they'll get the war Istam wants. They'll get that and more, I promise you."**

Touraine closed her eyes against the warmth that threatened to overwhelm her. It hadn't even occurred to her that she'd be in physical danger. She worried more that she would like it too much. Already, she missed Balladaire on an animal level—a homesickness for meat and the flavors of Balladairan herbs. For the autumn chill as the leaves turned, and the first snow. She didn't want to want them, but she did. And she was afraid that if she left, all of the comfort she'd built here in Qazāl would be stripped away. Even her fluency in Shālan—how quickly would she forget the language this time?

What else would she lose?

Touraine wasn't stupid. Balladaire never gave anything without taking something away.

She couldn't say any of that to Jaghotai. To her mother. Their relationship, their trust, was too new. And a part of her, a legacy of Cantic and the Balladairan instructors who had raised her, that part of her wanted to do as she was asked. To do what was needed.

She heard the heavy weight of her mother's weariness as she stood. Then Touraine felt that weight on her shoulder. A squeeze. "Think on it for me."

Touraine shrugged out of the half embrace. "Yes, sir."

Praise for

# *THE UNBROKEN*

"C. L. Clark gives us an unflinching story of colonialism and revolution and the people caught between. *The Unbroken* grabs you by the collar, breaks your heart over its knee, and mends it. An astonishing debut."

—Andrea Stewart, author of
*The Bone Shard Daughter*

"Rife with political, familial, and romantic tension, *The Unbroken* is a riveting epic fantasy about a city on the knife's edge of rebellion, a tangle of alliances, and a desperate search for magic and hope."

—K. A. Doore, author of *The Perfect Assassin*

"Get ready to fall in love with Touraine and Luca in one of the best fantasy debuts I have ever read!"

—Matt Wallace, Hugo Award winner and author of
the Savage Rebellion series

"A bold and exciting work that helps steer the evolution of the genre into the next decade."

—Marshall Ryan Maresca, author of
the Maradaine novels

"*The Unbroken* grabs you by the throat and doesn't let go. A perfect military fantasy: brutal, complex, human, and impossible to put down."

—Tasha Suri, author of *The Jasmine Throne*

"With its incisive look at the irreconcilable conflicts that colonialism wedges between desire, duty, individuality, and community, C. L. Clark's *The Unbroken* is a compelling and persuasive reimagining of both heroism and heroics as something inseparable from identity, perspective, and history. It's a deeply needed look at the myths we make, the stories we tell, and the bitterly binding ties of both blood and bondage."       —Evan Winter, author of *The Rage of Dragons*

"*The Unbroken* is a thrilling examination of love and loyalty under the crushing weight of empire. It's high adventure on a human scale—don't miss it."

—Alix E. Harrow, author of *The Ten Thousand Doors of January*

"C. L. Clark's epic fantasy debut reveals all the ugly, painful, deeply personal complexities of revolution against empire, captured in shimmering pointillist detail. I'm in awe!"

—Shelley Parker-Chan, author of *She Who Became the Sun*

"It doesn't take long to realize *The Unbroken* is something special. I'm going to need the second book ASAP."
—David Dalglish, author of the Shadowdance series

"This strong debut is filled with exciting action and worldbulding, intriguing characters dealing with themes of colonization, military conscription and indoctrination, and an explosion of feelings. Readers will be clamoring for more of Touraine and Luca before they finish."
—*Library Journal* (starred review)

"Clark's debut introduces a remarkable LGBTQ+ culture amid a story of colonial conquest, exploitation, prejudice, and brewing revolt in a land with a lost history of mystical powers.... Fans of epic military fantasy will eagerly await more from Clark."       —*Booklist*

"Clark conjures an elaborate fantasy world inspired by Northern Africa and delves into an international political conflict that draws on real histories of colonialism and conquest in their excellent debut.... Clark's precise, thorough worldbuilding allows this remarkable novel to dive deep into the intricate workings of colonialism, exposing how power structures are maintained through social conditioning and exploring the emotional toll of political conflict. The result is a captivating story that works both as high fantasy and skillful cultural commentary."

—*Publishers Weekly* (starred review)

# THE FAITHLESS

## By C. L. Clark

### MAGIC OF THE LOST

*The Unbroken*
*The Faithless*

# THE FAITHLESS

## MAGIC OF THE LOST: BOOK TWO

# C. L. CLARK

orbitbooks.net

Copyright © 2023 by Cherae Clark
Excerpt from *The Lost War* copyright © 2019 by King Lot Publishing Ltd.
Excerpt from *The Foxglove King* copyright © 2023 by Hannah Whitten

Cover design by Lauren Panepinto
Cover illustration by Tommy Arnold
Cover copyright © 2023 by Hachette Book Group, Inc.
Map by Tim Paul
Author photograph by Jovita McCleod

Orbit
Hachette Book Group
1290 Avenue of the Americas
New York, NY 10104
orbitbooks.net

First Edition: March 2023
Simultaneously published in Great Britain by Orbit

Orbit is an imprint of Hachette Book Group.
The Orbit name and logo are trademarks of Little, Brown Book Group Limited.

The publisher is not responsible for websites (or their content) that are not owned by the publisher.

The Hachette Speakers Bureau provides a wide range of authors for speaking events. To find out more, go to hachettespeakersbureau.com or email HachetteSpeakers@hbgusa.com.

Orbit books may be purchased in bulk for business, educational, or promotional use. For information, please contact your local bookseller or the Hachette Book Group Special Markets Department at special.markets@hbgusa.com.

Library of Congress Cataloging-in-Publication Data
Names: Clark, C. L. (Cherae L.), author.
Title: The faithless / C.L. Clark.
Description: First edition. | New York, NY : Orbit, 2023. | Series: Magic of the lost ; book 2
Identifiers: LCCN 2022026622 | ISBN 9780316542760 (trade paperback) | ISBN 9780316542838 (ebook)
Subjects: LCGFT: Fantasy fiction. | Novels.
Classification: LCC PS3603.L356626 F35 2023 | DDC 813/.6—dc23/eng/20220609
LC record available at https://lccn.loc.gov/2022026622

ISBNs: 9780316542760 (trade paperback), 9780316542838 (ebook)

Printed in the United States of America

LSC-C

Printing 1, 2022

*To my 'armoury, S and Jess*

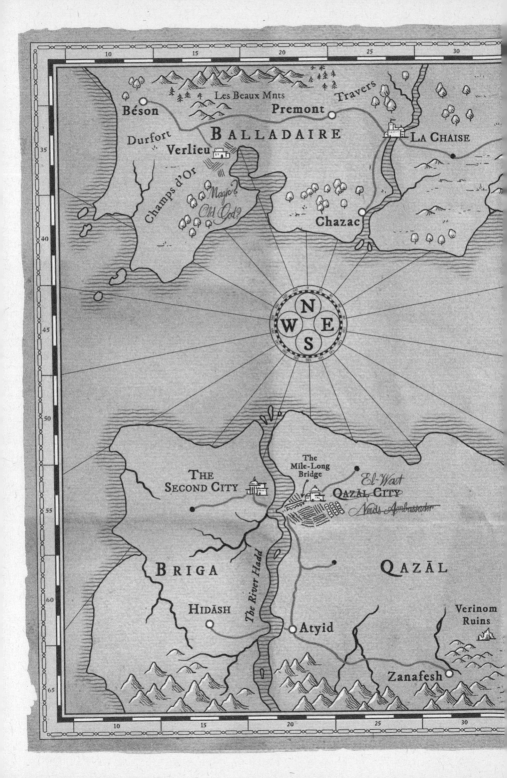

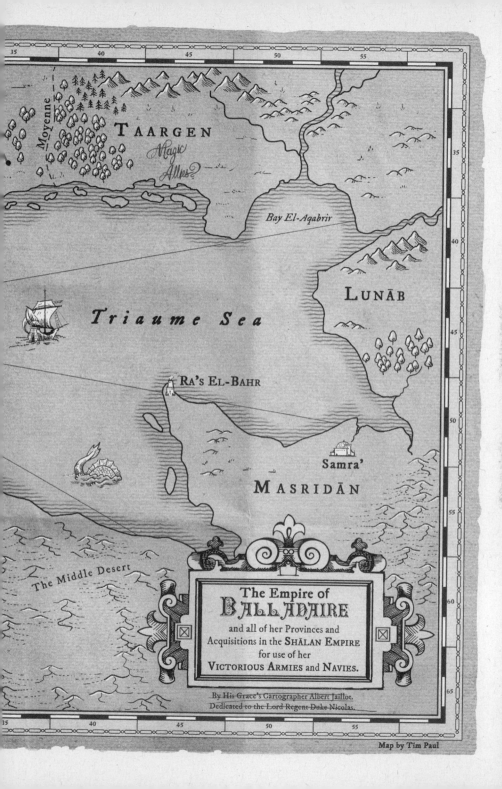

Moyenne

TAARGEN

Magic Allies?

Bay El-Aqabrir

LUNĀB

*Triaume Sea*

Ra's El-Bahr

Samra'

MASRIDĀN

The Middle Desert

### The Empire of
# BALLADAIRE
and all of her Provinces and
Acquisitions in the SHĀLAN EMPIRE
for use of her
VICTORIOUS ARMIES and NAVIES.

By His Grace's Cartographer Albert Jaillot.
Dedicated to the Lord Regent Duke Nicolas.

Map by Tim Paul

# PART 1
## THE BOARD

# CHAPTER 1

# ON MOURNING

It wasn't every day that Luca woke from nightmares of burning ships and the funeral pyres of her city, but it was most days.

It wasn't every day that Luca woke with a spasm of pain shooting through her right leg and up her spine, but that was also most days. She groaned and shifted until she was on her back. Her arm flopped limply against something warm with a fleshy slap.

It wasn't every day that Luca felt the poke of someone else in her bed, either. Not every day, and not all that often, and as she unstuck her body from the sweat of their closeness, she remembered why.

She reached groggily for the cup on the night table beside her bed. Her mouth came away full of warm, stale wine. She clamped her mouth tight rather than spray it across the room in surprise.

The figure beside her groaned at the sound of her gagging.

"Luca?"

"Ugh—looking for water."

She rolled back and placed a hand on Sabine's pale, solid waist. Little freckles dotted the skin around her shoulders in the gray dawn light.

Sabine snorted. "You'll need more than water, I should think."

"How do you mean?"

Sabine, marquise de Durfort, turned into Luca's touch. The back of her short dark hair stuck up at a ridiculous angle. She raised an

eyebrow that made her look even more scandalous. It belied the tenderness of Sabine's hand snaking around Luca's own ribs.

"The funeral?"

"Oh. That." As if it weren't the first thing on Luca's mind.

Sabine's hand drifted down to Luca's left thigh, and she curled into
Luca. "You'll do wonderfully." She kissed Luca's hip. "Your Highness."

"Of course I will."

Of course she would.


It also wasn't every day that Luca spoke at a funeral for hundreds of
citizens she had murdered.

Outside, the swelter of summer, which reminded her all too much
of Qazāl, had given way to autumn breezes. The trees in La Chaise's
greatest public courtyard were just beginning to turn colors, though
the branches still clung to the leaves desperately. Not unlike the way
Luca clutched her cane with nerves right now.

Inside the Grand Hall of the Palais La Chaise, however, the swelter
continued. Two fires burned low at either end of the hall, and sweaty
bodies crammed in a room that should have been big enough but felt
like a hat box. The audience's body odor was masked by expensive oils
and noxious perfumes. Along with the smoke from the fire and the
oily smell of the candles lining the walls, it was enough to dizzy and
nauseate.

Luca replaced the scowl on her mouth with something dignified
and somber.

In front of her, stirring and gossiping, her audience, like a single
creature, its voice a wave, its gaze crushing. Were they staring at Luca
or at the hulking, tarpaulin-covered statue on the dais behind her?

The monument memorializing the Balladairans killed in Qazāl's
Rain Rebellion.

Nobles from the five regions of Balladaire rustled in their silks and
jackets, the comtes and marquises and their smaller, regional lordlings.
The merchants rich enough to buy a place. Just as she had a year ago,

Luca felt smothered by the need to gain these people's approval. To pull them to her side. Unlike last time, however, she had little hope she could. She had just lost them an inordinate amount of money.

The captain of her guard, Guillaume Gillett, stood to her right, while the other two guards flanked her. All three of them stood utterly silent and still. Behind them, Duke Nicolas Ancier, her uncle and regent, cleared his throat brusquely.

*Stop wasting my time*, that sound said.

The great clock that hung on the north wall, above one of the fires, ticked merrily, its naked gears shifting, oblivious to the pressure mounting on Luca's shoulders.

Luca stepped forward to address her citizens.

"Balladaire."

The word came out as a squeak. The hall had been designed lovingly for acoustics, and still her voice was swallowed by the space. She cleared her throat, pushed down her nerves, and tried again.

"Citizens of Balladaire."

Silence rippled through the crowd as she caught their attention.

"It was my honor, last year, to oversee our interests at the farthest corners of our great empire while my uncle held us strong here, at home."

Luca tightened her stomach against the rising nausea. This was the first time she had spoken publicly about the fall of the colony.

"I ordered Balladairan soldiers to pull out of Qazāl for the safety of Balladaire and her people.

"I also witnessed the tragic treatment of the people there, people who counted on Balladaire to bring them civilization and its benefits. Instead, we brought them—"

A heavy hand landed on her shoulder. Her uncle glared down at her, under the guise of a tight-lipped smile. Her uncle, who still sat on her throne. Her uncle, who had given the order to sink the ships with the Balladairans on them before they could dock in Balladaire and spread the Qazāli plague through the heart of the empire.

Luca shrugged his arm off.

"Instead," she repeated, "we brought them pain. When I take my place upon the throne, I commit to forging a lasting peace between Qazāl and her people, with a new hope of magical exchange—"

Her uncle's fingers dug deep into her shoulder, and he pulled with just enough force to unbalance her. Luca stumbled back.

And then dear Uncle Nicolas took Luca's place in front of the crowd and began to talk about "this preventable tragedy" and the "importance of caution" when it came to the "safety of our great nation," as well as "rebuilding damaged trade relationships."

Luca seethed behind him.

When Nicolas finished, he stepped back. The crowd applauded, the sound deafening in the hall. At the duke's gesture instead of hers, the workmen beside the statue gingerly pulled the tarpaulin down.

The audience gasped. Even Luca gaped in awe, and she had commissioned the piece herself.

A proud ship of black stone, sails unfurled, crested on a plinth carved in the shape of a wave. The detail was precise down to the rings of the rigging. It was called the *Fire of the Sea*, the name of the biggest ship that Nicolas had set fire to. A brutal irony, not least because the ship itself represented not just those who had died but those who had sailed to Qazāl and other lands that eventually became the empire. A symbol of Balladairan greatness.

The ceremony ended and the nobles swarmed her uncle, bowing and simpering. Luca's spit soured in her mouth as she watched. Most of the dead Balladairans who'd been sunk in the sea were related to the court in La Chaise. She knew at exactly whose feet the court placed their losses.

Luca had hoped to have help from Qazāl, specifically in the form of a delegation to show how a new alliance would make up for what they'd lost. Most specifically, she'd hoped to have help from Qazāl in the form of a certain ex-soldier.

Luca didn't think overmuch about Touraine. After leaving Balladaire, Luca had written Touraine several letters across the span of several months. Having received almost no response, she stopped writing entirely until the final, more recent letter a month ago. An official letter inviting a Qazāli delegate to be part of negotiations for the official independence of Qazāl. If Luca had written another, smaller note within, asking Touraine to be that delegate, what of it? And what of it, that Touraine had not responded to say she was coming? Nothing.

"Your Highness." Ghislaine Bel-Jadot, comtesse des Champs d'Or, startled Luca out of her thoughts. The comtesse plucked a glass of dark wine from a passing servant and handed it to the princess with a slight bow. "You look thirsty." She smiled, beautiful as a dagger, and sipped from her own glass.

Ghislaine Bel-Jadot, one of the five members of the High Court, owner of the most expansive and expensive menagerie in the country. The woman's dark brown hair was framed with wings of white at the temples, and her skin was a dusky olive tone that some gossips attributed to ancestral liaisons with Shālans. All allegations denied, of course.

"Comtesse. My thanks." Luca drank warily, waiting for anger, but that didn't mean she didn't feel guilty.

"I blame myself, you know." Ghislaine stared at the stone ship. Her shoulders sagged and her eyes looked weary beyond reckoning.

"You can't have known, Your Grace."

The woman gave a small, tinkling laugh. Even in this shade of grief, the comtesse was enchanting. She pulled her shoulders back and tilted her head, an elegant gesture that bared a delicate neck.

"I should have kept Marie close. I can only hope that she wasn't ill before."

Luca nodded in sympathy. Ghislaine's daughter had made fun of Luca in a bookstore in Qazāl, but Luca wouldn't have wished the laughing pox on her. Or a death on a burning ship.

"I'm sorry for your loss, Your Grace. As I said, I'll do everything in my power to make sure our losses were not in vain—"

"You are well, however, and we should all be grateful for that. I do wonder if more experience would have brought my daughter home safely, but that can't be helped." She cleared her throat, shucking her grief as if she'd been given a stage cue.

"It's good of you to encourage Qazāli immigration. If we must lose the colony, this will at least make up for some of the losses."

"That's exactly what I was thinking." Luca smiled invitingly, tapping her wine glass with the tip of her fingernail. "If you have any ideas about how these new relationships could strengthen Balladaire, I'd love to hear them."

Ghislaine's sharp smile returned. A predator's smile, enticing. "As a matter of fact, I do. I was thinking of a development project. We have so much land in Champs d'Or. It could come cheaply for building a home if the crown subsidized it. An incentive to stay, to contribute to the empire."

"That would be very generous, Your Grace, though of course I expect nothing less." In the back of her mind, Luca tallied up the ways this would benefit Champs d'Or: Ghislaine would get Qazāli labor more easily, and the bulk of the cost would come out of the crown's coffers. "I'll consider it. Let's speak in more depth soon."

"I would like that. Until then, if you'll excuse me, Your Highness. I also need to speak with your uncle. A matter of my donation to his Droitist project. Will you be going to the opening?"

Luca covered her initial grimace with a sip of the wine. "The opening of the school?"

"Yes, of course." Ghislaine's dark eyes studied Luca carefully. Ever and always a performance, and everyone waiting for her to miss a step.

Luca smiled. "I wouldn't dream of missing it. Please, don't let me delay you."

As soon as Ghislaine was gone, Luca cast about for Gil. He appeared at her side out of nowhere.

"What did she want?" He furrowed his thick, graying eyebrows.

"To help the Qazāli, apparently," Luca murmured into her goblet as she finished the last of the wine. "Which means she wants to use them." She handed the cup off to the next passing servant. "Shall we leave? I would like to leave."

"Isn't this *your* memorial project?" Gil didn't quite chastise her, but something in the tone of his voice put Luca's defenses up.

"Not anymore. Look around," she grumbled. Pockets of nobles gathered and talking among themselves, elbowing to get to her uncle, and not one of them there for her. It reminded her just how tenuous—less than tenuous—her grasp on the throne was.

As Luca said that, however, Sabine de Durfort swaggered over to them, her left hand on the sword hilt at her hip. She gave Gil a salute so crisp it was a joke. "Sir!" Then she bowed low over Luca's hand and kissed her knuckles like a chevalier in the stories. Her lips lingered on Luca's skin, and she smirked.

Luca raised an eyebrow. It was hard to be cross with someone as ridiculous as Sabine.

"Shall I come by this evening then?" Her jaunty smile faltered just a hair as Luca shook her head.

"No. Not today. Not—I just—I don't want—" Luca clamped her teeth together so that she could properly filter her words without the rush of her mental chaos slipping out.

Sabine's expression cooled as she saw something over Luca's shoulder. "Don't look now, but your friend from the south is coming this way."

Luca's heart leapt in her chest. Touraine, so soon? She turned casually, however, and disappointment made her feel heavy and foolish at the same time.

"Bastien!" Luca said, forcing herself into joy she almost felt. It had been a long time since she had seen the new comte de Beau-Sang.

"Your Highness." He smiled at her and bowed. He looked marginally more comfortable in the Balladairan court than he had been the last time Luca had seen him.

He sketched a slightly shallower bow to Sabine. "Your Grace. Am I interrupting something?" His smile was charming, unassuming, and he really did look like he would leave if Luca said yes.

Luca had the manners not to. Sabine, however, did not. "Yes," the marquise said, pursing her lips.

Luca arched an eyebrow up at the other woman and put a hand out against Sabine to hold her back. "It's all right, Bastien. You're welcome to join us."

With an annoyed noise in her throat, Sabine said, "We were just speculating on what we think the Longest Night Masquerade fashions will be this year."

Bastien blinked, startled and a little confused. "So early? It's a couple of months away, yet, isn't it?"

He peered at the milling nobles as if he could divine what the next fashions would be in the clothes people were wearing now. But the Longest Night fashions were unpredictable and came at the whims of tastemakers. Once, a brown diagonal slash of fabric had become all the rage when Sabine had been splashed by a muddy carriage. She hadn't had time to change, she'd said, striding into whatever function it was. She'd looked so dashing despite the mud-spattered trousers and jacket that the fashion stuck for a season.

"It's not important," Luca said. "How was your trip to Beau-Sang?"

Bastien looked askance at Sabine. "It was different than I expected, Your Highness. But fine. It was fine. Nothing that would interest Her Grace," he said stiffly, "but perhaps another time I could tell you about it, Your Highness. Balladairan history, you know, the things you and I researched together in Qazāl."

Luca inhaled sharply. "Sabine, could you give us a moment?"

The marquise's eyebrows lifted in surprise, but she bowed graciously. "Of course, Your Highness. My lord."

"What is it?" Luca asked, her pulse quickening. "What did you find?"

"Will you come with me to Champs d'Or?" he asked in a low murmur. His eyes were bright and eager behind his spectacles.

Luca leaned closer. "What for? Did you find something?"

"I think so. I won't know, though, unless—You were talking to Lady Bel-Jadot just now. About what?"

"Nothing important, why?"

"We should talk to her. I think she knows. If anyone would, she would." He stroked the blond strip above his lip as he considered the comtesse. The mustache was new.

"Why?" Luca said again, impatient now. "What does she know?"

"I think—and I can't be sure, I would actually like to speak with her tenants and the older farm families in the heart of the Champs—Luca, I think Balladaire's magic—it comes from the land."

"We already know that, though. You wrote it yourself."

"No, I discovered that we once kept a god. This is different. That god of harvests...I suspect that Balladairan magic manifests similarly."

Luca hissed him quiet, looking furtively about them, but everyone was still enamored with her uncle.

"We can't talk about this here. And if I'm honest, Bastien, I don't think this will come well from me. Can you talk to her? You're one of her people and—"

"And I have less to lose by asking members of the High Court about magic because I'm already an outsider." Bastien smiled ruefully. "Of course, Your Highness. Is there anything else I can do for you?"

"Bastien..."

The last time he had been in the city, they had been somewhat casual lovers. In Qazāl, he and his father had both separately urged her to consider taking him as her royal consort, and she'd been amenable at the time. It had seemed like a good alliance.

He took a deep breath and held up both of his hands, staving off the excuses Luca struggled to muster.

"No need, Luca, no need. Consider this a favor."

"Thank you."

# CHAPTER 2

# A SCHISM

W e will not let El-Wast govern all of Qazāl without the other cities having a say."

"We weren't—"

"And yet that's exactly what you have been doing up to this point."

Touraine wearily watched Qazāl's bickering leaders volley shot after verbal shot from side to side.

This war room had once belonged to the Balladairan Colonial Brigade. Touraine had been court-martialed here—the first time she was accused of betraying the empire, but not the last. Now she sat with the other traitors, the fledgling government of a newly independent nation. Well. Partially independent. Touraine shifted her hand to cover the letters she'd taken from the packet ship. One was addressed to the Qazāli Council. The other was addressed to her specifically.

The other members of the council from the Rain Rebellion remained: Malika sat across from them, her long black hair twisted up in a bun that told everyone she was simultaneously the most elegant person in the room and too exhausted to care. Beside Touraine sat Aranen, who, despite her best wishes, remained alive. Her golden eyes were dull, the bags beneath them dark.

At the head of the table sat the Jackal, Jaghotai, resting her head against the stump of the forearm Balladaire had taken from her. She closed her eyes and sighed.

"We've been busy putting our own city back together." The Jackal bared her teeth like her namesake at the latest three to grace the council table.

"And ignoring the rest of us."

Of the three strangers present, it was the gray-bearded man from southeastern Zanafesh who spoke this time. He pressed himself to standing, leaning over the table as if Jaghotai would be cowed by him. She only blinked blearily at him.

"We sent messengers, Basim," Jaghotai said through clenched teeth. "To be specific, we sent them during the rebellion when we needed aid, and this is the first you've deigned to respond. You're a little late if you want to start dictating orders."

"Enough."

Aranen's voice was quiet, listless, but she injected enough disappointment into her gaze as she looked from the new delegates to Jaghotai that Touraine could practically see everyone's hackles fall.

"Haven't we lost too much, all of us, to fight like this?"

The group's chagrin lasted for only a second.

"Some of us lost more than others," Jaghotai growled.

Even as Basim bristled, turning his shoulder to Aranen, one of the other delegates sniffed sharply. An older woman, thickly curved, tall for a Qazāli, with a heavy gold ring through her septum. She narrowed her eyes at Aranen—and for that matter, Touraine. Dina, she'd said her name was, from El-Tarīq just south of El-Wast.

"And some of us lost our way," Dina said.

Aranen jerked still, eyes wide and staring as if Dina had struck her.

Now that really was enough.

"Fuck off." Touraine pressed herself up to loom like Basim and almost upset a decanter of pale green olive oil in the process. It lurched, wobbled, and then came to a stop. "Don't you dare. You don't know a thing about what Aranen din Djasha sacrificed to free your cities." Touraine spoke slowly, trying to pronounce each Shālan word carefully.

"That's noble, coming from the empire's whore," Basim spat at her.

"You come in with them, abuse our magics, and then expect us to be grateful? You're no better than the empire you sailed in with."

"Why don't I invite them back, then, shall I?" Touraine growled. She didn't look down at the pale envelope addressed to her on the table.

The Jackal slapped her hand against the table and made everyone jump. "Shāl take your fucking eyes, shut up!" she roared. "All of you, shut up!

"You." Jaghotai glared at Touraine, her message clear: *Don't dig yourself into a hole I can't dig you out of.* Then Jaghotai turned to Basim and Dina. "If you want to negotiate anything with us, you will treat all members of the council with respect."

"You can't expect us to come to the table in good faith if you laud someone who has perverted Shāl's teaching." Dina pointed to Aranen with her lips.

"As if you could claim half of her faith—" Jaghotai started.

Aranen held out her hand to stop Jaghotai's defense. When she looked at Dina and Basim each in turn, and included Istam, the third of the new arrivals, for good measure, they each shivered under her golden gaze. To avoid Aranen, they looked to Touraine instead. Their spite rolled off them in waves. Aranen frightened them—what the priestess stood for frightened them, too, but Touraine didn't understand enough of Shāl or the odd schism between the Qazāli and Brigāni branches of the god's magic. Touraine, on the other hand— she was an empty page they could write their hatred and anger all over. Whatever Aranen had done to the magic, Touraine had done it, too, and she was an outsider, an easy target who hadn't used the killing magic to save anyone but herself. She tilted her chin up and took the brunt force of their fury head-on.

"I will not argue about the gifts Shāl gave us in our desperation," Aranen started. "I pray often to understand what I have done and how I'll proceed. However, I understand your fears."

"But—" Jaghotai interrupted, but Aranen continued over her.

"I did what I did to save my people, and I do not regret it." Then she stood, looking down at Touraine and the other council members. She inhaled deeply and closed her eyes as she exhaled. "However, in the interest of peace over all, I understand that you need me to step away." She raked her hand through the short, loose curls on her head. They were more gray than brown now.

"Aranen, you don't have to comfort these Shāl-damned scavengers."

"Peace, Jak. Peace."

Aranen closed the door behind her with the softest snick. Touraine wished she had that kind of poise.

She quirked an eyebrow at Jaghotai: *Should I go, too?* The Jackal gave a minute shake of her head, then slouched back in her seat.

"Are you happy now?" Jaghotai asked the delegates from the other cities.

Istam remained neutral, but Basim frowned. Dina turned her haughty gaze on Touraine.

"She stays," Jaghotai said sharply. "If you didn't want to deal with us, you shouldn't have come. Keep acting like festering asswipes, and we'll take our chances as a city-state." She gripped the arm of her chair tightly with her left hand, nails digging into the wood.

Jaghotai's words made Touraine sit up straighter. Stare down the strangers a little harder. It made her feel a little—just a little—less out of place.

Istam cleared her throat. She was the delegate from Atyid, a city straight south down the river at the border of the Southern Mountains.

"What are your plans for food?" she asked. "The Many-Legged have granted us fishing rights, but the drought has caused difficulties."

Malika Abdelnour, daughter of the premier seamstress of El-Wast and current master of logistics, took over. She plucked up a piece of paper from the stack in front of her and referred to it. "We're struggling. We sacrificed many of our goats and fowl for the rebellion, and the crops were eaten by birds."

Touraine winced inwardly. That had been part of Djasha and Niwai's plan—using the Many-Legged priest's affinity for animals to create a food shortage for the Balladairans. It had worked, but now the Qazāli were paying the price.

"We've divvied up the remains of the Balladairan stores, and we're doing our best to stretch it until the next crops come in, but there are no guarantees. With the possibility of future Balladairan aggression..." Malika looked from her papers to Touraine, her thick, arched eyebrows knit together in worry.

"Training is coming along," Touraine filled in. It wouldn't be honest to say it was coming along well, even a year later. "We just don't have the numbers. As we said before, we sacrificed a lot to get them to leave."

The youngest Qazāli recruits, who hadn't even reached their majorities, watched eagerly at the edge of the training fields Touraine and Pruett had staked out. They practically begged to join, but seeing their faces, some still round-cheeked with youth where hunger hadn't sharpened the edges—it made Touraine sick to her stomach and sick at heart. She couldn't do what Cantic had done to her. *But their childhoods have already been taken away. You think the slums were fun for them?*

"But the Balladairans won't come back." Touraine unclenched her fists and pressed her palms flat against the table. Thick Balladairan wood from Balladairan forests, the grain smooth and polished beneath the pads of her fingers. "Not for war."

Basim narrowed his eyes at her. "What makes you so sure?"

"Because." Touraine met his eyes. He pulled back warily, like a cobra. "I know them."

"Ha!" Basim gestured incredulously at her. "I'm sure you do. Jackal, you let this traitor train your fighters?"

"This 'traitor' has proven her worth and her loyalty a thousand and a thousand times more than you have. How will *you* make yourself useful?"

Basim's nostrils flared. He lowered his brow over his eyes. "We didn't feed our food to the crows, did we?" The wide sleeves of his dazzlingly blue robe billowed as he crossed his arms smugly.

His threat was clear: they had food in Zanafesh. El-Wast needed food.

Malika, Jaghotai, and Touraine shared a look. Touraine didn't have the finesse for this. She was a blunt instrument. Malika, on the other hand, had a way of softening people.

Malika straightened the papers before her and smiled up at Basim, who still attempted to loom. The smile tugged at the scar on her chin. "We would appreciate your aid, then."

Before she could continue, though, Istam pointed two fingers at Touraine. "You train the soldiers."

Touraine startled. "'Soldiers' is a bit strong, we don't—"

"If Balladaire comes back, you don't have what? Enough people? Enough weapons?"

"Enough people. The Balladairans left weapons, but what good are muskets without people to shoot them?" What was the woman getting at?

"If you had more fighters, do you think you could attack them?"

"What?" Touraine looked to Jaghotai in alarm, but the other woman just looked bewildered at Istam.

Istam clenched one fist and screwed it into her other palm. "You said it yourself. They've taken plenty from us. But we have fighters, we have weapons. We have our god. If we reach out to our sister nations, to other allies—we'd have more than a chance."

Touraine was already shaking her head. "That would be suicide. We've got a few guns, aye, but Balladaire has an empire full of career soldiers."

"You and your Sands are career soldiers. You've been training the cadre in El-Wast. Atyid will send more."

"They won't be anything but cannon fodder. And the other Shālan nations are still occupied, aren't they?" Touraine looked to Jaghotai and Malika for help. She didn't expect to see Malika's thoughtful expression. The elegant seamstress put a painted thumbnail against her lip.

"Actually, if we did enlist the Many-Legged and—I know you don't like the Taargens, but they're Balladaire's strongest enemy—"

"No. We're not working with the jackal-fucking Taargens," Touraine said, raising her voice.

"They've already sent invitations." Malika shuffled her papers and pulled out another one. "It's not unreasonable."

"See?" Istam said. "If we join forces, we have enough skilled fighters to help the Masridāni free themselves. From there, to Lunāb. A sovereign Shālan Empire—only let us call it a coalition or league, with no one above another. Together, with our allies, we could break the Balladairan Empire for good and all."

Touraine sat back, the wind thrown from her chest.

To end the Balladairan Empire. To topple it? To conquer it themselves? To parcel it out among Shālan, Many-Legged, and Taargen? It was a heady thought, headier than Qazāli liquor. It terrified her. Not least because it filled her with something like sorrow.

"I refuse to be a party to perverting Shāl's gifts for violence." Basim scowled down at Istam. "I thought we were just clear on this? What good is saving the Shālan Empire if we forget the tenets it was founded on?"

"Our ancestors built this empire through the unity of both, in case you have forgotten. In Atyid, our memories are not so short."

"No, just corrupted by the Brigāni witches you let succor in your city!"

The meeting devolved into shouting, the representatives from the other cities arguing while Malika tried to justify herself to Jaghotai. Half of it was blame for grievances Touraine was too distant from to understand. Her head throbbed. She would have hidden behind her hands if she weren't trying so hard to look as if she belonged here, as if she could take the strain of leadership with the rest of them.

She took a deep breath. What would Djasha have done? Or Cantic? The two women were not so different from each other. Ruthless. Single-minded. And yet, it was Cantic who'd slashed Djasha's throat open, ending Djasha's lifelong quest for vengeance.

*Oh, Shāl. Oh, sky above and earth below.* She flicked the corners of the envelopes before her with her finger, letting them catch and snap under her fingernail.

"Excuse me," she said, trying to cut through the noise. She knocked hard on the table, but the rap disappeared in the onslaught. "Council members!"

The letter had come weeks ago, but it had gotten lost in the shuffle of bickering, and Touraine had struggled over whether or not to bring it up again. It felt safer to pretend it didn't exist, as Touraine had pretended with Luca's first letters. This was a more formal invitation, though, to ratify the treaty and attend her birthday and coronation. The council had been waiting so long for word that even Touraine had begun to wonder if the princess had forgotten her promises. Apparently not. She hadn't forgotten any of them, even the ones that brought a flare of heat to Touraine's face. Another letter, this time from Niwai and the Many-Legged asking if Qazāl intended to attend, meant that Touraine could no longer avoid the decision.

She pounded on the table with her whole fist. "Hey! Would you all shut up for one second!"

Everyone turned to her, mouths in tight disapproving lines or half-open in mid-speech.

She jumped into the silence before someone else did.

"Fighting isn't the only option. It might not even be the best. We still need to answer the princess." Touraine held up the envelope from Luca and pulled out the letter. She tossed it to Jaghotai. There had been a second letter in the envelope, but that was private. Touraine had taken it out and stuffed it in her pocket. She would burn it later, or throw it into the river and let the ink bleed away. Eventually.

"She's ready to ratify the treaty," Jaghotai said softly. Her voice was thick. "Is she serious?"

"She wouldn't lie about this." Touraine shrugged, palms up. "If it's a chance for peace, proper peace, shouldn't we at least try it? We know they have food. In exchange for priests who can wield Shāl's healing magic—"

"I'm not giving them my priests," Dina snapped. "Their faith isn't coin for a few Wastiyīn to piss away with bad judgment."

Jaghotai's face was hard as a brick, but Malika winced. Another thing El-Wast was short of: priests whose faith in Shāl was strong enough—and their knowledge of human bodies great enough—to heal. The losses—from the death to the destruction of the temple—were enough for anyone to question the strength of their god. The things Touraine and Aranen had done against the Balladairans in the attack on the compound had been the stuff of legends, right enough. But for every person who treated Aranen like a savior, many more in the city looked at them like Basim and Dina did. Abominations. Perversions of the faith.

"We don't need priests, yet, but we need food and...They won't destroy what they think they can use." Touraine closed her eyes against another pain in her chest. She wasn't so sure she shouldn't agree with Istam and Malika.

Peace first. Everyone was capable of surprising.

"I'm not saying we shouldn't fight," Touraine said. "I have just as much reason as any of you to want that. But fighters or no, Qazāl cannot take another war. Not yet. Think of it as strategy if you like. Biding our time."

Gratefully, Touraine saw that Jaghotai was nodding along with her words.

"The mulāzim is right. Only an idiot starts a war without steady ground beneath them."

"Not only idiots. The desperate, too—" Istam started.

"And we're not desperate. We were when we started the rebellion. Right now, we have peace, however tentative. We hold."

"And why should we listen to you?" Istam asked.

The others nodded along with her.

The Jackal rolled her eyes. "Let's put it to a vote, then. Raise your hand if you'd like to go to war against the Balladairans. Priests, Taargens, Many-Legged. Drain our resources beyond their dregs. Eh?" Jaghotai encouraged them to raise their hand with a harsh jerk of her head.

Istam jabbed her hand stubbornly into the air. She was probably in her forties, but she wore her age like a younger woman. The set of her mouth was petulant. The only tip-off was a few streaks of silver in her long, dark braid and the fan of lines around her eyes and mouth. She didn't look like a warrior, but Touraine didn't assume. She'd thought the same thing about Malika once, and the seamstress's daughter had pinned Touraine to the wall with a pair of throwing daggers just for fun.

Basim folded his arms pointedly across his chest again, and Dina laced her fingers together on top of the table.

Malika gave Touraine an apologetic look before steeling her face. She raised her hand, too.

"I say no," Jaghotai grunted, "so there'll be no war, not yet. Secondly." She waved the parchment Touraine had given her through the air. "We'll need to give this some thought. But we're not going to get anywhere now. Go get some rest. The rest will be as Shāl wills."

In a parade of dissatisfied huffing and sniffing and grumbling, the council members filed out until only Jaghotai and Touraine remained.

"Well." Jaghotai laid her head against the back of the chair. She closed her eyes and rocked her head back and forth as if the motion were soothing her neck.

"Well," Touraine echoed.

"You really think your princess wants to make good on this?"

"She's not my princess."

"She is to everyone that counts. You brokered this deal."

"I broke a lot of deals."

Jaghotai snorted with a grimace. Touraine couldn't tell if that was a laugh or not.

"I'm sending you back."

Touraine's head snapped up.

"You made the deal, you keep the deal."

"What? No. Absolutely fucking not."

"Yes. You"—Jaghotai waved her hand at Touraine, encompassing her whole body—"can hold her to it."

Touraine frowned. "Use her feelings against her, you mean."

Jaghotai shrugged, but she didn't meet Touraine's eyes. "We already have citizens there, trying to live on the promises in that half treaty.

All Qazāli have a right to live and work and settle freely in Balladaire, blah blah. It all sounds too good to be true, and we need someone over there to make sure they're all right."

"I never told them to go over there."

"You as good as did. It's in the treaty. Besides. No one knows Balladaire like you."

"Malika went to a proper Balladairan school. She knows the etiquettes they're looking for."

"But she doesn't know the princess. Plus, she never wanted to please them like you did."

Touraine's objections sputtered to a halt in her throat. The edge in the Jackal's voice had diminished over the past year, but it was a reminder of sharp teeth over fragile necks. At odds with what Touraine had felt when Jaghotai came to her defense in front of the other delegates.

"That's not who I am anymore."

"I know. All the more reason to send you in."

"I'm not going. I have command of the Sands—the military *you* just said we need."

"Pruett can take over." Jaghotai had had a small soft spot for Pruett— very small, she was still a Sand after all—ever since she'd watched Pru shoot a chicken skull off a building at over a hundred paces.

How to explain that Touraine and Pruett were already struggling with the half-fledged militia as they were? She couldn't, not without sparking the very trouble for the Sands she meant to avoid.

She stared at the table in silence for a while. Jaghotai's eyes were a steady weight on her. Pressure and pressure and pressure.

"Did you ever think," Touraine said, throat thick, "that I might never want to go back?"

"It's a risk, and it might be hard for you, but you are the only person I trust there. If they hurt you, they'll get the war Istam wants. They'll get that and more, I promise you."

Touraine closed her eyes against the warmth that threatened to overwhelm her. It hadn't even occurred to her that she'd be in physical danger. She worried more that she would like it too much. Already, she missed Balladaire on an animal level—a homesickness for meat and the flavors of Balladairan herbs. For the autumn chill as the leaves turned, and the first snow. She didn't want to want them, but she did. And she was afraid that if she left, all of the comfort she'd built here in Qazāl would be stripped away. Even her fluency in Shālan—how quickly would she forget the language this time?

What else would she lose?

Touraine wasn't stupid. Balladaire never gave anything without taking something away.

She couldn't say any of that to Jaghotai. To her mother. Their relationship, their trust, was too new. And a part of her, a legacy of Cantic and the Balladairan instructors who had raised her, that part of her wanted to do as she was asked. To do what was needed.

She heard the heavy weight of her mother's weariness as she stood. Then Touraine felt that weight on her shoulder. A squeeze. "Think on it for me."

Touraine shrugged out of the half embrace. "Yes, sir."

# CHAPTER 3

# OLD FRIENDS

The air outside was warm and humid. The rains would come soon, and come and come until Touraine's skin was puckered and her feet muddy more often than they weren't. That meant months yet until good harvests came in to fill out the meager stores from the past year's weak one.

Qazāli strode through the compound, and though it wasn't as busy with organized chaos as it had been when it was full of Balladairan blackcoats, Touraine's shoulders itched at how similar it was. The barracks were filled with Qazāli now—fighters and those who needed a place to stay—and sometimes the latter led them to becoming the former. When you lived in proximity of those training for violence, it was hard not to join them. Aranen was rubbing off on her.

Today, the fighters—Touraine was probably never going to be able to call them soldiers—were working rifle drills. Pruett's swearing echoed from all the way on the other side of the barracks.

Touraine should have been over there with her. They should have been running Qazāl's army together. When Touraine was a lieutenant under Captain Rogan, that was all she wanted: to be in charge of her soldiers, to be able to take care of them in a way the Balladairan officers never would.

Now, though, she was the military's mouthpiece on the Qazāli Council, delivering reports and making plans, and she was far from the camaraderie of her soldiers.

She turned away from the noise of the training yard and headed toward the compound gate. She focused on the road. If Touraine's eyes strayed, it was all too easy to see—*there*. Between the administrative building and infirmary was an alley, and Djasha had died not ten paces away from it.

Touraine shuddered. *Sky-falling miracle Aranen can even step into this place.*

A few Qazāli flicked her lazy, mocking salutes in the Balladairan style. Others nodded curtly at her, acknowledging her new place on the council but not ready to forgive where she'd come from.

Still, she was *the mulāzim*. It was more an epithet than a rank, but her place was with the soldiers. Not running back to Balladaire at Luca's call or Jaghotai's say-so.

Touraine peeled off her path and left-faced toward the barracks, cutting between them and walking to the training fields.

Pruett stood there in a Qazāli-style vest, lean arms bare and crossed in front of her, one hand tucked beneath her armpit and the other hand at her mouth, where she chewed on a thumbnail. Touraine winced as Pruett tore the nail with her teeth and spat it onto the ground.

Pruett noticed Touraine and her wince and grunted in greeting before looking back out over the yard. "Out of jackal-fucking cigarettes," she explained. She spoke Balladairan, like they usually did when they were alone. "Should have thought about that before we sent all the assholes packing. Put that in the new trade deal, would you, council member?"

Touraine grunted back. "I'll see what we can do. How are the new recruits?"

The new recruits in session were just finishing up a rifle-loading drill. Touraine's fingers twitched at the muscle memory of it.

"Target practice in a second. Thinking about taking a special squad with good eyes if we have enough."

"For what?" Touraine raised an eyebrow suspiciously.

Pruett laughed dryly, and she side-eyed Touraine. "Don't get hot in your trousers, Mulāzim. No new uprisings."

"Nothing new from the scouts?"

Trouble would be excuse enough not to leave.

"Infantry! Form line!" Pruett yelled. Her face was thoughtful as the recruits scrambled from their loading exercises and into a battlefield line.

Pruett looked Touraine full on. "No news. Why? You gold stripes expecting something?" After a quick once-over, she added, "You look like shit. What is it? No, wait." She held up a finger.

Pruett surveyed the field, her storm-colored eyes steady and all-encompassing. Assessing. The recruits faced the target lines, stacks of barley hay covered in marked cloth.

Pruett raised her left arm, the arm that would have marked her an officer with solid or striped gold. In another life. If things had been different. Touraine watched the other woman count down silently, lips tracing the numbers.

Touraine should have been ready. She should have expected it. But when Pruett called the order and a score of muskets fired, Touraine's breath stopped. Her heart, too. She cringed in on herself, eyes shut tight, arms wrapped around her stomach.

It took a second for Touraine to register Pruett's arm on one shoulder, the other hand gripping Touraine's other arm firmly.

"Hey. Hey." Pruett snapped her fingers.

Touraine opened her eyes to see Pruett staring down into them.

"There we go. You're all right." Pruett's hand on her was careful.

"Yeah. Yeah, I am. Thanks." Touraine crossed her arms across her chest, and Pruett's touch fell awkwardly away.

"Not any better yet, then?" Pruett said softly.

"Don't really think a year wipes out kneeling on the ground while a firing squad lets loose on you," Touraine muttered.

"Fair enough. Sorry." Pruett dug the heel of her boot into the dirt. She made eye contact with one of the other Sands; Touraine couldn't tell who from this distance, but she suspected it was Noé. He'd become Pruett's second. Pruett flicked him the signal for exchange of command, and then gestured for Touraine to follow as she left the training yard.

They walked in silence, out of the compound and down the road toward the noisy little souq that had sprung up. Some things found a way to grow no matter what.

As they walked, Pruett didn't look Touraine in the eye. Pruett used to be better at this, better at the comfort—at least, better to Touraine.

"So. How's the council?" she asked. "What happened?"

It was easy to lower her voice below the chatter of the hawkers.

"The reps from the other cities all have some problem with us or one another. One is mad about the magic, one doesn't like Jaghotai in charge, and the other wants to go to war again now before we've got more than a half-cocked militia." Touraine shook her head. "Even Malika wants to fight. I don't get it."

Pruett shrugged and swiped an apple from a fruit stall, flashing the pips on her shoulder. They were Balladairan rank pins, but they still held weight: it would go on the "military's" tab.

"Because it's not your home the Balladairans fucked over."

Touraine glared over at her. "They also don't like us."

"Oh. I'm so surprised." Pruett crunched through the apple. Chewed and swallowed while waving the fruit carelessly. "I thought the Qazāli would love to have a few dozen military-trained traitors—no, double-traitors—or is it triple? I forget." Another bite, spraying juice.

"How are we supposed to earn their trust?"

"Can't. They either do or don't. I've got better things to do than bow and scrape for a few…" Pruett trailed off on whatever unflattering swear she'd invented. She spat an apple seed like a bullet across the dirt.

The Qazāli locals' reaction to the Sands had hit some of them hard. Even though some Sands had fought and died in the rebellion, many Qazāli had neither forgotten nor forgiven the role the Sands had played in the bazaar massacre.

While Pruett crunched through the core of her apple, Touraine paused for a sugar tart filled with sweet custard and brushed with honey. A Balladairan legacy. Bees flocked around it as if they recognized their stolen goods. The baker refused the quart-sovereign Touraine offered with a reverent bow.

Touraine's eyes were as recognizable as any lieutenant pins. The gold earned her scorn or adoration, but her anonymity was gone. She left the coin on the baker's table anylight and moved on.

"We've...also had word."

The way Pruett's back went stiff told Touraine Pruett knew exactly who from.

Pruett sucked her teeth. "Aha. That's why you've been acting so weird."

"I told Jaghotai no."

"No what?"

"No, I won't go back."

Pruett's eyebrows rose in shock, but at Touraine's clouded expression, her eyes narrowed. "But...?"

"She says I have the best understanding of both sides."

Pruett snorted. "Bearshit. She knows the princess is weak for you and no one else. We all saw the way she dropped on her knees for you that day."

The bitterness in her voice.

"Can't have made that much of an impression. She did leave me to die."

They locked eyes, straight-faced for one, two, three beats—and then they burst with laughter so loud the hawkers near them went quiet.

"Shh, shh," Touraine said, gesturing for quiet with the sticky tart. She waved an apology at everyone nearby and the two of them slunk away, like naughty children. For a moment, things felt like they used to. Then she remembered what had set them laughing in the first place.

Pruett did, too. They both sobered.

"You're always leaving us, Tour."

"I don't want this, Pruett. I swear under the sky above, I don't."

"I know, I know, but you have a *duty*."

"Tell Jaghotai you need me here, then, or—would you come with me?"

Pruett barked another laugh. "Fuck no. I may not like it here, but you'd have to drag me back there by the balls. Anylight. With you gone, someone's got to mind the army." She flicked her rank pins again. "Speaking of. Got to get back to the recruits. Listen to your mother." She winked, but there was a cruelness in it. "She's a smart woman. Enemy has a weakness. Get your head out of your ass and use it."

"Luca's not our enemy. She may not be a friend, but she's not our enemy."

Pruett blew Touraine a kiss. "Keep telling yourself that, darling."


Touraine procrastinated for a day before visiting Aranen in the tiny temple the priestess had taken to using for prayer and healing. It was nothing compared to the glory that was the Grand Temple, but Aranen had said, "Shāl does not care for temples; it is only us who gloat with our might and skill."

This temple was little more than a one-room cylindrical building, at odds with the square buildings of clay brick all around it. Incense wafted from a small window, but it had no spires, no marble, and no glass. Probably why it survived the Burning Night unscathed.

Almost unscathed. Char marks stained the outer wall where a wooden door might once have hung. Funny, the little things you could convince yourself to ignore.

"Aranen din?" Touraine called as she ducked through the swath of crimson fabric that was the new door. It took a moment for her eyes to adjust to the dark room.

Walking into the temple gave Touraine a cool sense of peace. An escape from the heat and the sun, she'd been telling herself. Over the past year, though, as she studied with Aranen, it felt more and more like sloughing something off.

"Here," Aranen said in Shālan. She spoke to Touraine almost exclusively in Shālan now, slowly when necessary. No grammar primers like there had been with Luca, just a year of conversations and corrections. Between Aranen's lessons and the swearing in the training yard, Touraine was pleased with her progress.

"Would you light a candle, please?" Aranen asked.

Touraine did, hands sure in the darkness at one of the small altars. She knew the shape of the room by heart.

When the flame kicked to life, Touraine saw Aranen sitting on a cushion with her legs crossed, leaning against the wall. Her eyes were red rimmed, and drying tracks lined her cheeks. The fingers of one hand traced the bone prayer beads looped double around the other wrist.

"How are you?" Touraine asked uselessly.

"Grateful. How are you? You missed your anatomy lesson yesterday." Aranen tilted her head to the stack of Shālan instruction books for physicians.

Touraine bared her teeth in a sheepish smile. "Would you believe me if I said I had a lot on my mind?"

Aranen snorted delicately and pushed herself upright. She ran a hand through her short, loose curls and then beckoned toward the books. "Bring them here, then."

Touraine brought the books, but said, "I still don't think I have the head for it today."

"All the better. You should be able to heal someone even when you don't have the head for it."

Touraine flinched at the mention of the magic, but she covered it up by twisting into a stretch before flopping onto her own cushion across from the priestess.

Aranen laid one of the books between them. It was an old book, bound in leather, the pages delicate and colored with age. The page Aranen opened to was an intricately drawn diagram of a human torso with various top layers removed: one without the skin and fat, baring the muscles; one without the muscles, baring the top layer of organs and bones; and another baring the heart and lungs.

It was fascinating to see the body like this. To have it all exposed, its failures and its miracles explained away as so many levers and pumps. The books were clean compared to how Touraine had seen the human body pulled apart on the battlefield. They made order out of the chaos of the body.

Aranen pointed. "What's this?" It was a coiled mass of flesh in the image's lower abdomen.

"The intestines," Touraine answered. "One for pissing, one for shitting."

One corner of Aranen's mouth twitched.

"Aranen," Touraine started, "I wanted to ask you something."

The wry disapproval on Aranen's face disappeared, replaced with a patient tenderness that made Touraine feel even more vulnerable. She didn't interrupt or prompt, though, just waited for Touraine to find the words, or the courage, on her own. Sometimes, Touraine wished she wouldn't, and that Aranen would just drag out whatever Touraine was afraid of.

"The executions are tomorrow," Touraine said. "Ironic, isn't it? I started my time here with an execution, and I'll end it with one, too."

Not to mention the executions punctuating the months in between.

"You sound upset by that."

"Should I not be?"

"You're a soldier. Death is your purview."

That halted the breath in Touraine's chest. When it came back to her, she shook her head. "It's a politician's. They set the objectives, the enemies. The closed rooms, the treaties—they sign the lives away. As a soldier..." Touraine flexed her hand into a fist, marveling at the shape of the knuckles, the lines of tendon and vein. "As a soldier, it's about the body."

Aranen cocked her head. "Then it seems like you're in an interesting position. You're a politician now, a soldier, and a healing priest. What do you make of that?"

Touraine stared at the diagrammed bodies until her eyes lost focus.

"I don't know how to balance it all," she whispered. "Isn't that one of the tenets? How do you balance it? I'm supposed to want peace, but I want Beau-Sang dead as much as Jaghotai does."

A shadowy look passed Aranen's face. "I also wouldn't mind letting his corpse rot in the open sun."

Touraine jerked up in surprise.

"What?" The other woman grimaced and shrugged one shoulder. "Perfection is not one of Shāl's tenets."

"Then it's okay?"

"Killing? Or executions? Or justice?" Aranen turned her hands up. "I can't answer that for you."

"Then what's the point of any of this?" Touraine waved her hand bitterly at the temple. The incense had burned out, and the scent was slowly mellowing.

Smiling ruefully, Aranen said, "I've been asking myself the same thing for a year." She gazed steadily around the room, settling on an altar there, a prayer cushion over there, the mat in the corner where she cared for the ill and injured. "Why any of it? I have to believe that Shāl would not have given us a gift he didn't mean us to use. It has rules and we were not meant to break them, but it is not blasphemy to kill. There is no peace without justice, after all."

"Unlike the leaders from El-Tarīq and Zanafesh. I thought Istam said something about hosting the Brigāni?"

"Yes. The Brigāni have been nomadic since Shāl's curse, but more of them settled in Atyid because El-Wast was full of more...purist Shālans. I'll admit to being one of them before. There's a reason I didn't let Djasha bring them up to fight with us." She pursed her lips in disapproval. Apparently, this belief wasn't so easily thrown out. "Istam might have Brigāni there who would use the killing magic to fight the Balladairans."

"Do you think we should trust Luca instead of fight, then? You know her as well as I do. We've both been in her jail." Then, in a quiet voice, Touraine asked, "Shouldn't we want to make her pay more than anyone else?"

"I do. And yet. I had a chance to kill her and I didn't. Think about why."

Touraine looked down at the book between them, uncomfortable. "We were in a bad position. They had soldiers, but you had magic and they were scared. You could have had your way with them."

"Then, after the mainlanders had gotten their wits about them, we would have been plunged into another war we couldn't hope to survive. We're still on that same precipice. Also, I do believe her."

"You trust her, then?"

"That is absolutely not what I said." Aranen lowered sharp eyebrows. "You shouldn't, either. But," she relented, "I do think she's our best chance at a peace that leaves Qazāl on its feet and not its knees. Which is why I'm coming with you."

"You—what?"

"To Balladaire. I'm coming with you. Jaghotai is not going to let you out of this, and she won't admit it out loud, but she's worried for you to go back alone."

"All the more reason for me *not* to go."

"It will also ease diplomatic matters here if you and I are gone for a little while. It will be easier for Jaghotai to smooth things over with the other cities." She looked troubled as she said it, though, as if she didn't believe her words.

"Dina and Basim."

"Mm. They won't come to any agreements while the 'abominations' are part of the council. We can do more good elsewhere, at least for a time."

Touraine's stomach twisted. She'd thought Aranen of all people would understand. Instead, the last line holding her to Qazāl was slipping out of her hands.

# CHAPTER 4

# BEASTS

There were times that Pruett didn't hate the desert.

Sunrise, for example, when the touch of night still chilled the air and she could stand on top of the city and watch the sun crest over the dunes.

This was not one of those times.

Pruett closed her eyes and inhaled, letting that stale smell of dust coat her lungs.

"Good morning," Noé said when Pruett met him at the compound gates. His perfect voice just the right amount of subdued for an execution day.

"Is it, though?" Pruett raised both of her eyebrows.

"A day for justice, anylight." Noé stared at the sky somberly. "That's good, isn't it?"

"To justice, then."

Pruett's body still went hot with anger every time she stepped into the compound. Every time she passed the spot where Rogan had held her hostage, with a gun pointed to her head so that Touraine would surrender. The spot where they'd opened fire on Touraine. Where her body jerked like some sick marionette as she fell. Where the princess cradled Touraine in her arms. That, in particular, was galling.

"You all right, Lieutenant?" Noé said softly beside her. He cast her a sidelong glance.

"Never better," Pruett muttered as they passed the new gallows. It was smaller and more functional than its predecessor, built from wood taken from the last.

"I hate this place, too," he murmured.

It was comforting, to have her feelings read back to her like that.

When Pruett and Noé arrived at the jail, Jaghotai and Touraine already stood outside. Touraine nodded in greeting, but her expression was subdued. Troubled. Time was, Pruett would've known exactly what was going on in that head just by the cant of the other woman's lips. Another thing Pruett had lost to this sky-falling place.

Touraine and her mother made quite a pair, standing side by side with their arms crossed over their chests. Touraine's mother was a few fingers shorter than Pruett, like Touraine, but stockier—thick torso, wide hips, powerful legs. Her right arm was cut short and twisted at the forearm, a legacy of her time working at Beau-Sang's quarry, but her arms were thick and muscular, and it was easy for Pruett to see where Touraine got her strength from. And her rotten temper. They both had the same heavy jaw, good for taking punches. Broad, muscled shoulders—good for throwing punches. Together, they looked like they could take on the world.

Jaghotai's creased face relaxed marginally. "Pruett. Good. The daughter here?"

Pruett stuck her hands in her pockets. "Haven't seen her. I'll bring him out, shall I?"

The Jackal grunted and took the key off her belt. She swung it on her finger, holding it away from Pruett. "Be careful with that bastard. He's..." She frowned and spat into the dry dirt.

Pruett plucked the jail keys off the other woman's finger. "Understood."

Touraine looked like she was going to say something, but whatever it was, she bit her tongue.

Pruett stomped into the cool walls of the jail thinking just how much was now in the Jackal's power. Even though representatives from the other cities in Qazāl were still present, they didn't have near the sway that Jaghotai had, and even Pruett could tell it was causing problems.

"Casimir LeRoche de Beau-Sang." Pruett stopped in front of his cell. "Good morning."

"It's today, is it?" Stripped of all his lacy finery and his titles and all but the most basic of foods, Lord Casimir looked somewhat diminished from the arrogant prick Pruett had seen dragged through the city on a rickshaw by poor Qazāli. Like most flaccid pricks. However, you wouldn't know it by the way the bastard talked down at Pruett through his nose. At some point, it had been broken. By whom, Pruett didn't rightly care, except that it was a good shot. No one had reset it and no one had healed it, so it was squashed and crooked and his breath whistled through one side. Only thing left of his cultured voice was the nasal whine.

He was pitiful. Unfortunately for him, Pruett was out of pity.

She expected him to fight or put up some resistance when she opened the door to put the iron cuffs on his wrists, but he held his hands out willingly. When she told him to move them behind his back, he did. She locked him in and led him out with a jab to the back.

"I know my daughter has put you all up to this," he said. "I know you won't intercede. However, I'm willing to wager what's left of my life that these so-called leaders of this so-called nation can't even run themselves yet."

Pruett said nothing.

"You're a Sand," he added, looking back at her over her shoulder. He turned back to his footing and added, "I can see it. You walk like you have some pride. You're better than the rest of them and you know it."

Her lip twitched.

"I don't know what you want to get out of baiting me," she said.

"I don't know what you expect to get out of scraping from one master to another." He sniffed as they stepped out into the sun where Jaghotai was waiting. In a mutter, he added, "Especially one as coarse as this."

Pruett shoved him forward, rough enough for him to trip and land face-first in the dirt. He squealed in pain as he landed on his broken nose, probably breaking it again.

Touraine raised an eyebrow at Pruett, and Pruett blinked innocently.

Jaghotai looked down at Beau-Sang, eyes narrowed and her lips parted, as if she wanted to say something down at his back. She rubbed her poorly healed stump with her hand and shined her teeth with her tongue. She drew back her heavy boot as if she were going to kick him, but only nudged him onto his back.

On his back, hands under his ass, he looked like nothing so intimidating as a nasty cockroach. He glared up at Jaghotai with his watery blue eyes. His basket-colored blond hair was overlong and dark with grease. He smelled like he'd been buried in the latrines, dug up, pissed on by a dozen cats in heat, then put back.

None of that stopped him from leering at the Jackal. "You uncivilized bitch."

Jaghotai sucked her teeth again, hand still cradling her forearm. She looked up at the sky and then around the stolen compound, as if considering. Or, judging by the slow, deep breaths she was taking, she was tamping down her anger.

"I remember you and that stupid boy. You should have let the rock take him. Then you'd be good for something, still. I wouldn't even let my overseers have their way with you."

Even Noé stilled at that. Touraine looked like she was one step away from doing whatever she had done to Rogan to Beau-Sang. The Jackal, though, looked down at him, and her lips spread in something that wasn't quite a smile, but definitely showed teeth. Then, like a flash, her boot shot out. It connected with Beau-Sang's chin with a loud crack, and his head slammed into the hard-packed dirt.

Pruett no longer wondered how Beau-Sang had come by his broken nose.

Noé helped the man to his feet, but he was too woozy to stand. Pruett grabbed his other arm. Before they dragged him away, Pruett met eyes with the Jackal and tipped an imaginary cap. There were some things you just understood.

They led him to the gallows, a small scaffold with its single noose. His daughter, Aliez, had come, dressed like a Qazāli from her sandals to the sand scarf wound around her head. The mask of the scarf was pulled down so that everyone, even Beau-Sang, could see the hatred on her face. The leaders from the other cities (Pruett couldn't keep them all straight) stood before the gallows, too. Waiting for justice.

Waiting for her to kill for them.

Before Pruett could drag Beau-Sang up the gallows stairs, Aliez strode up to him and spat in his face, so hard a fleck of it reached Pruett's own cheek. The slimy glob clung to the comte's ruddy face, sliding down his squashed nose. The young woman looked like she wanted to say something more, but in the end, she kept it to herself.

It was a quiet, unremarkable thing, the comte's death. No cry of defiance, like Aimée's hanging. No confusion, like the hanging that had started all of this mess a lifetime ago. He didn't even sputter for his life. Just the thunk of the wooden floor beneath him falling away and the crack of his neck under his own weight. Quick and quiet.

Pruett descended, and a few unranked soldiers pulled him down.

His swollen face was still smeared with his daughter's spit.

Touraine came up beside her.

"Is this all we're good for, Pru?" Touraine's voice was low and pained, for Pruett alone. "Are we just executioners?"

Pruett frowned and tried not to let her face show the sudden bitterness that reared up in her chest. She couldn't keep it out of her voice, though. "Obviously not *all* of us. But me? I think so."

Touraine looked sharply at her, her expression so wounded that Pruett couldn't take it.

"Just fucking go, Touraine. You have a chance to get out of here, to do something worth a runny shit. Stop moping about it like some tragic little hero."

Pruett turned from them all, Touraine's eyes burning into her back like the sky-falling sun above. She didn't look back. If she did, she'd have to reckon with the other emotion she'd seen warring in Touraine's face alongside the pain: fear. If she had to acknowledge it in the other woman's face, Pruett wouldn't be able to hide from the fear in her own heart.

# CHAPTER 5

# ON STRATEGY

A few days after Beau-Sang's execution, Touraine and Aranen loaded onto the ship that would take them back—take *Touraine* back—to Balladaire. It was a small ship, and in Qazāli style, with triangular sails instead of the square sheets of Balladaire's transport or navy ships.

Crocodile Harbor smelled wet and green. Touraine's feet squelched in stagnant puddles clogged with mold or river moss or seaweed. Overhead, noisy seabirds squawked their discontent. Around her, the dockhands bellowed back and forth as they loaded Touraine and Aranen's trunks, food and water for the journey, and nothing else. A very pointed gesture not to come with gifts or tribute. The entire council, including the newcomers from the other cities, had agreed on that—their first unanimous decision.

Touraine scanned the docks for Pruett, scrubbing her freshly shorn head anxiously, her stomach sinking. Pruett hadn't come to say goodbye. Touraine couldn't blame her, but still—she stood on her tiptoes, just in case she had missed—

"Mulāzim." Malika appeared in front of her, one thick, perfectly sculpted eyebrow raised.

"Malika. What did I do?" Touraine craned her neck away, eyeing the woman warily. Touraine wouldn't admit out loud that the seamstress's daughter intimidated her, but that didn't make it less true.

Malika tossed her head, and thick, dark waves of hair flipped behind her shoulder in a cloud of jasmine-scented oil. "I'm only here to see you off, don't worry."

Then she wrapped Touraine in a fierce hug that took Touraine by surprise in its suddenness, the lack of hesitation. Though Touraine could have considered the young fellow council member as something like a friend, it had felt a step too far. She sighed into the embrace, rubbing Malika's back.

When they slid apart, though, the other woman gripped Touraine's elbows and in the small space between them said in a low voice, "I know you're no good at politics, Mulāzim—"

Touraine squawked indignantly. "I'm on the council—"

"Hush. You're no good. Balladaire will be sniffing for weaknesses—"

"Luca wouldn't—"

Malika gave Touraine such a look of pity that Touraine clamped her mouth shut. "Shāl take my eyes, you innocent babe, why are they sending you? Let's just pretend for a moment that Luca's perfect—she's not the only piece on your little shataranj board. They will *all* be looking for ways to exploit our cracks." She cast a subtle glance to where Jaghotai and Aranen were saying their goodbyes and around to where a few Sands were waiting for Touraine. And behind Malika, looking suspiciously on, as if they didn't believe Touraine would really leave, the delegations from the other Qazāli cities. In an even lower voice, Malika added, "It's what they did before."

"See? Then why don't you go instead? I told Jaghotai that you'd—"

"No. She needs me here more than she'll admit aloud. Besides . . . we aren't the only ones with weaknesses to exploit." At this she raised both of her eyebrows at Touraine as she slid her hands up Touraine's bare arms and squeezed the thick muscle there.

First Jaghotai and Pruett, now Malika? Touraine set her jaw. "I don't want—"

"She didn't hesitate to use you. All is fair in the game of empires."

And with that, she kissed Touraine on either cheek. "Good luck." She left in a swish of jasmine and red fabric, holding her hems elegantly above the damp and dirt of the docks.

Stepping nimbly out of Malika's way despite his bearlike stature, Saïd approached with a smile and a packet wrapped in waxed paper.

"Mulāzim!" He dropped the packet in her hands and then crushed her and the parcel against his chest.

Touraine shrieked a very undignified giggle, unbecoming of the broody, golden-eyed mulāzim. Her feet were dangling in the air, but he didn't let her down until the whole line of her spine had popped.

"Shāl take you," Touraine grumbled when he returned her to the ground. As embarrassing as it was to be swung around like a toy, her back did feel amazing. She waved the parcel curiously. "More books?"

"More books, sister." He gave a self-satisfied smile, but his eyes were tender with something Touraine couldn't place—sorrow? Affection? "So you don't forget us this time, sah? So you come back."

Touraine couldn't tell if the reminder was supposed to be chastising or not. "Thank you, Saïd. I'll—try."

"Good," he rumbled. "That's all I ask. Now, let me find that priestess."

He left Touraine alone, and she ran her fingers along the wrapping of the package. *And what is going to keep me from forgetting?* More poetry? A history? The claws of premature homesickness gripped into her stomach.

She dropped the book to her side and craned around again for Pruett. She wouldn't not say goodbye, would she?

The next shape that came barreling toward her shouting her name—"Mulāzim! Mulāzim!"—was young. Ghadin, one of the older slum children, was all gangly energy and excitement, and she had a pack on her shoulder. Over the past year, she had shot up a few inches.

Touraine narrowed her eyes, looking immediately for the girl's grandmother. A stern woman, Imm Zami wouldn't let Ghadin do anything as stupid as—

"Ghadin, please tell me that's a gift for me in that pack."

"I am a gift to you." She smirked like someone who'd already gotten what they wanted.

Jaghotai and Imm Zami were coming along the pocked and muddy dock road, Jaghotai matching her steps to the older woman's.

"Jaghotai," Touraine said, drawing her mother's name out in warning. The Jackal's smile was only a hair less smug than Ghadin's.

"You'll need a page. It's unseemly for a diplomat to go without the proper assistance." Ghadin sniffed, speaking with an exaggerated Balladairan accent. "The Jackal agrees and my grandmother said I could."

"Did anyone think to ask me?" Touraine growled, looking at Jaghotai.

Touraine liked the kid. She liked the kid a lot. Too much to want to drag her into Balladaire. Not to mention, how was she supposed to keep track of her *and* Luca?

She stepped closer to Jaghotai and muttered, "I can't take care of her, Jak. I'll be busy."

"And she'll be there, watching. Helping. A body servant all the other nobles have."

Touraine narrowed her eyes at Ghadin, who was still grinning. "She's a troublemaker."

"She's clever. And whatever happens," Jaghotai said in a low voice, "we need to think about who comes after us. That's how we got as far as we have."

In a louder voice, she said, "Ghadin's one of our best young fighters." She pressed the stump of her forearm against the young woman's back with something so like pride that Touraine had to fight down a surprising spike of jealousy. "Keep up her training. And you"—she gave Ghadin a level look, and the girl sobered—"will obey the mulāzim and the priestess in all things."

Ghadin ducked her head. "Of course."

Touraine rolled her eyes. "Fine. Get on the Shāl-damned ship. Go on."

The girl whooped and sprinted up the gangway, her long, dark braid bouncing behind her. Touraine couldn't help but chuckle even as the anxious pit in the bottom of her stomach grew.

Imm Zami gripped Touraine's arm, pointed fingernails digging into the flesh. "Bring her back safe."

Touraine gritted her teeth against the pain and bowed. "I will, Imm Zami. I swear it."

The older woman's grip released just a tick. "She deserves to get out of here. She could be so much bigger than this city, than our little tent. Ever since my son died in the rebellion…"

Zami, Ghadin's uncle. He'd died that night, too. With Djasha and countless other sacrifices.

*Sacrifices must be made.* The bitter echo of Rogan, Touraine's shit of a Balladairan captain, made Touraine shudder.

Touraine patted the older woman's shoulder in a way she hoped was reassuring. "I won't let anything happen to her."

"Good. Or don't bother coming back. I'll string your guts out so far even Aranen din Djasha can't put you back together again."

Touraine waited for the laugh, the smile, anything to signify a joke, but Imm Zami just hiked up her robe, spat at Touraine's feet, and headed back up the road. Before she'd gotten too far, though, there came another shout, and Ghadin came careening off the boat to ambush her grandmother and say final goodbyes. Touraine turned to Jaghotai for their own farewell.

She clasped her mother's left forearm and felt the other woman's strength leach into her as she squeezed back with strong, work-gnarled fingers. Jaghotai glanced up at her freshly shorn hair, soldier-short again for the first time in over a year.

"I'll wait for your reports," the Jackal said.

Was Touraine only imagining the wariness in Jaghotai's gaze? The *don't come back a failure this time* warning in her grip?

She didn't get an answer, because that was when Pruett showed up, glaring sullenly from beneath her old Balladairan field cap.

"Give us a minute, Jackal?" Pruett growled.

Jaghotai's glance flicked to Pruett and then back to Touraine. She cocked her head and hissed in that *glad it's not me* way, then released Touraine's arm and whispered, "Good luck."

When they were alone, Pruett mostly looked everywhere but at Touraine's face. To their boots, she said, "You're going, then."

"I am, yeah." Touraine's answer was just as stiff.

To Touraine's hairline, Pruett said, "You cut your hair for them."

Touraine cleared her throat roughly. "Promise you'll be all right here? No new wars while I'm gone."

Pruett scoffed. "Wouldn't dream of it, Lieutenant. Ah, sky-falling fuck, come here."

Relief washed over Touraine as Pruett pulled her into a tight hug, the bill of Pruett's field cap knocking against her temple. Pruett smelled like gunpowder and her favorite mint-flavored smoke from the smoking cafés.

When they pulled away, Touraine sniffed hard and Pruett scrubbed at her eyes, as if Touraine hadn't felt the wetness when their cheeks were pressed together.

"The Jackal will keep you busy."

"And the princess will keep you busy." Pain passed over Pruett's face. "For sky's sake, please be careful with her."

"I—"

"I don't care. Just be careful. I love you."

The words had a different punch now that Touraine and Pruett were…what they were now. Instead of what they used to be. They hadn't said it in so long that Touraine fumbled the words as she said them back. "I love you. Be safe. Stay on Jak's good side and she'll look out for you."

"I know." Pruett backed away. "Get on that boat before they toss you in with the cargo."

"I'll be back," Touraine said.

"I know." Pruett returned Touraine's little wave.

When the ship pulled away from the docks, drawn by the tide, Touraine stood by the railing until the city she'd begun to think of as home wasn't even a speck in the distance. Ghadin bounced around the deck, terrorizing the captain and the sailors with questions. Aranen had escaped to her cabin. Touraine was alone.

Everyone's hopes rode heavy on her shoulders, and she already felt herself buckling.

And despite everything that had happened, the people she'd found in El-Wast had come out to remind her that some of them, at least, cared for her. A thorny, complicated sort of caring, but it was there nonetheless.

Aranen reappeared and rubbed a comforting hand across her back, and Touraine took a long, slow breath.

"And so, we go," the priestess said softly.

"And so, we go."


"Hello, my dear uncle."

Luca found Duke Nicolas Ancier in the King's Library, which he'd claimed for his own study when he took the regency. He sat in his usual position at their usual table, the échecs board already set up with gray-white granite and onyx pieces and cups of steaming tea beside it.

Luca's cousin, Tiro, sat at another table off to the side, writing. His feet dangled above the ground. She suspected that, at eleven years old, he would rather have been out riding instead of being locked in this stuffy room.

Tiro brightened when he saw her. "Luca!"

"Tiro!" She held out an arm, and he was halfway out of his seat to run for her when Nicolas barked his name.

"Roland!"

The boy froze. "Yes, Papa?"

"Are you finished?"

"Almost, Papa."

"Finish. A steady mind sees everything through to its final conclusion."

"Yes, Papa." Tiro deflated back into his seat, took up his pen, and continued to write with painstaking precision. For a long minute, the silence was broken only by his pen scratching against the parchment. Luca spent the minute glaring at Nicolas, while he hummed contentedly.

Finally, the boy stood and went to his father's side, handing him the marked parchment. "I'm finished, Papa. May I be excused?"

"Of course," Nicolas said, giving the boy a warm smile and an affectionate stroke across his head. "Say hello to your cousin on the way out."

"Yes, Papa." ·

The boy hugged Luca tightly, but the joy had seeped out of him. He barely met her eyes. She knew exactly how he felt. He pulled away quickly, and though she wanted to press him close again, she let him go. The door shut behind him, and then Luca and Nicolas were alone.

Luca took the empty seat behind the pale pieces today.

"Hello, my dear niece. How are you? You look tired."

"And you look cheerful." That was never a good sign, not for her.

"My son is clever, and I'm playing échecs with my favorite niece. Of course I'm cheerful." He gestured at the board for her to take the first move. "How are you?"

Luca rolled her eyes and carelessly placed a pawn. "I'm your only niece. All things considered, I'm doing well. Dealing with the matter of the Qazāli treaty."

Their échecs games had been a tradition since before her parents died of the Withering. It had started out as a daily diversion or lesson, and Luca had enjoyed the special time she spent with her uncle, who doted on her—or rather, who doted on her when she answered correctly or chose the right plays.

Now every time they played was a chance to size up the other's weakness, the other's preoccupations, their habits.

"The treaty? Ah, that sovereignty business." As if he had let the document that would reshape the empire slip his mind for a moment. "Is that really the way you'd like to go?" He moved one of his own infantry.

Luca moved again. Without a response, Nicolas filled the silence, as he usually did.

"They'll be coming here, then, to negotiate properly. Unless you're going to do it one line at a time by carrier pigeon?" He chuckled. Made his move. "Do they even have a ruler? Who's their king now? Or queen?" Nicolas looked sharply at Luca. "Did that soldier of yours have the stones to make a claim?"

"They rule by council," Luca said, eyes on the board. She moved one of her chevaliers.

"Even better. That means you'll need ten pigeons and it will take ten times as long to get anything done. There's a reason we rule with a single king." He moved a scholar, then tapped his king for emphasis.

"A queen has specialists and advisors, even spies. Who's to say a council cannot function in the same way?" Without looking up at her uncle, Luca gestured at the back row of pieces: the scholars, the chevaliers, the nobles' keeps, the king and queen together.

She thought of Djasha, the leader of the rebel council, her fierce ruthlessness, the coldness in her golden eyes. How Luca had admired that woman. She even grieved her now.

"As it happens, I have sent for an ambassador," Luca added. She glanced up at him, just in time to see his smile widen knowingly.

"Good. I'm looking forward to meeting the conscript worth losing a colony over."

Luca glared and took one of his foot soldiers with her chevalier, on the way to trapping his queen and his scholar only for him to counter by taking the chevalier.

Her uncle folded his hands across his large stomach deliberately. "Ruling means knowing when to sacrifice something inconsequential for the good of the empire."

"Exactly." Luca tapped her fingernails along the edge of the heavy stone playing board. "The longevity of the empire is greater than a single colony. The lives of the empire's people are greater than a single colony."

"That's naive, dear niece. How much did that colony impact the lives of our people? Their livelihoods?"

Livelihoods. Lord Casimir LeRoche de Beau-Sang had also been concerned with Balladairan livelihoods over Qazāli lives, and now he was dealing with Qazāli mercy—and knowing the Jackal, there wasn't much mercy to be had.

"When I'm queen, the people will see. With allies who have the power to heal, we can avoid another Withering or Black Ships. That will have a greater impact than one lord getting rich off Qazāli stone and spice."

Nicolas paused with his hand on one of his own pieces. "It will be difficult, however, for a nation to accept a queen responsible for mishandling a situation so badly that it escalated to the burning of those ships." He placed it on a new square, close, too close to the imaginary defensive line Luca had created.

She countered with her own piece. " 'Even the best plans rarely survive—' "

" 'Contact with the enemy.' Don't quote the books back at me, I gave them to you." Another exchange, Luca's queen taken by Nicolas's chevalier. Her king was suddenly very alone on the whole wide board. "It will be more difficult still for the people to accept a queen who is so enthralled by the barbaric cultures of the south. This infatuation sounds as if you believe in this god and its magic."

Luca's face burned, but she tightened her mouth in resolve. His patronizing smile spread. Let him think he had her beaten, then. She had time.

Gently, so gently, Luca tilted her king to the board in surrender.


The journey across the sea felt like it would never end. It felt like it would end too soon.

In the darkness, against her will, Touraine's mind went to Luca and the ways they had almost been. In the darkness, Touraine stopped telling herself to stop thinking about her.

It was a raw wound, not near as healed as it should have been, and Touraine hated herself for picking the scab of it, for longing to see the blood.

There, against the darkness of Touraine's closed eyes, was Luca. Luca at the desk, ink on her fingers as she took notes. Luca, curled on the chaise reading. Luca, humming as she beat Touraine, or Gil, or even Lanquette—Guérin didn't play—at échecs. The straight lines of her, practicing with her rapier. The spark of her blond hair in Qazāl's dazzling sunlight, blowing across her face in the dry wind. Her eyes, deep blue green, constantly curious and probing.

The look on her face when she visited Touraine in jail before Touraine's execution after the failed attack on the compound—as she said she couldn't, wouldn't free the Sands, the rebels, Qazāl. Furious and tear-streaked and all the more heartbreaking because Touraine could see her determination to do what she thought was right. And any other day, any other goal, Touraine would have loved her for it. Instead—

*Stop.* Touraine opened her eyes and rolled onto her side, as if she could banish the memories that way. But part of her wanted to hold them close, because Malika was right: Touraine couldn't let herself forget what Luca was capable of.

# CHAPTER 6

# ON CHARITY

Nicolas's Droitist school was pristine, and Luca hated it for that fact alone.

There was also Nicolas himself, who ushered Luca and the other courtiers onto the grounds with smug pride. He smiled at her discomfort, swanning about in a fur-lined cloak, thrown open as if the chill didn't bother him.

She hated that, too.

The school was a square mix of wood and stone, squatting in a cleared field surrounded on three sides by trees. A wooden fence surrounded the place, rising up to the height of a tall man, and sharpened to points at the top. It looked more like the fortification of a small town than a fence for a school. The hairs on Luca's neck prickled. Touraine had talked often about feeling trapped by Balladaire, and this fence embodied that too closely.

"The fence protects them from the wolves." Nicolas gestured to the woods. It didn't help that his smile was so wolflike.

A large party made mostly of sycophantic minor nobility had gathered to see the duke's project. The comte de Travers had begged off, citing business in the city surrounds, but Sabine was there. The marquise looked around with bland curiosity that bordered on disinterest. Ghislaine des Champs d'Or was also in attendance with a small retinue.

What Luca hated the most as the schoolmistress showed them the facilities, pointing here and there with a thin wooden rod, was that the school actually seemed sound. In the main room of the schoolhouse, the children sat at the long tables, copying quietly from their Balladairan grammar books. They were round-cheeked and looked well nourished, except for a few of them with the shortest hair. The newest ones. Time, Luca assumed, would fill them out.

"How charming," Ghislaine said with a beatific smile.

The schoolmistress was a tall, shrewd woman with pinched lips and round spectacles. She slapped the thin wooden rod against her palm once, and the children stood at their desks immediately.

"Yes, Madame Tomier!" they said.

"We have guests," Madame Tomier, the schoolmistress, said.

The children greeted Luca and the others in eerie unison, bowing.

Madame Tomier called out to one of the older children: "Cécile! Come greet the court. It is a great honor."

A young girl stepped back from one of the long tables. Like most of the children, she wore a gray jacket over a sack-like gray dress. The jacket was overlarge, with room for the girl to grow into it. Her short-cropped hair was just beginning to curl.

The girl—Cécile—bowed first to Luca. "Hello, Your Highness. Your Grace." She greeted them all by title, with the proper honorifics; her Balladairan was as pristine as the school. When she was finished, she looked at her flat black cloth shoes.

The schoolmistress dismissed her with a nod. "Thank you, Cécile."

"Thank you, madame. It is an honor," Cécile added to the rest of them before returning to her place.

Luca did not want to be impressed with the girl, with the progress she'd made. She couldn't deny, though, that Cécile very likely would integrate into Balladaire with time. She could pick up an apprenticeship, learn a trade, open her own shop. All of the children could. That was what she'd promised Touraine, and it was Nicolas following through on that promise.

Then Madame Tomier snapped the rod against her palm again.

More than one of the children flinched minutely, and as the school-mistress dismissed them and they filed from the room in an orderly line, Luca felt the roll of revulsion in her stomach.

"Charming indeed," Ghislaine mused with a dainty finger against her painted lips.

"Tell me, madame," Luca said sharply. "What happens to the students who don't learn so well as that girl?"

The schoolmistress's lips pursed even tighter. "We work with them until they do learn, Your Highness." The awful certainty of her terrible efficiency.

"I see." Luca caught the look Ghislaine shared with Nicolas and the slight nod she gave him, but Luca was still missing something.

The schoolmistress said, "Please, follow me this way, Your Graces, Your Highness."

They followed her outside through the back, the same way the children had gone, passing two closed rooms and what Luca imagined were the kitchens.

Outside, the children were lined up in neat, military-like rows.

"Do you wish to examine them?" The schoolmistress looked at the duke before belatedly including Luca.

"No," the duke said. "I'm pleased with what you've accomplished so far. I look forward to further results."

"Thank you, Your Grace." Madame Tomier bowed, accepting the dismissal.

"Wait," Luca said, stopping her. "I'm not finished." She had to know, she had to make sure. She had to settle the unease crawling up her back. It felt like she could see the edges of a scare-specter, but the full shape wouldn't come to her unless she looked at the right moment, in the right place.

She walked over to one of the newer children, hair dark bristles against the scalp and cheekbones still sharp. The child's large hazel eyes were alert. Luca bent as low as she could to level with the child.

"Will you lift your sleeve for me?" Luca asked softly. She mimed the process with her own coat, baring her pale arm to the chill air.

Wordlessly, the child complied. Pale brown, unmarked skin on each arm, at least up to the elbows. The knuckles hadn't been bruised by the rod, either.

"Thank you," Luca said, straightening.

"You are welcome, Your Highness." The child's accent still rang with the music of Qazāl. That music would be snuffed out soon, like a songbird's snapped neck.

Luca sighed inwardly as she returned to the rest of the gathered nobles who watched her. Ghislaine, all false brightness. Sabine—was her curiosity a little sharper than before?

"Are you satisfied?" Nicolas asked.

"I have nothing further at the moment," Luca said.

Though Luca knew the child could be marked in other places hidden by clothing, the child had seemed remarkably whole. She tried to find something wrong that she could remark upon, but she couldn't. She had never seen a Tailleurist school, but could it be much different than this? Perhaps her uncle had changed his methods. The children had food and clothes, they were clean and learning. Other than the fence and the sharp schoolmistress whose manner left something to be desired, it didn't look anything like what Luca had read Droitism to be: cruel, restrictive, undignified.

Though Touraine had never shared the full details of her life as a young conscript, Luca had gleaned bits and pieces. Whatever Touraine had gone through had been worse.

As much as Luca hated to say it, it seemed like her uncle was doing something right.


Instead of returning to the palace with the others, Luca took her carriage to check on her concerns in the city. While Uncle Nicolas's school was isolated in the forests east of La Chaise proper, the carriage now took them deep into the southern heart of the city, across the bridge to La Gouttière—what everyone, even the nobles, called the western bank of the river farthest from the palace. It was easy to see how it got its name.

The commerce that sprang up on that bank was questionable and the public houses maintained with less diligence than the way-houses on the Queen's Bank. The western side of the city took its cue from La Gouttière—rickety tenements pressed together, holding each other up and sheltering sky above knew how many people inside.

Luca looked up at the sky from the carriage window. The sky was all over gray, the clouds thick and dark. It matched her mood too well. She shut her eyes tight against a wave of despair.

Gil gave her knee a reassuring squeeze. "You're doing the right things. One step at a time. It's enough."

Luca laughed, a shrill, bitter exhalation. "It's not." This city was broken, but she would fix it. Soon. Until then, Gil was right. She was doing what she could. Here, now.

They arrived in the morass of La Gouttière, and Luca's boots squelched unpleasantly. She didn't look down. It reminded her of the Puddle District in Qazāl.

Since she'd returned to Balladaire, she'd grown more familiar with the puddles in her own city. She squelched to the door of the one building that looked like it would actually stand up to a stiff wind. A wet drop hit Luca's nose, and she hurried into the Hand of the Queen.

Luca founded the Hand of the Queen to serve the district, with a special emphasis on seeking out the newly arrived Qazāli and giving them a place to find food and a few nights' lodging, until they could find work and a new footing. Its endowment came from Luca's own allowances. Imagine what she could do when the throne was hers!

The proprietor of the place, a middle-aged Balladairan woman named Madame Béryl, greeted Luca immediately.

"Your Highness," Madame Béryl said with a curtsy, "we weren't expecting you today. How can we serve you?"

"I…" Luca's unease from the school had filled her with the need to see her own work for the Qazāli reap benefits like her uncle's. With that revelation, she felt foolish. "I only wanted to check in and make sure you had everything you need?"

"Of course, Your Highness. We've been able to feed many of the"—she coughed delicately—"newcomers." The older woman pressed her hands against the front of her dress nervously.

"And?" Luca nudged. "What else?"

"There are—there have been—some disturbances."

"Has someone been bothering you?"

"Not me, Your Highness, but people—Qazāli—have come in hurt. I bandage them up and try to find them safer places to stay, but the city isn't as welcoming as one might hope."

Sky above. This was the last thing she needed. "Thank you for taking care of them. I'll see if there's anything I can do. I did speak with the comtesse des Champs d'Or. She mentioned positions in the comté. That would help move the Qazāli somewhere less..." Luca waved her hand. Less what?

"Oh yes!" The older woman brightened and bustled toward a small office. Luca followed as the woman spoke. "We received a letter from her. Her Grace has been most generous."

Madame Béryl gave Luca a piece of parchment from a drawer. Luca's eyes went immediately to the seal. It was Ghislaine's. A chill ran down her spine. No one was supposed to know about Madame Béryl and the Hand of the Queen. She'd kept it secret so that no one would try to sabotage it—or tell her uncle so that *he* could sabotage it.

The letter itself was innocuous, encouraging Madame Béryl to send Qazāli needing work to a man in the Place de Fer, one of the labor districts.

"Lovely." Luca smiled tightly as she refolded the letter and gave it back. Yet another reason for Luca to meet with Ghislaine for a private conversation.

Madame Béryl beamed. "It's so good that we can help them. Is there anything else?"

Luca shook her head, her false smile still in place. "Do let me know if anything changes. And if you need anything, contact me first, not the comtesse."

The rain started as they rode back to the palace. Luca stared blankly out the window, lulled by the rhythm of the water of the cabin roof, until Gil tapped the toe of her boot with his.

"What are you chewing on over there?" He said it with concern, though his face was as grim as ever.

Luca released her bottom lip from her teeth. "I was wondering what I would do if... he wins."

"Nicolas? If he wins what?"

Luca gestured widely at the city as they passed through it. "Everything. Balladaire. The throne. Qazāl."

"What happens if he wins, or how to keep him from winning?"

Luca smiled at the wryness in her guard captain's voice. "Both?"

"I can't tell you what happens if he wins—that's up to you, I think. And to him. I suppose if you just surrender, there might be less blood than there usually is with these types of affairs."

"You mean coups?"

"Mm-hmm. How much bloodshed typically depends on how much resistance. Bloodless—" Gil made a small pinching gesture with his finger and thumb, and then made a bigger gap with both hands. "Bloody. Very bloody. Civil war."

A nauseating fear seized Luca's stomach. "You think it'll truly come to civil war?"

When he spoke again, the wryness was gone. Luca was sitting not with the second father who had raised her but with the king's champion.

"It's hard to say. If he tries for a Trial of Competence—"

"He can't," Luca interrupted. "He'll need a unanimous vote from the High Court, and he won't get one." That much, at least, she was sure of.

Gil stroked his mustache thoughtfully. "If he doesn't... Right now, Nicolas has the field set up in his favor." He leaned forward and held up a finger, but he said nothing, waiting for Luca to fill in the silence.

"He has the nobles?"

Gil nodded and held up another finger.

"He... is already on the throne."

"Mm. It's easier to defend a strong position than attack."

"I know. And I have nothing to attack him with."

"That depends," Gil said gruffly. He closed his hands back into fists and rested them on his knees as he leaned back in his seat. For a silent moment, he looked out the carriage window, watching the city pass.

"Depends on what?" Luca said, impatient.

"How much is the crown worth to you?"

Luca bristled. "It's my father's crown. It's my place. It's worth everything."

He looked her in the eye. Luca read the weary tension in his shoulders. "How much blood?"

"I don't—it's my place, Gil. I'm what Balladaire needs. I'll do what it takes."

Gil nodded, his body slackening into the curve of the seat as if he'd expected that answer. "Then you'll need things he doesn't have."

"You mean the magic," Luca said quickly, eagerly. "Balladairan magic. I'm close—I spoke with Bastien, he's going to—"

"I mean friends, Luca. Not magic. Friends. Allies Nicolas doesn't have."

Luca sagged. "You said it yourself. He has the nobles. I have Sabine and Bastien and that's all."

"They're a good start. They are. But believe it or not, Luca, Balladairan nobles aren't the only people in the world."

"I know they're not," Luca groaned. "There are the Qazāli, too, and Touraine—" She closed her eyes and exhaled slowly through her nose. "Maybe it won't come to it. Nicolas isn't a warrior. He's a scholar, like me."

The word *war* was hard to say now that Gil had made it so real in the air between them. Trapped in the box of the carriage, it felt too large, as if it were taking up all the air and leaving it harder to breathe. "The Qazāli delegation should be here soon. We can ask for their support then." Any day now. Not that she had been counting the days. She added quickly, "And the delegations from the Many-Legged and the Taargens."

Her head was full when they returned to the palace. No sooner had she arrived at the stable, though, did a sweaty messenger scurry up to them and bow.

"Your Highness! You asked to be notified immediately? The ambassador from Qazāl has arrived."

Luca jumped back into the carriage, with a shout to the driver.

She prayed for Touraine.

# CHAPTER 7

# A WOUND

The Qazāli ambassador's ship arrived to port under rain and thunder. Touraine's stomach churned like the river below them. She wondered again if she'd made a drastic mistake. Very probably yes.

Some called La Chaise the city of gold, not because of the gold and bronze that the sun bounced off of, but because there were so many people that the lanterns at night turned the city into a glowing gold orb. Even in the middle of the night, one could be forgiven for thinking the sun was only just setting.

In the dingy gray of the stormy afternoon, that's not what Touraine noticed first.

She noticed the bridges. The River Nervure curled around the city, snaking in and out like veins, cutting the city into districts, unlike the River Hadd, which separated Briga from Qazāl. Here, the Balladairans stretched leaps of stone pavers. They were over a hundred strides long and wide enough for two four-horse carriages to pass each other going the opposite way, and for pedestrians to walk on either side. Monstrous stone faces decorated the sides.

Chilly wind nipped at Touraine through her now-sodden jacket.

"This is where you grew up?" Ghadin stared up at the stone buildings, mouth hanging open. Her long, dark braid dripped water onto the ground. The girl shivered.

"Not quite," Touraine answered. "We were garrisoned outside the city. They only brought us in to show off—make us watch a hanging or two, march in the autumn parade for Her Royal Highness's royal birthday. Shit like that."

"I can tell you're thrilled to be back." Despite her amused sarcasm, Aranen's eyes were hooded, and she scanned the city warily. On this side of the Nervure, the establishments catered toward those who could pay. Captains and crews funded by rich merchants to bring their goods safely and profitably back to civilized shores. The sailors called it the Queen's Bank.

"Ecstatic," Touraine said dryly.

Despite the rain, the docks were busy, full of merchants and fishermen. The sky was full of gulls. Even a small, river-friendly naval ship docked down the way, flying Balladairan colors: the golden horse blazing on a black field.

Touraine nodded up at the birds even as rain plocked into her eye. "Brings a new meaning to the phrase 'sky-falling shit,' eh?"

Ghadin laughed, but Aranen only pursed her lips as she continued to scan the purposeful crowd.

"Where is she?" the priestess asked.

Touraine sniffed. "I'm sure she has better things to do than escort us in the rain."

"Don't try and pretend you haven't scanned the road a hundred times over."

Touraine stuffed her hands in her pockets and hunched into her shoulders. "Colder than I remember here—"

She was saved from having to come up with a better distraction by a familiar gray mustache.

"Guard Captain Gillett!" Touraine raised a hand to catch his attention, then dropped it awkwardly to her side. When he reached them, she said, "I don't think it's appropriate for me to salute anymore, sir."

"Perhaps not." Gillett gave a brief smile. He offered a thick-knuckled hand and gave her a soldier's clasp. "Welcome to La Chaise, Ambassador de Sable." He bowed to Aranen. "High Priestess Aranen."

"El-Qazāli," Touraine cut in. "Ambassador El-Qazāli. Sir."

"And High Surgeon, if you please, Guard Captain," Aranen corrected. "I think that's best here."

"As you say. And...?" Gil raised a curious eyebrow at Ghadin.

Touraine clasped the girl to her side. "This is my body servant, Ghadin."

Gil gave the girl a small bow, too. "Welcome, Ghadin. Follow me."

Touraine bit her tongue on the question at the front of her thoughts. She would see Luca soon enough.

He led them away from the bustle and damp of the ships and the river and to a wider road where a carriage bearing the royal horse waited. An escort of four mounted guards surrounded the carriage, shining and jangling.

Touraine looked right past them. Princess Luca Ancier climbed down from the carriage and found Touraine immediately. Touraine thought she saw the ghost of shock or relief, but it was gone now, either swiftly contained or a trick of the gloom.

In front of Guard Captain Gillett and Aranen and Ghadin, pelted by rain, Touraine found herself at a loss, her throat dry and full at the same time, so she simply bowed.

"Your Highness."

Luca looked as Touraine had remembered—tall, despite her weight on her cane. She wore her hair in a loose tail instead of a tight bun. Strands of blond hair whipped across her face, slowly darkening with the rain. That self-assured certainty. A thrill ran down Touraine's back and into the deep of her gut. Back straight, gaze steady, Luca knew exactly where she belonged. Her lips slightly parted. Touraine searched the other woman's face for anything beyond that cool neutrality. Something to hint at what Touraine was getting herself into.

There was nothing. Luca only acknowledged the bow with a nod, just as formal. "Ambassador de Sable. High Surgeon Aranen din Djasha. Welcome back to Balladaire. I would be honored if you would allow me to accompany you to the palace."

Luca held her empty hand out, toward the open carriage. Waiting for Touraine to get in. Touraine still couldn't speak, not even to correct her name. The moment drew on, an awkward silence.

"Thank you, Your Highness." Aranen gave Touraine an exasperated sniff and glided around her, stepping into the carriage with a polite hand from the footman. Ghadin bounced into the carriage next.

That left Luca waiting for Touraine, arm still out, unwavering. "After you, Your Excellency."

The honorific sent another surprising thrill down Touraine's back. She held Luca's gaze until she ducked into the cab and slid into the seat beside Aranen.

Touraine's palms itched with the awkwardness of the ride. She felt like the others were there to chaperone her and Luca. The silence, the missed glances. Touraine had imagined their first meeting a million times in the secret dark moments of the ship's belly, but none of it had prepared her for this riot of feelings.

The princess was beautiful, impeccable, completely untouched by the last year, where Touraine felt ragged. To see her here, like this—Touraine wanted to hurt her, so there would at least be a record. Some way for the Rain Rebellion to scar her like it had scarred Qazāl and every Qazāli.

The city, too, was as pristine as its princess. La Chaise and its monuments, its bridges intact. How many of these roads, these buildings, these boats were paid for with money made off Shālan backs?

Even the irritation at her name—Touraine de Sable. Touraine had never given Luca a surname for her citizenship papers. Now Luca had taken the liberty to assign her one. Maybe it was meant as a gesture of goodwill, but it felt like possession.

Touraine closed her eyes and pressed her forehead against the cab. *You're here to make it right.* Even though right now all she wanted to do was watch it burn like she'd watched El-Wast burn under Balladairan torches.

"Are you all right, Ambassador?" Luca's voice was cool and polite.

So Touraine put on her own mask, too, the best she knew how to. She was headed into a viper's nest of people as cunning and ruthless as Luca, and Touraine would bet most of them didn't have the same stupid, hopeful, idealistic streak that Luca did. Or, once had. Maybe Qazāl hadn't left Luca completely unchanged. Touraine met Luca's eyes and looked again for a hint of anything out of place. A single crack that meant she cared at all.

Touraine couldn't see it.

"I'm fine," she lied. "It's just the motion—me and ships don't mix well. And—" She tilted her hand side to side and nodded at the carriage. "Sorry."

"Ah. Of course. We can have the physicians examine you if you like."

"No need. I just try not to talk."

Then she clamped her mouth shut and closed her eyes while Luca and Aranen talked carefully about absolutely nothing consequential.


Touraine waited with Aranen outside of the Grand Hall doors, shuffling from foot to foot. A faint murmur of conversation escaped from behind the closed doors; it had to be deafening inside.

"I'm not ready for this." Touraine wiped her damp palms on the sides of her trousers.

True to Gil's word, their belongings had been taken care of. In their appointed rooms—which were *well* appointed—Luca had provided clothing of Balladairan and Qazāli designs, and even a few fusion pieces that reminded Touraine of Malika Abdelnour's work.

Tonight, she wore a deep burgundy Balladairan coat, a gold waistcoat, and night-blue trousers with a cream blouse beneath, leaning carefully away from anything resembling Balladairan colors. Aranen, by contrast, was wearing an expensive-looking green Qazāli-style sleeveless shirt embroidered with gold, over black trousers. She'd taken off the prayer beads she usually wore on her wrist. They'd both lined their eyes in dark kohl, a Shālan fashion Touraine had grown fond of.

The priestess cocked her head at Touraine. She said flatly, "I'd have thought you'd be used to it by now."

"How do you mean?"

Aranen gave a minute shrug. When Touraine still looked confused, Aranen gestured at Touraine's entire body.

"You were a commander, weren't you? Aren't you used to the attention?"

"Hmm." Speaking of command. Touraine looked down at Ghadin. "You know where to go? There'll be—"

"—a line of body servants behind the High Table, and I'll stand with them until I'm called for." Ghadin sighed her great suffering. "I know."

"Follow their lead and listen for any interesting gossip."

Ghadin finished Touraine's sentence with her this time, and this time, it was Touraine who rolled her eyes.

"Sounds like we're ready," Aranen murmured.

The doors of the Grand Hall swung open, and the herald announced them.

Instead of noise, the Qazāli were met with silence. They walked forward together, the priestess, the soldier, and the youth, backs straight, pace steady.

Two long tables lined the left and right sides of the room, filled with the lesser guests. Ahead, stretched across the room, was the table for the royals and upper nobles. The row of body servants stood unobtrusively behind them, while a line of palace guards in their formal half cloaks stood at attention just behind the servants.

They approached the royal table, and only at the last minute did Touraine remember to bow, not salute. One empty chair waited beside Luca, with another seat directly across from it, between an older nobleman with a well-manicured snow-white beard and a barrel-chested younger man.

A handsome, heavyset man with thick gray-brown hair sat on Luca's other side, at the center of the table. Duke Ancier. He grinned, showing small teeth. The hairs on the back of Touraine's neck prickled.

"Welcome, Ambassador Touraine de Sable," the duke said. "Welcome, High Surgeon Aranen din Djasha."

When Aranen didn't speak first, Touraine said, "My thanks, Your Grace? We're honored?" Sky above, she had no idea how to talk to nobles, let alone royals.

A servant ushered Touraine into the seat next to Luca. Ghadin pulled out her chair with a hilarious mask of concentration before scampering to her post.

"Your Highness," Touraine said softly as she sat.

"Your Excellency," Luca murmured.

The awkwardness from the afternoon crackled between them still.

It was a relief when the handsome woman to Touraine's right said, "I'm Sabine LeMarchal, marquise de Durfort."

The woman's dark eyes were appraising and curious. Touraine only vaguely remembered Luca mentioning a Sabine last year, but Durfort was the region Inès Guérin, one of Luca's previous guards, had come from.

Luca cleared her throat sharply. "Ambassador, High Surgeon. Allow me to present my dear friend the marquise de Durfort, duelist extraordinaire and protector of our northern reach. And"—she gestured toward the older man to Aranen's right—"philosopher and financier Lord Evrard Castide, comte de Travers."

"And I'm Brice LaVasse, marquis de Moyenne." The burly man to Aranen's left seemed a little older than Luca and Durfort, but he had the cocky bluster that came from too few falls in the training yard. Where the marquise had a sleek duelist's build, Brice was built thick across the chest. His curly red hair was thinning a bit at the back, but his beard was thick and cut close to his chin.

Luca cleared her throat again. "This is the marquis de Moyenne, protector of the Taargen border."

"You're a veteran of the most recent war, then," de Moyenne said, angling over the first course at Touraine. A creamy red soup; it smelled like tomatoes and herbs.

"I am. Are you?" Touraine knew exactly how much action the noble soldiers saw. There was a reason the Sands existed, after all.

Luca shot Touraine a warning glare, but Touraine ignored it. Harder to ignore Aranen's level stare. The marquise de Durfort smirked.

"Of course. We'll compare scars another time. On the practice fields, perhaps? I would like to see how the great Cantic trained up her conscripts." De Moyenne leaned back, a small, satisfied smile on his face.

*Ah.* Touraine remembered. Cantic was from Moyenne.

"Her death was a tragedy," de Moyenne pressed.

Aranen picked up her glass of wine in one long-fingered hand and examined the contents with an eyebrow raised. Luca busied herself with a spoonful of soup.

"I learned a lot from her," Touraine evaded. How much did the nobles know about Cantic's death?

"She was a great general. We'll need a strong hand to carry her sword. So to speak."

"Balladaire will need a strong general," Luca said softly. She met Touraine's eyes briefly, but Touraine gave her a flat look. Shāl take her eyes if she would be pulled back into Balladaire's military, even as a general.

*Are you sure?* a small voice nudged in the back of her mind. *That's only everything you ever wanted. You'd pick the battles and the methods and—*

Touraine busied herself with the next courses. She was eating meat incidentally for the first time in a long time, and she savored the roasted chicken and medallions of venison—she'd never eaten like this as a soldier, and she had to keep from gorging herself. Aranen passed up the meat dishes entirely.

While they ate, Balladairan musicians played songs that sounded like versions of Shālan songs several times removed. There was even a Balladairan marching song, as if to remind Touraine of her soldier origins, on the off chance that she'd forgotten. All the while, Luca barely said five words to her.

It was agony to sit this close and not be able to look Luca in the eye, not ask any of the questions she'd held back for these long months. What she couldn't write. *Why do you keep haunting me?* And hardest for Touraine to answer herself, why did she feel drawn to come back? She didn't like any of the answers she came up with. *Use her weakness for you*, Jaghotai had said.

Instead, Touraine let the marquise lead them into harmless distractions. Sabine de Durfort kept up a steady conversation about horses—"Can you ride? No? Well, I must teach you, I ride as well as I duel"—and Durfort the region—"the finest wine in all of Balladaire, I swear to you"—and Touraine sat, amused despite herself, while Durfort and Moyenne tried to out-boast each other's conquests.

Durfort was just implying that Moyenne's conquests over horses were sexual in nature when Duke Ancier pushed himself away from the table and stood.

"Now that we've all been fed and watered." He raised his wine. "A toast to our esteemed guests, whose wisdom, I am told, has no end. My dear niece, Princess Luca, brings back stories that I can barely give credit to, they boggle the imagination so."

A nervous catch tickled the back of Touraine's throat, and she tried to cough it out discreetly. The duke hadn't spoken to her or Aranen at all during dinner. She caught the priestess's glance. She looked like a deer caught by the hunters' hounds, golden eyes wide and fearful. They both shot fierce glares at Luca. The princess eyed her uncle warily, her fingers pressed against the table.

"I grew up with stories of mythical healers in the southern deserts," the duke continued, waving his hand mockingly across the crowd of nobles to signify magic. They chuckled and smiled in agreement when he asked, "Haven't we all? My brother, King Roland, was so fascinated that he went on a fool's journey for this mystery, believing the Shālans would share their great gift with us." He waved his fingers. "Unfortunately, he died of a sickness, with no such aid." His voice went dark, and the laughter stopped.

"My niece, however, claims otherwise. She says that, despite the tragic loss of the Black Ships, she brought us something else in return. An alliance with the Qazāli, whose god grants them the power to heal." His tone was genteel, but the words were mocking. Touraine could hear the word *uncivilized* beneath it all.

He looked down at Touraine and Aranen. All around her, from every corner of the hall, she felt curious eyes, derisive and disbelieving smiles. This was a chance for him to make Luca look small, and it came at her and Aranen's expense.

Touraine was suddenly very aware of her eyes. She had hoped they would fade back to brown, deep and simple, giving away nothing about her, but after a year, they were the same burnished gold as Aranen's were. As Djasha's had been.

The duke's gaze stopped on Touraine. "I've heard much about your friendship with my dear niece. I would be honored if you would favor us with a demonstration. Show us what your alliance will bring that it couldn't bring before."

His smile didn't match the backhanded welcome.

Touraine's heart beat in her ears. It drowned out everything but the panic. Luca sat rigid in her chair, and Touraine understood, sickeningly, that no help would come.

In a low voice, Luca asked, "Can you try?"

"I don't heal," Touraine hissed. Panic rose inside her. She hadn't managed to heal a single scratch since the day she'd blown Rogan's head to pieces.

Touraine pleaded silently with Aranen, a white-knuckle grip on her trousers. The priestess bowed her head, eyes closed. When she opened them again, she turned that same hollow, disappointed look on Luca. The princess shrank back. Then Aranen shook her head at Touraine, looking pointedly at the dishes of dessert on the table. The last of the summer berries, the first of the apples, flaky pastries fluffed with cream. All delicious. All utterly useless.

Sky-falling shit. Aranen hadn't eaten any meat at all during dinner. Which left Touraine. Who still had no idea what she was doing, despite months of studying with the priestess. And this was Balladaire. The seat of all that was civilized. Sky above, she was still fighting off the idea that believing in gods was uncivilized, and she had seen—had felt!—Shāl in action through her own body.

Touraine started to stand, hands trembling at her sides, but Luca touched Touraine's thigh—briefly, a whisper of contact—beneath the table, bidding her sit. Instead, Luca gathered herself and stood beside her uncle.

"Your Grace, my lords and ladies," she said, with the smile of self-assured self-deprecation that nobles deployed so well. Their eyes all turned from Touraine to Luca, and Touraine felt the pressure ease a hair. "Unfortunately, my uncle misunderstands the limits to the healing gifts, and our guests are tired and unprepared. Just as you can't expect a surgeon to operate at the dinner table—"

The duke realized he was losing hold of the room. "Nonsense," he interrupted. He snapped one hand, and a servant in black and gold Ancier livery bustled to the duke on quick feet. He was young, no more than fifteen, one of the serving boys, and judging by his darker skin, he'd probably come from Qazāl or one of the other Shālan nations. But the way he looked at Duke Nicolas and then at Luca reminded Touraine of another frightened child that she'd met once: Beau-Sang's servant boy with his little fingers lopped off.

Like that boy, this one was afraid, and he knew that if he showed that fear, he would be punished.

Touraine leapt from her seat half a second before the duke took a dagger from one of his guards, grabbed the boy's arm, and slashed the blade across the pale inner forearm.

Touraine lunged for the kid as Luca reached for her uncle's arm. They crashed together uselessly, chair legs tangling with their own legs. Nicolas held the boy's arm high so that the whole hall could see the blood dripping from the deep gash. A collective inhale sucked the air out of the room. The kid's eyes were wide with shock. It happened so quickly that he hadn't even resisted.

Touraine separated herself from Luca first, kicking herself free from her own chair so that it toppled. She took the boy away from the duke, snatched several of the cloth napkins from the table, and pressed them around the boy's arm. She couldn't even look at Nicolas, because if she did, he'd see the murderous rage she felt—

The kid stared at his arm, teeth clenched as he registered the pain. No surprise; Touraine was squeezing his arm as tight as she could. His chest was rising and falling rapidly as the shock gave way to panic.

She locked eyes with him. "Breathe with me, okay?" She led him in a deep breath. His chest hitched and stuttered. "Again." In. Out.

Blood soaked through the cloths. She tried fleetingly to pray to Shāl. *If you're listening, help us.* She closed her eyes and tried to still her thoughts. The hot blood. She connected that warmth with the flesh of his body and willed the wound to close, to knit back together. *Shāl, help us, please.* Of course, nothing happened. No surge of heat through her hands, no beam of holy light. Nothing.

"Is he all right?" Luca asked, her own hands joining the pressure around the boy's forearm, lacing between Touraine's.

Touraine grunted. "Needs stitching. Infirmary?"

Before Luca could answer, Aranen made it around the table and stood before Duke Nicolas.

"With all due respect, Your Grace, this was foolish. You have endangered this child's life for something you do not understand." Aranen leveled her hard stare at the rest of the guests in the hall. "We're here as potential allies, not animals in your menagerie to perform tricks for you at will."

Aranen guided the boy away from Touraine and Luca, wrapping one arm around the kid's shoulders and holding the makeshift bandage on his forearm closed tight.

Nicolas's hand shot out to pull her back. Something flashed in Aranen's eyes, though, and Nicolas let his hand fall. Maybe he remembered the rumors of General Cantic's death at the hands of a certain Qazāli doctor. Maybe he was less skeptical than he claimed.

"A pity." The duke forced a smile. "We were all hoping for something to come of Princess Luca's diplomatic skills. Luckily, we have doctors and surgeons enough. A servant will lead you to the infirmary."

Nicolas dismissed them with a wave, and another servant appeared to lead Aranen and the boy away. Then he handed the bloody dagger back to the guard, wiped his hands against each other, and sat down again. He didn't even look at Touraine.

Touraine picked her chair back up and slammed it in place, leaving bloody handprints on the upholstery. The nobles sitting at the High Table flinched as the sound echoed through the silent hall.

Luca still stood with her, posture stiff and upright. When Touraine met the other woman's eyes, though, she was surprised by what she saw there. The cold princess, who was brilliant and in control of every échecs piece on the board, was afraid.

With one final glare around the room, Touraine followed on Aranen's heels, with Ghadin just behind her.

# CHAPTER 8

# A SCAR

Ambassador!" Luca limped after Touraine as quickly as she could. Touraine stopped, but didn't turn until Luca had caught up to her. Her eyes still burned like molten gold surrounded by a smoky cloud of kohl liner. It was disconcerting, to say the least. Stunning, to say the truth. Irrelevant.

"Let me accompany you."

"If you wish, Your Highness." Touraine glanced up the hallway, where Aranen had already disappeared. "Ghadin, catch up to Aranen. See if she needs help."

Touraine's young shadow speared Luca with a suspicious look, but she said, "Yes, Mulāzim," and then jogged away.

They spent the first steps in more silence. Touraine's anger radiated from her, her shoulders rigid. This meant, of course, that Luca couldn't stop her mind from spinning self-consciously over the small things:

The decorations in the corridors were garish. Centuries of obnoxious royal taste and ego covering the walls in the form of portraits and imaginary renditions of famous battles.

Rich carpets on the stone floors to minimize the sound of their boots. An extravagance.

The sharp cut of Touraine's hairline at the nape of her neck. Its gentle curve around her ear.

"So?" Touraine looked over with a raised eyebrow. Unamused.

Luca swallowed. "So . . . what?"

"Your uncle."

"What about him?"

"Don't play stupid, Princess. It's beneath you. What was that stunt at dinner?"

"I didn't know he was going to do that."

"I've never seen you hesitate like that. Are you afraid of him?"

Luca's boot caught on the marble floor and she stumbled. Touraine's hand shot out, but Luca had already steadied herself.

"Of course not."

Touraine grunted. "Then why didn't you stop him? Sky above. This better not be just like Qazāl." She laughed incredulously. "We're not worth protecting if it loses their approval, hein?"

Luca flinched. "It won't be like that." She had expected a few days before Touraine backed her on her heels like this. Touraine had changed. It wasn't altogether unpleasant. "It won't, Touraine. I reacted slowly because I was surprised, that's all. I'll make it up to you. And to the boy."

Touraine stopped and turned to face her, eyes probing Luca. "Your Highness. Why am I here?"

This close, Luca noticed Touraine's hollow cheeks, shadowed eyes. She'd lost weight. Luca saw the way Touraine had attacked the food tonight with new eyes.

"To sign the treaty between Balladaire and Qazāl. To make sure Qazāli immigrants are content here. To show that this alliance—"

"To show everyone that you didn't make a mistake."

*Well. In short.*

Touraine didn't look away. "That's why there's a Qazāli delegation here. Why am I here? You asked for *me*."

*I don't know, why are you here?* Luca wanted to retort. But she was afraid of how Touraine would answer. Afraid it would be too much and not enough all at once.

Luca made sure the corridor was empty before taking a deep breath. "The things I wrote to you in those letters—the first letters. Consider them forgotten."

Touraine nodded slowly. "Okay."

"My birthday is coming soon. In theory, I would be crowned then and could make Qazāli independence official. Nicolas has balked over the treaty for months. He's even stopped acknowledging it, and he mentioned sending the marquis de Moyenne into Qazāl with more troops."

"What?" Touraine growled. "*No*. We've broken our asses trying to rebuild our country. If anything, you bastards owe us!"

Luca held her hands up. "I am willing to talk about what we owe you in exhaustive detail. I hoped that having you here would stop him from erasing all the work we did."

"All the work *we* did?"

Luca's face went warm. "You know what I mean."

"Wait." Touraine's face went blank. "What do you mean 'in theory'?"

"I mean..." Luca leaned close to murmur in Touraine's ear. "He's not getting off the throne without a fight. I need your help."

Touraine's face paled with horror or fury or perhaps a mixture of both. She cursed and spun on her heel. "Where's this sky-falling infirmary?"

"This way." Luca limped after her again. She couldn't tell if Touraine's burst of speed was deliberate. Either way, the sudden disregard hurt and not just in Luca's leg. If she could just *start over*.

"Touraine—"

"Ambassador Touraine, if you please. Ambassador El-Qazāli if you prefer."

Touraine might as well have shoved her back physically.

"Ambassador El-Qazāli, then," Luca said around the lump in her throat. "I—How are you?"

Touraine's step hitched. "I'm—fine, Your Highness. Other than all of this." She waved a scarred hand at the palace walls and very pointedly did not look at Luca. "You?"

"Yes. Me, too. I'm fine."

"Look," Touraine said after a few slower steps. "I don't know what you expect from us. I came here thinking we were sovereign diplomats, not playing pieces for you and your uncle to bat back and forth. More fool me, I guess. But it's bad tactics to squat in an open field with no defenses. I don't want to feel helpless again."

It was hard to tell what Touraine was referring to. Just now in the Grand Hall? Back at her own execution? Or her entire life as a Balladairan conscript? Luca remembered how helpless she had felt while Touraine bled to death in her arms, her blood warm and sticky on Luca's skin, all the way through her clothing. If she never felt like that again, it would be too soon.

"You're under my protection," Luca said firmly. "I apologize for tonight, and you have my word: I won't let something like that happen again."

Touraine grunted, and they walked the last stretch in silence.

The palace infirmary was a small, mostly empty room. Luca wasn't very familiar with it; whenever she was ill, doctors tended to her in her own chambers. The three individual beds were curtained off, but Touraine led Luca unerringly to Aranen, her young body servant, and the boy.

The youth lay quiet, skin pale, breathing stable. If his eyes weren't staring fixedly at Aranen, Luca would have thought he was asleep. His forearm was wrapped in a length of cotton.

When Luca stepped forward, though, it all changed. The boy flinched up in his bed, eyes wide.

"Your Highness." His voice cracked, skewed high. "I'm sorry, I'm so sorry, please. I didn't know—"

"No," Luca said. "I—"

No one could hear her, least of all the boy, who was still panicking, while Aranen tried to calm him. The priestess shot a glare at Luca over her shoulder. The bottom dropped out of Luca's stomach.

Touraine stepped in front of Luca, blocking them from view.

"Your Highness," Touraine said softly. "It's probably best if you leave."

Luca stumbled back. She hadn't even managed to work her voice around the lump in her throat. But Touraine's eyes were weary and wary, both.

"As you wish," Luca said. To the head of the ward, a plump woman with a severe expression, Luca said simply, sharply, "See that our guests have anything and everything that they ask for."

Touraine stared after Luca a long while, even after the echo of her cane had gone. Touraine didn't expect the wrench of longing that sound would cause. It made her miss the quiet, hopeful times in Luca's Qazāli townhouse, as they'd tried to build peace from the same side.

"What did she ask you?" Aranen's voice broke through Touraine's thoughts.

Touraine jumped. She had forgotten she wasn't alone.

"Nothing. How is he?" Touraine went to the boy's side.

He was fast asleep now, an empty cup on the table by his side. Aranen had probably drugged him. That, or exhaustion had caught up to him. Ghadin sat in a nearby chair, knees tucked up to her chin, and chewed quietly on her bottom lip.

"He'll be fine."

Touraine nodded absently. A thread on the boy's blanket had unraveled itself partway. Touraine helped it along. "What about the duke?"

"What about him?" Aranen asked. "Obviously the princess wants our help getting rid of him."

"How do you know?"

"She can't handle him," Aranen said. "I've seen her when she feels like she's in control." She held up her finger and pointed to the door, toward wherever Luca had gone. "This evening was not it."

Touraine tugged the thread free. She flicked it back onto the sleeping boy's legs.

"She can't give us Qazāl," Touraine said, deflated. She found another thread. "Even if I tried to—to take advantage of her weakness."

Aranen's jaw tightened. "Of course she can't. It wasn't hers to take in the first place. She can't give us what was already ours."

"She says the duke wants to send more soldiers back in. Not conscripts. De Moyenne's troops. He was testing us. What are we supposed to do? Stay and play their games? Go home and get ready for more war?"

Aranen grabbed one of Touraine's clenched fists and squeezed it tight. The priestess sat on the edge of the boy's bed.

"I know it's scary to have someone's life in your hands and feel like you have to be the one to fix it." Sometime since dinner, Aranen had slipped her prayer beads back on, and they rubbed smooth on Touraine's skin as she stroked Touraine's forearm.

"I'm responsible for this. People will die if I can't do my job to prevent it."

"Mm-hmm. And now you've found this power. And it's beyond anything you imagined. It should be able to right all the wrongs in the world, let alone this one inconvenience of broken flesh. And since you found it once, you should be able to find it again, shouldn't you? When you can't, it's hard not to feel like the breaking is your fault."

Touraine blinked away the dampness in her eyes, not sure if Aranen was speaking about the magic or the measure of control Touraine had managed to get over her own life.

She twisted away from Aranen's touch. "I never asked for it."

"Oh, but you did. Shāl doesn't come if you don't ask."

"Then I'll give it up, like Djasha."

And just like that, Touraine realized she *had* decided it. She would give up trying to reach for Shāl's gift.

Fury split Aranen's face, sweeping over the grief like a storm. "You know nothing about what she went through."

"She made her own choices, didn't she? I can make mine."

"She didn't make her own choices. Don't you know how this works by now? We were all shaped by Balladaire, by necessity and survival. Not just you."

"If this is about necessity," Touraine started, slapping her temple to indicate her eyes—but she stopped when she saw Ghadin's wide eyes looking between the two of them. The girl sat and watched and absorbed it all. *What does she think of Shāl? What does she think of me?*

"Being back here..." Touraine started, trailed off, and started again. "I grew up in the one place you're not allowed to have a god. Despite everything you've tried to teach me, it feels like something I can reach for but never touch." *Uncivilized.* "And Djasha..."

Aranen closed her eyes. Touraine saw the ache as it spread through the other woman. She felt the prick of it in her own chest. She put her hand on Aranen's and squeezed.

"I'm sorry."

Aranen opened her eyes again, but the tears didn't fall.

"She lost her faith after her family died." Aranen stared, unfocused, but she pressed Touraine's hand back with her thumb. "If she had faith in Shāl, she thought, why hadn't Shāl protected them? When she lost the faith, she lost the gift."

"Which gift?" Touraine whispered. She knew this much, by now: all of the gods were as two-faced as a sovereign. What they gave, they could take away. A gift of blood, a gift of peace. Shāl would mend and rend the body. With Niwai's Many-Legged god, the Taargens' bear god, animals could maul or be tamed.

Touraine had only used one of Shāl's gifts. The one that marks its user by the eyes. She wondered if Aranen thought of Djasha every time she looked into Touraine's eyes. Touraine did, every time she looked at Aranen.

"Both." Aranen lowered her eyes, ashamed. That answered Touraine's question.

*Why do you hate it so much?* Touraine wanted to ask. The priestess seemed too fragile, the question too invasive. Instead, she pulled her fear closer so that it wouldn't break the priestess any further.

"Do you—could you heal him, if you'd eaten meat at dinner?"

Aranen raised her chin and eyed Touraine down her proud nose. "Shāl is still my god and I still have my faith."

"What if I don't?" Touraine looked at the boy's arm. The duke had slashed across his forearm the way one of Touraine's soldiers had cut his own wrists with a boot knife he'd stolen off a dead Taargen. She hadn't been able to save her soldier, but she should have been able to help the boy.

She didn't realize she'd said the words aloud until Aranen answered.

The steel in her gaze had gone. "You have to find your own path. Djasha's took her all the way down to the Southern Mountains, and she still came back without it." Aranen shrugged heavily. "Perhaps Balladaire is your way."

Touraine thought of the lonely thunk of Luca's cane echoing through the palace corridors. *The things I wrote...Consider them forgotten.*

Maybe Balladaire was Touraine's path. Maybe it wasn't.


Luca was dismayed but not surprised at all to find a certain tall marquise outside of her quarters. Sabine leaned against the wall, one shining boot propped against the white stone wall.

Lanquette made a face of long suffering. "I asked Her Grace to come back in the morning, Your Highness."

Luca pursed her lips.

"Why do you put my employees in this position, Sab?"

Sabine smiled coyly and kicked herself upright. "It's fun. Sorry, Lanquette." She winked at him. "Now. I have it on good faith that the reason you're late to bed is a certain conscript—ex-conscript, excuse me." She looked up the hallway. "As a matter of fact, I'm a bit surprised that you've come back alone."

"Your Grace." Lanquette stepped forward. Innuendo, apparently, was a line too far for him.

"It's all right, Lanquette." Luca sighed. She considered asking her friend to come back in the morning, begging off with exhaustion, but she wouldn't get rid of Sabine that easily. "Come on, then."

Inside Luca's quarters, Sabine helped herself to one of the cushioned chairs in front of the échecs table. The board was still set up in their last game. She started resetting the pieces.

"I don't have the head for it tonight, Sab." Luca sank into the chair opposite.

Sabine froze, a scholar piece hovering in her hand above the board.

"You? No head for a game?" Sabine put the piece in its place beside the queen. "Sounds serious. We should definitely play so I can win."

Luca looked balefully at Sabine. Then Luca huffed and moved a pawn.

"There we are, love." Sabine grinned at the board like a child in a pastry shop.

After she made her move, Sabine asked, "So did you invite her specifically or...?"

Much like her échecs strategy, Sabine jumped boldly into the conversation. She'd never been a subtle person. She had never had to be. She was an only child, and her marquisate was secure. She even had Luca's favor, so there was never a competition with others in the court for position.

While it worked fine for her in the real world, it was abysmal for her échecs.

"She's the ambassador for Qazāl. I sent for a delegation—"

"Yes, yes, for the treaty. Is that all she's here for?"

Luca scowled. "I don't have any designs on her."

"I do declare bearshit." Sabine said it fondly, even though Luca had just taken two foot soldiers in a row.

"I mean it. She led the revolution. Helped, anyway. She and Aranen din Djasha are the perfect people to serve as a delegation, and frankly, I didn't request anyone in particular." A lie. "They sent who they thought would be best, and they made good choices. Aranen is level-headed and respected in Qazāl. Touraine has been our intermediary since she...defected. She knows Balladaire." The truth. Some of it.

Sabine snorted. "She knows Balladaire as a conscript. She was as lost as a fish in a vineyard at that table."

Luca tried not to let her worry show on her face. That was exactly what she was afraid of, and if Sabine had noticed, everyone else had, too. It would be only a matter of time before the others took advantage of Touraine's naiveté.

Or worse, for Touraine to leave because she was ill positioned. Luca needed her to stay. At least long enough for her uncle and the rest of the court to see how beneficial a cordial alliance could be, instead of the colonial system.

"She'll learn. She just needs time. And"—Luca drew the word out, wheedling—"someone who can teach her?"

Sabine raised an eyebrow. Instead of saying anything, she took one of Luca's keeps and put Luca in check.

Luca grunted in surprise, and Sabine sat back, smiling smugly.

"You two would get along. Probably." They could also end up like two headstrong cocks scrabbling in the yard. Only, Touraine was subtler than Sabine. She had managed to dupe Luca, after all. "Welcome her. She'll need a friend who isn't . . ."

"Who's not you?" Sabine said softly. She wasn't gloating anymore.

Something thick welled up in Luca's chest. "Things ended badly. Being on opposite sides of a rebellion tends to do that."

Sabine cocked her head. "And now that you're allies?"

"No," Luca said sharply. "Too much is at risk with both of our countries. There's no room for mistakes."

"Good. You're in a delicate position. You'll be under even more scrutiny over the next few weeks." Sabine said the last in a hushed tone.

"I need the Qazāli, though. I don't think Nicolas is going to just hand me the crown, and I'm short on allies, in case you haven't noticed."

Sabine looked uncomfortable at that. "They're staying for your birthday?"

"If we don't frighten them away first. You saw what my uncle did. He'll dissolve any trust I've built with them." She made her final move across the board.

Sabine glared at the board. "Oh, fuck off, I had you."

"That's 'fuck off, Your Highness.'" Luca smirked. Then she softened. "Will you help her?"

After a long pause, Sabine huffed and then nodded. "Only because we're such good friends. You'll owe me for this."

Luca snorted. "I hardly think so. This makes up for that time I covered for you when you ran off with that traveling—what was she, a traveling singer?"

"That was ten years ago!" Sabine threw her hands up in the air.

"She was twice your age."

"Ten. Years," Sabine repeated.

"You've got heavy debts, my friend."

Very unexpectedly, Sabine sobered. She shrugged off whatever heavy thought crossed her mind, though, and quirked a smile. "At least I understand now. She's..." She whistled, low. "I'd cut off half my empire for her, too."

They locked eyes over the échecs board. The silence stretched. Then they broke into loud peals of laughter, and it was just like they were before Luca had ever gone to Qazāl.

Before everything began to crack.

# CHAPTER 9

# AN OPEN HAND

The night was dark and the streets were surprisingly quiet as Fili followed her master through the winding streets of La Gouttière. Intermittent lanterns lit the dockside district, leaving deep shadows in foul-smelling alleys that made the hair on the back of her neck stand up. There were no beggars on the streets in La Gouttière. There'd be no point—no one here had spare coin to throw. Plenty of unconscious drunks who'd gotten started earlier in the evening, though.

She hoped they were only drunks. She hoped they were only unconscious.

"Are you sure about this, master?" Fili stuck close to her master's comforting bulk. Despite his steady pace, he was practically bouncing on his toes with excitement. Not the *"Measure twice—twice!"* patience he tried so hard to instill into Fili.

Maître Gaspard laughed softly. "No, Fili. I'm not. But you and I share the same frustrations, I think, no matter the years between us—and no matter your mam—and so we're visiting a friend of mine."

At the mention of her mam, Fili raised a skeptical eyebrow. "If you say so, master."

They walked until they came to a public house that should have been bright with light shining from the windows like the other occupied pubs along the quay. Instead, it was shuttered, light filtering out through cracks and a broken slat here and there. A rumble of muffled chatter escaped, too.

When Maître Gaspard opened the door, the light and sound and warmth of a fire and the bodies crammed into the public house washed over her. Someone pulled them in quickly and slammed the door shut behind them. The woman at the door exchanged a familiar handshake with Fili's master before ushering them both in. Without asking, someone else pushed a mug of ale into their hands, and her master shuffled them off to the side of the room, squeezing between paunches and hips and bony elbows until they found a space large enough for them to stand and breathe.

"A friend?" Fili looked up at her master suspiciously.

"Aye, a friend. Just so happens he has more than one friend himself."

Fili grunted and settled against the wall with her drink. It was lukewarm and sour, not in a good way, but it was free and that alone surprised her. The people around them were a mix of nervous-looking craftspeople, tough-looking laborers, and seedy-looking everybody else. Through the cracks in between other patrons, she saw a tall man jump onto an empty table that had been pushed up against the bar. She cringed at the sight of his boots on the table. She wouldn't be coming back, if that's how the patrons were allowed to treat the furniture. The barkeep only looked up at him, in awe like everyone else in the room. Expectant silence fell.

"My friends!" the man said. He had the broad shoulders and thick forearms of a heavy laborer, and his long hair was streaked with gray. "My beloved friends."

"I take it that's your friend?" Fili muttered skeptically.

Her master grinned down at her. His grin wasn't all that different from the man on the table's.

"You can call me Brother Michel. Because that's what we are. Siblings in struggle."

Fili rolled her eyes. He sounded like any other street mountebank, gearing up to sell an easily deluded populace something they didn't need—or worse, something that could kill them. Charlatans. "I'm getting out of here. I told my mam I would—" She started to push past her master.

Her master grabbed her sleeve between his thumb and forefinger. "Wait," he whispered.

So, she waited. She found another gap so she could watch the man enrapture this gullible crowd.

"Too long have we let the High Court parade above us. Too long have the royals walked upon our backs."

Fili's back went stiff, her eyes wide. She looked furtively up at her master, who nodded silently down at her. Now this was worth listening to. Someone else speaking out loud the words she'd only grumbled to herself.

"We're hungry!" Brother Michel said.

"Aye!" the thick crowd said in unison.

"We're cold!"

"Aye!"

"The merchants pay us one penny and the landlords take five!" He held out his hands to either side in confusion. He was a performer, drawing the crowd in. Drawing Fili in. "We complain, we're out of a job, we're out of a house. No one in the court will hear us because the merchants and the landlords are their friends! Their own purse strings!"

"Aye!"

More murmurs of grievances from the crowd spouted up like steam from a kettle. Expensive food. Dirty Qazāli coming from the colonies. Labor injuries. Fear of the crowding leading to disease—a return of the Withering. Fili shuddered at that; she'd not been born for the last Withering, but her mam had been a young soldier at the time, and her pa spoke of it with fear.

As the crowd cried their own complaints, Brother Michel nodded grimly as if he heard every one. "And what, my friends, shall we do about it?"

Here, the crowd went silent, and Fili waited for someone to answer and make a fool of themselves. It was a trick question. Wasn't anything you could do in a world this big, against people so rich or influential they could order you crushed with a flick of their finger, and then order someone else to mop up the smear you left.

"Join us, friends. Together, we'll turn La Chaise—and all the rest of Balladaire!—into a place that values the work of its hands. Join the Fingers. Individually, we are weak, yes. Easily broken in one of the palace's torture cells." He pulled one of his own fingers at an odd angle to illustrate. "But together"—he clenched his fist—"we can hold a hammer. Together, we are a fist. We don't need them. They need us! Together, we will pull them down!"

Fili inhaled sharply. *We will pull them down.* Fili had a comfortable life—she lodged with Maître Gaspard above the carpentry shop. He treated her well and she loved her work. She understood the problems in La Chaise through her friends, and what she could see plainly as she walked through the streets. This, though, was tangible. The thought of justice for her mam, who'd lost her leg at the whim of the princess... It wasn't fair, what the nobles could ask of everyone else. It wasn't even asking because no one could say no. All because of an accident of birth?

"Aye," Fili whispered with the rest.

"We have a place for all of you," Brother Michel said. "Simply speak to Sister Velte and tell us your skills, and we'll figure out how you can best help the Fingers build a new order in Balladaire." He pointed to the table next to his stage where a large woman hunched over a table with an ink pot and a small stack of paper.

The shuffle toward Sister Velte was immediate.

"They aren't afraid that someone will tell the gendarmerie?" Fili asked her master. The gendarmes would fight in defense of the city's pockets. Her master shrugged and then nodded there, to a woman in a dark corner, and over there, to a man smoking a cigarette.

"Some of them are tired, too."

Fili grunted. "Let's see what Velte has to say, then." It felt dangerous to let herself get excited, and even more dangerous to show that excitement. She couldn't deny the wild beat of her heart, though.

As they waited for the room to clear and the queue in front of Velte's table to shrink, people came up to her master to greet him, shaking hands and patting backs, offering his apprentice a nod before moving on. She recognized some of them and greeted them in turn, but she was surprised by how many she didn't actually know. In and of itself, that wasn't a surprise. La Chaise was the largest city in Balladaire, easily home to hundreds of thousands of people. But she practically lived with her master, except for the days she went to visit her mam, or even farther, her pa. It was like he had a secret life unveiling before her eyes.

"How long has this been going on?" she murmured to him.

"The Fingers have been working up to this for months, at least. Finding the right folks for the jobs they need."

"What kinds of jobs?"

Her master shrugged again. "We'll know when they need us, I expect. Look lively, now." He jerked his head before them.

They stood right in front of Velte.

"You ready to join the Fingers, young friend?" Velte asked. She was a sun-darkened woman with a thin scar across her forehead and knobby, dry hands that held a pen with the confidence of a scribe. She looked Fili up and down. "How old are you, exactly?"

"Old enough," Fili said, bristling at the woman's tone. Fili was sixteen. She'd taken her apprenticeship with her master over a year ago, just after her mam went south to the colonies.

Velte chuckled. "Is this one yours, Gaspard? I like her."

Maître Gaspard laughed and clapped a warm hand on her shoulder. "I wish. Some of the best carving I've seen in an age." He added in a false whisper, "Might even be better than mine, but don't tell her that."

Fili scowled and pushed her master off, but she went all warm at the praise. "I want to help. Will it be safe?" Fili nodded at the papers.

"Oh, aye. It's my own shorthand I invented working as...well." Velte winked. "We'll find a job for you. Everyone deserves a say in how the country gets built up." She scribbled something in her shorthand. "Why do you want to join the Fingers?" Velte looked Fili up and down, from her crown of short tawny hair to her scarred and calloused hands.

"Because," Fili said, clenching her fists tight at her side, "I owe the princess a debt."

# CHAPTER 10

# AN EDUCATION

The duke regent summoned Touraine before Luca did.

The morning had found Touraine sitting in the nook of the window in her palace room, knees tucked up to her chest, her arms wrapped around her shins, her head resting on her knees. She had already dragged Ghadin through her normal exercise regimen, though without the aid of the heavy stones she had taken to using in Qazāl. As they'd gone through the motions, she felt a stab of longing for the Jackal and their wagers to see who could carry the heaviest rocks the farthest.

Still, she felt stronger today than she had yesterday. Something about having faced Luca and walked away, yet again. She had been harsh with Luca and it had felt good and it was also the opposite of what Jaghotai had asked her to do, and that also felt good.

Then the palace messenger came, and Touraine's ease leaked away like water in a cupped palm.

The servant in her black and gold livery bowed slightly. "Ambassador. The duke requests your presence."

Touraine looked the woman over for some sign of disdain or other disrespect. It wasn't until she found none—not in the cant of the woman's head or the tilt of her shoulders—that Touraine realized her own shoulders were tight with the expectation.

"The duke?" Touraine repeated.

"Yes. At your earliest convenience." That final addition gave Touraine the sense that it meant "now." So did the fact that the messenger didn't leave.

"I'll put on something appropriate and follow you?" Sweat prickled across her forehead and under her arms.

While Touraine deliberated over whether to dress in Balladairan clothing or Qazāli, Ghadin poked her head out of her room.

"Can I come? I *am* your page."

Touraine scowled. "I thought you went back to sleep."

The girl shrugged. As much as a part of Touraine didn't want to bring the girl anywhere near the duke after last night, another part of her couldn't deny that it could be useful. Another pair of eyes. A witness. A chance to learn.

"Fine. Get dressed."

Touraine wore a Balladairan cut, and she and Ghadin followed the messenger through the corridors. She wondered how long it would take before she had memorized the palace enough to travel unescorted. If they ever let her travel unescorted.

Touraine had expected someone a hand's breadth away from usurping a throne to hold court in some grand and gilded hall. Instead, the servant led Touraine to a small, private library. Little braziers kept the room cozily warm, not stuffy. The duke sat at his ease, twirling a glass goblet of wine in his hand. He flicked his eyes upward without lifting his face from the book he was reading.

The resemblance to Luca was uncanny, only she usually read with a cup of Qazāli coffee. Touraine bowed, though probably not as deeply as a royal regent deserved. Ghadin imitated. Touraine gestured toward the door, and the girl hung back.

"Ambassador. Welcome." He smiled, satisfied, and set the glass down gently before placing a strip of silk into the book and closing it. He stood and came around the desk, the better to greet her.

He was a large man, and carried an air of certainty and control to match it—you wouldn't move him unless he wanted you to. At the same time, he had the same perpetual squint as Luca behind his round spectacles, and the same forward lean that Luca had when she found something especially interesting.

His eyes, however, were brown, and his hair darker. He wasn't as coldly intense as Luca, either; he had the warm approach of someone used to working with frightened animals.

"My apologies for yesterday evening. I was led to misunderstand the breadths of the Shālan gifts."

He took her hand—to shake it, she thought. Instead, he yanked her closer to him, subtly enough that she could almost believe it was an accident, an off-balancing from a misjudged distance. Almost.

He stared at her eyes. "How peculiar."

Touraine slid her hand out of his and held his gaze even though it made her feel small. "How may I be of service, Your Grace?"

The duke released her and leaned back against his desk. It was a heavy but plain piece of furniture. "How can I put this…" He poked his bottom lip out thoughtfully. "I've been very interested in you since news from the colonies came back to us in trickles—and then in the abrupt flood saying that the princess had granted Qazāl independence." He gave an indulgent chuckle that put Touraine's hackles up.

"You were Cantic's, yes?" he asked.

"General Cantic was my first instructor after I was taken, yes."

"How did you find the experience? The classes, the training, and so on." He swept a palm out in front of the desk. "Stand there."

Taken aback, Touraine stepped closer to the desk. A half-finished charcoal drawing on paper was waiting for its master. Nicolas went behind the desk again and pulled out a fresh sheet and picked up his charcoal. He swept the other used paper aside and began sketching something new.

The turn of his questioning was unexpected. "I was young." She had to look down awkwardly on him. "It's hard to say."

It wasn't hard to say. She had loved it, after the initial bouts of fear and confusion. She learned to please Cantic and the other instructors well. She hadn't known any better.

"Do your best," the duke said. "Did it help you as a soldier?"

"Of course, Your Grace."

"What aspects, specifically?"

"Er—mathematics?" Touraine said. "Reading and writing? Combat skills."

She frowned as she realized what he was drawing on the paper. It was her. The rough shape of her head, the proportions of her shoulders, arms, legs. Her facial features.

"Very good. And would you say your treatment was fair or poor?"

Touraine eyed him warily. "Fair, Your Grace." As if there were another answer she could give in his company.

He made a curious grunt in his throat. "How peculiar."

His expression left Touraine wondering if he had seen through her. The more pressing question was what it had shown him and what he planned on doing with the information.

"Now, lift your arms up and out."

Touraine complied automatically and hated herself for it. Now she saw where he was going with this. *She* was the animal, some exotic species he'd never seen before. If he had been anyone else, she would have walked out immediately. Probably would have added a fist for good measure. But her conscript training still held fast. He was the duke regent.

Laid over it all like a too-warm blanket in sweltering heat was the overlay of a different memory of Balladaire. A different time, a different cold and steady eye.

She remembered standing under inspection for Instructor Cantic under a bright spring sun, the day she got her first Balladairan military uniform. Not the simple gray children's uniforms that kept them clothed and identifiable, but a proper soldier's jacket and trousers, real boots. Cantic looking her over with grim satisfaction. The ghost of Cantic's fingertips brushing her jacket's shoulders and straightening the collar. Touraine had been young—she'd only had her monthly courses for a couple of years—but she had known that Cantic was leaving, and so, when Cantic gave her a nod of approval, a hint of a smile, Touraine had flushed with gratitude and pride. With...love.

Here, now, in front of the duke, her face burned. She wished she could call that heat anger, but that would have been a lie. It was shame, hot and true.

*Leave*, Touraine told herself. Begged herself. But her boots stuck to the wooden floor. Sky above, she was a free citizen, wasn't she?—a Qazāli citizen! Sovereign. And yet, she had her papers for Balladaire. Luca had made her a Balladairan citizen. She dropped her arms to her sides and held them tight.

"I must confess, when I first had the idea to start the conscript program, I didn't think it would take. The inferior physiques and mental abilities we found in the colonies didn't seem like they could support the more rigorous training and education of a Balladairan."

"You started it?" The words burst out.

The duke smiled humbly, nodding, and continued, "I said to the generals, at least they would make serviceable infantry."

*Use the pawns first, and spare the more valuable pieces.* The first lesson Luca had taught Touraine.

"We're the reason you still have the Moyenne," Touraine said coldly. "*We* pushed the Taargens back. *We* held off their bear-priests. We were more than serviceable."

Duke Ancier scribbled notes on the page and retorted without looking up, "And yet, you're the reason we no longer have Qazāl and why the other Shālan colonies are in danger of infection with sedition. You rebel against civilization itself."

He looked between her and his notes before nodding at his paper with satisfaction.

"You'll be glad to know that you are a fine specimen of our first efforts to educate the primitive, and your...overall success has inspired further research. I've already opened a new school for Shālans and other immigrants from throughout the empire. It will use the most recent research in the Droitist theories. Especially useful now that my niece has invited this influx of"—he paused and gave a small smile, as if handing out alms—"seekers of a better life. I would love to show you and Aranen our progress. I also understand she has a strong command of the Qazāli physiognomy. She can share what she knows about the needs of your kind. I'm also curious to see how they compare with your young friend there. You are a Qazāli native, are you not, child?"

Nicolas's eyes roved curiously over Ghadin, and Touraine felt sick. She should never have brought the girl with her.

Touraine made a low cutting motion with her hand. *Don't answer.*

The cloying, sweet pity of his smile twisted Touraine's stomach even more. Luca wanted Touraine to convince this sack of bearshit that an alliance with Qazāl was worth it?

Luca always asked Touraine for the impossible.

Luck was with Luca the next morning. When she marched on the infirmary, Touraine was nowhere to be found. Aranen din Djasha was alone, tending the boy from last night. He chatted happily with the priestess in Balladairan.

Had he been cut off from speaking Shālan until he'd forgotten it, like Touraine? When had he come to Balladaire?

She knocked before stepping through.

"Good morning, Aranen din." Luca bowed her head. "How are you?"

Despite everything that had happened between them—small things only, like having Aranen jailed until she gave up the secrets of her god, or Aranen holding Luca's life in the vengeful grip of said god—Luca admired the woman. Though she was soft-spoken and otherwise not very physically intimidating, Aranen was the strongest person that Luca knew. Jaghotai had bluster and muscles and could lead her followers, but when Aranen whispered, a room went silent. A city obeyed. What a pair she and Djasha must have been.

And Luca would never forget the searching way Aranen had pulsed through her body, deciding whether or not Luca should live or die. She had spared Luca, though she had no reason to.

For that, Luca owed her everything.

Aranen stood and bowed. "I'm well. To what do we owe the pleasure?" She gave a polite non-smile.

Luca crossed her hands on her cane in front of her and focused on the metal of the horse head handle. She took a deep breath. She was not especially good at this part.

"I came to apologize. To both of you." She bowed to the boy in the bed, too. "If I had known my uncle's intent, I would have stopped him."

"It was very poorly done." Aranen frowned.

"I know." Luca tried to relax her face and let her guilt show, fighting the instinct to hide her feelings. She turned to the boy. "What's your name?"

He and Aranen shared a look, and the priestess gave him an encouraging nod. "Mounir, Your Highness," he said softly. He didn't raise his eyes to hers.

"Mounir." A Shālan name. Luca strongly doubted that was what he'd been called in the palace. "You'll be well compensated for your pains. Where do you normally work in the palace?"

"I'm one of the duke's pages, if it please you, Your Highness."

"It doesn't please me. Would you like another job?"

His eyes went wide, then he trained them on his lap again. "If it please you, Your Highness."

Luca almost pinched her nose in exasperation. *Don't lose your temper with the boy. You're the sky-falling princess; what do you expect?* a voice in her head challenged her. It sounded annoyingly like Touraine's.

She stepped closer to his bed, and Aranen moved slightly to make space while hovering protectively.

"You misunderstand, Mounir. I'm giving you a choice. Do you have parents in the city?"

He shook his head at his lap, lips tight.

*Ah.* "Is there something else you've wanted to do? Train for the palace guard, perhaps?" Like every other youth Luca knew. Even Sabine had wanted to be one of Luca's royal guard before she realized the benefits of her own rank. Everyone dreamed of glory like the old chevaliers. Even Touraine. A smile tugged at her mouth at the thought.

Mounir's face went slack with surprise. He looked shyly at Aranen.

"I don't want to fight." He looked at his arm, still wrapped in bandages. The cut must not have been serious enough to merit the healing magic.

An inexplicable tenderness warmed Luca. "What, then?"

He looked between Luca and Aranen again. "I . . . I like the pastries, Your Highness?" Mounir said hesitantly. "I could learn to make them? If not, though, I could help Lady Aranen and Lady Touraine—"

Luca snickered. "Lord, if you must. She'll kill you if you call her lady."

Aranen smirked, too, but the poor boy swallowed, and Luca realized she could have perhaps chosen her words better.

Luca looked to Aranen with a raised eyebrow.

"I'm afraid we already have a page," Aranen said softly. "And if you don't like fighting it would be a tricky place for you."

"Not to worry, though," Luca said before the boy's face could fall. "You'll have a place in the kitchen. Aranen din, may I have a word in private? Back in my own office."

The priestess sobered. "Of course. If I can change Mounir's dressing, first."

"Of course."

Luca and Aranen sipped their small cups of bitter coffee in a moment of silence.

"I wanted to ask you some things." Luca's hand trembled. The coffee in her cup sloshed like a tiny, dark ocean in a tempest. Like her stomach. She wished she had had luck doing this on her own, but she needed a lead. She opened her mouth again, but Aranen cut her off.

"About magic."

When Aranen said the word, her newly gold eyes seemed to flash. Certainly it was only Luca's overactive imagination. She sipped her coffee and nodded. It was difficult to find her composure. Anylight, the priestess would see right through any facade Luca built around herself.

"My magic?" Aranen said stiffly.

"Yes. I'm...pausing my search for the Balladairan magic. I've turned up nothing so far, and I need to put my attention elsewhere."

"You found nothing at all?" Aranen said, her voice surprisingly gentle.

"Nothing." No sense in going into Bastien's lead just yet.

"It makes an ironic sort of sense. Balladaire tried to uproot everyone else's religion like a weed. You probably did the same to yourself."

Luca grimaced. She had come to a similar conclusion. The absence was too clean. The history hadn't been lost to time; it had been purged.

"You don't know anything, do you?" she asked.

Aranen shook her head, hands held out helplessly. "Djasha was the scholar. I learned the body. I learned my art. That's all. I'm sorry."

"I understand. Thank you. I actually came to speak to you about our own alliance—"

"How would you use it, if you found it?" Aranen interrupted. She cocked her head over her delicate coffee cup. "You aren't a believer, are you?"

"No," Luca said quickly.

But she remembered so clearly the feeling of Aranen probing her with her magic. It hadn't been Aranen alone. Something else was there, seeing her, judging her. If that was Shāl, how could she deny it? And if she couldn't deny it, did that make her a believer?

She put her cup down and signaled for two more. "I thought I could strengthen my claim to the throne by strengthening Balladaire."

The priestess's gaze was steady, and Luca had the feeling she was being tested again.

She straightened. "I've just cost my empire. Drastically. I'm afr—" Luca stopped. She couldn't admit that aloud. A queen couldn't say she was *afraid*. Especially not to a powerful priestess of the country she hadn't even properly freed.

"There are already whispers that it was my incompetence that caused it, fanned, no doubt, by my uncle. Balladairan magic would have been an alternative. Something else to give my people."

"And lacking your own magic, you turn again to ours. Hence, yesterday's demonstration."

Luca leaned forward in her seat, opening her mouth to continue, but Aranen held up a hand and frowned. The chain of prayer beads she wore slid halfway down her thin forearm.

"Why are you talking to me about this?"

"To talk about what it means to trade your healing with us. Hospitals, acolytes, all of—"

"No. Why are you talking to me and not Touraine?"

Luca clamped her jaw tight. She felt herself blushing. "Because. I wanted to know what's possible before I bring a complete offer to the table. You're the High Priestess."

"I am a member of the ruling council. But so is Touraine, and we're here together." Aranen stood. "Next time you want to talk about this, bring us both. She's a council member, too. She deserves to be treated as another sovereign, not a friend you can ask for favors and then cut out when it's convenient. Or when you're afraid."

Luca sat back in her chair. "I'm not—I wouldn't—"

"Thank you for the coffee, Your Highness. I'm looking forward to your parade."

# CHAPTER 11

# NEW FRIENDS

No one escorted Touraine and Ghadin from the duke's library. Touraine felt like a post-battle drunk, weaving, unsteady, nauseous. She leaned against a wall when she'd finally gotten far enough away that she didn't think Nicolas would turn up to look her over some more. Give him something else to say about "the Shālan constitution."

After her breathing calmed and her stomach stopped trying to empty itself on the marble floors of the palace corridor, the anger flooded in. Her fists balled up in rage, not fear.

Touraine knew how to aim anger.

"Are you good, Mulāzim?" Ghadin asked quietly.

"I'm good." Touraine scrubbed her face. Touraine couldn't bear to look at the girl. "Come with me."

If you know what you're looking for, a garrison and its training yard aren't hard to find.

She looked for the out-of-the-way corridors, the ones that could stand the grime and dust of working boots instead of scholar's buckles and silk slippers. She followed them toward where her heart knew boasts and bruises waited. There, she could remind herself that she was strong on her own—without some lord or commander to tell her so.

Ghadin practically ran to keep up with her, matching Touraine's silence.

They spilled out onto a courtyard large enough for the palace guard and a few squads of local soldiers to cut their teeth. It was only after they arrived that Touraine realized she was still dressed in the fine clothes she'd worn to see the duke. Pulling his face back to mind set her blood burning all over again, and she stopped caring about the clothes. Let Luca throw more at her.

Touraine unbuttoned her jacket, ready to throw it on the ground, ready to throw everything on the ground, when she stopped.

All around her, pale Balladairans, pink and shining with exertion, wrestled, punched, swiped at each other. Some ran in pairs around the outer edge or taunted each other through calisthenics.

Her heart seized with so much pain that she almost doubled over. Tibeau and Aimée should have been here. They should have spent the last year sparring with her. They should have been alive. Aimée might even have come with her, back to Balladaire. Sky above, how she would've loved strutting around the palace.

"Why did you let him do that to you?" Ghadin asked quietly, punching through Touraine's grief like a cannon.

The girl was half a hand shorter than Touraine and probably wouldn't get much taller, but when she met Touraine's eyes, Touraine felt even smaller than she'd felt in the duke's library.

Touraine opened her mouth—a strangled moan came out, cut off by the thickness in her throat. She didn't have an answer she wanted to give the girl. *Because I was afraid. Because it felt normal to me.* Now that she'd seen the duke's scrutiny turn to Ghadin, there were even more reasons that she would let him do it again—*So that you won't have to. So that he forgets you even exist.* She blinked up at the sky.

"Sometimes you just have to," Touraine answered, voice hoarse.

Ghadin looked like she was forming a retort, so Touraine tossed her jacket aside and snapped her fingers. "All right. First forms. Get in position."

"But we already did them this mor—"

"First. Forms."

Ghadin obeyed. Touraine grounded herself in the dirt beneath her boots. The cool breeze felt bracing after the stifling heat of Duke Ancier's library.

One set of the forms, slow and repetitive to warm up the joints. At least she had maintained these in Qazāl. Moreover, her body was hers now.

It did not belong to either of the lords Ancier.

Or so she told herself as she led Ghadin from one strike to another.

Somehow, she'd lost herself so deep in the movements that she was startled when she turned and a young soldier stood a few paces away, watching her. She held herself, mid-strike, her whole body coiled to kick. She imagined spinning the blow into the side of the man's body. He had a soft face and hadn't approached with the brash arrogance that so many Balladairan soldiers took around the Sands. (*There are no more Sands.*)

"What do you want?" Touraine asked sharply.

"Would you like a sparring partner?" he asked. "My name is Valmorin." Valmorin had tufts of blond on his upper lip and along the base of his chin. He wasn't tall or broad, so she wondered what he was going to bring to any fight. An eye with a musket? Or money for a horse.

It might have felt good to knock a Balladairan into the dirt, but Touraine was too aware of Ghadin's presence.

"I don't need one," Touraine said quickly. She nodded to Ghadin. "I'm training her."

A taller guard with a proud, unshaven day of dark beard-shadow swaggered up behind Valmorin like a hound who'd caught scent of its prey. He had familiar lieutenant's wheat sheaves on his collar. He propped an arm on Valmorin's shoulder. The shorter man flinched at the other's presence and then refused to meet Touraine's eyes again. She took it that Beard-Shadow didn't just pick on Qazāli.

Even though the new soldier didn't have Captain Rogan's narrow horse-face or long hair, there was enough familiarity in his bearing that he put Touraine on edge. She shifted her weight. Just in case.

"What would it take," Beard-Shadow drawled, "to get you to fight a couple of us?"

Touraine said nothing, waiting.

"We've heard things about the princess's Qazāli," he continued with a shrug. "We wondered if they were true."

This wouldn't go anywhere good. Touraine stepped back, pulling Ghadin with her.

She backed into someone very solid. Animal fear near broke her. The feeling of being hemmed in. Men like him thrived on fear. Sky above knew she'd learned that lesson time and again with Rogan. She fought down the panic in her chest and turned slowly to face the guards surrounding her, making a point of showing the others her back.

Instead of another guard, though, the marquise de Durfort stood, tall and broad shouldered, wearing tailored training clothes that showed the strength in her legs and backside.

"Marquise." Touraine dipped her head.

"Your Excellency." Durfort flashed a gleaming smile. "I thought I might find you here. Her Highness mentioned you have a fondness for the physical arts. Were you about to show Fougaire and these lads a thing or two from the colonies?" She feinted her shoulders, exaggerating a dodge from imaginary blows.

"No, Your Grace. This soldier graciously invited me to train with him." Touraine nodded curtly to Valmorin. His cheeks were flaming, probably with as much embarrassment as Touraine felt.

"I prefer to train on my own," she lied, "but thank you."

"Oh, nonsense!" Durfort clapped her hands together. "Surely you must." She beckoned the young man over and then shouted to one of the children waiting along the edges to ferry and fetch for the soldiers. "Two practice blades, a duel!"

"Wait, Your Grace—"

The marquise wasn't listening. She was busy conducting the field of play, moving the gathering crowd of soldiers and guards several steps back so that Touraine would have a chance to humiliate herself a second time today. Durfort waved to the sky, and Touraine's stomach dropped in horror. There was a glassed-in viewing corridor above the courtyard. Any noble in the palace could look down and admire the strength of their protectors. *Shit.*

"Your Grace." Touraine squeezed Durfort by the arm. "I don't know how to use a sword," she hissed.

That brought the marquise up short. She kept smiling that charming grin and said through her teeth, "You don't...what?"

Touraine bent her head closer to the marquise. "The Sands don't use swords."

"Then what under the sky above do you do? Spit at the Taargens?"

Touraine looked at her incredulously. "We didn't duel the Taargens, Your Grace, we shot at them! Muskets. Cannons. Fuc—fists if they got too close."

Durfort frowned, as if it had been Touraine's choice to go to war under-armed. "That sounds dreadfully dull."

"Take it up with the generals another time, Your Grace. I'm not making a fool of myself right now."

"No. You really can't afford that," Durfort muttered.

They scanned their growing audience, both above and on the ground.

"Do you trust me?" Durfort said softly.

"What—?"

Before Touraine could properly object, the kid with the blunted practice steels—definitely some noble offspring still too young to be training formally—shuffled eagerly up to Durfort.

Durfort took the blades and made a show of studying them. Liking what she saw, she ruffled the kid's hair. "My thanks, young chevalier." The child beamed.

With one, she pointed Touraine and Valmorin into the center of the area she'd cleared. They obeyed. Then, capriciously, she threw the practice steels to the side. The poor kid who'd brought them looked near to tears, confused, lip quivering. Touraine empathized.

"I've changed my mind." Durfort held her arms out to encompass everyone watching, though the nobles in the palace corridors above would hear nothing. "I want this to be interesting. No swords. Let's see them get creative."

This time, Valmorin looked uncertain.

It was the asshole Fougaire who spoke, though. "You want them brawling like common infantry?"

"Now, now, Fougaire." Durfort patted the air in front of her. "I want an interesting show."

Touraine met Valmorin's eyes. He looked hesitant but he nodded. He looked like he'd never been close enough to an enemy to smell their sweat, let alone punch them.

They squared off to his compatriots' dark comments. Fine by Touraine. It wasn't the first time Balladairans had been upset about a challenge they started. At least here they couldn't sneak up on her when she went to piss in the middle of the night.

"On my say. Stop at surrender." Durfort raised her arm. "Ready—"

"No head blows," Touraine interjected.

"Of course, of course. No...head blows," Durfort repeated, as if the words were foreign. "Ready—and—fight!" Her arm fell down like a flag.

Either Valmorin was nervous, or he really had no idea what he was doing, but whatever it was, he jabbed at her straight on, his feet awkwardly placed a step too far apart.

Touraine grabbed his outstretched wrist and used his own momentum to pull him close to her, his arm twisted behind his back between them. Touraine's other arm barred his throat. His other hand scrabbled helplessly against the muscle and bone of her forearm.

He tapped her arm frantically. "Yield," he said hoarsely.

She let him go and he fell to his knees, purple faced. He massaged his throat and shoulder alternately. All told, it had only taken a few seconds and she hadn't done him any lasting damage. Touraine considered that a success.

Fougaire the Asshole did not. He scowled. "Again. Another one. Valmorin is new. A child."

If Valmorin took any offense to that, he said nothing from the ground. Durfort's mouth, however, was open in an excited grin, full of bright teeth.

"It's true. Valmorin, though noble in his effort, was not enough to test the ambassador. She'll take two challengers!"

Everyone's eyes widened, including Touraine's. She didn't have a chance to say no. Two more of the palace soldiers stepped up, this time eager. Their odds just improved.

Touraine scowled at the marquise. The other woman smiled jauntily and sauntered out of the area of play.

It took a little longer, and the cheering against her was louder, but in the end, she left both soldiers on the ground, one clutching his balls and the other dry heaving to the side.

This time, Durfort wasn't surprised. She stepped in immediately to grab her new champion's arm.

Touraine had won. Again. Something felt off in the pit of her stomach. She had the feeling she'd been turned into a puppet again. She just couldn't figure out how, or whose, or why.

"Surely that was still too easy." Durfort grinned at the crowd. "How about three?"

"No." Touraine had to draw the line somewhere.

"Are you afraid?" Fougaire stepped forward. "The great desert beast can't handle a few soldiers after all? It's my turn."

Touraine shook off Durfort's arm and met Fougaire in the middle. She was close enough to see the texture of the hair beneath his shirt and to smell the sour sweat that dampened it. She had not murdered Rogan only to have this half-cocked piece of bearshit talk to her like this.

"Three people in a contest to surrender doesn't work. You want me to fight three of you and it's broken skulls and flattened throats. Your soldiers would be done for months. Unless you're volunteering?" She spoke loud enough for the closest audience. It included not a few of the middling nobles who had come down from the viewing corridor despite the growing chill and the clouds overhead. Fougaire said nothing.

Touraine turned to Durfort. "I'm done."

Touraine found Ghadin holding her jacket. This time, the girl was beaming. Whatever Touraine had broken in the girl by not leaving Duke Ancier's grip, maybe she'd just fixed it. Touraine draped her coat over one sweaty shoulder and—politely—shoved past the nobles.

She was only half-surprised when Durfort caught up with them.

"That was indeed quite a show," Durfort said, eyebrows raised with interest. "Very impressive."

"Glad I could entertain you," Touraine said darkly. "Your Grace."

"Mm?" The marquise had sensed the shift in Touraine's attitude. They weren't coconspirators anymore.

"I know your mother." Touraine finally placed Durfort's title, recalling the dowager marquise with unfortunate clarity—or at least, her words. She'd called the Sands dogs. *Easily trained and begging for a master.*

"Not well, I hope."

Touraine snorted. "Thankfully, no. We met at a dinner with the governor-general when I first got to Qazāl."

"You?" Durfort's eyes widened. "Dined with the governor-general? Who did you pay off for that?"

"I was a good soldier."

"Until you weren't, or so I hear." She smiled crookedly at Touraine. "I would love to hear the full tale sometime."

"You mean the princess hasn't already given it to you?" Touraine was genuinely surprised. Right now, she felt like nothing was her own, not even her own history. That, at least, was worth a silent *thank you* to Luca, wherever she was.

The ready charm on the other woman's face was replaced with careful study. "No. She keeps your secrets close."

They walked in awkward silence through the palace corridors until Durfort broke it abruptly.

"Let me teach you to duel."

"What?"

"Duel. Sword. The pointy ends." Durfort lunged, brandishing an invisible rapier. Her own sword knocked at her hip.

"Why?" Touraine looked at her skeptically.

"Well, I would normally never give Fougaire credence, but he's right. Brawling is for common soldiers. You are an ambassador. While it's not strictly necessary, it will earn you some respect to be a creditable duelist."

Touraine grunted. She liked fighting. She liked the rush of blood, the thrill of her own strength, the heavy breath of victory. She would never deny a chance to learn a new method under better circumstances. These were not better circumstances. They were suspicious ones.

"Why do you want to teach me?"

"Because I'm the best in the empire." Durfort said it simply, as if it were an incontestable fact. "I even helped train our beloved princess when we were young. When I'm in the mood, I teach private classes."

She gave Touraine a rakish look that left Touraine in little doubt about what those private classes could entail.

"More importantly," Durfort added in a low voice, "I can tell you more about the court and how we do things around here."

Now that would be useful. Something uncertain still sat in the pit of Touraine's stomach, but the lessons would help her do her job. And, if she would admit it to herself, it also gave her a—well, if not a friend, a companion.

They'd reached a branching hallway, ready to go separate ways.

"What do you think?" Durfort asked.

"All right, Your Grace. Teach me how to duel."

"It would be my pleasure. Will you be in La Chaise long? I expect we'll both be busy with Her Highness's birthday festivities next week, but after that, I am at your leisure."

Touraine didn't know how long she and Aranen would be in Balladaire, but she was already suspecting it was going to be longer than the Qazāli Council had planned.

# A HEALER'S INTERLUDE 1

Aranen is alone in every way that counts.

None of her friends or the friends who she calls family are nearby to reach for. The child in her care lies in a fitful sleep. The Balladairan doctor has also retired.

Aranen sweeps the boy's loose, silken curls off his forehead, gently arranging them about his face.

It is a distraction.

An empty plate sits on the simple bedside table beside her, along with one of Djasha's journals. They offer little comfort in comparison, but her wife's words inspire Aranen to *try again*.

Aranen scans the room, self-conscious in a way she has never been before. There is a jarring dissonance in her mind: the room, with its Balladairan decor—curls of leaf, curves of blossom, carved and pressed and sewn into wood and metal and fabric alike—is so foreign and yet utterly familiar. She has never seen an oak tree, and yet she recognizes its acorn. Though Aranen had never been to Balladaire, Balladaire had come to her and infected like a disease.

She can remember a Qazāl before Balladaire, but she remembers it as a dream, not as a fact.

Aranen is alone and so she prays.

She seeks the beat of her heart, the press of blood and breath through her body. Her pulse is quick. Once, it was calm and certain, even under the pressure of life and death. Once, it was—

Panic is a distraction.

She reaches out and places a hand on the boy's bandaged forearm. A practiced flick of her wrist brings the bone prayer beads down her wrist and into her other hand. She concentrates on the chicken she's just eaten, its small sacrifice. She pushes this life, this sacrifice, and her own life to the boy's wound. His blood, his flesh.

She tries to be a conduit.

Her hands remain cold. Something in the familiar ritual dies, as it has every time since *that day*.

Alone. Truly alone.

Even Jaghotai would not understand the desperation Aranen feels. The shame. If losing a wife is an amputation, losing Shāl's gift is evisceration. Aranen has lost Djasha before. She has never lost this.

Aranen has not forgotten how Shāl's light burned away the threads holding the Blood General's body together. It makes her shiver, not entirely with revulsion. Drunk on the lifeblood of her wife, Aranen had burned with power and she had liked it. There had been nothing peaceful in her.

But she has faith in Shāl and faith in Shāl's tenets: peace above all.

The boy's eyes flicker beneath his eyelids with unquiet dreams. When she looks at him, she sees the duke's smug smile: the mundane arrogance of someone so accustomed to dominance that he cannot conceive of defeat.

It is hard not to think like Djasha when she thinks of that smile. *You have the power to end them all.*

Aranen jerks at the sudden vehemence of the thought, putting a hand to her lips as if she can muffle her already quiet sobs.

There is a new feeling there, wrapped up in the cold shame, or if it is not new, it is one she sees at last for what it is: fear.

Not fear that her god has abandoned her. Not fear of Balladaire.

She is afraid of herself. She is afraid of what she is capable of.

# PART 2

## SCHOLARS AND
## NOBLES AND PRIESTS

# CHAPTER 12

# FAUX PAS

Thunder rumbled in the distance as Touraine faced down the giant beast from her saddle and prepared to do battle.

"You're not so scary," Touraine muttered.

The horse blew in irritation before turning away from the two-legged nuisance on its back.

Beside Touraine's leg, a stablehand tried to broker a peace between Touraine and the horse that she was meant to ride in the autumn parade.

It wasn't the horse that made her nervous. It was the height, and the fact that the horse could take her anywhere it wanted, or buck her off and break her neck, or trample her—

"Is everything all right, Your Excellency?"

The stablehand's eyes went wide with panic as Princess Luca approached them. He bowed deeply. "Your Highness! I'm sorry she's late. We're trying. I swear, Cendre here is the sweetest girl we have, but—"

Luca smiled. "It's all right. You explained to the ambassador the basics?"

The boy knuckled his forehead. "Aye, Your Highness."

"I'll take it from here, then." She dismissed him with a nod.

Touraine looked on warily. When they were alone, Luca craned her neck to look up at her. Touraine started when she saw the thin circlet around Luca's brow, gold and silver vines entwined. It was the first time Touraine had ever seen Luca wear anything to indicate her royal status. It fit her.

"You look well up there." Luca's voice shook with mirth even though her expression was as smooth and cool as ever.

Touraine scowled. "Not funny." She clutched the reins tighter, and the horse whinnied in disapproval.

"Easy, Ambassador." Luca put her hand on the saddle beside Touraine's thigh. The horse settled beneath the princess's hand. Touraine hoped Luca didn't hear the sharp intake of her breath. Touraine knew how much Luca disliked horses, so Luca's quiet certainty as she calmed the animal tightened something deep in Touraine's belly.

To the horse beneath Touraine, Luca said, "I'm sorry that we haven't had time to talk since you arrived. With the Taargens, the Many-Legged, and the Southern Mountain delegations arriving, I haven't even had the chance to piss." Luca ran her thumbnail along the sewn seam of Touraine's saddle. A moment of nerves showing through. Was it Touraine who made her so nervous, the horse, or the politicking?

Then, abruptly, Luca looked up and asked, "Would you ride beside me today? It's tradition that a close friend rides to the right of the royal being fêted."

"A close friend?" Touraine said, trying, and failing, to mask her surprise.

Luca dug her nail back into the saddle as she nodded. "I know you feel...precarious here. I—let me help. It's a place of honor. People will see that you have royal favor. It will be especially useful with the Taargens, I think. And the Balladairans, of course."

Touraine raised an eyebrow. "The court already knows I have your favor. Doesn't seem like it's doing *us* any favors."

Luca pressed her lips together. "They'll know you have my protection. Besides, I mean the Balladairans in the city. And the Qazāli."

If seeing her beside a royal raised the standing of others like her, it might actually be worth making a fool of herself. Something about the thought felt familiar, but she couldn't place it. "I can barely ride," Touraine warned Luca.

"Can you make her move forward?" Luca asked.

"And keep my seat at the same time? Doubt it."

"Nonsense. Try." Luca stepped well out of the way.

Touraine made a skeptical sound in her throat but nudged the toe of her boot tentatively into the gray's ribs. The horse shook its head and took one step forward. It whickered and shook its head again.

From down the stable, the same stablehand called, "She's laughing at you, sir. Give her a bit more than that."

Touraine scowled at the boy, who bent back to his pretend task with a smile, keeping one eye on his four-legged charge. Touraine nudged the horse again, harder this time. The horse took a few more steps this time and made another whickering sound, like it approved. The last of the stablehands cackled appreciatively from inside the stables.

That wasn't so bad. Touraine flushed with pride and somehow convinced her horse to follow Luca and Gil to the front of the parade.

Above, the clouds teased them all, floating just distant enough and slowly enough to let everyone hope that the procession would proceed without rain.

The parade included the nobles from the High and Middle Courts and an array of impressive soldiers: Brice and Sabine on horseback, Ghislaine and Evrard in carriages bearing their house symbols— a golden cockerel and a red boar with black bristles—and the duke himself, in a carriage with the Ancier horse. After the soldiers came the Low Court, not nobles at all, but dancers and musicians especially chosen for the day and honored with positions at court throughout the winter.

Met with the most anticipation were the meal wagons. As the procession passed through each quartier of La Chaise, one wagon stayed behind and a contingent of mighty quartermasters dispersed a meal of fowl and stewed grains, baked apples and fine wine to everyone. An easy way to buy the people's loyalty for a little longer. Luca had tried that in Qazāl, too, handing out food and money to the Qazāli who had suffered under the Balladairan rampage through El-Wast, buying them away from the rebels. It had almost ended the rebellion.

The procession moved through the upper and middling quartiers, populated with old families and merchants who'd made their fortune trading—stealing, more like—from the colonies. Artisans and shop-keepers stood in front of their storefronts dressed in their best hose and jackets, all to see Luca.

That changed when the procession crossed the bridge into the labor quartiers. In the streets of La Gouttière, people turned out in their caps and coats and held eager children on their shoulders. Some shiv-ered in their shirtsleeves or, worst case, in rags. Qazāli stood out in the crowd—one even carried a large metal kettle, selling drinks of coffee. Touraine clenched her jaw against the sudden ache of familiarity.

Through it all, Luca waved, a tight smile fixed to her face.

"They look hungry," Touraine said softly.

"This is a festival day." Luca frowned up at wet drops falling from the clouds and pulled her cloak up over her head. "They'll be well fed, play music and dance, put their work away."

Touraine grunted. Sounded more like Luca was trying to convince herself than anything.

A rush of motion in the corner of her eye dragged Touraine's atten-tion backward.

"Shit." A block behind them, where Luca's coin throwers were toss-ing half sovereigns into the crowd, a fight was breaking out. Touraine wobbled violently in her saddle and swore again.

Luca hissed her quiet, grabbing Touraine's arm to steady her. "What is it?"

Touraine jerked her arm away, and it almost sent her tumbling again. The gray mare snorted in annoyance. Then the angry shouting reached them.

"Balladairans." Touraine swore. "They're fighting the Qazāli for coins."

"A scuffle is normal, Touraine. It's money."

"Maybe that's the problem, Highness."

The "scuffle" rippled through the line of the crowd as civilians on both sides of the road grew more interested in the conflict than the procession.

Touraine yanked at her reins, trying to turn her horse around. The horse pulled against her with its better judgment.

"They're going to beat one of my people to death for some of your stupid coins, Luca! Stop them!"

In the pause before Luca answered, the rain crested like an incoming wave. The crowd scattered, ignoring the chance to catch coins or taking the opportunity to push closer. Luca reached for Touraine's arm again, but Touraine twisted out of reach.

"Touraine, you are making a scene in front of every Balladairan noble"—Luca leaned over to her and hissed—"the Taargens and anyone else you want respect from. You are *not* a soldier anymore. You can't brawl in the dirt and bash in heads whenever you feel like it."

Touraine hesitated. She was supposed to be wooing Luca, getting the princess to help the Qazāli, but if Luca wasn't going to help the people Touraine was here for, what was the point?

"You mean anyone *you* want respect from." Touraine clumsily swung her leg around. She yelped as she slipped on the wet stirrup and crashed to the mud. Not the graceful punctuation she'd hoped for.

She scrambled to her feet and loped toward the fighting, ignoring the sharp bruising of her ass. *There.* The Qazāli with the steel kettle. He was being piled on by a ruddy Balladairan man in a heavy apron. A cluster of Qazāli tried to pull the ruddy man off, and other Balladairans tried to shove them back. The steel pot lay on its side, dented, black-brown liquid pooling out to mingle with the rain.

No one from Luca's procession came to help, not the guards and not the cavalry on their fine horses, and no sign of the gendarmerie.

She drew her long knife and waded into the din of grunting and swearing. She added her own shouts, in Balladairan and Shālan both. She yanked the Balladairans off the Qazāli, and they rounded on her— then they took in her finery and her bared weapon. Her face, her skin. They looked back to the procession.

Thunder clapped overhead.

"In the name of Her Royal Highness Princess Luca, stop this immediately." Touraine squared herself between the aggressors and the Qazāli man on the ground, her blade pointed at the Balladairans. The last thing anyone in this Shāl-forsaken city needed was the Qazāli ambassador poking holes in Balladairan citizens, but her people didn't deserve to be beaten, either, and Touraine was sore and out of patience.

The Balladairan in the apron sized her up. His rain-dark hair was soaked to his red face, his chest heaving. Bright silver and gold flashed as he slid the coins into his apron pocket. Then he spat at her feet and left, and the Balladairan support shrank away.

The procession itself had moved on without her. *Well, fuck you, too, Princess.*

Touraine dug into her anger so that she could avoid the hurt, and that same shame she'd felt in the duke's library, shame that she even cared. This was why she held Luca at a distance.

*This is why you have to get close to her. She won't change this for anyone but you.*

Touraine snorted in disgust. That was seeming more and more unlikely.

Touraine hoisted the man up from the mud with matching groans. A little Qazāli boy darted forward nervously, chasing down tin cups and the steel pot with its clever little spigot.

"Thank you, sister," the man said in Shālan. He winced as he spoke. His thick beard was dark with shots of gray. His back was slightly stooped without the weight of the pot. He sighed at the pot the boy carried and the smashed contraption that had helped him carry it.

"Are you all right?" she asked. "I can escort you to the palace and have you seen by Her Highness's physicians."

The man shook his head sharply, then winced again, pressing a hand to his temple. "I've been in a fight or two, sister."

The last wagon was well up the road. The Balladairans edged away from them, but slowly, like wolves waiting for the sheep to be left unattended. The few Qazāli who had come to the man's rescue glared around them like an honor guard. Touraine almost laughed. She should start traveling with protection, like Luca. Her own gendarmerie, if Luca wouldn't help.

"Let me escort you home, at least." She took in the rest of them with a look. "All of you."

The man considered her and then the wary Balladairans around them. He nodded. "My name is Sulmain."

"I'm Ambassador Touraine El-Qazāli." Touraine hoisted the steel kettle from the boy.

The man tried to take it from her, but flinched before he could even take the full load of its weight. "It's all right, I've got it." She considered its bulk as she followed him. "What is this, anyway?"

For the first time, the man brightened. "I made it. Well, I made the tray and the straps. The pot, I had a friend make. Good with metals. It holds coffee. More watered down than proper, but these people can't handle coffee the way it's meant to be. No problem." He grinned. "I make more money when it's watered down."

They wound between leaning tenement buildings, and Touraine found herself uncertain if she should pay more attention to where her feet went or to what was above her. She'd imagined herself dying in a lot of ways, but under a building in Balladaire was not one of them.

They stopped in front of a building that looked like it was one dropped match away from taking the whole street out in flames. At least, it would have if it weren't sheeting down rain. Anyone living on the upper floor was probably getting as wet as Touraine was outside. A bold rat skittered over her boot and she bit back a screech, even though she couldn't see it with the pot in her arms. Just a rat. Nothing she hadn't seen before. She'd even slept with rats. Not by choice, but still. She took a deep breath.

"You live here?" Touraine asked dubiously.

"It's good to even have a room in this Shāl-cursed city, sister," he said defensively. "There are even Balladairans who don't have a room. Better than sleeping out in the cold." He nodded at the Qazāli who'd come with them. Touraine thought they were escorts, but the man said, "We all live together. Chip in. There's safety in the numbers, too."

"If living in Balladaire is like this, why are you still here?"

Someone laughed darkly. "How would we even get back? I'd be on the first ship home if I had a spit-soaked sovereign."

Touraine grasped at that. "I can get you passage back."

"Back to what?" someone else said sourly. "To hunger? If you can get a job, it's more money than I've seen in Qazāl."

Touraine wanted to sink to the ground and bury her face in her hands. She and the council were trying so hard, and they were still failing.

Gathering herself together felt like trying to hold a fistful of musket balls in one hand without letting them spill out. "Go to the food wagon. The gendarmerie will protect you, and you'll get a good meal."

One of the younger Qazāli scoffed. "The gendarmerie? They're more likely to hold our arms so those pork-faced bastards can get a better punch in." She spoke in the quick-fire combination of Shālan and Balladairan that was common in Qazāl but near indecipherable to outsiders.

"Besides," another piped in, "that's half the problem. That bastard picking on Sulmain? Kept saying the crown doesn't owe us shit."

Touraine growled low in her throat. The empire owed Qazāl—and all of the other Shālan nations—more than a few coins and a roasted bird. She set the large kettle on the ground.

"I'll make sure the crown gives us exactly what's owed." Touraine wished she had a coin purse on her. "I'll speak with the princess." She looked up at the apartments again, squinting against the rain. "In the meantime, I'll see what I can do about the meal."

It was their turn to look at her dubiously. A weight settled on Touraine's shoulders and she straightened beneath it, giving them her best impression of the famous rebel mulāzim.

Touraine trudged back toward the palace, boots sloshing, wet fabric chafing. She would do whatever it took to make sure that Qazāl was given its due. Luca owed them.

*     *     *

Touraine's anger kept her warm for the long walk back to the palace, but by the time she arrived, she was sodden and shivering, with cold mud splashed up her ass, and she'd had time to think about Luca's words. She stalked through marble halls like a furious, half-drowned kitten, avoiding the scandalized glances, noble and servant both. Touraine had embarrassed herself, and by extension, Qazāl. She was here to represent them and she'd gone against all decorum in front of Balladaire, Taargen, and Many-Legged alike.

Now she was going to be late to Luca's birthday banquet. After a rushed wash in freezing water, she raced to the banquet hall. It was already full, abuzz with drink and whispered scandals (of which Touraine was certainly one). Everyone had taken their places. The Lower and Middle Courts sat at tables along the walls and in rows throughout the hall, while the High Court sat at the High Table. Luca's and the duke's seats were still empty.

"There you are." Aranen appeared beside Touraine out of nowhere, everything about her sharp with disapproval.

The priestess was elegant in a long, sleeveless red gown belted with slashes of yellow and orange silk up the torso. Her short, gray-streaked curls were slicked back behind her ears, and the ears themselves were studded with a few golden rings. She reminded Touraine of the desert sunset. An angry sunset. Ghadin trailed behind Aranen in a long shirt the color of the desert sky at midnight and white trousers.

"Swear to me on Shāl's name that the rumors aren't true," the priestess asked in Shālan. "Tell me it's just gossip and we can start repairing the damage."

Touraine sucked in a breath. "Depends on the rumors."

"The rumor," Ghadin piped up, "is that you beat the jackal piss out of some Balladairans over the coins the princess threw."

"Okay, that's true enough." Touraine waved her hand in the air— *sort of.*

Aranen's nostrils flared. "Touraine, could you possibly be any more—" She pressed her palms together and put her fingers to her lips as she visibly tried to calm herself. "Touraine. I don't think what you did was wrong. But this is not going to help your reputation."

"As the traitorous, street-brawling rebel conscript that the princess keeps around as a pet," Ghadin added unhelpfully.

"Thanks, I got that," Touraine muttered in Balladairan. "Sounds like you'd be better off sending me back?"

Aranen sighed. "Don't be so eager. We're Qazāli. We represent Qazāl. It's better if we stick together. We rise together, we fall together. We'll be that much more likely to survive together."

Despite the growing ball of dread in the pit of Touraine's stomach, Aranen's words steadied her. She stood a little straighter. "Let's go fall together, then."

Touraine's neck burned with the feeling of eyes on her. She took the empty seat at the end of the table, where a small placard held her name in curled script. Her Excellency Ambassador Touraine El-Qazāli.

Aranen took the chair to her left, and Ghadin took her place against the back wall with the other young pages. Touraine's face fell when she saw Brice de Moyenne across from her. Durfort was on the far opposite corner. Touraine tried to catch the marquise's friendly eye, but Durfort had turned the charm of her crooked smile on Niwai. The Many-Legged priest looked odd without their personal menagerie.

The orchestra changed its tune from gentle to strident. Everyone stood up, as if at a signal everyone but Touraine knew. She fumbled to right herself as the duke entered the room. He strode down the aisle nonchalantly and took his place at the table beside the comte de Travers, leaving the empty seat next to Aranen for Luca.

The song segued from a march to something celebratory yet dignified as Luca walked into the banquet hall.

Touraine's mouth went dry. The princess wasn't wearing her usual formal garb in dark, imperial colors. She wore a cream blouse under a startling turquoise coat that matched her eyes exactly. The stiff collar brushed her sharp jaw, set with determination. The gold embroidery sparking along the coat matched Luca's hair and the golden circlet nestled there; and her hair and the embroidery, the circlet and her gold buttons and the gold handle of her cane all glinted in the light of the chandeliers. And though her trousers were simply gray, they fit her perfectly.

Aranen cleared her throat sharply at Touraine's elbow. "Try not to be so obvious."

"Euh?"

"Your mouth is hanging open."

Touraine closed her mouth.

Luca approached the table without expression—or at least, what someone who didn't know her well would say was without expression: she scanned the room dispassionately, holding herself aloof.

Touraine could see she was nervous, though, and fighting hard to hide it. For a moment, the anger she'd nursed for the better part of the day was lost in a wave of tenderness. When Luca took her place at the table, though, the look she gave Touraine was cold.

# CHAPTER 13

# THE BEAR QUEEN

At dinner, Touraine found a new love for men who never shut up. De Moyenne was so determined to impress the solemn man and woman from the Sanshir Monastery in the Southern Mountains that he wouldn't stop talking. It meant no one had a chance to do more than stare at Touraine. No chance to get a prying word in, to ask her why she had jumped off her horse and into the mud to rescue some shabby Qazāli.

Luca came for her after dinner, looking like a storm passing through the summer sky in her gray and turquoise. Touraine braced herself for an upbraiding. Instead of chewing Touraine out, though, Luca asked, her voice strained, "How is he?"

Touraine pulled a quick rein round her half-formed defensive retort. "Better than he would have been without help."

Luca nodded sharply. "Good."

With suspicious timing, Ghadin appeared with two glasses of wine. She looked like she wanted to linger nosily, but Touraine shooed her away.

"Thank you for attempting to take care of the people in my city." Luca pressed her glass to her bottom lip. "However, you need to understand how things work here, who you are here, now, and who I am. We're not playing in the provinces. The stakes are higher."

Luca's aristocratic accent seemed stronger here, where she was surrounded by people like her. Or her irritation at Touraine was cutting her syllables short.

"Those provinces are my home," Touraine said tightly. She sipped the wine. It tasted sweet. Good, she guessed. "You're not in a position to judge those stakes for me."

"I didn't mean—"

Jaghotai was depending on her. Sulmain and the other Qazāli in Balladaire were depending on her. *Use her like she wants to use you.*

"Never mind. I'm sorry. I'll be more considerate next time." Touraine touched Luca's arm and gave her a subtle, apologetic smile.

Touraine wasn't expecting the warm smile Luca gave her in return, nor the rush of heat to her face that followed. She cleared her throat. A quick glance showed that Durfort was in animated conversation with the young Taargen princess, while de Moyenne let the young prince size him up.

"You're nervous," Luca murmured. "It's all right. It takes getting used to. It's just échecs." She gestured with her wine at the wide hall, full of the pieces on the great board of nations. Or rather, the players who moved the pieces like Touraine.

Only, Touraine *was* a player now. She just didn't know what to say, or who to say it to. The last time she'd tried her hand at "playing the game," she'd gotten her friends killed. She'd done more damage than she ever had as a pawn.

"Or, if you're like Sabine and Brice, it's all cock-waving and armflexing." Luca rolled her eyes, then sighed ruefully. "Will you be all right if I leave you? I've got to make some moves of my own."

Touraine remembered the time Luca rescued her from Captain Rogan on a dance floor. Touraine had the feeling that, if she said no, Luca would stay with her. She wanted to cling to the security of Luca's presence.

Instead, she bowed. "I'll be fine."

When Luca left, Touraine had to count her breaths and consciously ease her clenched grip on her wine glass with each exhale. She had reached ten twice and was about to start again when the Taargen priest approached her. Touraine stopped breathing completely.

The priest was a large man built like Tibeau: wide shoulders, belly big and hard as a wine cask, and hands so large he probably could have picked Touraine up by the head with one. Unlike the twins, who wore only fur mantles, Albric wore a full bearskin cloak despite the pleasant warmth of the palace hall. A silver torc of a hollow circle hung on his chest.

Taargens like him had ripped shreds through the Sands' brigades during the war. With their god—and the unwilling sacrifice of Touraine's soldiers—they could change their forms. Touraine tried to suppress her shudder, but she could tell from Albric's abrupt smile that she'd failed.

Times changed.

"My lord," Touraine said through clenched teeth.

"The mysterious ambassador from the south." Albric smiled behind a long gray beard.

Touraine jutted her chin up. "I am. Touraine El-Qazāli."

"We have you to thank for destabilizing our neighbors. You Shālans were fierce enemies in the wars. I hope that we can be even fiercer friends." He stuck out one of his massive hands. When Touraine extended her own, expecting a soldier's clasp, he squeezed it too tightly in his own. She gasped, bit down on the sound, and squeezed back.

*It's just cock-waving and arm-flexing.* Right. Cock-waving. Touraine understood that well enough. That was half of being a soldier. She puffed out her chest and pulled her crushed hand from Albric's.

"Tell me, Your Excellency, are you a soldier or a politician?" he asked, smiling as he lowered his voice. "Or something else entirely?"

The gleam in his eyes gave Touraine pause. A glassy look like the one Niwai and Aranen sometimes had. Like he was seeing beyond her. The probing regard of a priest.

"I'm whatever my country needs me to be," she said.

"Such patriotism! But it looks like you've taken up some things I know you didn't learn in Balladaire." Albric raised a hand as if he were going to tuck a lock of hair behind Touraine's ear—only she didn't have enough hair for that, and his hand stopped short of touching her. He only pointed, indicating her eyes.

Touraine stiffened.

It was so easy to forget them.

Albric pulled back. "As they say, a bear sleeps through winter, but she wakes hungry in the spring."

Touraine raised her eyebrows. *Priests and their riddles.*

"Are you tired, then?" she said as smoothly as she could. "I'm sure a servant can escort you to your chambers."

The big man laughed deep and clapped Touraine on the shoulder, her spine creaking under the force. He used the motion to sweep closer to her and make a secret of their words.

"This is a nice peace," he said softly, "but it won't last long. Balladairans don't accept people like us. Taargens, Shālans, the Many-Legged. Even those monks. They don't trust in anything but themselves— they're not willing to sacrifice for something bigger than their petty selves. They think they're better than us, and it shows in the backstabbing they call 'peace treaties.'"

Touraine ducked out from under his hand as if she could get away from the words, but they had hit too close to the mark. Albric saw.

"We hope for peace, of course, but we also understand the Cycle. Nature demands it and only fools ignore it. Don't be a fool. Know your own power." He tapped the side of his own eyes this time. They were brown, as ordinary as her own had been. But then, Touraine had never seen a bear's eyes up close.

She was out of her depth. She needed Saïd or Malika. *They aren't here. No one is here but you.* And she needed to get out of what was feeling more and more like the closing jaws of a trap.

Touraine stepped back, straightening her coat. "I hope that isn't a threat, my lord. Under the royal roof, no less."

"A threat?" Albric's smile widened. "Of course not. It's an offer of friendship. In Taargen, your people practice their faith without restraint. Imagine what you could do without them looking over your shoulder, calling you 'uncivilized.'" He gestured subtly this way and that, taking in the Balladairans present. The ones who had stared at her with so much disdain all evening, whispering behind their hands. *The savage Qazāli.*

"I understand you," he said again. "More than any of them will. You and your countrymen will be welcome in our halls should you find yourself in our woods." With that, he strode past her, giving her one last knee-buckling pat on the shoulder. Touraine watched him go with equal parts relief, terror, and excitement.

The Taargen priest was offering her an alliance that could help her people. One that didn't rely on an uncertain succession or the grace of a duke whose contempt for her people was as plain as the scars on her back. Albric was offering her a place away from the stigma of being "ill-bred." She might even be respected. She wasn't completely stupid—like Luca and the duke, Albric's Bear Queen would probably want to use Shālan healing magic. If they were *sharing*, though, an equal partnership—that would change the lives of everyone in Qazāl. If Qazāli wanted to settle in the north, what difference would it make if they went to Taargen instead of Balladaire? It wasn't as if the Balladairans were welcoming them with open arms.

All he was asking for in return was an alliance when Balladaire and Taargen inevitably clashed again. Not the possibility of war, but the certainty. He was asking her to betray Balladaire. To betray Luca. Again.

Touraine scanned the hall once more. There. In her vine circlet, leaning on her cane, talking now with the Taargen twins. Luca was all grace and gravity. She looked like a queen.

Touraine didn't want to betray her again. She hadn't wanted to the first time, but it had been for the Sands. *This time, it would be for your whole country.* For all of the Shālan colonies still in Balladaire's hands. *Aren't your people worth it?*


"Cousin!" the young Taargens chorused in unison as Luca approached them.

Though they weren't strictly cousins—not to Luca's knowledge, anylight, and wouldn't that be a fascinating discovery—it was a bit of a joke among the Taargen royals that Luca's mother had Taargen ancestry, and not even so far back. Queen Étienne had come from a minor noble house in Moyenne; the territory there was so disputed that it was hard to say if anyone's family hadn't intermarried on one side of the border or another.

Luca embraced the sister, Linsel, first, warmly kissing her on either cheek, before embracing the brother, her lips meeting rough beard. "Roric, where did you find this dead animal, and why have you stuck it on your face?"

He grinned, and she could see the blush creeping up his face—such that wasn't covered by this beard. The last time Luca had seen him, he was a spotty teen, tall and big for his age. Linsel, too, was more assured in the way she carried herself. They both wore the sides of their heads shaven, in the fashion of royal Taargen adults.

Sky above, Luca was getting old.

"Happy birthday, cousin!" Roric's deep voice no longer cracked. He reached out for the customary Taargen back slap, and Luca deftly pivoted to avoid it. She could do without having bruised shoulders for the rest of the week.

"My thanks. How are things on your side of the Moyenne?"

"Not near as eventful as they have been on your side," Linsel said. She smiled smugly, as if she had a secret.

Luca relaxed her face into a blandly curious expression. "Oh?"

If there was one thing Luca had learned she could count on, it was a young courtier's eager inexperience. The need to sound smart too often manifested in an eagerness to talk, and an eagerness to talk meant they would say anything. Too much anything. And Linsel thought she was very clever indeed.

"Yes. Unlike some people, we make good investments instead of picking fights we can't win. Trade with Lunāb has never been better. Roric and I even visited. Your governors were practically on their knees to sell to us. Have you ever worn Lunābi silk?" Linsel plucked at a panel of her dress and pointedly ran her thumb along it, inviting Luca to touch it.

Luca humored her. The green-dyed silk was paler than the rest of her dress, an accent feature. It was very fine. However, Lunāb was a Balladairan colony, and so Balladaire had no shortage of the silk they produced. What was more interesting, though, was that Luca hadn't heard about this visit from the governor, and she didn't think her uncle had, either. At least, he wasn't acting as if he knew the Taargens were making a move on their easternmost colony. What with the loss of Qazāl, another lost colony would bring the empire to its knees. *At least this one won't be my fault.*

Luca brushed the silk between her fingers and smiled. "You look lovely in it. I'm sure you'll have even more when your mother convinces them that the Taargens make better masters than the Balladairans."

Linsel's mouth dropped open, and Roric's smile vanished. The horrified glance they exchanged cemented Luca's suspicions.

"That's not what I meant," the young princess said, mortified.

"Did your mother send you here to show me your entire strategy, or are you just that clever, cousin?"

The young woman's face went pink with frustration, but she closed her mouth. Good. It might have stoppered the flow of free information Luca could have goaded out of her, but that was what Balladaire had spies for, surely. It was more important for her to seem like she had all the information already. If she knew more, she had the advantage. And judging by the dismayed expression on both of the princelings' faces, they knew it, too.

They shrank even further into themselves as their high priest approached. He was probably as much their chaperone as a delegate in his own right.

"Your Highnesses. May I join you?"

"High Priest Albric. The princes and I were having a fascinating conversation. Probably as fascinating as the one you were having with my ambassador over there."

The priest's eyes were sharp and his smile sharper, set in a face that looked like it had been hacked into a tree by a hatchet. He didn't look back to Touraine. "El-Qazāli. Yes. Fascinating woman. Do your best to keep hold of her, otherwise I might steal her for myself." The smile didn't touch his eyes.

If the Taargens took Lunāb and wrested Touraine and the Qazāli away, civil war would be the least of Luca's problems.

"I'd rather you didn't. As I'm sure you've heard by now, I'm rather fond of the Qazāli." She made a self-deprecating smile back, but she didn't let it reach her eyes, either. Let him take the warning. *You can't use her against me.* Even though Luca wasn't at all certain that he couldn't.

Luca glanced back over his shoulder to the other woman. Touraine looked around the room like a hare hearing the dogs on her trail. The ambassador sought refuge up the nearest staircase.

"What did you say to her?" Luca asked Albric icily. "If you were rude to my guest—"

"I only made her the same offer I would make you, Your Highness." He held up an open palm. "It looks like you need friends."

Luca inhaled sharply. *Friends.* Luca didn't think this was what Gil had in mind. She glanced up to follow Touraine's progress to one of the balconies that jutted from the hall. If Touraine listened to Albric—

"We should talk—" he was saying, and Luca interrupted curtly, stepping away. "Excuse me."

Albric, watching her, watching her watching Touraine—

Luca made her way up the stairs, her heart stuck in her throat as she imagined how Touraine would answer. If she were Touraine, she knew which ally she would choose. She tried to remind herself that the Taargens had slaughtered the Sands on the battlefield, but a nastier voice reminded her that it was Balladaire who put the Sands there in the first place. Luca's clenched jaw ached.

The last thing she wanted was Bastien, coming to waylay her. She couldn't avoid him gracefully or even politely, but she didn't break her stride.

He stopped her with a gentle hand on her elbow, their bodies close. Closer than they'd been in quite some time, her shoulder nestled into his chest as he leaned down to speak softly in her ear.

"Will you meet me in the rose garden later?" Bastien's voice was rich and eager. He wore a bright cologne that reminded Luca of a sweet biscuit with a hint of citrus. It was the kind of smell you pulled close. The dove-gray fabric of his coat was soft velvet. "I have a gift for you."

Luca looked again toward the balcony, impatient. Then she said warily, "Bastien, I don't think we should—"

"It's nothing like that, I promise." His face fell. "I found it when I was back on the estates. Only we haven't had time alone since I returned." Despite the hurt, he buzzed with the same excitement he'd had on the day of the Black Ships funeral.

Luca felt a twinge of guilt for putting him off.

"Yes?" he said, sensing her softening. "Meet me tonight?" He cocked his head. The slight quirk of his lips said he knew he'd won.

Luca raised her head, keenly aware of the crowd of people watching her but pretending their attention was elsewhere. This was his way of snatching private time with her, bribing her with the hint of what he knew she couldn't leave alone.

"I'll try and get away," she said. She smiled just enough.

He straightened, and the happiness in his face made Luca feel even more guilty. Whatever else they were or weren't, they were friends. She had missed him. After the delegates were gone and when she could breathe again, they would catch up properly.

He stepped back, hand sliding from Luca's elbow to her hand. He squeezed it as he bowed. "You'll love it, I know." He left, a new bounce in his step.

The cool air on the balcony lifted the oppressive air of the hall. The autumn breeze played along the damp hairs clinging to the back of her neck. The clouds were still thick in the night sky, but the storm had stopped. Below, puddles littered the walking paths leading to the garden and its hedge maze.

A handful of others were taking advantage of the fresh air, and Luca noted them—a noblewoman deep in...conversation...with someone whose face was too occupied for Luca to distinguish. Evrard speaking to Aranen, though Luca could tell the priestess was keeping the comte at a distance. Even young Ghadin had managed to sneak away from her page duties to lean on the balcony railing and stare forlornly over the edge.

None of them, however, were Touraine.

# CHAPTER 14

# AMONG THE ROSES

If the fresh air on the balcony had felt like surfacing after drowning, seeing Aranen talking to that older noble—Travis? Traverte?—was like getting pushed back under. Touraine slipped back inside.

*Please, Shāl*, she begged. *Get me out of here.* What use was having a god if they couldn't help you out with the little things, too?

It turned out that it wasn't so hard to be at a princess's birthday and avoid talking to nobles. Not when you'd made yourself even more of an outcast by scrapping in the mud in La Gouttière over a few coins.

Instead of being bombarded by people trying to manipulate her like she'd feared, no one but the Taargens had approached her. That felt even worse. She was fucking up. Her empty wine glass—empty? when?—trembled in her hand.

And then the glass was deftly taken from her by surer fingers than her own. They replaced the empty cup with a fresh one.

Touraine looked up. The marquise de Durfort grinned down at her, holding the empty wine glass and her own full one.

Was she Shāl's answer?

"You look like you need to make a hasty retreat, Your Excellency," Durfort said. "Or reinforcements?"

"I could do with both, Your Grace," Touraine said. She nodded back to the balcony. "Too crowded out there, though." She saluted Durfort with her glass before taking a sip.

It was sharp, tart, and fizzed pleasantly on her tongue. "*Oh.* That's good."

Durfort cocked her head smugly. "I'm glad you think so. It's from my own vineyards. We're trying something new to develop these bubbles. Here, come with me."

Durfort led Touraine back down from the mezzanine and outside, launching into a winding tale of grapes and seasons and harvests and cellars, and the more she talked, the more Touraine's mind fizzed and sparked like the wine.

"Have you seen the Rose Maze yet?" Durfort gestured to the gardens. "The last of the roses are blooming."

Touraine took a bracing breath of the cool air. "Not yet, Your Grace. I've been busy."

"Please, call me Sabine. Or at the very least, Durfort. Believe it or not, even I tire of hearing 'Your Grace' this and 'Your Grace' that."

"As you like."

Durfort stopped on the garden path before one of the three entries to the maze and seemed to consider Touraine, a bemused smile on her face in the light of the stars. "Which path shall we take?" she asked.

Touraine wondered if the wrong choice would be yet another false step, but compared with the stuffy anxiety of the crowd, feeling constantly and contradictorily both watched and dismissed, she would take this. She answered by stepping into the middle hedge opening.

It took Touraine's breath away.

"Isn't it a marvel?" Durfort said as they wove their way deeper into it.

It was. Taller than Touraine by an entire pace and still thickly green. She couldn't even see through them to gauge how deep they were—at least a pace in that direction, too.

And roses, everywhere. They sprouted from the thorny hedges sporadically, and though some were beginning to wilt, Touraine and Durfort walked through a cloud of their perfume.

The sandy dirt path was littered with puddles to dodge. Little glass lanterns holding candles on hooks extended from the ground, lighting the way.

"It's beautiful," Touraine said, mouth slack.

"Mmm."

They walked a little farther in companionable silence before Durfort said, "You don't understand your place at court, do you?"

The question came so out of the blue that Touraine blinked stupidly. "Euh?"

Durfort had that bemused look on her face again. "You're a foreign ambassador. You speak with your king's voice here, which makes you like to a prince at the very least."

"We don't have a king, we have a council." Touraine scowled. "And we're barely considered sovereign enough to be foreign."

Durfort tilted her head. A dark curl fell across her brow. "Are you on the council?"

"Yes?"

"Well then." Durfort walked on in silence. Touraine didn't know the marquise all that well yet, but she suspected that long stretches of quiet weren't normal.

"I've never been in a court like this." More to herself than to Durfort, Touraine voiced the fear that had been plaguing her since she arrived. "How am I supposed to know where I fit?"

Durfort sipped her wine and smiled. "You've been around Luca too long. I'll give you a beginner's tip—start by knowing the other players. Do you?"

Touraine sighed and shook her head. It spun a little with the wine. "Barely. Not as well as I should. I expected Luca to—" She cut off in a frustrated growl. "It'll take more time. I'm working on it."

"Allow me to give you the basics." Durfort took another drink and gestured with her hands as if to make a wide table. "In Balladaire, you have the upper five noble houses that support the crown and the lower counties' nobilities that support those houses, and everyone has someone here to represent their interests at court—"

"Not that basic. They did teach us about the government in the barracks."

"Did they now?" The other woman smiled, teasing.

"And history, and mathematics, and reading."

Durfort's expression turned thoughtful. "I didn't realize."

"No one ever does."

"To the people, then. First, there's Evrard. He's a sneaky bastard and probably the richest family in the empire except for House Ancier. He's so clever that everyone thinks Ghislaine is the richest, with her little menagerie." Durfort shrugged. "It's possible he's even richer than the royals. He pretends at being smarter than everyone, and the duke tolerates him because they like to debate each other."

That sounded interesting. "Debate what?"

"Sky above only knows. Old men's bearshit. Cock sizes, I expect. Or who is losing potency quickest." Durfort held her hand up and let it droop slowly until it pointed toward the ground. "Either way, I want nothing to do with it."

Touraine snorted. "And what about Moyenne?"

"I'm sure his cock is just fine, but again—I want nothing to do with it." This time, Durfort's smirk included an appreciative once-over at Touraine's form.

Durfort reminded Touraine of Aimée, if Aimée had been born into silver boots. It made her heart sore. She raised a pointed eyebrow. "What about the rest?"

Durfort acknowledged Touraine's dodge with a conceding head tilt. "The rest of him…" she started gravely, "is not so bad if you like redheads." For several long seconds, she looked serious. Then laughter bubbled out of her.

Touraine cracked a smile.

"Ah. There. That's better." The other woman grinned and then tossed back the last of her wine, more like a soldier quaffing her beer. "Brice was fine when we were children. He idolized King Roland, and he wants nothing more than to piss in the Bear Queen's bed and expand Moyenne.

"Ghislaine…She's rich, as well. The menagerie is worth visiting, but she has a cruelness in her. You could see it in her daughter, and it's even worse now that the girl died in that Qazāli plague business."

Touraine stiffened. Touraine had helped start that "plague business" in a desperate effort to push the Balladairans out of Qazāl. She
made a mental note to avoid Ghislaine at all costs. If Durfort noticed
Touraine's reaction, she didn't let on.

"And finally," the marquise said, skipping ahead of Touraine and
bowing with a flourish, "the marquise de Durfort, at your service. The
most charming of the High Court, the best swordsman in the empire,
renowned seducteur, and loyal servant of the future queen."

Touraine played along, cajoled by Durfort's energy. "And your best
exports are...wine, swords, and sex? I have a hard time believing that
from your mother."

"Ha! She is unpleasant, I'll grant you that. However, a true lord
would never allow an insult to blood or crown go unanswered." Durfort cast about as if looking for a weapon—even though her rapier was
belted at her side. "You're lucky we're not evenly armed. Unless..." She
stepped closer, close enough that Touraine had to look up to meet her
eyes.

Whatever Durfort was going to say, she didn't finish it.

"Here." Durfort took Touraine's chin, and Touraine went rigid
again, arms ready to—to what? To push her away? To lash out with
her fists? The marquise's thumb was soft but firm on Touraine's skin.
They were so close that she thought Durfort was going to kiss her.
Instead, the marquise simply tilted Touraine's chin up. "If you want to
look like you belong, you first have to believe it." Durfort dropped her
hand, but the touch lingered.

Touraine hadn't realized how drawn into herself she had been, how
hunched her shoulders. She straightened, settling into her full breadth.
Then she met Durfort's eyes squarely. "Why are you helping me?"

"Ha!" Durfort's face broke into a dazzling open-mouthed smile as
she laughed at the sky. "If it's not obvious, I must be slipping."

Touraine chuckled. "No, that part is—but—" Nothing in Balladaire came without a price. Not for Qazāli. Durfort might want a night,
or she might want the same things everyone else did. Shālan magic.
Influence in shaping Qazāl, whatever it became.

"And you and Luca?" Touraine asked.

Durfort cocked her head. "What about me and Luca? She asked me to look out for you when she couldn't. So."

*Oh.* That sent an entirely different warmth through Touraine's chest, further dampening the anger she'd held close this evening.

"So."

"So." Durfort stepped closer still, so that their chests were touching. "Would you like to know a little more about our other export?" Her eyes flicked down to Touraine's lips.

Touraine put her hand between them and stepped back. She felt dazzled by the wine and wasn't ready to take such a large step onto an unmarked path, even one as handsome as Durfort. "Maybe another time, Your Grace."

"Of course." Durfort made more space between them, bowing her head in apology. "Forgive me—"

A scream cut through the night and Touraine tensed, breaking the wine glass in her hand. She didn't feel the pain as the glass cut the meat of her palm. She knew that voice. Judging by the pale, slack fear in her face, Durfort did, too.

"Luca," they said at the same time.

They ran.

Luca winced her way to the Rose Maze to find Bastien and call her duties done for the night. She hadn't found Touraine, and her poor mood was only temporarily alleviated when Guérin had found her.

Luca's old guard was doing well, growing soft and happy without a willful princess to follow around, and her carpenter daughter was headstrong and too busy to make an appearance but she was also magnificent, and would Luca do them the honor of accepting the new cane her daughter had made, as a gift?

Not that Guérin had said it in so many words. Guérin had been taciturn as a royal guard, and that hadn't changed. She'd greeted Luca and then departed, refusing even the offer of rooms in the palace.

Outside, Luca felt apart from the whole celebration, especially as she passed couples on promenade along the hedges.

The Rose Maze was also known as the Queen's Garden, for Luca's mother. It had been her project, her fondness for roses and games that had grown the hedge maze. Luca knew this maze better than anyone in the city, except perhaps the groundskeepers. She had walked it so many times with her mother, and then after her mother had died. She relearned to walk after her accident in the hidden safety of the hedges, where no one could see her falter. Luca brushed the roses she passed by with her fingertips in gentle greeting. Their petals were so soft and the fragrance... By the sky above, she missed her mother.

*What a loneliness this is.*

The Royal Oak grew at the heart of the maze. It was ancient, wider around than four large men could reach, and above, the leaves were turning every shade of fire, from copper to sunshine and everything in between. As a child, Luca had thought it was silly to have a giant tree at the center of the maze—you could never get properly lost if you could just look for the tree. Still, she had ignored the question of logic and spent as many days as possible reading under its shade. When she was in her Fruit Chevaliers phase, it was where she slept, certain that a smaller, Luca-sized tree would spring up where she rested her head. It was one of her favorite places in the world.

She inhaled the earthy scent, how it mingled with the roses and something else she couldn't quite place. She grinned and called out, "Bastien?"

Luca limped around the tree. "I swear, if you try to frighten me, I'll have you—Bastien?"

He was bent over the thick wall of the hedge, heedless of the thorns. His gray coat was pale against the dark green of the foliage. Sometimes there were bird nests in the hedges, with eggs or bald little fledglings, but it wasn't the season for that.

Deniaud, Luca's newest guard and Guérin's replacement, came up close behind Luca. "Your Highness, wait—"

"What are you looking for?" Luca asked Bastien, smiling at his ridiculousness.

As she neared him, though, her eyes began to understand what the prickles of fear along the back of her neck already knew. Something was wrong.

"Bastien," she whispered hoarsely.

He wasn't moving. He wasn't digging through the hedge branches. His legs were splayed, and it was clear that the hedge wall and the thorns were holding him up.

She stepped closer, but Deniaud was already pulling her back. "Your Highness, I don't think—"

Luca yanked her arm out of Deniaud's grip and pulled Bastien from the thorns. She couldn't hold his weight, and his body fell to the ground. As he sprawled on his back, she could see the bloody gash opening his throat. His blood striped the pale roses crimson.

She screamed, loud and piercing.

"Your Highness, get back." Deniaud again.

Luca couldn't. The ground hit her knees before she realized her legs had given out. She knelt beside his body, Bastien's body, thick, dark blood coating the gray front of his waistcoat and still oozing from his neck. His blue eyes stared at the night sky.

She didn't stop screaming until Deniaud clamped a hand over her mouth, hauled her back, and whispered in her ear:

"Whoever did this may still be here. Come, Highness. Now."

Too late. Thundering footsteps found them, and Deniaud dropped Luca unceremoniously to the ground to pick up her sword and face their attackers.

"Luca!" Two voices Luca knew, mingled in fear.

"Your Grace, Your Excellency," Deniaud was saying, "it's not safe—"

She tore her eyes away from Bastien and looked over her shoulder.

Touraine, with her belt knife, and Sabine, with her rapier, both drawn and ready.

*Oh. So that's where they went.* Luca started to laugh even though it was the absolute last thing she should have been doing, it wasn't right at all, it was absurd—*Sky above. Sky above!*

Sabine stared at her, horrified, as if Luca were the one whose throat had been slit.

Touraine, on the other hand. Touraine had been to war. She had led a revolution. She made a quick lap of the perimeter. Sharp. Alert.

"Clear for now," she told Deniaud.

Then Touraine went to—to the body. Checking it. For what? It was obvious what had killed him.

"Your Highness, can you walk?" Deniaud was saying. By her tone, she had said it more than once already.

"I—" Luca groped for the guard's shoulder, and together they got her to her feet. Her leg ached, but it held.

*Whoever killed him could still be here.*

"I can walk, I'm fine, let's go."

As soon as Deniaud tried to step away, though, Luca's leg threatened to give out again.

"I'll take her," Touraine said brusquely, slipping under Luca's other arm, leaving her cane to dangle in the air. "You cover our rear. Durfort. Durfort!"

Touraine snapped sharply with her free hand until the marquise started, pulling her eyes away from Bastien's bloody corpse. "Can you use that thing, or what?" She nodded toward the rapier. "Go in front of us, make sure the path is clear."

"Yes? Yes, of course, I can."

With new purpose, Sabine led the way down the fork Luca had taken, back to the palace.

Touraine was warm against her. "I have you," she said. "Put your weight on me."

It was not the first time Touraine had said that to Luca, and it touched something deep inside, just like it had before. Touraine's grip on Luca's waist was solid. It was real. She met Touraine's eyes, the gold soft and fiery with the lantern light.

"Ready?"

Luca grimaced and nodded, taking the first step. Touraine stepped with her. Steady. But as Touraine looked back at Bastien one more time, Luca saw fear flash across her face. Then it was gone, and she focused on their course.

Somehow, they made it back into the palace and into Luca's chambers. They ran into no one but Gil, Lanquette, and a handful of palace guards. Someone had thought to ring the palace alarm bells. Perhaps they had been ringing. Perhaps they had already cleared out anyone who had heard her scream. She hoped the Taargens hadn't seen her. If they got wind of this—

*They might have* done *this.*

No, she couldn't think about the politics of this yet, she couldn't—

At Luca's rooms, Lanquette went in first. After he deemed it safe, Luca shrugged herself off Touraine's arm and limped inside. She shivered in the sudden absence of the other woman's heat. Gil followed, while Deniaud and Lanquette posted themselves outside of the door.

Adile ushered them in, already reaching for Luca's outercoat. She didn't even gasp at the blood on Luca's empty, spasming hands.

Touraine halted, as if the threshold were made of fire, her battlefield confidence ebbing away. Her broad shoulders seemed to fill the doorway, at odds with the nervous hesitation. Another time, it might have softened Luca. Tonight, there was nothing in her to soften. The first wave of shock and grief had passed. She only felt empty.

"Come in if you like." Luca's voice sounded raw in her ears. "I'm fine, though. You don't have to stay."

Adile eased Luca into a chair, but instead of helping with Luca's shoes or the rest of her clothes, Adile held an envelope in her hand, and she looked anxiously between them all.

"What is it?"

"Your Highness, it's a letter."

"Can it wait?" Gil asked gruffly.

"I don't think so, sir."

"From whom?"

"The duke, Your Highness."

A small correction: Luca was capable of feeling something else. Dread quickly filled the emptiness Bastien's murder had left behind.

She held out her hand.

The large ivory-colored envelope was sealed with the wheat stalk and pen, her uncle's personal seal. Inside, the parchment was as fine, heavy and smooth against her skin. She unfolded it and skipped all the way to the bottom, where the five names were signed, five sigils stamped in wax:

*Duke Regent Nicolas Ancier de La Chaise*
*Evrard Castide, comte de Travers*
*Ghislaine Bel-Jadot, comtesse des Champs d'Or*
*Brice LaVasse, marquis de Moyenne*
*Sabine LeMarchal, marquise de Durfort*

She stopped at the last name. Stared at it before jumping back to the top of the letter and reading it straight down.

"What is it?" Gil asked.

"Nothing we didn't expect. He plans to hold the throne." Luca tried to sound nonchalant, but her voice cracked. The members of the High Court would vote on her suitability for the throne, her competence tried like a criminal's innocence. If she didn't prove herself, she would have to surrender the throne, with no legal recourse to take it back.

"But how? Everyone knows you're the heir." Touraine. How little she understood.

"He can, though it's not done often," Gil growled. "Trial of Competence. Last time it happened, there was civil war."

"The one against L'Atroce?"

"Mm-hmm."

Luca ignored them both. Sabine had followed them in. The marquise's hair was damp with sweat despite the cool evening. She was disheveled from their flight to the palace; her face was bloodless. Her dueling steel was sheathed at her hip again, but she was shaking. Luca was shaking, too, her teeth chattering uncontrollably. Throughout the palace, the bells still rang.

"Sab," Luca whispered raggedly. "Sabine, how could you?"

# CHAPTER 15

# ON SELF-INTEREST

W hat do you mean, he blackmailed you?" Luca asked coldly.

Sabine sat on a chair across from Luca. The marquise had steadied some thanks to a glass of wine that Adile brought from Luca's personal stores.

Gil was gone now, meeting with the captain of the palace guard while Lanquette and Deniaud kept guard outside. Touraine had gone to make sure Aranen and Ghadin were safe. That left Luca alone with her oldest, most trusted friend.

"He offered money, first. I swear, I told him no. When I did, he...Durfort is in debt, Luca. Badly." Sabine's voice was thick with the confession. "We lost all of our investments in the col—in Qazāl. Your uncle knows. He says—he said that we'd get them back. If I supported him now, he wouldn't strip our holdings from us. My father would beat me bloody if he were alive. My mother would, too, if she were in the city, the old shrew."

Sabine sat on the edge of her seat, elbows on her knees, gripping her hair in her hands. A spark of silver shone amid the dark brown hair. She wore no grief rings on her nimble fingers: her father had died peacefully in his sleep several years ago. "I've been trying to earn it back, the new wine had promise, but I mortgaged half the sky-falling estate to develop it, and—"

"I don't understand, Sab. How are you in so much debt? Why didn't you come to me?"

Sabine dug the heels of her palms into her eyes. "I didn't want anyone to know. I suppose he nosed about at the banks."

Luca took in the soft cotton of Sabine's shirt, the silk of her coat. The tiny diamonds that sparkled in her decorative rapier and her one dangling earring. The promises made from hand to hand, across nations and between cities, to make this outfit alone possible, let alone whatever else Sabine had done. Luca had thought it a front, that Sabine used her reputation as a fop as a mask to keep people underestimating her, but that she was in control of it all.

The mask was hiding something else entirely.

Luca forced her hands out of their fists, but then they wanted to tighten around her thighs, so she let her fingers tap out a mindless rhythm, back and forth, back and forth. She tilted her head back again and sighed. "'Self-interest rules us all.'"

"What?" Sabine said, blinking bewilderedly.

"Yverte. 'A ruler does not have friends. They cannot, because self-interest rules us all.'" Luca cursed herself for forgetting Yverte's most important lesson. It was so important that he mentioned it in every book, from *The Rule of Rule* to *The Price of Peace*.

Sabine dropped to a knee beside Luca's chaise and took Luca's hand. "Luca, I am your friend. I swear it, but—I'm—I was scared."

Luca suspected that losing her title and her land wasn't the only thing Sabine was afraid of. "What else does he have on you?"

Sabine didn't look up, only clenched her hand tighter around Luca's and pressed it against her forehead.

"Sabine," Luca growled. "I can't help you if you don't tell me what you need."

The other woman shook her head jerkily. "Nothing else. It's just... every time he and I spoke, it felt like there *was* something else. A threat."

The words clarified the stomach-turning idea that had been coalescing at the edges of Luca's mind. She didn't want to believe it possible, but what would she do for her throne? What would her uncle do to keep her from it?

"Do you think it was Nicolas? Tonight." Luca couldn't bring herself to say *My uncle killed Bastien.*

Sabine flopped from her knee to sit on the floor, leaning against the chaise. "Not that he wielded the blade. I don't understand, though. What would he have to gain by killing Bastien? He has no influence in court."

"Exactly." Luca ran her fingers through Sabine's hair. The affectionate gesture made the words she spoke seem less horrible. "He's—he was no one. Just someone that I cared about." Luca swallowed. "He wants to hurt me."

Luca wondered if her uncle knew that Bastien was helping Luca get closer to Balladaire's magical and religious past. That didn't seem worth killing him over, especially not when Luca could easily do her own research.

"Why him, then? Why not—" Sabine's voice cracked and her throat bobbed as she tried to finish the sentence. "Why not me, or your ambassador? If he's willing to have someone killed at your birthday with all the nobles and the foreign dignitaries in attendance, why not just kill you?"

Luca's mind buzzed around the pain that filled her. Only, the hole inside her was ravenous. It would never fill. She clamped down the urge to vomit and lolled her head against the back of her chair. If it had been Sabine in the garden, her throat gaping and red and—

Luca lunged for the basin of red-tinged water Adile had left for her to clean her hands and threw up. Sabine jerked, her dark eyes fear wide.

Luca shuddered. "Because we're all too big. Too noticeable." She wiped the corner of her mouth with a handkerchief and rinsed her mouth with a swill of wine. "Nicolas wants this to look legitimate, or he wouldn't have bothered with the Trial of Competence. He hopes I'll step down quietly."

"Will you?" Sabine clutched one knee to her chest. Her expression seemed torn, uncertain which answer she wanted.

Luca met Sabine's fear with a hard stare. "No."

146

C. L. CLARK

If history had taught Luca anything, it was that competing heirs rarely survived a contested succession. Even if this didn't go to war, even if Nicolas hadn't had Bastien killed, Luca wasn't safe anymore. And if her uncle *had* had Bastien killed... none of her allies were truly safe. The fear inside her settled. Her heart had stopped trying to beat its way out of her chest, and a small part of Luca could admit that part of her reaction to Bastien's death had been fear for herself. In its place came the need to act. The need to make her own move.

"Then what do we do?" Sabine asked. *It's "we" now.*

"You'll need to vote for me in the Trial," Luca said. "I won't strip you of your titles or your land. And"—she cut Sabine off before she could question—"I'll keep you protected as best I can. Travel with guards. I need to talk to Gil, make a plan."

"Are you going to kill him?"

The question gave Luca pause. Did she have it in her to have Nicolas assassinated? She had to. She'd left Touraine in jail to be executed in the name of her throne. She'd condemned Shālans and Balladairans to death during a rebellion in the name of her throne. She could kill one man. Even if he was her uncle. The man who had taught her everything she knew.

"Why wouldn't I?" she said. "If he would do the same to me? To the people I care about? It isn't my first choice, if it makes you feel better."

Sabine sighed and scrubbed her face with one hand. "All right. Okay. All right. I'm with you. This is all rather a lot, though, and I need to lie down. Can..." Sabine looked hesitantly at the door, and for a moment, Luca thought she was going to ask to stay with her for the night. "Can I borrow one of your guards?" Sabine didn't look so much afraid now as wary and determined. "If it is someone in the palace..."

"Of course. I'll be fine. Be careful."

"I will."

For a moment, they looked at each other, Sabine nervously tapping her thigh with the side of her fist. The silence was full of everything that had just spilled between them, full of the entire night preceding. Full of the things they hadn't even spoken of yet, like her and Touraine arriving at the maze heart at the same time.

Sabine heaved herself up. "Good night, then." She headed for the door.

As Luca watched her go, though, something wrenched painfully in her chest.

"Sab? Why didn't you come to me?" Luca asked again. She wrapped her arms around herself, tight and protective. "I would have helped." *A ruler does not have friends. They cannot.*

Without turning, Sabine barked a laugh that was full of self-loathing. "Because I didn't want you to see me like this."

When Luca woke up, she wondered why her mouth tasted sour and her body felt weighed down by anchors. Why her head ached.

Then she remembered. After she remembered, she promptly tried to forget. When the memory of Bastien—

*—splayed on the hedge—*

She pushed it into the back of her mind. Locked it up and buried it with the things that needed her attention.

*A ruler does not have friends. Only pieces upon the board.*

*Pieces that can die.*

She stretched. She dressed. She broke her fast. By the time Gil arrived, immaculate in a fresh uniform coat, she was considering changing into her training clothes and going to the salle.

She needed to gather her strength. There was precious little of it, right now.

Gil narrowed his eyes when he found her pacing in her study.

"I didn't expect to see you...up."

"Why not?" Luca said sharply. "We have work to do."

"That's true. A young nobleman was murdered in the palace last night. One of your friends. Have you given a thought to that?"

*—blood sprayed across the roses—*

"Oh, yes, a little," Luca bit sarcastically. "Did you learn anything from the palace captain?"

Gil shook his head as he thumbed his mustache. "No one found on the grounds."

"I talked to Sabine last night. It has to be Nicolas."

His lack of surprise was disappointing. A part of her had hoped that she was wrong and the blame would fall at some other, distant feet. Instead, Gil nodded.

"It makes sense with the Trial of Competence. A warning."

"He doesn't think that I can win the Trial." Luca gripped her own hands hard as she paced, twisting her palms until the small bones ached. "If I can win, maybe none of this will go to war."

"I think he does believe you can win. Else why kill the lad? But you'd have to convince all of the High Court that they should support you instead of Nicolas," Gil said dubiously.

"I already have Sabine."

Gil's expression went even more skeptical.

"I have Sabine," Luca repeated. "I trust her."

Gil grunted. "And the rest? Travers, Moyenne, Champs d'Or?"

"Give me time."

Luca released her hands and leaned over the chair at her desk. Her nails dug into the lush upholstery. "I don't want to force a civil war on our people," she said quietly. "If there's hope it won't come to war, I will fight for that hope."

"That's a battle worth fighting," Gil said, "and you know I'll stand beside you. Nicolas controls the royal soldiers, but more than a few remember my name. I'll spread a quiet word. Not enough to mount a full war, but enough to keep you safe."

That triggered a memory Luca had lost in the horror of last night.

"The Taargens. High Priest Albric made an offer—they would support my bid, I think. With soldiers. Or if I need somewhere to run."

"No. Absolutely not."

"Only if it's necessary, Gil. If we're desperate—"

"We will never be desperate enough to invite an enemy army into this city."

Luca wasn't so sure about that. "We're not enemies. We signed a peace treaty"—Gil snorted—"and they want someone on the throne who isn't afraid of the gods and their magic."

Gil threw his hands up. "You're as stubborn as your father. Talk to me before you send them anything. I'll let you know if we're 'desperate enough.'"

The old man huffed his irritation behind her, and Luca was struck, as she sometimes was, by the strangeness that Gil knew her own father more than she did. Gil had known the man's habits, his thoughts, his fears, his private idiosyncrasies.

"Gil? How did you handle it?"

*—Touraine, pocked with bullet holes—*

Gil made a sound like he'd been punched in the stomach, and Luca turned to find him staring at the ornate plaster of her ceiling.

"Not well. I was an utter asshole to everyone. Except you, I hope. You gave me something to hold steady for." He stepped over to her and held her face in his hands. "The one good thing the three of us made."

Luca collapsed into his chest, and he tucked her under his chin, pressing a kiss against her loose hair.

"There's as much me in you as there is Roland and Étienne," he murmured. "Who taught you how to fight?"

"You," Luca said against his chest.

"Me. We'll get you on that throne, my dear."

# CHAPTER 16

# A CAGE

W e shouldn't leave without speaking to the princess." Aranen scowled at Touraine from below her hood. "At least sit down with her. Talk this over."

"I sent her a note," Touraine said shortly. A note and the medallion she'd found on Bastien's body.

They were in La Gouttière, it was dark, and they were alone. Touraine's every sense was on the alert, and she didn't have time to think about Luca right now. She held her head up high and pretended to look like she knew where she was going. Aranen glided behind her along with Ghadin, and their porter who dragged their two chests on a flat cart.

"A note."

"I know that I don't have the best track record with negotiations," Touraine said through gritted teeth, "but I have a lot of experience with being a Qazāli when a Balladairan gets murdered, and I can promise you, it never ends well for us. If they still want to negotiate, we can do it from the other side of the Triaume." *If Luca even has the position to negotiate.*

The sky above the docks was a riot of gulls and pigeons fighting over scraps. Their screeching drowned out all the other noise. The sun had barely set, leaving the sky darkening blue with a haze of pink on the horizon. The lanterns in the dock district were lit, some held by children, who would offer to escort you for coins—or they would escort you into an ambush and take your coins anylight.

She wondered if the Taargens would be under as much suspicion, if they, too, were hitching their wagons and racing back to their own city in this clusterfuck of diplomacy. They might have been behind it. She thumbed the priest's offer in her mind like an old coin in her pocket.

A man with a tablet and the pinched look of an underappreciated administrator stood near the quay, supervising the unloading of a cargo ship.

"Excuse me." Touraine approached him with as nonthreatening an air as she could. She felt herself shrink into something more palatable to Balladairans. An old trick that she'd picked up back when she was a Sand. The performance was deliberate now. She hadn't felt so aware of it with the nobles, because they were allowed to have oversized personalities, to be good at everything, like Durfort. Around them, she didn't have to shrink—she already felt small.

He looked her up and down suspiciously. "There's no passenger ships leaving right now."

"We need to be on the first ship to Qazāl. May I speak to the harbormaster?"

"That's me," he said. "Who are you?"

"I'm Touraine El-Qazāli, and this is Aranen din Djasha; we're ambassadors of Qazāl."

As if the title were a key, his eyes brightened.

"You want the last boat at the end, there." He pointed to a ship that looked quiet.

"There, with the sails furled?" Touraine squinted skeptically.

"Well, aye, and I said no one was leaving tonight." The harbormaster shrugged. "Might be you can speak with the captain and get a berth, though."

Touraine grunted. "Fine. Thank you."

"You're welcome, Your Excellency." He bowed a little over his tablet, but when Touraine turned back to him in surprise—he'd used her title!—he was already grousing at a grubby urchin of an underling he'd conjured up from nowhere.

"Well, I suppose that's good news," Aranen grumbled. She hadn't wanted to leave at all. *Who would look after the Qazāli?* she had asked, and Touraine retorted that no one would if they were locked up in Le Fontinard. It took half a day to convince her that it might be better to regroup and talk about the change in situation with Jaghotai before sending someone back to the palace to maintain some semblance of good relations with whoever was on the throne. Someone who wasn't Touraine.

They padded down the street, the porter and the flat wagon bumping along behind them on the cobblestones.

They were almost at the ship when Touraine realized that the ship wasn't just quiet—it was empty. There were no sailors moving or even drinking raucously on board.

"Aranen—" she started. Touraine turned to see the gendarmes—no, they were in the palace uniforms with the white piping on the breast to differentiate them from the general military—spreading around them. She backed toward the ship, only to bump into another one.

The man she'd backed into held his hand on the grip of his pistol. A captain's wheat sheaves glinted on his collar. "Your Excellency. High Surgeon." He ducked his head to each, respectively. "His Grace Duke Nicolas would like to see you before you depart."

"What's the duke got to do with this?" Touraine said before she could stop herself. She eyed the man's gun. *Should have asked Luca for one of those.*

"We're to escort you back." He said it with the kind of tone that meant the three of them would be going nowhere if not to the palace.

"Very well," Aranen said coolly. She stepped close to Touraine and put her hand on Touraine's forearm. Touraine gave her the slightest nod. Ghadin caught the gesture and nodded, too, her eyes hooded as she feigned disinterest.

With a heavy sigh, the young porter wheeled the flat wagon with their chests around.

Instead of returning to the palace and being taken to the duke regent, however, they were escorted back to their quarters.

Touraine scowled at the captain. "I thought the duke wanted to see us."

"I beg your pardon, Your Excellency." Again, he ducked his head. "You're to wait on his pleasure in the morning."

"I presume your escort will stay outside our doors throughout the night?" Aranen said tartly.

"I'm afraid so."

"Thank you, Captain." Aranen pulled on Touraine's wrist. "Come. We should get some rest." They entered the joined quarters through Touraine's door.

Her room hadn't changed at all in the few hours since she'd left. The brazier that kept the room warm had only recently gone cool and dark. The thick carpets and figurines in gold and ivory from the Shālan Empire—stolen or extorted, most likely. The chairs with their plush silk pillows, still rumpled and tossed where she left them as she hunted for all of her effects. A beautiful place. More than she'd ever dreamed of as a soldier.

The door closed on them, locking them in their opulent cage.

The next morning, a knock on the main door of her quarters woke Touraine from the restless sleep that she'd only just fallen into. A heavy knock, to be heard all the way in her bedchamber. She jerked upright in the bed, groping for her knife. Her eyes were thick with exhaustion, but her body was alert.

After a moment, she heard soft murmuring at the door, and then it shut again. Then, on Touraine's bedroom door, a softer knock.

"Mulāzim?" Ghadin called.

"Come in."

The girl shuffled in on bare feet, still scrubbing her eyes. "You have a meeting with the duke—less than an hour." She spoke around a jaw-cracking yawn, the Shālan-Balladairan mix of the language slurring. "You don't need help getting dressed, do you?"

Ghadin looked hopefully back at her own small bedroom.

"Oh no you don't. I suffer, you suffer," Touraine grumbled back in Shālan. "Besides, I'm just as likely to go in with my shirt on backward right now. What time is it?"

"Early." Ghadin went to the other side of the room to rummage through the clothing Touraine had packed to take back to Qazāl.

Touraine got up and went to the armoire instead. It was full of the clothing she'd intended to leave behind. Things Luca had given her that were too Balladairan, something she wouldn't want to wear in Qazāl or something so fine it was clearly a gift.

"You should wear something like this," Ghadin said, pulling out a long, square-cut midnight-blue coat embroidered with Qazāli geometries and a long shirt.

"I was thinking something more like this." Touraine fingered the sleeve of a Balladairan coat. It was almost the same color blue as the one Ghadin held up. The cream chemise beside it was soft. Fine enough to pay half of Rose Company's salary for a month.

"Why?"

Touraine turned at Ghadin's petulant tone. The girl was scowling down into the chest of Shālan clothing, and she wouldn't look up to meet Touraine's gaze.

"What's wrong?" Touraine asked her, though she could already guess.

"I don't get why we have to dress like them."

Touraine frowned. Sky above. She could see it happening like it had happened to her, like it had happened to the other Sands when they'd first been brought to Balladaire. Ghadin was learning the complicated double-speak of being a Shālan in Balladaire. The theater of it. Of being the "right" kind of Shālan. In a way that would hurt for decades to come, she was learning to be ashamed of herself.

Touraine was the one teaching her.

Touraine let the sleeve of the chemise fall and sat on the edge of the bed near Ghadin and the open trunk. Ghadin glared at her.

"The duke is dangerous," Touraine said simply, "and dressing the part will make this all easier." In the end, it was that simple. Give the Balladairans what they want, and they won't hurt you. Speak the way they speak, and you'll get sweets. Pray to your gods, and they'll beat you. If you act like them, they will care for you. So Cantic had taught Touraine.

"He's going to shit on you no matter what you wear. Besides. We're dangerous, too."

Touraine had to concede the former, but she answered the latter. "Not here we aren't."

"We are, too. You have Shāl's gift, and you can fight."

"I can't fight my way out of this palace by myself."

"You're not by yourself. I can fight, too," Ghadin said matter-of-factly. "And Aranen din Djasha has Shāl's gift, too."

Touraine raised her eyebrow at the girl.

Ghadin relented. "All right, all right. I know we can't fight our way out. You could at least remind him that we're not weak."

"Mm." Touraine grunted. It was a risk. If she pissed him off too much...She took the Qazāli coat from Ghadin. "All right. Let's remind this jackalfucker who we are. Stay here this time."

The captain who'd brought them back to the palace was waiting in the corridor. He was tall and solid, straight backed and blank faced. The perfect soldier.

"You were serious about the escorting thing," Touraine muttered.

"Of course I was, Your Excellency. My name is Captain Perrot." The man saluted. "Please follow me."

Captain Perrot led Touraine to the duke's library, where she'd met him before. Touraine's hackles went up immediately. *His analytical gaze, his grasping hands.* A whole meeting so that he could determine whether or not she was enough of a person for him to take seriously. Time to find out what he had determined.

The captain rapped three times sharply on the door. A moment later, Touraine was escorted in. As before, the room was innocuous. The books and papers on the desk had shifted, perhaps, but the heat was the same. Despite the early hour, the duke's hand darted black ink across the page.

"Your Excellency," Duke Ancier said. His voice was flat. "Thank you, Captain. You may go."

Captain Perrot bowed and departed, but not without a curious glance at Touraine.

"Your Grace. We were on our way home."

"Yes. So soon. And without saying your goodbyes to your host. I was surprised. I thought you would have learned better manners under General Cantic."

He eyed her up and down, taking in her Qazāli clothing.

"I said the goodbyes that mattered. I didn't think anyone especially cared whether we were here or not."

The duke tsked softly. "Then that is my fault. I should have made you feel more welcome. I know you think it's only my niece who wants the alliance with Qazāl, but that's untrue."

That didn't put her at ease at all. "Your Grace?"

"I wish to embark upon a deal with the Qazāli," he said slowly, as if Touraine were too stupid to understand him. "Are you not the ambassador of Qazāl? Should I not be speaking with you?"

"We agreed on a treaty with Princess Luca. It's ready to be signed."

He tsked again. "Unfortunately, the princess's grasp on the empire's needs isn't as strong as mine. I've made some changes."

Horror crawled up Touraine's back. Everything she and the rebels had argued for, the financial reparations, the grain stores and seed, engineers to update and maintain the farming equipment and work with the River Hadd and its floods...

"What changes?" she asked stiffly.

Nicolas held out a sheaf of papers for Touraine to take. It wasn't the original; at a quick skim, Touraine realized many of the points the council and Luca had agreed on were reduced or outright missing; the aid agreements for grain were cut by fully three-quarters—that wouldn't even feed the people in El-Wast, let alone the rest of the new nation.

"What?" Touraine gasped as she came to the last line on the first page. "You want *us* to pay *you*?" The equivalent of thousands of sovereigns a year, either in coin or precious metal and jewels or stone.

Nicolas folded his hands and nodded simply. "You owe us. We brought Qazāl civilization—look at the schools we built, and the improved architecture in the New Medina. The weapons technology, the irrigation systems—"

"The irrigation systems were an exchange from before you colonized us," Touraine snapped. She remembered that much from her days with Luca, listening to the princess mutter about treaties and magic. "We gave you medicine and taught you surgeries."

"The price of advancement, Your Excellency. And, speaking of medicine."

The ball in Touraine's stomach curled even tighter on itself, heavy as a stone.

"Despite your reticence to demonstrate at the dinner we held in your honor, my niece seems quite determined to believe that you and the priestess"—he spat the last word—"can in fact heal. She believes it so strongly that she's staked her claim to the throne to it."

Touraine opened her mouth to deny it, but caught herself. Luca's Trial of Competence. If she lied and said the magic didn't exist, it would jeopardize what little leverage the princess did have. Qazāl might be able to keep the holy magic out of the duke's hands, but that wouldn't keep Qazāl safe. If Touraine told him it was real, though, he would find a way to exploit them.

"I will admit that I find it very hard to credit," the duke said when Touraine refused to answer. "And if it weren't for..." He tapped the corner of his eye with one finger. "I wouldn't even consider it. However, I am a curious man, and I have heard interesting tales of what transpired in El-Wast last year. Tales that make me feel more open-minded to the potential of the... more primitive beliefs."

How much did he know about what Touraine had done to Rogan, and Aranen to Cantic? About Niwai's control of the animals? It was hard to believe if you hadn't lived through it.

The longer Touraine stayed silent, the harder Duke Ancier's eyes grew. His dark eyebrows lowered. "Of course, I would be happy to study you and the priestess further. Perhaps it's something in the blood. Or the diet. Away from the food or your grubby patch of sand, are you disconnected from the source? Is the magic itself replicable in civilized people?"

He said it as if he were musing, not making threats. Hot anger burned in Touraine's belly, and she thought of Ghadin, waiting for her in their rooms. To keep herself from clenching her fists, she folded her hands behind her back, faking her ease.

"Study us all you like. It won't help you. Didn't Princess Luca tell you that?" Better for her and Luca to fight from coordinated fronts.

Touraine might have imagined the slight narrowing of the duke's eyes. Aloud, he said, "Then you'll stay here until I've satisfied myself one way or the other. Either you show me this healing of yours and we include it in this treaty, or Princess Luca repudiates it and, with it, her suitability for the throne."

Alarm shot through her. "The Qazāli Council will wonder why we haven't returned. I've already sent word to expect me," she lied. There hadn't been time. She'd known in her bones something like this was bound to happen.

"They'll have to be disappointed, Your Excellency." He leaned forward again, smiling coldly. He smelled her fear. Touraine took a half step back unconsciously. The resemblance between his and Luca's mannerisms made Touraine's skin crawl. Matching ink stains dotted their fingers.

"There's nothing stopping me from sending the marquis de Moyenne and the King's Own from taking back the entire rabble of a colony you call a nation and turning it to better purpose. However, I'm a practical man. I know you're practical, too—you would never have been able to rise so high if you weren't. I meant what I said before: you are exemplary for your kind. Show that same pragmatism now and we can find a mutually beneficial solution. If you can't..." He drummed his fingers on the desk, then shrugged. "I can only make the best decision for the Balladairan Empire."

If Touraine could have used Shāl's gift to unknit the duke right then, Shāl take diplomacy—she would have. She took a shaky breath and straightened.

"We're hostages."

The duke tsked again. "Of course not, Your Excellency. You're Qazāl's ambassador. You're our honored guest." He bowed his head respectfully and then nodded toward the treaty in Touraine's clenched fist. "Don't take too long."

Touraine stalked back to her quarters with Captain Perrot close behind her. "Are you going to ride my heels forever, then?" Touraine asked as she yanked open her door. Two palace guards waited outside of her door, arms crossed and bored looking. They shared a look with their captain.

Perrot shrugged in answer to Touraine. "Until I get orders otherwise, Your Excellency."

Touraine rolled her eyes and slammed the door shut behind her. She knocked on the door between her rooms and Aranen's. No answer. She pounded on the door again with her fist and was about to take her fury and frustration and fear out on the door once more when the door swung open.

"What in Shāl's name is going on?"

"We have to help Luca. I need you to teach me how to use the magic or we're all fucked. We have to get Luca on the throne or we're all fucked—"

Aranen hissed her quiet. Ghadin stood in the middle of Touraine's sitting room with a tray of midmorning snacks. The dark, bitter smell of coffee wafted from the cups.

Seeing the girl's surprised face siphoned away the hot, energetic fear that was burning in Touraine to act, to fight, to flee. It was replaced with a helpless dread that made her feel listless. She flopped onto the couch.

"Ghadin knows the score already. Not like she wasn't 'detained' with the rest of us."

Aranen scowled between the two of them, but eventually she sighed, resigned. She joined Touraine on the upholstered wooden chair across from the couch. She nodded for Ghadin to bring in the coffee and set it on the small table between them. Touraine's stomach growled. She hadn't eaten before running at the duke's whistle. She grabbed one of the pastries and bit a chunk out of it. Sweet, buttery. It flaked into crumbs down her front, and Touraine took a perverse joy in the mess it made.

"So? What happened?" Aranen asked in Shālan.

First, Touraine turned to Ghadin. "You understand what it means to be here with us? Everything we say here is secret."

"I'm not a child." Ghadin crossed her arms.

Touraine explained everything Nicolas had told her and everything he had threatened. When she showed Aranen the new treaty, now stained with buttery fingerprints, the priestess let loose such a string of curses that Touraine didn't even recognize some of the words.

"I told you something like this would happen."

"It's not that I'm surprised," Aranen said. "I just thought he would be more subtle. We have to let Jaghotai know, though. Just in case... something happens to us."

Ghadin still hovered near, but she didn't look frightened at Aranen's implication. Only determined. She tugged on her long braid, and when she caught Touraine watching her, she tossed the rope of hair behind her shoulders.

"We can ask Niwai to take a message, if they're still here. They'll have to go back through Qazāl to get to the rest of the Many-Legged," Touraine said.

"You assume they aren't going to spend more time visiting with their brethren."

The Taargens. There was one possibility that would neatly cut the knot of her Balladairan problems apart. Touraine could reach out to them and see if their offer was genuine. Leave Luca and the duke to fight their own petty battles, and when the victor came back for pieces of Qazāl, the Qazāli would have the Taargens on their side. But what price would the Taargens carve from them?

"We can ask them, at least."

Aranen nodded. "As for the rest..." The priestess looked at her open hands and shook her head. "We should stay for now. Without giving the duke his 'demonstration.'"

Touraine crossed an ankle over her knee and rested her head on her propped hand. "What about if we said yes, though? If I let you cut me, heal me up. We show him, we show everyone. That might be enough to help Luca with her Trial. It proves she did a good thing by making us allies instead of subjects—"

"No," Aranen snapped. "Better we observe without giving away our last coin. If you would learn patience—"

Touraine bristled at Aranen's tone. "Oh, is that one of Shāl's tenets?"

"No, it's just good sense, which you—" The priestess's nostrils flared, and she closed her eyes and breathed silently, in through her nose and out through her mouth. "We need to discuss this with the princess before we make any foolish moves. We're bound together now. I'll leave that to you. In the meantime, I'll continue to help in the infirmary. If I learn anything useful, I'll tell you." She stood. "Please don't do anything that either of us will regret."

Aranen went back to her own rooms and left Touraine popping her knuckles through her thoughts.

She only had the one bargaining chit: Luca's feelings for her. Touraine didn't know how far that would take her now that Luca was battling for her succession. How did Jaghotai expect Touraine to use a woman with no power? Moreover, what would Touraine have to give Luca to play Jaghotai's game? The princess was a greedy ally.

The only other coin Touraine had to play was the one she didn't know how to use, despite all of her studying.

She startled when she noticed Ghadin still hovering. "Go help Aranen in the infirmary today."

"I always help her. I'm *your* page. I'm supposed to help *you*." Ghadin crossed her arms.

"You can help me the most by helping her."

"I—"

"Please, Ghadin. You swore you'd listen when I let you come."

Touraine thought she was going to argue, but the girl turned and stalked off. After several long minutes, when even the sounds next door had vanished, Touraine got up and went to find her knife from the beautiful rack hanging in her room just for daggers and swords.

She drew the weapon out of its sheath. The weight was comfortable now. She'd practiced with it every day in Qazāl; it had been a welcome escape from the arguing of the council.

The brazier pushed back the morning chill, and she was over-warm in the dark blue Shālan coat. She shrugged it off and pushed up her shirtsleeve.

The silvery scar on her left forearm, the one that had started all of this a year ago, the day Touraine first arrived in Qazāl, had shrunk to the size of her smallest finger. She placed the edge of her knife just beneath it and hissed as she drew the slightest line of blood. Then she closed her eyes.

Touraine may not have been trained to be a healer, but she knew the body. Even before she'd started studying the inside workings with Aranen. She knew the steady timbre of her heartbeat as she ran, and how different that was from the erratic pulse of sparring. She knew the tearing of muscles and wrenching of tendons and the slow, limping regrowth.

She let herself sink into the heat of her body.

*Shāl.* She screwed her eyes up tight and waited for the moment to come, for the tingling of her skin sealing itself back up. She tried to envision it, closing like the buttons of a shirt. She imagined the layers of skin, each one separate and with a purpose, like she'd seen in Aranen's books.

*Shāl, please. We need help.*

She felt nothing. She opened her eyes. Blood leaked down her wrist, trailing toward her trousers. She growled and cupped her hand beneath the arm and went to the washbasin. The water clouded pink as she rinsed herself off.

How had she killed Rogan if she couldn't heal such a small cut? She hadn't even had the consciousness to pray, let alone to focus on what she wanted to do to him.

As she sat there, Touraine's thoughts kept turning back to Luca. If Touraine wouldn't trust the Taargens, Luca was the only solution. They needed to talk.

# CHAPTER 17

# SCAVENGERS

Pruett was heading back to the barracks for a piss when a sloping shadow started circling the ground around her. She looked up. A vulture. Excellent. Her life was such shit that a fucking bird thought she was carrion.

"Fuck you, too," she muttered up at it.

Only, instead of waiting for her to die like any respectful scavenger, the little shit-eater swooped lower and lower, its shadowed wingspan growing larger.

"What the—"

She shrieked as the large bird landed on the ground in front of her in a flurry of feathers.

"Mulāzim?" Alarmed shouts came from the training yard Pruett had just left.

Noé and a few other soldiers ran to her, and Noé tried to shoo the bird away. It hopped once and gave Noé an unimpressed rasp. Then the vulture cocked its head at Pruett, piercing her with its eerily intelligent orange eyes. It held her gaze like it knew her, and then she realized—it did. Or at least, she knew it. That Many-Legged priest's bird. She'd seen the vulture often enough over the past year. The priest was practically a member of Qazāl's council.

Pruett held a hand out to stop the others. "Wait."

The bird fluffed itself and scraped a claw against the hard-packed dirt, as if impatient. Pruett approached warily.

"Where's your master?" Pruett murmured.

Though she'd been talking to herself, the bird stuck out one leg, and Pruett saw the small pouch tied to it. She pulled out a tight, narrow scroll and recognized Touraine's handwriting immediately.

She scanned it and swore. She sprinted to the administrator's building, the bird flapping and hopping behind her.

"Jackal!" she shouted. "Jackal?"

"What in Shāl's name is the matter with you?" The one-armed woman stepped halfway out of a room, frowning. "And why is there a—fucking Niwai."

"Sevroush?" Malika's disembodied voice came from within the same room. "Niwai? Are they here?"

"Sevroush?" Pruett repeated, looking down at the bird. He gave a rough scratch of a sound and puffed his chest out again. Kind of cute for a scavenger. "Huh." Pruett held out the small scroll to the Jackal. "From Touraine. Some noble at the palace got killed, and she and Aranen are being held there. Hostages. The duke is keeping the throne, and it doesn't look good for the princess's treaty."

The need for a smoke curled up in Pruett's chest like—well, smoke. There was a smokehouse in the New Medina, back under Qazāli ownership, with the best tea and a handsome server. She'd let the smoke cloud out everything, and get something else besides.

Jaghotai ran her hand through her graying dreadlocks and sighed. "We were counting on that food."

Pruett snorted. "Well that was your first mistake. When it comes to Balladaire, better not to count on anything. I could have told you that."

"I wasn't counting on Balladaire. I was counting on Touraine."

That shut Pruett up, but only because she couldn't bring herself to say out loud what she was thinking: *Better not to count on her, either*. There was only silence for a minute, as both women sat with what they'd just read. Then the noise of the other council members came in from outside, and Pruett was glad to be pushed aside by their self-importance. She slipped away to find her smokehouse and her server.

Much later, when the door to the smokehouse opened, Pruett ignored it, sending a cloud of smoke to obscure the door. Tried to ignore it, anylight. Ever since that sky-falling bird came, she'd suspected her relaxation was coming to a sharp, swift end. So, in spite of the dread souring her gut, she focused on the broad-shouldered woman who was pouring tea and replacing coals on the water pipes, and made to catch her eye. She was feeling thirsty, all of a sudden.

Her focus was ruined by none other than the Jackal herself. A golden-eyed woman Pruett didn't recognize trailed behind her.

"Thought I might find you here," the Jackal said. "Hiding."

The Jackal slid onto the cushions beside Pruett. The golden-eyed stranger took a third cushion on the Jackal's other side and rested her elbow on her knee before ignoring Pruett entirely. Pruett took another drag of smoke and blew it out.

"Just waiting until the council gets its shit together. I've seen a room of black-and-golds with a better sense of direction than you, and that's saying a fucking lot."

"You've spent a lot of time with the Balladairans, I don't doubt it. You're welcome to scurry back to them—oh wait, we saved you from them, didn't we?"

"Funny. I remember it the other way around."

"Oh? Was that what you were doing when we climbed the compound walls? Saving us?"

That got the stranger's attention. She looked over, nostrils flaring.

Pruett clenched her jaw tight. Her left eyelid twitched. How fast would she have to be to pull out her pistol, she wondered. Before the Jackal could turn her into a paste? There were some things you just understood, and the Jackal *should have understood that you just—*

"Don't go there," Pruett growled.

"I thought so. Look." The Jackal held her hand up in surrender, backing off, *I'm sorry.* "I didn't come here to fight. I came to ask for your help. Touraine's letter..." The Jackal blew the air out of her cheeks.

"Aye," Pruett said.

"Yeah. It means Qazāl is in a tight spot and we're low on options."

"That's my problem?"

"It could be. You run our military. What do you think's going to happen when the city runs out of food and finds out you're still being fed?"

"Probably gonna be a whole lot of angry people. That sounds more like your problem."

"Actually, it is my problem. So I get to pick how to solve it."

"My heart gladdens," Pruett said flatly.

"You're Masridāni, right?"

"Dunno if I'd put it that way."

"Don't you want a chance to go home?"

"Not particularly, no."

Pruett ran her tongue along the sharp edges of her teeth, then took a long, slow drag. She knew why she'd grown up with the Balladairans. That place in her chest was scarred over and untouchable.

"That's a shame," the Jackal said. "We need you to go anyway. The Masridāni are our best chance to make it through the winter."

"Aren't they still Balladairan territory?"

The Jackal raised her hand and her stump in a shrug. "You and your soldiers can fix that."

A server came with a cup of tea for the Jackal. Not the woman whose attention Pruett was trying to catch.

"Fix it?" Pruett asked.

"Help them overthrow their Balladairans like we did ours. At the very least, convince them to send aid, if those scavengers even remember we used to be united under one call," the Jackal spat. "Revolution can come later."

"If I do go?" Pruett pursed her lips, tapping the pipe's mouthpiece against them. "What's in it for me?"

The Jackal clicked her tongue and grunted. "You don't have my daughter's sense of altruism."

Pruett bristled. She blew a ring of smoke, fighting the temptation to blow a cloud right into the other woman's face.

"Nope. Shouldn't have sent her away, I guess. Besides, you saw how much good she did, running from one side to the other. If she'd sat and thought for the time it would have taken her to rub one off, she wouldn't have caused half the damage she did. Me, on the other hand...I like to take my time. Enjoy myself." She glanced pointedly at the serving woman across the room.

The Jackal wasn't as affronted by Pruett's crass language as she'd hoped. In fact, she didn't blink at all. A point to the old bitch.

"Let me put it this way, girl." The Jackal took the pipe and inhaled deeply before sending a stream of smoke right through the fading remnants of Pruett's ring. "I like you. You do a good job, and you're right—you do think. Good qualities in a commander. My daughter likes you, too. I'm asking you one more time. The next time, it's an order or a dismissal. There's no reason we can't all work together anymore, but we all have to work. If you don't want to do the work, I don't have time for you."

"Huh." With the smoke pipe in the Jackal's hand, that left just the teacups for Pruett to fixate on. She twisted her small tin cup, covered with the usual Qazāli geometries, painted painstakingly by some hunched old man with a hard squint. The tea inside was a golden brown, and the mint and sugar mingled with the rose-flavored smoke. Sugar and smoke alike tasted stale in her mouth.

Up until this point, Pruett had made that oh-so-innocent mistake of thinking she was free here in Qazāl. That that's what all her fighting and bleeding and having Rogan's fucking pistol shoved against her skull had earned her. Welp. She wouldn't be doing it again, that was for fucking sure. She stood up and jammed her cap onto her head.

"Guess you've made your point. If that's what you want, *my lord*, have our supplies ready at the gates when it's time to march. I'll take care of the soldiers." She looked around one more time for the handsome woman. She'd been thinking the woman might even be able to hoist her up. Would've been nice to at least flirt. If Pruett came back, she would. It felt like looking for a lifeline to pull her back to safety. If she came back, she'd tell the Jackal exactly where she could put it.

Who was she kidding? Her cheek tugged sharply sideways in a smile, if a look like a fishing hook was snagged in your mouth could be considered a smile. If she came back, alive, she'd just find herself in the same situation. She had a particular set of skills.

"Glad we have an understanding." The Jackal kicked back in her seat and waved for another cup. The handsome woman came through with more tea, giving the council member a respectful nod.

The woman smiled at Pruett as she brushed by, but Pruett's fish-hook smile apparently was about as charming as—well, as a fishhook to the face. The woman's smile faltered.

"Before you leave—this is Kiras." The Jackal jerked her head toward the golden-eyed stranger. Kiras flicked the hand resting on her knee. Pruett guessed that was a wave. "One of the Atyidi. She'll be your second."

Pruett looked her up and down. Kiras looked a few years older than Pruett, just old enough not to have been taken by the Balladairans. Despite that, a handsome white streak wove through the braid hanging down her neck. The left side of her deep brown curls was shaved down.

"I already have a second."

"She'll be your third, then, I don't care. She knows the desert and she knows Masridān." The Jackal gave the woman a wary look from the corner of her eyes. "And a few other things besides."

Pruett held Kiras's eyes and grunted. The other woman grunted back, one corner of her lips twitching up.

"All right. Anything else, Your Majesty?"

"You'll be provisioned for fifty. Zanafesh, Atyid, and El-Tarīq are sending ten each. With some Sands and some of my own—"

Pruett glared down, incredulous. "Are you out of your fucking mind, woman? That's not enough to convince the Masridāni not to piss up wind."

"I'm not sending you to fight. I'm sending you to get help." Her expression fell, and for a moment, she looked like a woman with the weight of the fucking world on her shoulders. "It's all we can spare. If Balladaire comes back like Touraine said—"

"You're just like the Balladairans," Pruett snarled. "Don't fucking complain when you don't get what you want."

Pruett found Noé in the barracks, stretched out in a bunk and reading some book in Shālan. The sight of him all comfortable and wrapped up in this city, its words, its art made her want to scream, but she held it in because that's what she always fucking did. It never helped to let it out.

Noé closed the book on his finger and sat up. "Did something happen to her?"

Pruett laughed jaggedly. She didn't even know how to answer that, and it made her angrier that he had even assumed—!

"Jackal's sending us to Masridān."

"Masridān?" he said, a note of interest in his voice as he tried to figure out how she felt about that.

"Masridān," Pruett repeated. "The bitch is sending me home."

"That's . . . not a good thing, I take it?"

"I didn't ask to go. We're being sent."

"Ah."

And like a dog, Pruett was running.

# CHAPTER 18

# OF HEROES

L uca held the torch over Bastien's body, ready to light the pyre. Almost ready. Almost. His hair had been rebraided and lay over his shoulder. She had never gotten to tell him that she liked this style. She brushed her hand across his. And his fine coat and knee trousers, a pale red with gold brocade. The cravat around his neck made it look as if there'd been no gash at all. Someone had used heady perfumed oils and herbs to preserve and mask his body.

Nicolas hovered a respectable distance away, full of elegant gravitas, as if this wasn't his fault. The heat of the torch in her hand, licking out at her face, complemented her cold fury. Both were eager to consume.

Luca felt a soft touch on her shoulder. Sabine. The marquise nodded encouragingly, subtly urging Luca's torch arm forward. The flame took to the oil-soaked wood, and once her kindling caught light, the other torchbearers lit the pyre at other points.

"Thank you," she whispered to Sabine as they both stepped back.

Luca didn't want to watch Bastien burn. Instead, masked beneath the solemnity of the occasion, Luca asked Sabine to catch her up on the gossip. All these noble heads bent together, eyes darting suspiciously at the rest of their cohort.

The mood in the palace had changed drastically. Even here, on the royal pyre grounds, the guard presence was doubled, not including the personal guards that shadowed everyone who could afford them.

"Half of them are blaming El-Qazāli and the Lady Aranen," Sabine said softly as they stepped away from the heat. "It's no secret he came from Qazāl. They say it was 'lasting resentment.'"

"You'll stop those when you can?"

Sabine nodded, then raised her eyebrows to the side. The lady of Champs d'Or was heavily bundled and stood distant from the pyre, gazing alternately between Bastien's body and scanning the crowd. "The lady is returning to her estates after this. She claims she's afraid."

Luca scoffed. Ghislaine was within her rights to leave, but it was an insult to the crown. "Everyone's afraid." She gave Sabine a sharp look. "And you?"

"I told you, I'm at your disposal. I'll be here."

"Thank you—" Luca stopped.

Her uncle was leaving, without even speaking to her. She left Sabine and intercepted him. His personal guards bristled in their formal half cloaks.

"My dear uncle."

"My dear niece. I'm so sorry for the loss of your friend."

"Thank you," she said, gripping his elbows under the pretense of pulling him close for an affectionate kiss on the cheek. Instead, in his ear so that not even his guards could hear, she said, "You will pay for this, Nicolas."

Just as softly, he answered: "You've already lost, Luca. How much more do you want to risk?"


Touraine woke up to a yelp outside of her bedchamber. She was out of bed and lunging for the door with her long knife in hand just as Ghadin burst through holding a folded letter. It had already been opened.

Touraine sighed as her heart rate fell to normal. "Don't scream like that. I thought someone was murdering you."

"Sorry, Mulāzim. But you have an invitation—can we go? It's for this morning, if we want to go, we should get dressed now—"

"*We?* This morning?" It was still dark out, but if Touraine strained hard—really hard—she could see the sky paling at the horizon. "It's not even light out."

Ghadin waved the piece of paper under Touraine's nose and Touraine took it, blinking rapidly to un-gum the sleep from her eyes. The handwriting was all elegant loops and flourishes.

*Your Excellency,*

*I'm hosting a beginner's fencing lesson today in the training salle. You would be most welcome, as is your young shadow.*

*Ever yours,*
*Sabine LeMarchal de Durfort*

"See? I'm obviously the young shadow."

Touraine blinked from the letter to Ghadin. The girl stood in her nightgown, bursting with more energy than anyone had a right to at this hour. "You read Balladairan?"

Ghadin looked at her flatly. "Djasha din Aranen taught us. The marquise's handwriting is awful, though."

"Why are you so excited to train with her? I thought you didn't like Balladairans," Touraine said pointedly.

"Because one, I can't use a sword and I want to. Two, I know you're going to go, and three"—she counted off on her fingers—"I told you I was tired of getting left with Aranen din in the infirmary. It's boring. And anyway, I like this one."

Touraine flopped back onto the bed. "Fine."

She was going to kill Durfort for waking her up this early.

Captain Perrot led Touraine and Ghadin to the training salle through subdued corridors. It was the day after Bastien LeRoche de Beau-Sang's funeral. Though Touraine and Aranen weren't *not* invited, no one begged them to come.

The visiting nobles stayed in their rooms, and when they had to move about, they traveled with half a company of guards. Touraine didn't want to admit it, but she was glad the captain was there. There were already four palace guards outside of the salle. They shared some silent eye signal with Captain Perrot before knocking. Sabine de Durfort greeted Touraine with a broad smile at the salle door. She bowed—with a flourish, as usual—and ushered Touraine and Ghadin inside.

Touraine and Ghadin gasped in unison.

A large mirror the height of a tall man and three times Touraine's arms' breadth hung from the wall. It was polished to a shine. The flickering candles and the early sunlight bounced off it, brightening the room.

"Impressive, isn't it?" Durfort strode up to them, one hand on her hip. As usual, she looked and sounded pleased with herself.

There was one other student—a young boy of about seven or eight in neat white half tights and a tightly buttoned white coat. Touraine and Ghadin were in their Shālan training clothes, light and sleeveless and loose in the legs for kicks and flips.

"Your Excellency, please meet Tiro. He's had a few more classes than you two, so he'll help me demonstrate as necessary."

Ghadin crossed her arms and looked skeptically at the boy. In Shālan, she told Touraine, "I didn't know this was a class for children."

Durfort raised an eyebrow at Ghadin and then at Touraine.

Touraine cleared her throat. "You're being rude. Speak Balladairan," she said in Shālan. Then, to Durfort, "She didn't realize the age range of the class."

"Aha! Well, Ghadin, it's a class for beginners, in fact. No matter how old." She winked at Touraine. "Have you ever used a sword? A rapier?"

"No," Ghadin said sullenly. "But I can fight. Just ask the mu—the ambassador."

"Hmm. Let's see."

Durfort turned to the wall where a wide array of practice swords waited, leaving Touraine and Ghadin to follow curiously. Tiro already held his practice blade, a long, thin strip of metal blunted with a little bit of cloth on the end.

Durfort walked along the row, making noises to herself and shaking her head at the different weapons she passed until she plucked one up by the handle. With a deft flick, she flipped the blade into her hand so the hilt faced Touraine.

"Try this one." It was metal, long and narrow with a flat blade that tapered to a blunted point. Touraine swung it with her whole arm. The weight of it was pleasantly challenging.

"Close enough for now. You'll get stronger the more you practice."

Durfort plucked a similar, shorter one for Ghadin. The girl failed to conceal her excitement as she gave it a surreptitious swish.

"Now. First thing. This is a duelist's sword. Not a soldier's sword." Durfort stepped close and squeezed Touraine's arms to her sides. "No flapping about like a swan, pretty as you are," she muttered only for their ears.

Touraine blushed as she cleared her throat.

Durfort smirked and skipped away. She clapped once. "All right, my ducklings. Stand like this." She turned sideways and spread her legs shoulder width apart, her right foot in front, perpendicular to the rear foot.

Touraine mirrored her, her left foot forward instead, but the stance felt a bit off-balance. Durfort came over and poked Touraine's feet with her practice sword, nudging Touraine's legs until she was in the right position.

"Hold your sword arm out straight. Your right arm can balance for now. And then, lunge!" Durfort twirled her off hand and lunged forward like a snake.

It seemed simple enough. Touraine lunged. And she lunged, and lunged, and held her dull sword and lunged until her left shoulder complained and her left thigh screamed and her left knee groaned. And then Durfort made her do it some more. Then she made them all change sides.

"You never know when you'll need to trick someone with your weak hand. Best to show them that it's not weak." Durfort winked and they started again.

Touraine watched herself in the giant mirror. On her right, Ghadin's brow was furrowed in concentration, a light sheen of sweat covering her forehead. She kept throwing competitive looks at Tiro. To Touraine's left, the quietly determined boy accepted Durfort's critiques with an obedient nod.

Touraine lost count of how many repetitions they did, because she retreated to the place she had as a soldier a lifetime ago. Training to be better, to be good enough to be an officer. The pain had always been in service to that.

Now it was in service to something new. With every lunge, Touraine imagined herself moving through the palace like Durfort did, her unquestioned confidence and social grace. Everyone treated the marquise with respect. *So charming, how cultured.* Touraine would never have quite the same impact. She was a Sand. She still wanted respect. She still needed to know how to behave as a courtier, even if she never would be—

"All right, Ambassador, that's enough. That's enough, I said." Durfort clapped her hands sharply twice. "What focus," she said with wry admiration.

Touraine snapped her arms and legs back together at attention before she realized she wasn't at the barracks anymore. The children were staring.

Durfort walked to a tray of water, and she poured them each a cup herself. Durfort took a long drink and sighed as it quenched her thirst. A droplet of water clung to the corner of her mouth, and Touraine remembered the taste of fizzing wine. The other woman caught her staring, and a slow smile crept across her face. Without breaking eye contact, she wiped her open mouth with the back of her hand.

Then the moment passed and Durfort was poking and prodding Tiro and Ghadin with one of the wooden dowels until they giggled and set back to lunging—Durfort even pretended to spar with her, all seriousness until she swatted Touraine on the ass. Ghadin laughed especially hard at that while Tiro giggled behind his hand. Despite the burning in her legs, the mood in the salle was joyful, and Touraine began to feel some of the camaraderie that she'd longed for since she left the Sands for Luca's household. By the end of their session, the tension in Touraine's shoulders was replaced with the pleasant ache of a body well used.

Durfort escorted them all to the door. Her cream chemise clung damply to her chest, and her short, dark hair was slicked back with sweat. Even so, she looked effortless.

"Good job, lad. Off you go, enjoy your next lessons." She ruffled the boy's hair and he beamed up at her. There was something familiar about that look of utter worship in his eyes.

Abruptly, he hugged his arms around her hips before walking away with a quiet dignity. Three of the guards peeled off the wall and followed him.

Judging by her half-open mouth and wide eyes, Durfort was just as surprised by the gesture as Touraine.

"He likes you a lot," Touraine said, sidling up beside the marquise. "How long have you been working together?"

"Oh, a month or so. Since I came back to the palace for the season. He's a sweet boy. Shame about the father." Durfort crossed her arms and leaned against the doorway, heel kicked up.

"Eh?"

Durfort smiled wide and mischievously. "See, this is why you need a guide to the palace. That's little Roland Ancier. The duke's son."

"Hmph." Ghadin grunted from behind them. "I knew there was a reason I didn't like him," she grumbled in Shālan.

"Tsch." Touraine snapped her fingers for Ghadin to behave. The girl groused, but was distracted by doing more lunges in front of that magnificent mirror. "I didn't know he had a son. He's not like his father at all."

"Oh, I wouldn't go that far—he's a clever boy, like all the lords Ancier. I imagine the duke is a...demanding father. He was certainly a demanding uncle." Durfort's expression darkened for a moment.

It was odd to see Durfort look anything but sly or amused. Touraine had only seen it happen twice before: Durfort's horror when they'd found Bastien's body, and her fear as Luca read the Trial of Competence summons. The letter that Durfort had signed.

Touraine and Durfort had something else in common—one betrayal against the heir under their belts.

"Why did you do it?" Touraine asked softly.

Durfort stiffened defensively. "I don't expect you to understand—"

"You'd be surprised. But you're her friend. Why did you sign away her throne to her uncle? Is there something I'm missing? Or do I misunderstand the finer part of Balladairan politics? If I need to be on guard—"

"Of course you need to be on guard. You're a foreign diplomat in court during a struggle for succession that might well turn into civil war, and you and your people are one of the prime players, pieces, and bargaining chits." Durfort spoke through her fixed smile, and it came out almost a growl. "If you're smart, you'll make a move before someone else moves you." She sighed and ran her hand through her damp hair. "It's not always about who's your friend."

Then she kicked off the doorway and bowed. Her jaunty smile was back. "I have to prepare for my next student. Thank you both for joining me."

Touraine jerked her head to beckon Ghadin. As they left, Durfort saluted Touraine with her blade.

They'd barely turned the corner when Ghadin looked up at Touraine. "Can we go back?"

Touraine glanced back over her shoulder though the marquise was out of sight. "I think we'd better."

Luca loved the way the heels of her boots clicked on the marble tiles of the palace halls. It's why she never liked the slippered fashions that came in the spring and summer. The clicks added rhythm to her thoughts.

She was having a brilliant thought. The medallion that Touraine had sent with her note. Ghislaine. Bastien and his land. Ghislaine's estates. If she drew it out, a single line could connect them all to a point in the middle: Balladaire's god. Balladaire's magic. She just had to figure out what the connections were. Bastien had left her the clue, she was certain of it, even though she'd said she was done digging this up—

Luca stopped just short of crashing into Touraine.

"Tour—Your Excellency." Luca caught herself just in time, breathless in her surprise. She nodded to the young page at Touraine's side. "Ghadin. Hello."

The girl shot a glance at Touraine, who nodded encouragingly, as if she thought the girl were just shy. Luca read something else in the girl's sidelong look at her, though. Regardless of any misgivings, Ghadin bowed.

They were both dressed simply in plain loose trousers and sleeveless Shālan tunics. Touraine's was damp across the chest and under her arms, and they both smelled of exertion.

"Keeping your skills sharp?" Luca asked casually.

"Picking up new ones." Touraine frowned and shook out her arm. At Luca's questioning eyebrow, she added, "We were training with Durfort. She insisted."

"Did she? I hope you found it . . . stimulating."

"It's something to do while we're enjoying the duke's hospitality," Touraine said tightly.

"Ah," Luca said. "Actually, Your Excellency, could we have a moment alone? If you have the time. We need to talk."

Touraine and Ghadin shared another look, and this time, it was very clear what the girl thought about this.

"Fine," Ghadin said in a huff. "I'll go hide away in the infirmary. Again." She spoke Shālan in the Qazāli dialect, but Luca's skills hadn't rusted away entirely. Certainly not so much that she couldn't understand the girl's ongoing muttering as she stalked down the hallway.

"Ya, take Captain Perrot, here," Touraine called after her. To Perrot, who was flanking them, she said, "Would you escort her safely?"

The guard hesitated for a moment, and Luca could tell he was weighing orders. He considered Lanquette and Deniaud behind Luca.

"I'm not going to flee the palace," Touraine growled. "I'll be with Her Highness, and I'd rather not find my charge with her throat slit because your people can't do their jobs."

Luca added the weight of her imperious glare to Touraine's words and watched the guard's face harden as he relented.

"I will find you after I've delivered your page safely to Lady Aranen." The captain bowed deeply to Luca. "Your Highness." He jogged off quickly to catch up with the cranky youth.

"An interesting addition," Luca said as they both watched the pair vanish around a corner.

"She's a good kid. Has a killer spinning kick, and she'll probably be good with a sword, too. Not too keen on you lot, though." Touraine smirked with more than a little pride.

Luca pursed her lips and arched her eyebrow higher. "I meant the soldier."

Touraine's expression darkened immediately. "Captain Perrot. More of your uncle's hospitality."

"I see." Though it stung that Luca hadn't merited a goodbye when Touraine attempted to flee, she understood. "When my people told me the duke had brought you back, I feared the worst. Especially when you didn't come to Bastien's funeral."

Touraine sighed and shoved her hands in her pockets. "It wasn't my place."

"I also never thanked you for helping Deniaud get me to safety."

"It was nothing. I'm sorry I wasn't—I know you were close. I'm sorry."

It wasn't until the woman's face passed through that complicated flicker of grief that Luca decided.

"Touraine, would you like to see something?"

Quizzically, Touraine said, "All right?"

Luca led them along the corridor, taking a different turn than the guard and the girl. They were in a wing of the palace that was never used, but the corridor was spotless: the floor swept, the carpets and tapestries beaten, every curl of vine on the frieze and the baseboards lining the corridor dusted. She hadn't been down this way in ages, even though it was around the corner from the King's Library. Her uncle's library. There was an ache at the center of her chest even as something in her relaxed. If the Rose Maze was her favorite place, this was her most private of places, one of the few things she still had to herself.

Outside of the king and queen's chambers, Luca pulled the key on its leather thong from around her neck. She'd begged the old seneschal for it so she could make a copy. To many, the door would have been surprisingly nondescript. The undecorated wooden door was supposed to confuse assassins; it couldn't confound a disease that snuck into people's beds and stole into their bodies.

Luca watched Touraine put it all together. She took in the immaculate yet desolate corridor and looked back at Luca and her hesitation. Even when Touraine's eyes had been brown, they had shaken Luca with their intensity whenever Touraine looked at her—really looked, not out of obedience but with her full focus. The gold frightened her. It felt like Touraine could see even deeper, and Luca wondered if it was true—if the Shālan magic did let the Shālan priests see someone's thoughts. Sky above, she hoped not.

"We don't have to," Touraine said softly.

The gentleness spurred Luca on. "I want to." The door creaked with disuse as she opened it and stepped in.

Without asking, Lanquette went for the stash of candles in the dark, then he and Deniaud slipped discreetly out, shutting the door behind them. She and Touraine were plunged into the gloom of her parents' past.

The penumbra lightened just enough for her to see the rest of the room, its furniture covered in sheets. The dusty carpet muffled her steps to the table where her father's sword lay in its leather belt. It was simple and elegant: not a sword to show his wealth or his status, but to show his strength and experience.

Luca rested her cane against the table and picked up the sword. It came out of its scabbard smoothly, still well oiled from before she left for Qazāl. She moved through the steps, slowly, minding where she placed her feet and how she distributed her weight over her bad leg. Gil never let her practice with heavier swords, but these quiet moments were hers alone. When she held her father's sword, she imagined that he was here, guiding not just her steps but her actions outside of the room. A complicated turn and twist of her wrist and she ended in front of Touraine, with the tip of the blade pointed at the other woman's throat.

Touraine didn't move. The air between them was thick with tension, time, and words unspoken.

Slowly, Touraine pushed the blade down and away. "You know, if you wanted to be the one to give me sword lessons, you could have just said." The corner of her mouth twitched.

Luca chuckled and raised the blade to examine its edge. "My father wasn't a perfect king. Perhaps not even a good man. He made mistakes. He was never cruel to me, though. Not that that excuses anything he did to others," she added quickly.

Touraine leaned against one of the tall engraved columns separating the sitting room from the bedchamber. She crossed her arms.

"Then why do you want to be so much like him?"

"I just expected that I would rule after him. The crown, the sword, the charging warhorse." Luca opened her hands, as if those things she didn't have would fall into them. "And then..." She gestured at the lifeless room around them. At her leg.

"You wanted to be a warrior queen?"

"Is that so hard to believe?"

Touraine tilted her head, surveying Luca as if Luca were strange terrain and she was strategizing how best to position her troops. "No, actually."

"Anylight, maybe I didn't want to be a warrior queen per se. I wanted what any child wants. For her parents to approve of her. And I can't help but think that he'd be disappointed in me," Luca finished in a whisper.

"Ha!" Touraine laughed bitterly. "I know a thing or two about disappointed parents." She wandered around the room, examining the artifacts of Luca's childhood. She didn't touch anything.

Luca couldn't help but smile. "Oh? And how does the daughter of the Jackal get back into her good graces after fighting for the enemy?"

Touraine bared her teeth. The glint of them in the candlelight, with the dark hollows of Touraine's eyes and cheeks, sent a not unpleasant shiver down Luca's spine.

"Ah, yes. Get rid of the interlopers. And now? Is she proud of you?"

"Hard to say." Touraine paused at Luca's mother's violoncelle. "It's a far shot from threatening to kill me like she did the first day we met."

"That's harsh."

"I also hanged her brother."

"You did?"

"I did. Jak doesn't talk about him with me."

"Oh."

"Yeah. So, you can see it's complicated." Touraine shrugged.

"Do you wish you'd never met?"

A long pause, then a heavy sigh. "No."

They stood in silence for so long that Luca felt the ache in her bad leg start to clench. She limped over to the only uncovered chair in the room, where Queen Étienne once sat to play. The music stand was where Luca had left it, with the same pieces Luca had played before leaving for Qazāl.

She stroked the bout of the instrument as it lay on its side, then reached down and plucked the strings, expecting the discordant tones. The sound dredged up such a longing in Luca that she whimpered, the hitch in her chest threatening to come out in sobs. She held them back.

"Luca?" Touraine knelt beside Luca and placed her hand over Luca's, covering her grief rings. Touraine's eyes burned like embers, and Luca wanted to warm herself in their glow.

"They would be proud of you," Touraine said. "How could they not be?"

Touraine brushed a thumb along the back of Luca's hand. Luca gasped involuntarily. Touraine looked down at their joined hands, and returned her hand to her own knee with deliberation.

Luca cleared the sudden hoarseness from her throat, and her voice came out pitchy and high instead. "Because I'm parceling out their empire and fighting over the pieces with their brother?"

Touraine saw through Luca's thin, wry humor for the insecurity it was. "You're doing what's right, Luca," she said. "You're trying, anylight. If that's not something they would be proud of, why are you so intent on pleasing their memory? You know who you are. Be true to that instead."

Luca stared, her mouth gone dry, unnerved that Touraine could see right through her. *Was* it the eyes? Was it Shāl?

Perhaps it was something else entirely, something more mundane and yet altogether more.

"Anylight," Touraine said roughly, standing up, turning away. She held her elbows in her hands, emphasizing the strong breadth of her back. "You have an idea, right? One that involves us."

It was still seconds before Luca could speak. "Only if you want it to. Though I think my uncle has forced both of our hands. Having Bastien killed was a threat, and if he's keeping you here—"

Touraine whipped around. "He had Bastien killed?"

"I believe so, yes. He as good as confirmed it at the funeral."

"That sack of bearshit—he threatened us, too. He wants me to sign a new treaty. It would beggar us. He's going to use your connection to us 'barbarian witches' to show you're not fit to rule. That, or he wants to take the magic for himself. He says he'll study us," she finished with a growl. "Is killing him an option?"

Luca laughed. Touraine did not.

"No. For the same reason he—probably—won't try to kill me directly. Murdering rival heirs tends to leave a stain you can't wash away."

But Luca wasn't as sure as she sounded. *He wouldn't kill* me. *Would he?*

"Fine," Touraine grumbled. "What, then?"

"The long version: every week, my uncle and I play échecs. Since I was a child, I've watched him build himself enough support to take mine out from beneath me. I didn't learn to beat him by using his strategy against him. That always backfired. He saw it coming. He knew how to block it. He knew most of the strategies, actually. He thought he knew me.

"I only managed to beat him when I surprised him. It rarely worked more than once, he was too clever, but—I surprised him by doing things he didn't expect me to do—something he thought was beyond me, or a strategy too obsolete to be a threat. Perhaps he didn't think I was willing to take the risk. I'm willing to risk everything now, Touraine."

She waited for Touraine to say something. The other woman stood wolfishly, one hand on her hip and the other caressing the handle of her knife.

"The short version?" Touraine cocked her head.

Luca pulled the medallion out of her pocket. It shone buttery gold in the candlelight. On one side, in beautiful detail, was a field of barley. The goldsmith had even picked out individual kernels on a few of the plants in the foreground. A symbol of fertility, of good harvests. A bounty.

A pyramid of piled skulls was just as lovingly picked out on the reverse.

"Come with me to Champs d'Or. Bastien left me a lead."

# CHAPTER 19

# FIELDS OF GOLD

Champs d'Or was made of gold.

They'd traveled for several days across Balladaire, and everywhere Touraine looked from the carriage, wheat fields shimmered to the horizon.

It was also immediately obvious why the Champs d'Or colors were bright green and gold. Fields of squat green plants butted up next to large multihued squashes tangled in green vines, all of it ready for harvest, with tiny figures in the distance bending to the work.

Touraine would not have come if not for the weight of the Jackal riding in the back of her mind. She remembered Durfort's warning: the comtesse had little love for the Qazāli. Luca needed Ghislaine, though, and wanted Touraine's help to get her. As long as the Qazāli needed Luca, Touraine needed to keep the princess happy.

So much for avoiding Ghislaine at all costs.

They arrived at Lady Bel-Jadot's manor on the seventh day. After Touraine and the others were shown to their rooms and given time to rinse the road dust from their faces, they were escorted to the menagerie for luncheon.

"Welcome, Your Highness, Your Excellency." Lady Bel-Jadot curtsied to Luca and nodded politely to Touraine. The woman was decked in an emerald-green dress that complemented the olive undertones of her skin. The bodice and skirts were slashed with gold, just like her fields. "Let me show you our new additions."

The comtesse beckoned, and a ring on her middle finger caught the light. It was thin and silver with a blue-green stone in it. A grief ring for her daughter. She snapped her fingers, and servants came with warm drinks as they set off. Touraine expected tea, or even coffee—most Balladairans liked to show off with "exotic coffee from the colonies."

It was neither. It was something dark and brown, mixed with... warmed milk. Sweet.

"This isn't coffee." Luca smacked her lips delicately as she mulled the taste of the beverage over her tongue.

Lady Bel-Jadot couldn't help the smugness as she looked back at them over her shoulder. "No, it is not. It's called chocolate. Melted and mixed with sugar. Evrard gave me some to try; it's truly delicious, isn't it? I find honey so...dull in comparison."

The drink's bright, overwhelming sweetness made Touraine's tongue curl the same way a lemon did.

"It comes from a bean, like coffee. From somewhere even farther south than the Southern Mountains," the comtesse was saying. "The climate isn't right in Balladaire, but I think if the Qazāli could be—" She cut off and gave Touraine a tight smile. "That is to say, Your Excellency, it could be an excellent crop. I'm sure Lord Castide would be happy to give your farmers in Qazāl something to grow. He has ships and connections, I'm sure that would be useful."

"And I'm sure you'd pay handsomely for the privilege of a nearby source." Touraine saluted her with the cup and took another sip, savoring it.

From Lady Bel-Jadot's other side, she saw Luca's eyebrows shift up in surprise. The appreciative smirk vanished quickly, but it was enough to send a satisfied flush through Touraine's body.

Like Luca, the comtesse was too well versed to let her true feelings show. "We'd be absolutely thrilled to be trading partners," she said. "But, ta! Enough of business. First, we have the lions."

The menagerie was built in a circle, with hexagonal cells for the animals like honeycomb, fanned around the edges. Their enclosures were gated with iron bars so people could see them without getting mauled. A manicured, circular path planted with shade trees led them around in a loop. Servants waited at a table beneath the pavilion in the center of it all.

"Actually, Your Grace," Touraine started again, "I wanted to ask after my countrymen. I heard in La Chaise that many of them found work on your estates. How are they?"

No, Lady Bel-Jadot's face didn't change. Her relaxed smile didn't drop, her eyes showed no fear—her face simply froze for a moment before shifting into an appropriate look of concern. It wasn't that noticeable, but Touraine had spent a lifetime alert to her superiors' slightest mood shifts. Something wasn't right.

"I've been glad to help them find a place in Balladaire." Ghislaine waved at Luca. "The princess and I spoke about the good we can do with them here."

Luca made a noncommittal noise in her throat and sipped her chocolate.

"Anylight, later, later. Ah, here. Look at that mane! Isn't he mighty?"

If Touraine hadn't met Niwai's lioness, she would have thought this lion was mighty, if lazy. His mane hung thick about his head, and he lounged at his ease, licking his paws. The meaty, tendonous carcass of some unlucky beast lay cast off a few feet away. But Touraine had met Niwai's lion, and this one seemed soft in comparison. Slow and sullen. It looked up at them and gave a low chuff of a growl as they passed by.

"I've seen lions before," Ghadin said, whining in the way only a bored youth could. "Better ones than this, too."

Touraine caught the girl's shoulder and squeezed, shooting her a warning look. Ghadin shrugged off the squeeze, but she did go silent.

Ghadin's turn to be on the receiving end of one of Lady Bel-Jadot's smiles. "I suppose you must have, coming from the wild desert. What about this magnificent creature?"

The next animal did give Touraine pause. The lion in the previous cell was content in its indolence, but the next cat, just as large and with orange and black stripes all over, pulled back its lips and let out a roar that was a cross between something definitely animal and a large man's shout.

Luca gasped and stepped back against Touraine. She steadied Luca even as her own heart jumped into her throat. Instinct made her clench her fist, as if she could fight it. The beast's teeth were as long as her fingers, and it looked heavy with muscle and fur. Ghadin, on the other hand, was fascinated.

"That is called a tiger, Your Highness. From south of the Lunāb colonies. This one is new—still aggressive, you see. The Taargens," Lady Bel-Jadot continued as they walked, "have the practice of fighting the animals against each other." She shuddered and looked at Touraine and Ghadin, pretending to include them in the ridicule of that other "uncivilized" nation. "Simply barbaric."

They continued the circuit of animals, and though Touraine couldn't help but admire them—the odd little striped horse Ghislaine called a zebra, and the giraffes! How could an animal's neck even grow that tall? And sky above, why?—she had a feeling that Niwai would have been upset to see it. What would the Many-Legged think of their brethren, locked up for a rich woman's pleasure?

"I'm hoping to build a special water enclosure next," Lady Bel-Jadot was saying to Luca as they sat around the table beneath the pavilion. "Perhaps a crocodile from that river you mentioned?"

"My lady, might we have a word about things closer to hand?"

"The farms? As I said, Your Highness, the Qazāli are perfectly fine here—"

"I'm sure they are"—Luca shared a quick look with Touraine— "but there are other things. I'd also like to ask the seneschal about the yields. And—" Luca stopped when the servants arrived to serve a warming soup full of vegetables and some type of buttery-smelling fowl. Touraine's stomach growled.

After the servants stepped away, Luca continued. "Perhaps you'd be able to talk to me about something Paul-Sebastien de Beau-Sang was looking into before he was murdered."

Lady Bel-Jadot's spoon froze on its way to her lips. "That poor boy. I knew his father well. Unlike his father, he was actually pleasant."

Beside Touraine, Luca went taut. Another cup of sugar-sweetened chocolate came, and Touraine slid her new cup over to Ghadin without taking her eyes from Ghislaine.

"He was looking for our history, Lady Bel-Jadot. He was a great scholar, and I don't want his work to remain unfinished."

"Unfortunately, Your Highness, I have no idea what you're talking about." Ghislaine swallowed her spoonful and took another, but she was concentrating too hard on the bowl.

"Perhaps not, my lady. But he was your liege man, and since you're so close to the heart of the empire—the earth, our grain—I thought I would come and see if I could follow the trail he hoped to find."

"And what is that, Your Highness?"

"I think you know."

The comtesse put her spoon down beside her bowl, tightened her shawl about her shoulders, and then placed her hands gently in her lap.

"Your Excellency." Ghislaine's smile crinkled her eyes, and her voice was smooth and sweet as the chocolate, but she didn't fool Touraine for a minute. "I apologize, but it seems like Her Highness and I have some matters of Balladairan state to discuss privately. My seneschal would be happy to take you to the fields and see how your countrymen are getting along. I think you'll be quite pleased."

Touraine looked down at her half-finished bowl of soup. It was the first meal they hadn't had at an inn in a week. *You've gotten spoiled.*

Luca was watching her from the corners of her eyes while she faced Ghislaine. It was just enough to share a message: *Go. Take advantage of this.*

*So be it, Princess.* But Touraine was still pissed about the soup.

The silence between Luca and Ghislaine stretched while Touraine and Ghadin walked away. Their footsteps echoed on the stone slabs of the menagerie path. It was quiet enough to hear the birds and the chuffing of the animals in their cells. Quiet enough to hear Ghislaine's strained breath through her nose.

With a sharp gesture from the comtesse, her servants vanished, too.

"Ghislaine, does my uncle have a sword at your neck, too?" Luca said recklessly. "Anything that might keep you from supporting my rightful bid for the throne?"

"What does this have to do with the LeRoche boy?" Ghislaine frowned over her quickly cooling soup.

"Does he?"

"No."

"Then you'll support me with your vote at the Trial of Competence."

"Ha!" Ghislaine leaned back in her seat, full of cruel mirth. She had a substantial laugh, not a delicate court tinkle like so many nobles and want-to-be nobles affected, eschewing anything real at all. Like Luca. Though Luca didn't wear a tinkling laugh, either. She didn't laugh at all.

"Why should I do that, Your Highness? You come to me full of erratic suspicion, digging into Balladaire's uncivilized past—the duke regent knows to leave that sordid history where it belongs. The duke also has experience ruling the kingdom. A kingdom which is already stable. What good does it do to upend that with an impulsive youth?"

*Stability.* These were all facts, and strong points in her uncle's favor. In other circumstances, Luca would have chosen them herself. She addressed the other half of Ghislaine's objection instead. "If the duke is so certain that our 'uncivilized' history should stay in the past, then why has he threatened my guests"—Luca gestured in the direction Touraine and Ghadin had gone—"in order to use their so-called 'uncivilized' gifts for his own benefit?"

It was a small lie, woven from threads of truth Luca had plucked from Touraine's recounting of her encounters with the duke.

Ghislaine hesitated. "He wouldn't do that."

"He would. What he wants can't be taken by force, though, and the Shālans will not ally with him."

Ghislaine was shaking her head before Luca could finish. "We're better off without allies like that, Your Highness. There's only one way we can fit the Qazāli into Balladaire—they must be civilized and willing to leave their god behind."

"And if they choose to become our enemies, what then? I have the Qazāli, and reason to believe the Taargens would actually keep a peace with me."

Ghislaine's eyes flashed. "Are the Taargens planning to break the treaty?"

"I didn't say that." Luca tapped a nail slowly on the table. "I only mean that my uncle spends his time looking at just one area of the board. I have a wider view and better position with those who have reason to become enemies if we aren't careful."

Luca let it hang in the air for a moment what it meant to be "careful" and what else might turn these two neighbors of Balladaire into enemies. If Ghislaine came to think that these countries might march to war if Luca asked...what of it?

"We'll be better able to face the future with powerful allies." Luca leaned over the table. Heavy weight on the word *future*. On *power*.

"Your allies killed Marie."

"Disease killed your daughter, Lady Bel-Jadot. It was an unfortunate tragedy, but if we blame the Qazāli for that, we should also blame her for being there in the first place."

Luca and Ghislaine stared at each other over the four bowls of soup, all of them but Ghadin's practically untouched. Ghislaine's eyes shone with tears—of grief or hatred, Luca couldn't tell.

"You have my answer, Your Highness. If you will please excuse me." Ghislaine rose from the table. "Linger with the beasts as long as you wish."

Touraine heard the laborers singing before the wagon arrived at the fields. She pulled her cloak tight against the wind that carried their voices.

The song was mournful, but rhythmic, and the closer they got to the workers, the more she saw how they bent and reached with the music. The closer they got, the clearer the words became.

*Farmer Jean, oh, Farmer Jean, oh,*
*Tell me where has your daughter gone, oh,*
*I'll tell you men, oh, I'll tell you men, oh,*
*My daughter's gone for to reap the wheat, oh,*
*My daughter's gone for the wheat.*

"What was it you wanted to see, exactly, Your Excellency?" the seneschal asked. Surprisingly, he drove the wagon. She hadn't pegged him for the sort to dirty himself with the manual labors of the estate.

"The Qazāli. Are they being treated well, is the work fair?" Touraine gave him a hard look.

The seneschal bowed his head. "As you wish, Your Excellency. After you tour the fields, I can show you their lodgings, and you'll be welcome to speak to them at their dinner hours." He clucked his tongue at the horses.

One puffy-faced Qazāli man approached them, swinging his sickle and whistling to the tune of the song that echoed across the field. When he reached the end of the line, he looked up at the seneschal, gave him a nod, and went to the next line of wheat, this time marching the other way, sickle rising, falling, sawing a little. Rising, falling, sawing. She watched him as the seneschal drove them forward before she realized why the man had seemed familiar. She stopped the seneschal and leapt from the cart as she ran back toward the man, down his row of wheat.

"Sulmain?" Touraine's voice went high with excitement. She didn't mean for it to, but there was a joy, a relief, at finding someone familiar in a strange place. Even if that someone was a man she barely knew, had only met a couple weeks ago. Even so.

At his name, the dark man straightened in confusion and wariness. Then he saw her, and the confusion deepened. "Mulāzim? What are you doing here?" He spoke to her in Shālan.

"My job," she said cheerily. Her smile didn't change his expression. "You told me Qazāli were taking up the comtesse's offer? To work her fields? I'm making sure you're being treated well. What are you doing here?"

The portly man pushed his sweaty black hair up from his damp forehead as he looked around the field. It flopped back down, and he tried to wipe his forehead with his sleeve. He'd shaved his beard.

"It seemed like the safest thing to do. Better than getting beaten for a few coins of charity in La Chaise." He looked like he wanted to spit, but good manners held him back.

Touraine scanned the field again, more critically this time. The workers were a mixed bunch, still more Balladairan than Qazāli.

"Is it better? You're paid well? Should you even be working? Those men beat you—"

Sulmain kicked out one foot. He was wearing a simple but solid brown leather boot. He plucked at the shirt he wore, rough spun, but not patched or threadbare like the clothes she'd last seen him in.

"Well enough." Then he patted his belly with a smile. "I don't suffer too much." He didn't address the beating at all.

"And money? Where do you live?"

He pointed off to the southeast, over several fields. Back toward the manor, but far enough south of it that they wouldn't cross paths with the comtesse if she was in residence. There was a vague dark shape Touraine assumed was the housing.

"Tenements?"

"More like barracks, if you forgive my assumption. Not much privacy, but no holes in the roof. Important soon, I hear."

The comparison made the unease in Touraine's stomach sharpen to a point. She, too, had been given boots and clothing, food and shelter, and work to occupy her mind. She, too, had been grateful.

"Sulmain." Touraine stepped closer and lowered her voice. "Tell me the truth. Are you being paid fairly? If you wanted to leave, right now, could you?"

The apple of his throat bobbled. He struggled to meet the intensity of her glare. She remembered that her eyes were gold and tried to bore into him, force out the truth.

"And go where, Mulāzim?" He matched her low, fierce tone with his own bitter one. "We left Qazāl because we were starving, and when the council told us we'd be free to live here in peace—why wouldn't we take a chance in the better country?"

"Better? How did you even know what it would be like?"

"How do you think? They've only been shoving it down our throats for decades. Is it so hard to think some of us believed it? Besides. No one can afford to go back, remember? We spent all we had to get here." Sulmain's face reddened, and he put his fists on his hips as he glared, daring her to shame him.

Touraine had no right to shame him, though. She stepped back into her heels.

"I'm sorry. Things are—complicated here. In the palace. It's taking longer than I'd like—"

"They say the princess is going to get thrown out on her ear."

"Who says?" Touraine asked sharply.

Sulmain shrugged. "They say. Sounds like a mess to me. Enjoy your parades, though." He turned back to cutting the stalks of wheat with his sickle.

Though his tone was bright again, Touraine recognized it for the lie it was. She'd heard it enough in her life, especially from the other Sands when she started working for Luca in Qazāl.

"Wait, Sulmain. Is there anything else…people…say? Anything that could help?"

He looked her up and down, eyes grazing her face, her hands. They stopped on the little purse at her belt. It took Touraine a minute to understand. Then she reached into the purse and pulled out a couple of silver sovereigns. A high cost for whatever information, but then, she could recover it. It was enough to change Sulmain's life. Or, if someone else found out he had it, to end it. He made the coin disappear.

"Look at this." He beckoned her close to the wheat he'd just cut down. With a grunt, he knelt, and Touraine followed. He held up a stalk to her face.

"What about it?"

He hit her in the face with it.

"What the—!"

"Look at it. Does this look like their golden little flag to you?"

Touraine wiped the plant dust off her nose and looked closer. It was wheat. Funny little tufts of fiber around two rows of nested seeds. They were pale yellowish, pale greenish in parts, all with a peculiar dull grayish cast to them. The seeds were wrinkled and thin.

"I'm not a farmer. You mean it's not supposed to look like this?"

"I'm not a farmer, either. At least, I wasn't." He picked up another stalk and rubbed his fingers over the seeds and frowned thoughtfully. "But these Balladairans out here? They know their work. They say something's odd about it." He started to say something else, but he trailed off and shook his head.

"What? What is it? What's odd about the grain? Has it been making people sick?"

"It's probably nothing, Mulāzim. It's just..."

Touraine stepped around in front of him. "Let me decide if it's nothing. Tell me."

"We're not supposed to believe in Shāl here, sah? No praying, no beads, nothing. Even in Qazāl it was forbidden." Sulmain scratched at his chin with the back of his gloved hand. Pale flecks of chaff littered the dark stubble. "But I saw a couple of the Balladairan workers go off, the day they realized the wheat was wrong."

"I don't understand."

Sulmain looked at Touraine as if she were being deliberately obtuse. "We talked about it, the other Qazāli and I. There are only a few things to do when something goes badly wrong—you drink, you fight, or you pray and hope some god is listening."

He held up one finger. "They weren't drinking, or the rest would have gone, too." The second finger: "They weren't fighting, or else why do it in private?" He tapped his third finger.

"Or they went to fuck," Touraine said, exasperated. "Or they don't like the rest of their work crew, or—"

"It was different, Mulāzim." Sulmain was affronted. "Just different. Like I said, it's probably nothing, just a couple of hypocrites. That's nothing new with Balladairans."

Touraine stared up into the sky and blew out her cheeks, letting the air hiss out. "It's all right, Sulmain. I'm sorry, it's fine. Did you see where they went? Is there a...shrine? A temple? What are their names?"

"Can't recall their names." But he pointed with his sickle toward a small, lone cliff—a sheer drop on one side and a gently sloping hill on the other. "They went to the Lord's Seat."

"What's there?"

"I've never been. I'm afraid of heights." Sulmain bent down over his wheat again with a finality to his words.

"Thank you, Sulmain." Touraine handed him the rest of the coins in her pouch, half-guilty.

The man snorted. "Just remember me to the princess."

"I will."

"I mean it, Mulāzim. Don't forget us out here."

Touraine jogged back up to the wagon where the seneschal waited. Ghadin and Perrot were playing some sort of reflex hand game in the back and stopped as she approached. The horses hitched to the wagon were trying to crop at the wheat by the edge of the road.

"Did that man satisfy your curiosity, Your Excellency?" The comtesse's man blinked behind his oval spectacles as Touraine vaulted up to her seat. He picked the reins up from his lap and prepared to snap the horses into action.

"He did. He gave me much to think on. What's wrong with the wheat?"

The man looked like he'd smelled curdled milk. "Nothing," he said too quickly.

Touraine waited for him to remember that she came with the princess. She made herself look taller. She didn't know if the golden eyes trick would work on him, too.

Slowly, as if he were drawing a bayonet out of his own guts, he continued. "It isn't that the grain is...ill. But the crops aren't strong. The yields aren't where anyone predicted. And the last time the numbers were this bad with no directly correlated weather..." He trailed off, staring unfocused at the fields.

"What?" Touraine wanted to shake him. "What?"

The seneschal shuddered and shook his head. "The Withering came."

# CHAPTER 20

# A PRECIPICE

Touraine should have been out following up on Sulmain's hunch. If she told Luca about the hunch, though, the princess would get excited, and when Luca was excited, she got ideas, and when Luca got ideas, they usually put Touraine right in the line of fire when—not if—those ideas went ass up. Touraine didn't like being on the front line at the best of times, but she had Ghadin to worry about now, too.

Ghadin, who was dutifully following Touraine through Touraine's old conscript calisthenics routine, their breaths synchronized as they squatted, lunged, and did push-ups in their generously appointed room. Not as generous considering they had to share it, but Touraine didn't care enough to press the insult. She preferred to keep Ghadin nearby.

So much had changed, and yet Touraine was in the exact position she'd been in a year ago: fighting for the Balladairan crown because the lives of her own people were at stake. Last year, she'd been protecting the Sands. This time, the Qazāli.

None of it mattered, though, because she had no solutions to the crown's problems, which meant no way to solve her own. Unless she went to the Taargens or threw herself on Nicolas's mercy.

"Why are we doing this?" Ghadin asked the ground as she pushed herself up and lowered again.

Touraine held herself at the top of the push-up. "It builds strength."

"No, this." Ghadin balanced on one hand and waved the other vaguely at the ceiling, encompassing the whole empire.

Down. Up. "For Qazāl," Touraine said automatically.

"How is this for Qazāl? It's got nothing to do with us. Why do we have to be in the middle of their politics?"

Down. "You begged Jaghotai to come." Up.

"I thought it was going to be like when you came to Qazāl. There was more fighting then."

"Be glad there's no more fighting," Touraine grumbled. She jumped her feet to her hands and popped up. "Squats."

"I know, it's dangerous, people get hurt." Ghadin rolled her eyes and hopped onto her feet. Her squats were effortless in the way that only a kid's could be. "It worked, though. You won when you fought them. Now you just talk and stare at each other and nothing happens."

Touraine barked a laugh as she lowered herself on one leg. It was good to show off for the kid sometimes. Ghadin's assessment was annoyingly accurate, though. "That's politics, kid." Up. Down.

Still, it made Touraine want to do something so that it didn't feel like she was wasting her time at dainty luncheons where people hunted for the least offensive way to say "Go fuck yourself."

Touraine straightened. "Get dressed."

"Where are we going?"

"To do something. Hurry up."

Touraine slipped on her boots and opened the door to find Luca standing outside, her knuckles poised to rap on it.

"Touraine," Luca said, surprised. "I wanted to speak with you."

"I want to talk to you, too." Touraine gathered her coat. "To look for something, actually."

"Right now? It's night. It's cold. You're ... sweating?"

"I know." Touraine waved her coat in Luca's face. "Come on."


The night was chilly, but pleasant compared to the last blustery days in La Chaise. The moon hung high and heavy in the clear sky. Large and round, pale orange, it lit the path with an eerie beauty. From a distance, the hill seemed to stretch up like a thick finger making a grab for the moon, just barely out of reach.

As they walked, Touraine told Luca what she'd learned, from the seneschal's fear of the Withering to Sulmain's suspicions.

"But why would believers come up here?" Luca asked as they all trudged up the hill.

Touraine rubbed the back of her head in frustration. "Prayers? Balladairan magic? I don't know."

"You don't believe him."

"I don't know what to believe."

At the top of the hill, Touraine looked for a sign that Sulmain had been onto something. There were no footprints, no weird gouges in the dirt. No sign saying *Holy Magic Was Done Here.*

"I don't see anything," Touraine muttered, feeling sheepish.

"I don't ei—wait."

Luca half stooped over her cane to look at something on the ground. She stood close enough to the edge of the cliff that Touraine had the irrational fear that Luca would trip and fall over it. She approached the other woman slowly, positioning herself between Luca and the steep drop.

"There."

Touraine knelt where Luca prodded the ground with her new wooden cane. Large shards of clay littered the grass.

"Is it something?" Luca's words came out breathy and excited.

Touraine shook her head. They were stained dark and smelled unmistakably of sour wine. The edges were sharp, so the breaks were fresh—possibly as fresh as a few days ago. Sulmain's friends had just been drinking after all.

"That's it?" Ghadin asked, unimpressed. "That's what we were looking for?"

"Just a couple of farmers getting drunk." Touraine groaned and dug her knuckles into her forehead. "Never mind. It was stupid."

"It's not stupid." Luca offered Touraine a hand up. Surprised, Touraine took it. "This is how research works."

"I guess," Touraine huffed. Put research right next to politics, then. Touraine could do without either.

She stepped away from Luca, toward the edge. She didn't want to jump, but there was a rush in that sudden vertigo of standing on the brink. The height of the tor made the world feel so small, like Touraine could crush it with her thumb if she closed her eye, and at the same time so large that she wanted to cry out—the weight of it all was too much, there was too much she was responsible for, too many people whose lives rested in her hands, and she wasn't enough to handle it all.

"It's breathtaking, isn't it?" Luca whispered into the hush between them.

"All this space. I feel small."

"So do I."

The soft sentiment surprised Touraine. "That's not something you're used to."

"No," Luca said after a breath. "No, it's not."

"Well, you are small. Inconsequential. Join the rest of us." The joke came out wearing Touraine's bitterness.

Luca looked over at her. "You're not inconsequential."

"No? Tell that to the moon."

"To the moon, then. Not to anyone else. Not to the Qazāli. Not to Ghadin."

*Not to me,* Touraine waited for her to say.

Instead, Luca reached into a pocket and dug out a small box with a metal clasp. "I wanted to give you something." Her raised chin bared her throat, as if daring an assassin's blade, her neck long and beautiful, the cords stark against her jawline and the lip of her collarbone. Her throat bobbed as she swallowed, and Touraine couldn't look away. There was something about the moon here. Something fierce and magical. The moon.

Touraine took the box hesitantly and flicked the clasp open with her thumb. On a bed of velvet, two grief rings lay nestled together. One was a thick gold band with a black jewel and the other was thin and gold, the metal twisted and turning like a knot of rope. Touraine dumped them into her hand and traced them with her fingers.

"What..." she said hoarsely.

"For your friends. Tibeau and Aimée." Luca pointed at the thick one and the thin one, respectively.

"How did you know?"

"You talked about them a lot. Before they died. The ones you left in the guardhouse." Luca ducked her head, trying to meet Touraine's eyes, but Touraine turned, blinking away the sudden tears blurring the view from the tor.

"I want to apologize. I have wanted to apologize for a long time. For what happened in Qazāl last year and for my role in it. Sky above, for what happened before we even got there. I'm sorry that it cost your friends their lives and I'm sorry that Balladaire—that I ever made those sacrifices necessary. Please believe me when I say I want something better. Better for all of us. I will make right all that I can."

Luca sought Touraine's approval with wide eyes. What was Touraine supposed to say? That this was enough?

No. Luca's face didn't ask for that at all. The sorrow and guilt in her expression told Touraine that Luca knew it wasn't enough and that it never would be. Luca knew it, and that left a crack inside her that Touraine and Touraine alone could put her fingers into and pry open. Touraine could see it in the way Luca's lips parted, waiting for a response, her chest still as she held her breath, waiting for some sign, any sign that Touraine accepted the gift and the apology that came with it. *This is why Jaghotai sent me.*

Touraine could have scoffed at the rings. Said, *What good will this do my people, starving in your city? The people starving in* my *city?* Touraine could press into the seam of Luca's guilt, and Luca would respond. Luca would help. It was the perfect time to.

But the rings were beautiful, and Luca had thought of her. She had thought of Touraine's pain. There was no guile in the other woman's face, and for once, the court mask Luca hid behind was gone.

Touraine held the rings cupped in her palm, turning them and letting the moon catch them at different angles. The black stone wasn't actually black—it flared red at the edges, dark and deep, like a coal hiding a heart of heat. Passion buried under a Balladairan uniform. A lump rose in Touraine's throat as she slid first Tibeau's ring and then Aimée's onto her fingers.

*Look at us*, Touraine thought. *Look how we've failed.* She and Luca had failed, and somehow, they were the ones still standing, with the world stretched out below them.

Maybe there was hope for Qazāl. Maybe there was hope for her.

"Wait—where's Ghadin?" Touraine whirled around, but the girl was nowhere in sight. "Ghadin!"

"Down here!" Ghadin's voice came from below.

With her stomach in her throat, Touraine flattened herself against the ground and looked over. Ghadin was climbing down the dirt and stone, nimble as a goat.

"Ghadin, I'm going to kill you!" Touraine shouted down the cliff face in Shālan. "Perrot!" Without further instruction, Perrot sprinted down the hill to be there when Ghadin reached the bottom.

"Stop whining," Ghadin called up. "It's just like climbing in the quarry. Easier, even."

"I'm going to kill her," Touraine repeated, this time to Luca.

Luca smothered her laughter with a hand. "It sounds like she's all right; what's the harm—"

A shriek from below cut them off. It felt like ice-cold water down Touraine's back. It was followed a moment later by another cry.

"Ghadin!"

Touraine galloped down the hill, only barely keeping her feet beneath her. Captain Perrot's voice echoed through the night, but it wasn't until Touraine had reached the bottom of the hill and slowed to a jog that she could make out the captain's words above the mad rush of her heart.

"We're okay! She's okay!"

Touraine jogged after Perrot's voice. The captain and Ghadin were on the other side of the bottom of the hill, at the base of that sheer cliffside. Perrot stood over Ghadin, who was scraped up and sitting next to something in the thick, springy grass while she rubbed at her ankle. The guard looked like he wanted to pull the girl back. Another step and Touraine saw why.

Ghadin had found a skull. Part of a skull. A half-rotted skull. A decent bit of the rest of the skeleton, too, if not all of it. The reek of death was long gone—just the smell of the damp earth and grass under the moonlight.

"Don't touch it," Touraine snapped as Ghadin reached forward.

"But look." Ghadin pointed. "There's something."

At the region of the skeleton's chest—the ribs were gone, and Touraine briefly imagined some poor animal wearing them like a grisly corset—a curved edge stuck out of the dirt. It was irregularly smooth. Touraine crouched beside Ghadin and scraped at it, gingerly at first, and then roughly as she realized it was half-buried. She pulled out the large clay disc just as Luca reached them.

Touraine looked from the disc to Luca. The princess was breathing heavily from the quick descent and leaned more than a little on Lanquette's arm.

"What is it?" Luca asked. "What's happened?"

The disc was immediately familiar, even though it was made of fired clay and pocked with weathering. Its etchings were simple, not ornate, not done by any master. There was simply an apple—or peach or pear?—on one side of the disc, and a skull on the other.

She pushed to her feet and held the clay disc out to Luca, flat on her palm. Luca traced the outline of the fruit with a finger. Her touch tickled through the clay to Touraine's palm. Then Touraine flipped the disc, skull side up.

"Oh," Luca breathed. She made an abortive gesture, and Touraine suspected she had reached for her own version of the disc, the golden medallion that Touraine had found on Bastien's body.

"One question, Luca." Touraine kept her voice low. She looked back at the remains. They were old, definitely, but... "How long has religion been outlawed in Balladaire?"

Luca rolled her eyes up into her head as she did a quick calcula-
tion. "Officially? One hundred eighty-three years? Give or take a few
depending on if you count anti-religious popular sentiment and the
final dissolution of the practices in the outer counties—"

Touraine grunted. "Maybe there was no final dissolution in the
outer counties. If this person was a...sacrifice...it's a decade or so old
at most. There's too much of it here to be old as that. Someone here
still practices."

"We'll tell Ghislaine tomorrow," Luca said. She turned the disc
over and over in her hands thoughtfully. "I'll have her arrange for the
remains to be burned."

"Then what?" Touraine asked.

Luca gave an uncharacteristically mischievous smile and turned it
on Ghadin.

"I know how to get Ghislaine's vote."

"Why are you looking at Ghadin like that?"

The smile sharpened as Luca turned it on Touraine.

Touraine closed her eyes and groaned. "Oh, sky above."

# CHAPTER 21

# MERELY PLAYERS

The plan wasn't the worst plan Luca had ever had.

This time, no one was going to fall into a crocodile-infested river.

And yet, Luca was full of tense anticipation when they returned to Ghislaine's menagerie for lunch with the comtesse. Touraine was also on edge in that soldier's way she still had, as if an armed threat lurked behind every corner.

The three adults fell smoothly into pleasantries—which is to say, Luca and Ghislaine did, while Touraine brooded respectfully—as if Ghislaine hadn't insulted Luca and denied her claim to the throne the day before. As if Luca hadn't found a sacrificed skull on Ghislaine's land.

Ghadin was touring the animals again, according to plan. She teased them by walking on her hands. It was no way for a page to behave, but people like Ghislaine had lower expectations for the Qazāli. Ghislaine had given the girl one disbelieving look, and when Touraine did nothing and Luca didn't, either, she ignored the girl entirely. That was fine. For now.

"My lady," Luca started after Ghislaine concluded the disturbing description of how, exactly, she'd come by the tiger in her menagerie. "What about the growing season? I heard it's not going well."

Today's lunch was a selection of sliced, toasted bread with various pastes and creams, from butter to something that tasted of woodsy mushrooms and herbs to another of fresh fish.

"I've spoken with the duke about anything concerning," Ghislaine said. She patted the corner of her mouth clean of a delicate smear of fish pâté. "We have the situation in hand."

Luca picked up one of the toasts. Mushroom, with—thyme, it smelled like. It crunched deliciously in her mouth, delightfully creamy with an earthy richness that sat deep on the back of her tongue. She chewed slowly and watched Ghislaine wait. She swallowed.

"What do you think about the crop failures and their connection to the Withering?"

"I think that a scholar such as yourself should spend less time listening to farm gossip."

Before Luca could pry deeper, there was a loud crack and thud, and then Ghadin's cry of pain.

Touraine leapt from her seat, knocking toast and condiments from the table, and racing into place beside Ghadin, who lay supine on the ground. Ghislaine rose slowly at first, in her confusion, but Luca followed, urging the woman closer. She had to be there, she had to see, to be convinced—

Ghadin lay on the ground, sobbing, with her left leg twisted beneath her so that her foot was beside her backside. Luca's stomach lurched and warm spit flooded her mouth, her cheeks tingling, and for a moment, she had to look away.

The girl's terror sounded so real, and so did the panic that crossed Touraine's face. There must have been a mistake and Ghadin was really hurt. If she was and Touraine couldn't heal her, the plan would fail.

Touraine mumbled and waved her hands over the girl's twisted leg. Luca couldn't tell if it was theatrical or born of that same panic. Last night, while they plotted, Touraine had confessed to Luca: she couldn't heal, had never done it. The only magic she'd done was on Rogan, unknitting him from the inside out.

*Can you be convincing?* was all Luca asked.

The animals roared and lowed in sympathy in their cages.

*Something has gone wrong.*

Luca stepped closer, to see—

Ghadin's eyes shot open wide. A shriek tore out of her while her body arched up and her legs spasmed straight. Then she collapsed, back on the ground.

All went still. The animals hushed. Touraine's shoulders sagged, and she sat on her heels. She looked lost and tired, like the pantomime had taken a very real toll on her.

Ghislaine stared down, agape, from Touraine to Ghadin to Luca and back to Touraine. To Touraine's hands, now resting on her own thighs, full of—*false?*—potential. The two grief rings shone on her fingers.

"You foolish girl," Ghislaine snarled. Luca thought Ghislaine was speaking to Touraine until the comtesse glared at her. "You have no idea what you're meddling with."

"You speak to your princess and heir," Luca said tightly.

Ghislaine snorted in distaste. "You are just like your father. You want more power and you want it at anyone's expense. He wanted Shālan magic and so did you. Now you want to dig up a past that's better left buried. I'm warning you, Your Highness. Leave. It. Alone."

A shock like lightning blazed across Luca's mind.

*She knows.*

Luca limped toward the older woman, angling Ghislaine away from Touraine and Ghadin. Goose bumps prickled across Luca's skin.

"This isn't about power, Ghislaine," Luca said, low and urgent. "It's not about our empire. It's about the people and what's right for them. My uncle won't even come to peace with the Shālans even though their magic would save our people the deepest grief." When Ghislaine's face showed no sign of softening, Luca went for the vulnerable strike. "What if your daughter had had access to Qazāli healers? Healers who were bound to us by a treaty, by friendship?"

"How dare you?" Ghislaine hissed. The hatred she'd hidden so well now glittered in her eyes. "How dare you mention her and those

monsters in the same breath? You are the reason my child is dead."
Ghislaine glanced sideways. "Is this about magic or keeping your pet
Shālan happy?"

Touraine's arm gripped tight around Ghadin's arm as she stared at
them, her mouth in a suppressed line. Like her daughter, Ghislaine
knew where to place the knife of her cruelty, and Luca recognized
Touraine's way of shutting down all too well. The way her jaw went
tight, her whole body rigid with anger she could never risk letting loose.
Matching rage uncoiled in Luca's stomach. She caught Touraine's eyes,
golden and burning. *Let it loose*, Luca tried to tell her. *Be dangerous.*

Luca took a menacing step closer to Ghislaine. "Under my uncle,
the Shālans will continue hating us. I have seen what they can do to
the people they hate. Do you understand what a loss that would be?"

Touraine's boots crunched toward them in slow, deliberate steps.
Luca didn't take her eyes from Ghislaine's face, but she imagined
Touraine's approach like a wolf circling prey. They made a good pair.

"Your daughter died of illness," Luca said coldly. "You weren't there
when the rebels tore General Cantic apart from the inside, with just
a touch. I was. I watched the blood pool from her eyes, her ears, her
nose, her mouth, Ghislaine. I watched Ambassador El-Qazāli collapse
a man's skull."

Touraine was close now, coming in on Ghislaine's other side. The
loose skin at Ghislaine's neck tightened as the woman swallowed and
clenched her jaw. She tilted her chin defiantly. "And?"

"I'm the heir, Ghislaine. When I take my throne, I will give my
people every advantage, magic or not, Balladairan or not. I know the
truth: people on your land are still practicing religion. Tell me who.
Tell me how." Luca pulled out the two discs, gold and clay scraping
against each other.

"Or you'll set your hound on me?" Ghislaine tilted her head back
and laughed, dark and musical and condescending. And yet, Luca
caught Ghislaine's fearful glance at Touraine. It was working.

"The ambassador is not my hound. She's a very, very powerful
friend."

# THE FAITHLESS

THE FAITHLESS 211

"And if you want to benefit from the labor of my people," Touraine cut in, moving in another step so that she and Ghislaine were a hair apart, "you'd do well to support the rightful heir. Otherwise, I might think you don't actually give a shit. The princess told you what happened the last time you people exploited the Qazāli."

Luca held out an open palm. "Help me take my place, Ghislaine. Tell me what you know."

"If you want my vote, take it. It won't do you any good. But you tell me—*if* you take your throne, what will your people think of that advantage when you're asking them to slaughter their children again?"

Luca froze. She signaled Touraine to hold. "What do you mean?"

"You didn't know." Ghislaine laughed in disbelief, then she sneered in Touraine's direction. "See? Don't meddle in things you don't understand."

"Slaughter their children?" Luca pressed.

"For the magic you claim to want for the people's own good." Ghislaine folded her arms smugly. "Sacrifice their children for a good return on their crops? Ha! Oh, they would drag you out of that palace and tear you into pieces. All magic comes with a price. If you want to control the land, you have to put your blood into it. Ask your *friend*."

Luca shared a look with Touraine. The ambassador's face was grim but unsurprised.

It made a sick sort of sense to Luca. Blood and earth, connecting the two. The same way eating flesh allowed the Shālans to manipulate the body. *Sky above and…earth below.* She pressed a hand to her stomach.

"How do you know all this?"

Ghislaine scoffed. "I live too close to the source to be ignorant. It's my duty to keep it from taking root."

"Does my uncle know?"

Ghislaine gave her a pitying, obvious look.

Of course Nicolas had known. All of the threads of history she and Bastien tried to follow—from Balladaire to Qazāl and back again—to a conclusion that Nicolas had kept from her. Had her father known this, too? Is that why he'd hunted Shālan magic with such fervor, enough to pull the Shālan Empire under his sword? Had he really been hunting for the magic, or had he been trying to eradicate it? She dug her nails into her palms.

"More than that," Ghislaine offered, smiling at Luca's disorientation. "My house is tied to the land. Like the magic used to, we feed the empire."

"Your family were priests of the god?" Luca scrambled for purchase. "Then you know how we can use it to help—"

"No. My family helped kill them. How do you think we earned our place in the High Court? We made certain the 'how' is gone."

# A HEALER'S INTERLUDE 2

Aranen is not as alone as she thought, though she would not call the man drinking tea with her a friend. Not yet.

Guard Captain Guillaume Gillett sits back on the couch with one ankle crossed over his knee. The tea glass dangles from thick fingers. It is strange to see the man without his charge, but the princess and the ambassador are traveling west to woo an elegant snake.

"Does it get any easier?" Aranen asks.

The guard captain grunts. He is a man of few words, and they have exhausted the easy topics: the obstinacy of their charges, overdue apologies, projections on the political prospects.

Aranen dwells on two losses. The guard captain can only help with one.

"I've heard rumors," she says to him. "You and the king and the queen—"

The guard captain grunts again, this time quirking his lips beneath his mustache.

"They are not rumors," he says. "Is that strange to you?"

Aranen smiles back. "Hardly. Djasha and I had our own...guests." Dead, too, now.

"What, then?"

She avoids the man's probing stare when she speaks. "When they died. How long did it take—How did you—"

It feels like unwrapping a fetid wound and showing off the rot of it. She is both ashamed and afraid to let it go. The pain is the last thing she has of Djasha.

The guard captain stares into his tea. He chuckles. His thin lips twist into a frown. "I'm not over them, if that is what you mean."

"It's been decades. How do you do it?" Aranen asks him.

"Do what?"

Aranen closes her eyes, fighting the sting in them. She whispers: "I want to die every day."

He says nothing. She opens her eyes to see the blur of him, resting his forehead on his upturned hand. The tea glass is refracted into a million gleaming glasses through her unshed tears.

"Everyone keeps asking me that."

"What?" Aranen is momentarily baffled.

"I miss him," the guard captain says. His voice is rough and low. "But I never wanted to die." He laughs darkly at himself. "Well. Early, I did. It was hard and I was a coward. But there was Luca. She was ours. All of ours. I protect her because she is mine and because it connects me to them."

It is quite possibly the most Aranen has ever heard the man speak at once.

She thinks of Touraine and Ghadin. Of Jaghotai and the council. These things that Djasha cared about, that Djasha fought for. None of it makes her want to stay; it exhausts her.

She does not see, but she says, "I see."

A knock on the door startles her and the guard captain to their feet. She is not expecting anyone.

She opens her door to find a new blackcoat staring down at her. He is not her last guard, but there is something familiar about him that she cannot place. He is too old to be a rankless soldier: his pale brown hair is streaked with gray, his face weathered. He must be older than her, or perhaps her age and poorly used.

"Where is my chaperone?" she asks this new man.

"You are Aranen din Djasha?" he asks in a strange accent that is almost native Balladairan. He holds his hands empty and open at his chest: he means no harm.

"Who are you?" Aranen asks. The guard captain stands close behind her.

"Are you Djasha's wife? Is she here, by chance?"

"My wife is dead," Aranen says, as if the words are not her words but someone else's, given for her to say. "Who are you?"

The stranger blinks, his mouth opening. He is surprised by this news, but he pretends he is not. "May she be seen as she is." He bows his head solemnly. "My name is Roland Tessaud. I knew Djasha once. I wish to repay a debt."

Finally, Aranen recognizes the stranger: he is one of the delegates from the southern monasteries for Luca's birthday. On her birthday, he had dressed in loose robes and tight wraps.

His name, too, is familiar, and an odd shiver runs down her back—not so much fear as anticipation.

"Are you here to assassinate me?" she asks.

He tilts his head like an owl. "No, I am not. May I come in?"

The guard captain steps forward. "I will escort him out, Aranen din."

Aranen puts a hand on his arm. She wants to speak with this stranger. Roland from the Southern Mountains.

"Go," she tells the guard captain.

"I'll wait outside," he says.

Roland Tessaud from the Southern Mountains comes into the room, deadly graceful, but she is not afraid. If he kills her, so be it. If he does not kill her, she will have something else of Djasha's.

"You are Roland Tessaud, lieutenant in the Balladairan Colonial Brigade under General Rosen Cantic?"

"She was a captain at the time." A calm correction.

"You killed my wife's family."

He bows his head in acknowledgment, but there is no sign of guilt or grievance.

"I asked her forgiveness once," he says, "but she refused. I asked more than once. Each time she refused. The last time, she said, 'Do not ask me for another thirty years.' She is gone?"

"Cantic killed her," Aranen says. She attempts to wound him with the same blade that bites into her every day, and she cuts herself again. "And I killed Cantic."

He takes the news with the same stillness as he had the news of Djasha's death—more still, in fact. This time, he does not even blink.

"Djasha told you about me?" he asks.

"No. But I know of you."

# PART 3

## PAWNS AND CHEVALIERS

# CHAPTER 22

# THE WORLD, UPSIDE DOWN

Ghislaine's revelation was taking a toll on Luca. Despite having claimed one of the duke's pillars for her own, the princess had spent the return journey drawn and silent.

Touraine had helped Luca steal that pillar, with the threat of her magic and the threat of her body.

It hadn't felt good to pretend to heal with Shāl's gift. It had been necessary, and it wasn't against any tenet Touraine knew of, but the counterfeit had felt like an oily film in her mind. Still, she had done it.

For Luca, Touraine had also threatened Ghislaine with Shāl's killing magic, letting her body imply the horrors that Luca spun with her words.

It was as if Luca had given her permission, had spooled out a leash that let Touraine expand into her full size. Touraine hadn't done any magic, but she'd watched Ghislaine's face contort in fear as much as hatred, and by the sky above, that felt good. For once, Touraine was seen, not dismissed.

*And if she saw you but only as an unarmed woman sees a lion? If she fears you the way you fear a wild animal?*

The question she'd asked Pruett haunted her: *Is this all we're good for?*

"Is it worth it, Touraine?"

Luca's voice pulled Touraine out of her thoughts. The princess stared out the window with quiet intensity. She shook her head and laughed, self-deprecating.

"We sacrificed children, Touraine. We held ceremonies to sacrifice children. Is magic worth that much? What god would ask for that?"

"I don't know."

Luca didn't seem to hear her. "My ancestors stopped this. The religious purge was brutal and they murdered the priests, but they *stopped* this, even though they knew the magic it gave them. Why would they do that, if the magic was worth it?"

*What would it make me if I brought it back?* Touraine heard Luca's unspoken question in the worried set of her mouth and the fear that made her voice tremble.

Luca's eyes were red rimmed when she turned. "What would you do?"

"Shālan magic doesn't take the same toll—"

"No." Luca shook her head. "If you were a general and could guarantee peace in your lifetime—no, across generations—just by sacrificing a company of soldiers every year, you would do it, wouldn't you?"

Touraine leaned away, but there was no place to retreat from the question. "That's not fair, Luca."

"You would do it, wouldn't you?"

"A bad war, you might lose a single company's worth in one battle alone. How many battles in a year? The last Taargen War was three, four years long? And it was the *second* Taargen War." Touraine scoffed. "It's not even a choice."

"So, murdering them would be worth it?"

Touraine glared. "You know that's not what I'm saying."

They stared at each other over the narrow gap in the carriage, a handspan between their knees. Their boots fell in alternating patterns, Touraine's, Luca's, Touraine's, Luca's.

Luca surrendered first. She closed her eyes and leaned her forehead against the window again. "There must be another way."

A bump on rough cobbles slammed Luca's forehead into the window. The princess frowned, then opened the hatch to speak to Lanquette and the driver. "Where are we going?"

The guard's voice came small and distant from outside. "Apologies, Your Highness. The coachman had to make a detour. There was an accident. The horses couldn't pass."

Luca closed the hatch and sat back. "We're almost home. I need to make a plan to win over the rest of the High—"

The gunshot came out of nowhere. Wood splintered around Touraine's head, and she tasted blood, hot and metallic.

Time slowed.

Luca and Ghadin ducked in their seats, covering their heads with their arms.

The carriage lurched to a stop, slamming them against the walls like dice in a cup.

Deniaud pushed the door open, her sword half-drawn.

Another round of gunfire.

It wasn't that Touraine's body wouldn't obey her commands. Yes, her arms wouldn't move, and her legs stuck fast to the bench. Some prevailing animal part of her brain still reacted to the gunshots with a flinch, but a bigger part refused to participate at all. It was like her mind wasn't even there to issue orders. She was in a nightmare. She was kneeling on the ground in front of Rogan and his soldiers with the barrels of their muskets aimed at her—

Luca screamed as another bullet shattered the glass above her head. Blood trickled in thin lines down her forehead. They locked eyes.

"Touraine, get down!"

*I can't*, Touraine tried to say. Nothing came out.

Luca dived across the cab and dragged Touraine to the floor of the carriage, huddling over her, a protective arm arching over Touraine's back.

For a second, there was peace. Crouched beneath Luca's body, head in the dark crook of Luca's knees, Touraine was safe. Until the tight space began to press on her and she couldn't find enough air.

"No," Touraine whispered hoarsely. "No, stop, stop—"

"What?" Luca asked, her voice shrill with panic. "Are you hurt?"

The gunfire slowed, but Touraine still felt every shot as if the bullets were hitting her all over again, musket fire in her mouth, the hot iron and powder smell of the barrel of Rogan's pistol and—

"Touraine!" Luca shouted. "What's wrong with her?"

Above her, the princess's voice was raw with fear, or raw from screaming, or both. Luca yanked Touraine upright by the back of her coat and held Touraine's face in her hands. Blue eyes panicked and searching.

"It's the battle shock, Your Highness." A familiar voice, sieved through pain. Strong, careful hands lifted Touraine from the floor of the carriage and back onto the bench. Someone hissed in pain.

The darkness narrowing Touraine's vision slowly receded. Her jaw ached. Upright again, Touraine found herself seated across from Captain Perrot. He'd wrapped his left arm in his coat and held it awkwardly to his side. Blood speckled his face, and rivulets dripped down his fingers.

Luca looked between them both. She still gripped Touraine's coat tightly, as if she were afraid Touraine would collapse if she let go. When Touraine didn't collapse, though, Luca asked, "Was that another warning from Nicolas?" She eyed the big man's bloody hands. "Or are you here to make sure we died in a tragic robbery?"

The man's face was guarded. "I wasn't sent to kill either of you, Your Highness. I don't know who attacked us. Your man Lanquette is going to drive, and Deniaud is keeping the watch."

"Lanquette's driving?" Luca asked sharply.

"Your driver was shot."

Luca swore softly, then settled close to Touraine. "Are you all right?" she said, the way you'd speak to a spooked horse. "Touraine? I need to tell you something."

Touraine's erratic pulse eased. The quiet of the cab was wrong. She began to catalog what she could see. Luca, hands hovering close, still trying to speak. Feathers, shot out of the seat cushions. Perrot, his wariness. Blood. Splinters. There, in the corner of the cabin, where she'd been snoring—

"Where's Ghadin?" Touraine yelled. She lunged across Luca for the door, but Perrot hauled her back.

"Touraine, stop. Stop it. She's not here." Luca held her hands up, either to block Touraine from the door or to placate her. She looked grief-stricken.

"Where the sky-falling fuck is she?" Touraine growled.

Luca shrugged helplessly, gesturing toward the door. "She ran." Her voice cracked on the words.

"Then we have to go find her—"

"We can't," Perrot said, slicing his hand through the air. "We don't know who did this, and we don't know if there are more brigands out there. We need to get Her Highness to safety."

Luca was royal. Luca was the heir to the throne. Luca couldn't die. Luca mattered.

"Lanquette ordered some of the guards to stay behind and look for the girl," Perrot said. An inadequate offering, and the captain knew it.

"Then let me out. I'll go find her."

"You're in no condition," Luca said. "You can barely stand—"

"We're not turning around," Perrot said. "We report to the palace first."

Luca reached across their laps and gripped Touraine's hand, tight, but Touraine couldn't feel it.

"We'll find her, Touraine. I swear on my throne, we will find her."


"What happened?" Aranen din Djasha asked when Luca and Lanquette got Touraine to the ambassadors' suite. She stopped in front of Touraine and gazed into her eyes, gold to gold. Without receiving an answer, she nodded and ushered Touraine into Touraine's bedroom.

Luca followed, desperate to help, but Aranen started undressing Touraine and gave Luca a pointed look. Luca retreated.

In the anteroom, where Gil and her guards waited, Luca paced.

"Are you going to tell me what happened?" Gil growled. He'd

ascertained her well-being; now he was a thunderhead, angry that any-one had come so near to harming his—her.

"I'm all right." Oddly, she was. Luca felt calm, this time. Even though her knees were unsteady. She gripped her cane even harder and waited for the dizziness to pass. She sat. "Captain Perrot, the soldier Nicolas put on Touraine? He says Nicolas wasn't behind it."

"There was an accident on the normal road, sir," Lanquette added. "It forced us to divert, which seems intentional. The people shooting at us weren't wearing uniforms, though."

"That sounds like Nicolas to me." Gil crossed one arm over his chest and tugged angrily on his mustache. "It's calculated."

Luca rested her forehead against her cane. "It's easy to think so, but if he wanted me dead—he has Captain Perrot. The man could have killed me in the confusion. Instead, he was wounded protecting us."

"As far as I'm concerned, that doesn't rule Nicolas—"

Aranen stepped out of Touraine's bedroom, the frown lines on her face deep.

"How is she?" Luca leapt to her feet, but Aranen held a palm up to stop her.

"Where is Ghadin?" Aranen's voice was hot with anger.

A wave of heartsick shame crashed against the illusion of calm Luca had built. "We left the rest of the escort to search for her. May I see Touraine?"

Aranen's nostrils flared, but she angled her body just enough that Luca could push past.

Touraine sat on the bed in a clean black caftan with a deep V collar trimmed in gold. Her bare feet dangled from the bed, toes trailing against the thick plushness of the rug.

It was odd, to see how Touraine lived in her own space. An opened book lay flat on its pages. Her long knife had been hung on a small weapon rack. Other than these touches, it was an austere place.

Across the room, by the dressing mirror, a washbasin was filled with pink water. Large and small splinters covered in blood littered the plate next to it.

"I'm fine," Touraine said, tracking Luca's attention. She lifted her bandaged forearm, then let it drop listlessly back to her lap.

Aranen still hovered at the door suspiciously.

"Could we have a moment, Your Excellency?" Luca asked the priestess. She tried to keep the tartness from her voice.

"You aggravate my patience, Your Highness."

Luca marveled at the woman's audacity before she realized Aranen had said *patients*. Maybe. Aranen didn't leave until Touraine nodded her consent.

"May I?" Luca pointed to the chair by the dressing mirror.

Touraine's eyes were dull and unfocused, but she nodded again, so Luca dragged the chair over to sit beside Touraine's bed. She sat close enough for her knees to brush Touraine's shins.

"Do you know what happened to you?" Luca leaned forward, caught between wariness and the desire to hold Touraine close. The blankness in Touraine's face scared her. Luca hated being scared.

Touraine shook her head slowly, as if it hurt her. "I lost her." She focused on the steady circles she was tracing in the rug with her foot.

"You didn't lose her." If anyone had lost Ghadin, it was Luca. She should have grabbed the girl. But Touraine wasn't moving, and Luca had been so scared. "It's a miracle you weren't shot yourself. Captain Perrot said it was battle shock?"

"Like battle fear?" Touraine's foot froze in its orbit. "It didn't feel like battle fear. Battle fear is...I know battle fear. I've seen it, felt it. Freezing on the field, hiding from the fight. You're scared of the moment. That's normal, isn't it? Happens when you're new. This?" She held her hands out, and her voice cracked as she whispered, "This was different. I was terrified, but I wasn't even there. I was just...gone. It's been like this for a while now."

"What do you mean, gone? Was it Shāl's magic?"

"No. Gone like...like I was back in Cantic's compound. With the firing squad." She shut her eyes tight, digging her thumbs into the corners as she fought whatever visions haunted her.

Luca clenched her jaw. She understood that, at least. She still dreamed of holding Touraine's body as the other woman's blood soaked the sand. Sometimes the body in her arms changed—sometimes it was Gil, sometimes it was her mother or Sabine. When she woke up, her heart hammering against her chest and tears dampening her cheeks, Luca remembered what had really happened.

"But you survived that."

Touraine gave a strangled, high-pitched laugh. "You think that matters? Sometimes that's even worse."

"How do you mean?"

The other woman's face closed off, and she started popping her knuckles. "Nothing."

"It's not nothing," Luca blurted, hand darting out to take Touraine's. She stopped herself and put her hand back on her knee, curled in a loose fist. She swallowed. "It's not nothing. Tell me."

Touraine made a frustrated sound in her throat. "I'm the most useless of us, Luca. Every day I ask myself, 'What could Tibeau be doing for the Qazāli if I hadn't got him killed?' I think, 'Aimée would get along better with this person' or 'Djasha could still be teaching that child'—but they're all dead, Luca! I promised to keep Ghadin safe, and I—" She choked off.

Touraine's throat worked as she tried to force down the anguish. She failed. Her pain was written in the harsh lines of her face, the smooth cheekbones and the gentle slope of her lips pulled taut.

"It's not your fault," Luca said softly. "You didn't wield the blade, or the gun."

Touraine snorted and began counting on her hands. "First, that's not true. I, personally, have killed plenty. Second, I gave the orders or made the plans. I calculated the risks and decided their lives were worth it. Then those plans all went to shit."

When there were no more joints for her to pop, Touraine twisted her grief rings around and around.

Luca had come into the bedroom determined to make sure Touraine was all right, and if she wasn't, to fix it. She'd thought Touraine had broken, that she was no longer the brave, stoic soldier, loyal to her highest principles if not directly to authority. Someone that her troops looked up to. The woman in the carriage, the woman before her, was uncertain, frightened, hurt. Haunted.

But maybe Touraine hadn't been broken out of her normal shape. Maybe this was the first time Luca had taken the time to see Touraine. To see all of her.

This time, Luca didn't stop herself. She reached out and took both of Touraine's hands in her own. When Touraine's fingers curled around hers, Luca squeezed them gently.

"Touraine? Listen to me. If we're assigning blame, let me explain it like Cantic once explained it to me: if the soldiers are the arm, then the royals are the head. Balladaire's actions forced Qazāl into rebellion. If you want, we can trace that line of blame back a thousand years, even beyond Empress Djaya and my great-great-great whomever under the sky above. But you?"

Luca brushed her thumbs over Touraine's scarred knuckles. Some of the old wounds were as smooth and soft as the unmarked skin. She wanted to bring them to her lips. She didn't.

"You've done the best you can at every turn. You never stop trying to do what you think is right. Even when it's ill-timed or infuriating." Luca smirked, trying to coax some sort of smile out of Touraine.

Touraine only sagged further into herself, her gaze dropping back to her feet.

Someone knocked on the door.

"Come in," Luca answered automatically, releasing Touraine's hands.

Aranen entered with a glare for Luca and a cup for Touraine. "Drink this."

Touraine pushed the cup away without force. "Aranen, I have to—"

"Drink. This. You won't do that poor girl any good running through the city when you can't think straight."

"She's right, Touraine."

"I don't need your validation, Your Highness."

Luca bit her tongue on her retort. She had questions for the priest-ess. *Peace over all, my sky-falling ass.*

She bowed her head and stood. "I'll check on you soon, Touraine. Rest."

Luca flexed and clenched her hands while she waited. The feeling of Touraine's fingers laced with hers lingered. Finally, Aranen emerged from Touraine's chambers and closed the door gently behind her. She carried her medical tools with her.

"Is she sleeping?" Luca asked.

The priestess brought a hand to her chest in surprise, and for a moment, Luca feared retaliation. Aranen simply sniffed, though, and said, "Come. You're next."

"Me?"

Aranen gestured toward her own face, and Luca furrowed her brow in confusion. The motion sent a sharp, stinging pain across the tight, crusted skin of her face. Luca let out an astonished, weary laugh.

Aranen led Luca through the door that joined the two quarters. The difference was palpable. Though the decorations were similar—and all Balladairan—Aranen's rooms were warmer. They felt more lived in and comforting. They smelled of Qazāl: the incense and water pipes, sweet oils and dust. Luca didn't know how. One square of incense smoked on the sitting room table like an altar. It didn't seem like the room of a person who could murder General Rosen Cantic with a touch.

Aranen followed Luca's gaze to the incense. "Are you going to persecute me?"

"You know I'm not, Aranen din. I do have a question, though, if you're willing to answer."

"Whenever you have a question, Princess, I happen to be conveniently imprisoned. I'm beginning to suspect that it isn't a coincidence."

Luca bit the inside of her lip in irritation. "I'm not the one keeping you prisoner here."

"But that won't stop you from taking advantage of it. I understand."

Aranen pointed Luca to the couch and set up a medical station on the small table beside it. A tray, a pair of forceps, a cloth and basin of clean water, a jar of some ointment or unguent. She took the cloth, dipped it in the water, and tilted Luca's chin up. The touch made Luca shiver. When Aranen had killed Cantic, she had considered killing Luca. Her magic had coursed through Luca, searching. Luca had never been so bare.

"Tell me," Aranen said.

"In Champs d'Or, I learned...some things."

"About magic." With Luca's chin in her hand, Aranen dabbed the hardened blood, softening it before wiping it away.

Luca winced. "Touraine told you?"

"She doesn't need to. When else do you want to talk to me?"

Luca pressed her lips together. "Touché. The next time you'd like to talk about the finer points of Qazāli coffee brewing, think of me first. I stand ready."

That coaxed a slow, sharp smile from the priestess. "I will. Go on. Our magic? Or yours?"

"Ours."

"I'm listening."

"We killed people, Aranen din," Luca said. "We killed hundreds of people a year, maybe more—sacrificed in the name of a god for good growing seasons. I wanted—I thought—" Luca broke off, her hands upturned in her lap, beseeching. "If I could control the land like Ghislaine said, the empire would thrive. My people would eat, we would have grain to spare even for Qazāl and anyone else who wanted. If I had that, no one could choose my uncle over me."

Luca's hands began to shake in her lap, and she clamped them together. Aranen's eyes sharpened on the gesture.

"But you will have to ask them to sacrifice."

Luca nodded mutely. Then: "Unless you know a way—that uses less—asks less. Of us."

The priestess made a satisfied noise in her throat before picking up the forceps. Aranen studied Luca, from her eyes to her white-knuckle grip to the boot Luca was grinding into the rug. Back to her forehead.

"This is going to hurt," Aranen said simply. Luca imagined, perhaps, the note of glee in her voice. With no further warning, she plucked a piece of glass out of Luca's forehead and dropped it to the tray.

Luca hissed through the pain. She tried again. "Do all of the gods demand so much?"

"Every god requires sacrifice. It is the nature of faith, I think. But—" Aranen held up the bloody forceps to forestall Luca's interruption. She tightened her grip on Luca's jaw, and Luca groaned through her gritted teeth as Aranen dug out a splinter of wood. Then the priestess shook her wrist, indicating her prayer beads—beads the worn yellow white of old bone.

"I told you before: Shālan priests eat flesh, or lifeblood, to show that we have given Shāl something precious to us, something that connects us to the way we want to use the magic. It's why I don't eat meat so casually, like you do." She waved the bloody piece of wood dismissively. "But we also decided that some sacrifices were too great to bear. To unknit requires a greater sacrifice than to knit. After Djaya's Folly, there was a schism in the faith with the Qazāli falling on one side and the Brigāni falling on the other. Did you know that?"

Luca shook her head.

"Of course you didn't. Let's just say that there's more than one reason Touraine and I were chosen as your diplomats. We broke the Qazāli taboo."

"I don't understand. Because you killed with it?" That didn't make sense. Plenty of rebels had killed.

"No. Think." Aranen forced Luca's face back to hers. The forceps were so very close to Luca's eyeball.

What could be so terrible a sacrifice that two sister nations would divide because of it? Luca knew the basic tenets of Shālan faith: peace over all, balance, something else she couldn't remember—what taboo could Aranen and Touraine have broken?

"I don't—"

"What is the most sacred flesh, Princess?" Aranen hissed.

"I don't know! No flesh is sacred unless you have a god—"

Luca's throat closed and she gagged as she understood. She yanked herself out of Aranen's grasp and clenched tight on her stomach to keep herself from vomiting on the carpet. Bile burned her throat.

"You didn't—Touraine didn't—" She covered her mouth.

Aranen's golden eyes locked onto Luca's, and Luca cringed into the sofa.

"I saved my people and avenged my wife," Aranen growled.

"But how? *Who?*"

"What, under the sky above"—Aranen used the Balladairan phrase so mockingly, her voice so bitter and so heartbroken at the same time—"could be more precious to me than my wife's lifeblood?"

"And Touraine?" Luca whispered, horrified. "Her, too?"

Aranen's brow furrowed. She put her tools on the tray and dabbed gently at the fresh blood on Luca's face. "She said no. The only thing I can guess is that she used her own blood. She was definitely dying when I got to her. If she hadn't been using Shāl's magic herself, I don't think I could have healed her." The furrow went deeper. "She also never touched that man she killed. I was taught that contact was necessary. For healing. I assumed it would be the same with killing. Alas, the one person who might have pointed us to answers was murdered by your prize general, and I drank her blood. Have I satisfied your curiosity?"

The priestess held herself taut, but it was the tautness of a thing stretched to its breaking point.

"What about the Taargens and the Many-Legged?"

"Niwai is quite tight-lipped about their magic. I expect there was an exchange between them and their animals, but who am I to assume? Touraine would know more about the Taargens than I do."

Luca shook her head and stood. "I won't bother her with it. Thank you for your help, Aranen din. I'm sorry to dredge up these memories." She bowed deeply.

To Luca's back, Aranen called, "No, you're not."

Luca paused and considered, then looked over her shoulder at the priestess, whose face was now tear streaked, her kohl running down her pale brown cheeks in dark lines. "I'm not sorry I asked. I am sorry for the memories. Anything you need, please ask."

Aranen laughed bitterly. "Only this—don't ask anyone to give up what you wouldn't give up yourself. What are you willing to sacrifice, Princess?"

# CHAPTER 23

# A WOUND, REOPENED

If Qazāl was Shāl's city of art and learning and beauty—at least, when the Shālan Empire was an empire worth fearing and not the wheezing carcass of a flea-bitten jackal bitch (Pruett had no particular reference in mind, of course)—then Masridān was Shāl's fortress. Its ancient walls stretched up to the sky, a feat of engineering that Pruett couldn't quite fathom. How her ancestors had accomplished it, she had no idea. Anylight, they couldn't be all that impressive because now they were manned by Masridāni in the same black coats she and the rest of the Sands knew so well, so it wasn't like the walls were impregnable.

Still, it was enough to make Pruett draw up her mix of soldiers a mile away so they could reconnoiter. Fifty ill-trained fighters weren't going to waltz into a Balladaire-controlled city and liberate the masses. She took a deep breath. That was the problem with all of these rebellions and revolutions. They were hard and they were work, and you had to be willing to get bloody for them—maybe even die. Pruett was tired of blood. She didn't particularly want to die, either. Not for the Jackal and not for these Masridāni bearfuckers.

High above, Sevroush flew in lazy circles above one of the parapets. It made it look like the Masridāni blackcoats manning the walls were crow food, or would be soon. She liked that thought well enough, at least.

Admiration for the vulture swelled in her chest. He made it look so easy. He could stretch out his wings and be gone, if he wanted to. Just a few mighty flaps, and *whoosh*. Maybe that was a swell of jealousy, too. Pruett wasn't above admitting that.

"So?" Pruett asked Noé and Kiras. "What do you think?"

Despite herself, Pruett had taken a liking to the Atyidi fighter and her new third, because the woman was strong, silent, and mostly looked like she didn't care much for what the others said about her—which was a lot, and none of it good. Pruett also wasn't above admitting she had a type. At least, not to Noé, who had caught Pruett eyeing Kiras early on in the journey. Pruett blamed the odd white streak in the woman's hair.

The fighters from Zanafesh and El-Tarīq called Kiras and the two other golden-eyed fighters *ākilīn*, in Shālan. Eaters. Pruett gathered that was an epithet for Shālan priests. The other fighters kept their distance from all the Atyidi, even the normal ones, but they never did more than sneer at them, so Pruett had let it lie. If the ākilīn could do anything near what she'd seen Touraine and Aranen do in the compound that day, she wanted to keep them alongside.

Kiras shrugged and hooked her thumb around the jeweled dagger she and the other ākilīn kept at their waists. She wasn't as thickly muscled as Touraine or the servingwoman in the smokehouse, but she had a wiry strength and a dangerous glint in her eye.

"As I said before," Kiras said, her thick Atyidi accent rolling the way her body rolled in the saddle, "the Masridāni aren't like the Qazāli. When they bent, they bent in half." Kiras spat down from her camel.

Noé sat his camel easily, though not as easily as Pruett. The other Sands weren't too fond of the beasts and their bubbling and spitting, but Pruett thought if the camels were going to carry them across the desert, the Sands might as well get friendly with them. Be grateful, at the very least. She didn't envy anyone who tried to walk the desert leagues on foot.

Noé squinted up at Sev and then over at Pruett. He wore his scarf wrapped around his head, neck, and face, like Kiras had taught them. His nut-brown skin had darkened beautifully over the journey, where Pruett had mostly freckled and burned a little before tanning a pale reddish brown.

"I think this will be difficult," he said. "But I'm optimistic." She could hear the gentle smile in his voice, though she couldn't see it behind his scarf.

Pruett rolled her eyes, but she smiled. "Of course you are."

Kiras snorted. "Shāl save us all from optimistic soldiers."

They'd spent the journey trying to figure out how they would approach the Masridāni leaders. The Qazāli Council didn't have the greatest bargaining position. Which was to say, Pruett and her little company didn't have the greatest bargaining position. They needed help. They needed food. The Masridāni would have to be interested in pissing in the boots of their Balladairan masters, and the Qazāli had all made it clear how likely that was.

Noé nodded up at Sev. "I was thinking that you could use him. Send him with a note. Like he came to you."

Pruett grunted. "If he knew how to get to the Masridāni council. Governor. Whoever's in charge."

"What if…Do you think you could talk to the Many-Legged priest? Maybe ask them if they could…guide the bird? Or whatever they do?" Noé shuddered, and Pruett did, too. It reminded her too much of the Taargens.

Kiras frowned at them. "All this shuddering over a god. You're just as bad as *them*. Use the tools you were given."

As if the bird knew they were talking about him, Sev swooped down and landed on Pruett's saddle horn. She had even grown used to his smell. She chuffed him gently beneath his vicious hook of a beak. Blood stained it. Despite the bird-stink, there was something comforting about his constant presence as they traveled through the desert. She stroked his chest feathers with a finger.

"What do you think, then, friend?" she murmured idly.

He nipped her. "Fuck!" she yelled. She glared at him, sucking her bloody digit before realizing she'd probably just given herself some bird disease. "What the fuck was that for, feather-fuck?"

Sev cocked his head at her and blinked slowly. Then, very pointedly, the bird looked toward Pruett's saddlebags.

"That's creepy, Captain." Noé edged back in his seat, putting some distance between him and the vulture while trying not to lean himself out of the saddle and into the sand.

Kiras smiled wide and chuckled. "Shāl save me from the Many-Legged."

Pruett scowled at the woman, and her smile only grew wider. Yes, she was very attractive. Pruett didn't know why she hadn't tried to do something about that sooner. Oh, right. Trying to keep the balance in the camp.

She turned back to the bird. "You'll take the letter?"

He made a rasping chirp that sounded like a laugh, but birds didn't laugh.

She peered suspiciously into the bird's eyes. They were staggering and fearsome. Keen and sharp, like his claws. "Is that you, Many-Legged?"

Sev opened his beak, eyes still on Pruett. It looked like he was smiling at her, but birds didn't smile, either.

"All right, then." Pruett shrugged at Noé before she could find herself more fucked off than she already felt.


They waited all day for Sev to return with a message from the Masridāni. They waited until the sun rose too high and they had to put out tents to escape the burning heat. They waited until they grew too hungry for dried fruit and bread, so they cooked a meal of beans and couscous as the sun set. Pruett had enough of waiting and was fixing up her courage to see if Kiras was interested in the same thing she was when a familiar bird screech made her jump out of her sky-falling skin.

She ducked back into the small tent she shared with Noé and snatched up her pistol belt. "Noé," she hissed.

"She said no already?" he mumbled from his bedroll.

"No, asshole. Sev is back."

She left him wrapping his chest and getting dressed again. She stepped into the cool night, wrapping her scarf around her neck and clutching her shawl close to her.

Instead of a bird perched on her tent pole, however, she saw a trio of people dressed like Balladairan nobles flanked by a platoon of black-coats. Sands. Only they weren't Sands. According to Kiras, these soldiers never left for Balladaire. They were trained here, in Masridān, willing servants doing Balladaire's will in their own home.

She raised her pistol. Letting her voice carry in the night across the camp, she said, "Not another step. Introduce yourselves before you bring an armed platoon into my camp."

She closed the gap between them slowly, giving her soldiers time to gather themselves. Indeed, the camp shuddered like an animal waking up and giving its ass a quick scratch before getting ready to defend its lair.

Kiras was beside her in an instant, matching Pruett's step. "Captain," she said softly. "I'm here. My squad is ready. All of us."

As some of Pruett's soldiers brought out lanterns, the newcomers' faces became clearer. At their head was a handsome man probably a decade Pruett's senior, forty years old or so. Gray speckled his queue of curly dark hair. His brown face was smooth shaven, the common style for Balladairan nobles, though it made most of them look like weak-chinned children. This man didn't look like that.

Two more Masridāni, a middle-aged woman and a younger man, followed him, both dressed similarly in silks and lace. Both men wore those hideous half trousers and stockings like they hadn't come out to parlay with an armed militia.

*You're here to ask them for help, not to do battle with them*, Pruett reminded herself. She looked the man up and down. Not that it would be much of a battle if it came to it.

The man at the front sniffed at the camp, taking in the soldiers appearing from their tents.

"I take it the letter came from you," he said. He flicked his hand at her disdainfully. Fingers heavy with rings glittered in the starlight.

Most surprising, though, was that he spoke in clear, aristocratic Balladairan. He sounded like Rogan, Pruett's old brigade captain. They weren't going to be on good terms, then.

"Aye," she said. "We're envoys from—"

"Qazāl. Yes. We can read." The man looked her up and down. "You said you're Masridāni."

"Aye. One of the Lost Ones."

He snorted. "Lost Ones. Qazāli sentimentality if I've ever heard anything. We're all lost in this uncivilized land. My companions and I came to talk. Is there no such thing as hospitality among you sand fleas?"

Pruett shared an uncertain glance with Noé, who had emerged to stand at Pruett's other side. She muttered, "Do we have anything they can eat? Water?"

Noé tilted his head doubtfully but left to scrounge something up.

"Sir." She put her hand to her chest and bowed over it. "We didn't expect your company and we've traveled a long way. You'll forgive us if we aren't fucking ready for fucking guests. Especially ones who haven't even introduced themselves."

His eyes went wide and scandalized. "Why you—"

One of his companions stopped the ensuing loss of dignity with a hand on the man's arm. If he'd followed through on the hand he raised to strike Pruett, she would have shot him in the face. Pruett wasn't a brawler like Touraine and Tibeau. Too drawn out. Too messy. Too easy to get hurt yourself. She preferred a single, well-placed shot— from a distance, if possible.

The man pursed his lips as he took in the camp, from the tents to the mélange of Pruett's soldiers. "How did Qazāl end up with the loyalty of a host of conscripts?" Pruett couldn't tell whether it was the conscripts he thought were dubious or the conscripts' loyalty or the Qazāli.

Noé returned and nodded for Pruett and the others to follow him.

Noé led them to a small fire he'd brought back to life. There was a large but shallow clay dish of oil and flatbread to dip into it.

"Sit." Pruett gestured. She lowered herself first, crossing her legs. She grabbed a hunk of bread, tore it, and popped it into her mouth as if to say, *No poison, see?*

Noé and Kiras sat beside her and the three visitors. The older woman grumbled the whole process about proper chairs. Pruett left the Masridāni soldiers outside of the camp, surrounded by her own soldiers. Tension crackled through the camp like the static before a lightning strike. *Qazāl is counting on you*, she reminded herself. Not the Jackal, but the whole sky-falling country. People would starve if she didn't get Masridān to help. Pruett was a bitch, she could admit that, too, but she wasn't a monster.

Pretending she couldn't feel the pressure, though, she yawned.

"Let's start again. I'm Pruett, late of the Balladairan Colonial conscripts, and before that, Masridān. Now, I'm an emissary of the Qazāli Council."

After he'd taken a courteous swipe of the bread and oil, the man said, "I'm Lord Governor Yoroub, Governor-General of Masridān, and these are my assistants."

Pruett's eyebrows shot up, and she let out a low, impressed whistle. "Lord governor." It sounded ironic and probably looked disrespectful, but really, she was impressed. If the city was run by a Masridāni, soldiered by Masridāni...

Maybe Touraine had been right after all. Bend your neck low enough to the Balladairans and they won't feel the need to keep their boot on it. Was Touraine on her knees in the palace now, or was she still playing the rebel?

No, that wasn't fair.

"Indeed." Yoroub hmm-ed suspiciously. "What does a rogue colony want with us?"

"Qazāl is sovereign again, but they need aid." Pruett sat up straight, trying to be earnest and open, all of that bearshit Touraine liked. Seemed like the kind of thing this velvet sop might appreciate, if he appreciated anything, which Pruett doubted. He looked too full of his own accomplishments to be impressed by people who needed help.

"Balladaire stripped the land, and with the drought, food and water both are scarcer than they should be. They'll need grains and meat and any healers you can spare. With your help, they'll last the winter rains and the summer dry season, hopefully enough until the new crops can feed the entire country. In return, they offer help shifting the weight of Balladaire off your own shoulders."

Pruett finished and sat back, folding her hands together over her knees. She felt that fishhook smile tugging at the side of her face again.

For a second, Yoroub just stared incredulously. Then he burst out laughing, the laugh of a man who was used to being found funny and laughing charmingly at other people's worse jokes. His assistants tittered at his side.

When he finished, he leaned toward her, a hand on one knee, an elbow on the other. "We don't have healers," he said. "We have trained physicians. And Qazāl already had aid. You had Balladaire. Why should we waste our own food because you decided to throw away the resources you had?"

"Balladaire wasn't helping us, you fool," Kiras spat with venom Pruett hadn't expected from her. "They've been raping us. It's the same here, but you've convinced yourselves you want it."

Yoroub fixed his gaze on Kiras, eyes widening slightly before going hard as stone. "So Qazāl is harboring the cannibal witches." He made a sound of disgust in his throat and turned back to Pruett. "Tell this so-called council of yours that this is the price they pay. If they want to behave as the savages do, it comes with consequences. They had their chance."

He rose smoothly to his feet. Looking down on Pruett, his face went from disappointed to weighing. "You're not like them, though." He jerked his head at Kiras. "You were a conscript. We might be able to find a place for someone who can follow orders. Someone who's been taught civilized values. As you can see, the drought has not done so much damage here."

Something caught in Pruett's chest and tugged, so painfully that it stole her breath. Another fishhook, this one caught through her heart. She certainly hadn't hoped for anything resembling a welcome, here in the place where she'd been born. She hadn't ever, not once, wondered for a second if she would find someone, like Touraine had found someone. Not when she could still see her parents standing in the doorway of a shadowed home, the jingling exchange of a small sack of sovereigns as Balladairans led her away.

*Baba!* she had cried out. Probably. That's what kids did, right? *Amma!* No one had reached back for her hand.

And the lord governor's words sounded so much like Casimir LeRoche de Beau-Sang's last words. She definitely hadn't tongued that sore tooth over the journey.

Pruett stood to get level with Yoroub. She gave him her most charming grin, which, Aimée had told her once, looked more the grimace of a rat that had just been skewered on a knife. It had about the same effect. Yoroub and his compatriots all blanched and leaned back as if Pruett were going to bite them.

Around her, Pruett saw the Qazāli fighters, from every city, edge in. They were hungry for the same thing she was. They were also waiting to see what she said. Their captain. A coat-turning conscript. *Would she turn again?* She made a small "hold" gesture.

"Eat my shit, Lord Governor."

Lord Governor Yoroub's eyes narrowed to slits. "I see the conscript training experiment wasn't as successful as I was led to believe. Very well. Give the Qazāli 'Council' my regards."

As he walked away, back through the tents and past the glares of Pruett's fighters, Pruett murmured, "What if we capture him now? Get what we want that way?"

"I'm ready," Kiras growled. She cracked her neck. "Do we have to keep him alive?"

Pruett liked Kiras more and more.

On her other side, however, Noé shook his head. "Better we try and talk again." That pretty voice of his was like a tenor viol, taut as the strings. "They probably have a whole garrison in there. We take him hostage and they'll slaughter us."

Pruett made a frustrated sound in her throat. "Fine."

"Went about as well as I expected," Kiras muttered as Noé left. It wasn't quite an *I told you so*.

"Aye. Like slamming your balls in a door."

Kiras raised an eyebrow and glanced down at Pruett's crotch. She quirked that half smile of hers. She had a nice jawline, the kind you could . . . carve something on. Poetry was failing Pruett lately.

"You can do that?" the other woman asked.

Pruett snorted. "I'm sure some asshole has before. I wish Yoroub would." She stared off after him and his soldiers as they marched back to the fortified city. "It wouldn't help this ass-up situation any, but I'd feel better."

She turned back to Kiras to find her still watching her, golden eyes bright in the starlight. She had a nice mouth, too, Kiras did. It quirked up in a knowing smile.

"Huh."


Kiras had a *very* nice mouth, actually, and Pruett was close—*so close, fuck!*—to dragging the woman up from between her legs and telling her as much when that *fucking shrieking bird*—

*armed men in the sand, in my territory, armed men.* Pruett looked down and saw, far, far below, a company of Balladairan soldiers—no, not Balladairans but Masridāni blackcoats, twice as many as hers, marching, *marching*—

"Captain!"

Kiras's shout broke through Pruett's—vision? Premonition?

"Captain, you all right?" Kiras was naked, hovering over Pruett, concern in her eyes and a hand on Pruett's cheek. Pruett's face stung where Kiras had slapped her.

Pruett blinked hard, trying to bring the tent back into focus. Then the vision she'd seen clarified.

She pushed the woman off and shrugged to her feet, still tingling with the aborted orgasm as she jumped into her trousers and tugged on a shirt. "We're under attack."

The woman blinked, bewildered. "Under attack?" But she followed Pruett's lead and was dressed by the time the first gunshots fired.

Pruett ran out with her coat flapping open, a pistol in each hand, a musket flung over her shoulders, a bayonet at one hip, and a dagger in one boot, and she was still too outgunned for this firefight. Kiras was right behind her, and then, she wasn't.

Pruett's soldiers—she laughed, what a joke that was, they weren't soldiers, no matter how much she and Touraine had pretended, and thirty of her "soldiers" had barely drilled—

As if on cue, musket fire tore through the air. Pruett followed the sound. The Masridāni had formed a line two deep and were taking turns shooting at her fighters, who had taken cover behind tents and camels and were returning fire in spurts. A few unlucky Masridāni fell. The camels bellowed in distress, lurched to their feet, and fled, leaving Pruett's people exposed.

"Noé!" she yelled. Her second-in-command didn't answer.

Pruett stopped behind a tent and swapped her pistols for the loaded musket. Pistols were fun, but they didn't have the range. She poked her head out from behind the tent, hunting the square of Masridāni soldiers for someone with an officer's sleeve, a stripe, anything that made them look important—

There. A tall woman raised an arm to order the next volley. Pruett lined up the shot and stilled her breath. Slowed time down. The woman's arm dropped through the air, slow as honey. Pruett's bullet found the woman's chest.

Pruett moved before any of the Masridāni soldiers could follow her trajectory.

Problem was, this, right now, was the best case: the Masridāni sitting in one spot as their formations demanded, all nice and tight like fish in a barrel. Pruett's own company, taking shots from cover, but too spread out for the organized blackcoat volleys to have much effect.

The worst-case scenario, on the other hand, was if the Masridāni decided to—

"Charge!"

The Masridāni sprinted into Pruett's camp with their bayonets fixed. The Qazāli were still outnumbered two-to-one.

*Fuck me sideways.* Pruett shoved her bayonet onto her own musket and ran into the melee.

"Kiras!" she shouted. No sign of her, either.

Instead of Kiras, Pruett got a blackcoat barreling at her in the dark, bayonet glinting, bared teeth glinting, eye-whites glinting. Pruett batted the barrel of his gun away with hers and popped the butt of it into his temple. While he was stunned stupid, she ran her own bayonet up through his chin. Blood soaked down the barrel, her hands sticky with it. It was going to be a fucker to clean.

"Noé! To me!" Pruett shouted again, alternating between Shālan and Balladairan as she fended off another Masridāni. "Qazāl, to me! Anybody, Shāl damn you! To me!"

It was hopeless. The camp was chaos, every soldier fighting for their life. In close quarters, the Qazāli would only be as good as their hand-to-hand combat, and though that was good, flashy-athleticism good, fine-in-a-brawl good, it wasn't two-against-one good. It wasn't not-get-stabbed good.

In the tangle of two tents, one of the Zanafeshi was scrabbling backward on his ass while a blackcoat aimed down at him with a bayonet. Pruett sprinted over and shoved her bayonet through the blackcoat's back. Through fabric and muscle, scraping on bone. The soldier coughed blood onto the Zanafeshi's bright clothing, and for a second, the Zanafeshi just gaped at Pruett.

"Retreat!" Pruett yelled. She shook the blackcoat off her weapon to flop in a heap.

"Retreat where?" the Zanafeshi cried back, smearing the blood on his face as he tried to wipe it off with an equally bloody sleeve.

"I don't fucking know, just run!" Pruett was supposed to know. Touraine would have known.

The man ran, away from the bloody wreck of the Qazāli camp and into the desert. If he was smart, he'd stay close by. They would regroup.

Against her better judgment, Pruett ran the opposite way, back into the camp, weaving between the remaining tents to stay out of sight. She saw a flare of gold and hissed, "Kiras?"

It wasn't Kiras, but it was one of the Eaters, his golden eyes glowing in the darkness as he knelt over a dead blackcoat. With a butcher's precision and carelessness for blood, he slit the corpse open with his jeweled knife and reached inside the body. The Eater's lips moved—he was praying.

She couldn't look.

She stopped calling for Kiras.

The air was thick with gunpowder and blood and crying, and somewhere deep fucking down, Pruett wished that were her. That she could lie down somewhere and stop. Just stop. The sand leached its cold into her legs where she crouched. Hiding.

*You can stop*, a voice inside her said.

But Noé. Kiras.

Above her, the stars were numberless and oblivious, and the moon fat and uncaring, and fuck everything if this wasn't just another tiny, insignificant pissing contest in the history of the world.

She jumped up from her hiding spot and shouted, "Retreat!" Her voice was raw and barely carried, but she yelled it over and over. The Jackal wasn't worth dying for, not like this. She yelled and she ran through the camp, dragging the survivors she could. None of them were Noé or Kiras.

She did see that Eater again, though, and she watched him—his face oddly clean, fastidiously clean, but his teeth smeared red—come up against one soldier, and another, slicing with his dagger and reaching out for their flesh. Whenever his fingers connected, his eyes glowed and the blackcoat fell, shuddering and boneless. Like Cantic had.

Pruett retched and vomited. It splattered on the ground near a body she recognized. Thélieu. One of hers. Fuck these assholes. Fuck Masridān. Fuck Yoroub. Fuck the Jackal and fuck Touraine, too.

Touraine would have waited for everyone to get out. She wouldn't have left. She would have fought to get every last living soldier out, or she would have died.

Touraine was an idiot. A brave, precious idiot who had gotten Pruett into this mess.

What would Kiras say? *Shāl save me from noble warriors.* Somewhere, Kiras was eating some poor sod's heart out of his still hot chest.

Pruett ran.

The Masridāni didn't pursue them. That wasn't the message Yoroub wanted to send. He wanted them to return to Qazāl in tatters and remind the council—the rebels—why Balladaire had beaten them in the first place.

Pruett and the handful of survivors she'd found so far—one of the Atyidi, not an Eater, a few Sands, and a big woman from El-Tarīq—licked their wounds. They'd salvaged a couple of camels, too.

The fortress city loomed in the distance.

This was supposed to be her home.

"What is so wrong with me?" she whispered. Tears pricked at the corners of her eyes and she blinked rapidly. She tried to scowl them away, or at the very least squint like the sun was too bright, and not like a weeping sore inside her was being cauterized.

"Captain?"

"What?" she snapped.

It was Armande, one of the Sands, a tall woman with a knack for artillery. Which they didn't have. She narrowed her eyes at Pruett's tone.

"Sorry," Pruett mumbled.

"Are we heading back to Qazāl?"

How did Touraine do this all the time? Under Balladaire, it was easy. Someone gave them orders and Pruett carried them out. Touraine had had a strange way of smoothing things over with the whole squad. Pruett didn't have that knack.

"I—I need a minute," she said gruffly. "Keep looking for... survivors. Set guards. Sleep if you can."

Armande saluted and Pruett stalked away.

She scanned the sky for Sevroush, but there was no black shape blotting out a patch of stars anywhere above her. She whistled sharply. No answering caw came. She even held her arm out, the makeshift leather bracer waiting as his perch. Nothing.

He had left her, too.

She picked up a rock from the dirt, got a running start, and hurled it at the city walls. As the walls were now miles away and the rock stopped after about fifty yards, it didn't help. An animal sound ripped from her throat, wordless but utterly intelligible as it came out of the core of her being.

"Fuck you!" she screamed at the city. "Fuck! You!"

She sank to her knees and pressed her forehead to the ground. Her tears soaked the sand beneath her.

# CHAPTER 24

# THE DESPERATE

Touraine dreamt of Ghadin.

She dreamt of finding Ghadin shot and bleeding from the gut on a battlefield.

She dreamt of Ghadin kicking and flipping and twirling, kicking Touraine again and again, her kicks spinning faster and faster so that Touraine couldn't keep up.

She dreamt of Ghadin following her, lurking just behind a wall, dodging out of sight when Touraine turned to catch her.

Touraine woke in darkness, gasping.

*You lost her.*

A rapid pounding on the door woke her again. She blinked blearily around the room, swearing at the bright sunlight.

"Touraine! Are you here? Are you asleep? Touraine? I'm going to come in."

Luca. Touraine pulled the thick covers over her head.

Luca came in. "Touraine, wake up. Sky above, what did she give you, a horse relaxant?"

Touraine groaned but didn't pull her head out of the blankets.

"You are awake. Well, let's go. The carriage is waiting for us at the stables."

"Whatever you want, I'm not doing it, Luca."

"Whatever *I* want? We're going to look for Ghadin. Now get your ass out of bed, and stop wasting my time."

Touraine poked her head out of the blankets. "There's no point."

Luca made a confused sound in her throat. "What do you mean there's no point?" Luca's voice softened, and she took a tentative step farther inside the room. "This isn't you. I know it isn't. The Touraine I know would do anything—even something utterly stupid—before she would let down the people who trusted her to keep them safe." Luca tapped her cane on the floor sharply, two times, a summons. Her voice sharpened to match it. "I'll wait in the anteroom. Get dressed."

Touraine wasn't sure if it was the backhanded compliment or the pricked pride of Luca issuing orders that got her out of bed.

They took an unmarked carriage to La Gouttière first, and Luca stopped them at a building that looked too pleasant to belong. A line of people in patched jackets and shoes flapping at the toes stared at Touraine and Luca as they approached. And—Touraine's heart leapt— half of them were Qazāli. She scanned them for a familiar face, but they were all adults. Inside, an older couple doled out food.

Luca coughed slightly. The gray-haired woman noticed them, handed a bowl to the balding man with a whisper, and came over. She didn't look askance at Touraine until she made a double take at her eyes.

Luca took her aside and they spoke in hushed whispers, dropping so many names and locations that Touraine didn't recognize that they might as well have been speaking in code. This dock, those tenements. Luca and the woman took turns shaking their heads at each other, the old woman's face growing worried and Luca's growing grim, until Touraine was half-mad with frustration.

"Hello?" Touraine interrupted. "Does she know where Ghadin is?"

"Thank you, Madame Béryl." Luca pulled a small pouch of coins out of her pocket discreetly. "A coin each for those waiting outside, and you can use the rest to buy coats and blankets. I'm afraid winter might be a cold one."

Then Luca strode back out and climbed into the carriage with Touraine scrambling behind her.

"Who was that?" Touraine asked.

The carriage stuttered into motion again, the horses' hooves clopping on the cobblestones.

"Madame Béryl," Luca said, her tone clipped. "She runs this charity. I thought she could give us a lead."

"And?"

Luca didn't sag, but her eyes dropped to her lap, the muscle in her jaw clenching. "She hasn't seen her, she hasn't come for food or shelter."

"The docks?"

"She might have tried to sneak onto a boat; if so, they might have put her in a stowaway keep for the day as punishment."

"Then let's go check them."

Luca pressed a hand to her brow, massaging her temple. "I didn't think before, but Madame Béryl was right. She might be at the school."

"The school." Touraine didn't like the weight that had. Cold fingers gripped her heart. "*The* school. What school?"

Luca slid her hand from her forehead to cover her mouth. "My uncle has a school for Shālan children."

Touraine remembered the way the duke had prodded her. Looked down on her.

"No."

"He does."

"You didn't tell me."

"We were dealing with bigger problems—"

"There is nothing bigger than this, Luca! This is everything!"

"We've barely had time—"

"Stop."

"Touraine, please—"

"Shut up."

Luca closed her mouth and looked very hard out the window for the rest of the ride, while Touraine dug her nails into her knees and tried not to throw up.

They arrived at a well-made square building of wood and mortared stone surrounded by a wide grass lawn caged in by a fence of pickets sharpened to points.

Luca's hand hovered over Touraine's lap. "Stay here and let me—"

"I'm going to see what he's doing to us." Touraine boiled out of the carriage. "I want to know what you're letting him do to us."

Luca called her name, but Touraine didn't slow. Captain Perrot jumped down from his post and caught up to Touraine with long strides.

"What's going on?" He grabbed for her, and she slapped his arm away. He winced—it was his injured arm—but Touraine didn't even think to feel sorry.

She swung the door of the school open so hard that it slammed against the wall.

A group of children on their knees scrubbed the wooden floor of the large hall with fistfuls of straw. Others wiped the wooden tables with cloths. They were all carefully not looking at a conflict in the center of the room.

A grown woman held a girl by the arm, yanking her half-standing. She dangled toward the ground, her face contorted in pain or fear or both while the woman yelled at her. Strands of straw clung to the girl's upraised hand.

"What did you say?" the woman said, with the air of someone who had already asked the question.

"Nothing, madame, nothing!" the girl cried. She didn't even try to fight the grip.

"I know it was nothing because it was in that primitive tongue of yours." The woman shook her arm. A sickening pop rent the air.

The girl wailed.

The shock gluing Touraine's feet to the ground released.

"Put her down," Touraine growled.

The woman must have put the girl down, because here was her collar in Touraine's fists, here were her hands, both of them, scratching against Touraine's knuckles, and here, her body against the wall, with nowhere to run.

Touraine met the woman's eyes, her chest heaving. The woman's chignon was spoiled, and wisps of gray-brown hair fluttered between their faces, moving with their mingled fury. It would take nothing, nothing to end this woman's life right now. Touraine's fist could crush her windpipe. Touraine could throttle her, listen to her well-heeled shoes tap out her death song.

The woman tilted her head back against the wall, the better to look down at Touraine. She'd been wearing spectacles. They were gone, now. There was no fear in the woman's eyes, not even the rightful fear you'd have of a rabid animal, like Ghislaine had felt when Touraine menaced her. This woman felt only contempt, and that smug satisfaction that everything you'd ever believed was correct and righteous and justified. Touraine slammed the woman against the wall again, as if she could shake that conviction loose.

The children screamed. Touraine was scaring them. *Touraine* was scaring them.

"Put her down." A new voice. A deep voice.

Touraine turned her head slowly to either side.

To her left: Luca, eyes as wide as the children's. (Was Touraine scaring her, too?)

To her right: three burly men had come in through another door, each with fists thick as Touraine's face. One of them had spoken.

Lanquette, Deniaud, and Perrot—Perrot, the duke's man—didn't even wait for the order. They fanned out around Luca, their swords drawn. Their royal uniforms with their short cloaks made them a sharp contrast from the bruisers' workman's trousers.

"What are you doing to that girl?" Luca asked the woman, cold as winter night.

The woman's pale throat bobbed against Touraine's thumb. "It's called discipline, Your Highness."

"For what?"

The question followed logically, but it was the wrong one. There wasn't anything a child did to deserve that.

"Girl," the schoolmistress said, "why were you punished? Tell the princess from the beginning."

From behind her, Touraine heard a tremulous voice, and as the girl spoke, Touraine held the schoolmistress in place. They were in sync: the rapid tick of the woman's heart beating in time with the pulse in Touraine's hands, the slow rise and fall of their shared breath.

"We were cleaning the floors, madame. B-but—we started singing."

"And what were you singing?" The woman's voice was hard and she stared down into Touraine's eyes, matching Touraine hatred for hatred.

The girl murmured something so softly Touraine barely heard.

"What was that, girl? Speak clearly. Don't butcher the civilized tongue."

"A Shālan song, madame."

"There." The woman nodded. "She's been punished for her uncivilized behavior. She'll know better than to fall back into bad habits."

Each word fell like a lash on Touraine's back.

The children had gone quiet. The quiet of children who knew too well that it was better to go unnoticed, even when they were afraid. Even when they wanted comforting.

Touraine shut her eyes tight. *Oh, Shāl. Oh, sky above.*

Sensing Touraine's struggle, the schoolmistress relaxed in her grip, and Touraine opened her eyes to see a pursed-lipped smile creep onto her face as she looked between Touraine and Luca.

Touraine didn't like the idea of the kids exposed to this violence— to her. But it was too late. Their lives already were violent and this woman was part of that. In a perfect world, Touraine could spare them. This was not a perfect world. It was badly, badly broken, irreparably so. But she wanted to show them—they *deserved* to see that they were worth protecting.

Touraine pulled back a little more and the woman exhaled, somehow managing to make that sound smug, too.

Bone crunched beneath Touraine's fist, and blood gushed from the woman's nose like a warm, sputtering fountain. Her head snapped back into the wall and she collapsed in a heap on the ground, clutching feebly at her bloody face. The big men stepped forward, but the guards matched them—they didn't come any closer.

Touraine wheeled around to Luca. "We have to get them out of here." To the children, she spoke in Shālan, the language they were right now having ripped away from them, the language she had had to fight to take back. It felt thick and fumbling in her mouth as she said, "We're going to get you out of here."

Luca pulled up close to Touraine, though, and whispered, shaking her head, "And keep them where, Touraine? Turn the palace into an orphanage?"

The question was so mundane and so practical that Touraine blinked stupidly at Luca. Of course there was no place to take them. Who would raise them? Teach them? Mind them? They might as well be in the same hands as they were now. The duke's.

"Ghadin?" Touraine said thickly.

"She's not here. I'm sorry."

Luca reached out for her, but Touraine shoved past her outstretched hand and out of the schoolhouse.

She was burning. She pulled at her coat, struggling to shrug out of it. The green of the dying grass was too vivid; it swam in her vision. She misjudged the height of the stair into the carriage and fell to her knees. Luca knelt beside her, and Touraine snarled her fist in her coat. Buried her face in Luca's chest. Drowned herself in the smell of rose cologne and sweat.

Touraine had lied to the children, and worse. She knew that look in the woman's eye. She would punish them for what Touraine had done. Touraine should have killed her. But Luca was telling the bitterest truth—right now, that woman was the only thing standing between the children and starving to death this winter.

As she cried and cried, Luca held her and held her and held her.

# CHAPTER 25

# A SPARK

S ky-falling—watch where you're going!" Fili winced as someone hit her. Her knife slipped and gave Fili a narrow slice on the web of her thumb. She turned and saw what had crashed into her. A Qazāli girl with a thick, dark braid and suspiciously fine—sky above, she was in nice clothes. Dirty and torn and bloodstained nice clothes.

The girl sprang off her ass and onto her feet like the acrobats who flipped in the Place des Oreilles. Tried to spring to her feet, anylight. It turned into more of a wincing roll and scramble, though, as the girl clutched at her side. She backpedaled, her dark eyes wide with fear.

"Hey, wait!"

Fili swore. The lumber at her feet was expensive. Her master had ordered it especially for fancy projects, and he'd only let her take it outside of the shop because he knew not only what she could do with them in the right mind, but also that she would die before letting their materials get stolen.

Fili swore again, then tucked her whittling knife into her pocket along with the chunk of wood she'd been idly toying with, and sprinted after her.

The girl was hiding in the crook of the street, leaning against a wall to catch her breath. The hand clamped tight over her lower hip was smeared with fresh blood. Fili approached her like she would a feral cat.

"You need some help." Fili held her hands up. Empty. Knife gone. The girl looked Fili over. "I'm not going to hurt you. I swear it."

"I don't need help," the girl spat. She said something venomous in that language of theirs.

Fili couldn't speak it, couldn't make head or tail of it, but you could hear it easily enough if you went into the poorer districts, which she did lately when she went out with her master to gather recruits for Brother Michel and the Fingers.

"You want to die here?" Fili snapped back.

"I've seen Balladairan help." The girl's eyes flashed with sparking hatred. Her Balladairan was aristocratic and accented at the same time.

"Who did this to you?" Fili eased closer. Was she a noble's servant? Had she run away from her master?

"Piss off." The other girl kicked away from the wall and started edging deeper into the alley.

"That's a dead end."

The girl scowled at Fili and then looked over her shoulder. It was a wall. Her growl of frustration ended in a whine of pain.

"Look, I promise, I can get you some help. Follow me to get my wood or my master will kill me. Then we go. Can you walk okay?"

"I can walk fine," the girl said through gritted teeth as she passed Fili. Her stomach growled so loud that she jumped, winced, then flushed. Fili's eyes went wide. Then her stomach growled, too.

"Let me buy us some lunch?" Fili cocked one shoulder and tried a smile.

The girl straightened her coat and looked at the blood on her hand. She pressed it back to her side, muttering. Fili definitely caught the words "the fucking princess," or maybe it was "fucking the princess."

The Qazāli girl stalked past Fili and out of the alley, looking warily up and down the street before turning and hunching into her shoulders as if to become invisible.

Fili rushed after her. "I don't trust the princess, either." Then, in the same comradely whisper her master used with new recruits, she added, "I think the whole lot of them could drown in the river, and I'm not the only one."

The girl side-eyed Fili but didn't try to speed away.

"I mean, look at this place."

Fili gestured to the garbage in the streets. The smell of piss and shit from drunks and the sewage drains. The people, shoulders low under their burdens while Princess Luca pranced about in her fancy coach and exotic clothes. Fili's mother had been Luca's guard, and perhaps that should have softened Fili to the princess—her mother certainly seemed to like her, even after she'd lost her leg. That wasn't the kind of person who should decide what a country needs, though. The people should decide. Fili agreed with the Fingers on that.

"That sounds like . . . what's the word for when you kill the king? Or send them out?" the Qazāli said darkly. "I have been there, and I have done it."

"What? Kill? No," Fili said quickly. Then, softer, with all the heat she felt in her chest at the thought, she said, "I think the word you mean is *revolution*." That was the word the Fingers used. It stirred the heat in Fili's chest just to think of it.

The girl met and held Fili's eyes. In that moment, she looked older than Fili, older than some of the adults she knew. Her eyes were drawn in pain and exhaustion.

"You don't know what that means, it's . . ." She hunted for the words. The girl's eyes were dark pools. "Revolution is not a game."

Then her eyes rolled up into the back of her head as she fainted.

# CHAPTER 26

# GIFTS

Day after day after day again, Luca waited for word from Touraine's treks into the city with her escort, Perrot. They hunted for Ghadin, and Luca watched the despair hollow out Touraine's face more each time they returned to the palace empty-handed.

Luca wanted to stay by Touraine's side, but Gil refused to let her out until they figured out who was responsible for the attack on the carriage. That, and Luca's attention was needed elsewhere. With Ghislaine and Sabine in hand, Luca needed to pull Brice or Evrard to her side—preferably both. Still, her stomach twisted with guilt when the sun rose and she knew Touraine had already left the palace for the day.

Instead of riding into the city, she headed to the Rose Maze to intercept Evrard on his morning walk, Gil and her guards with her.

Evrard was not alone, and he was not happy.

"What are you going to do about it, hein? Wait until we're all attacked in our carriages? Or in this very garden?"

"Lord Travers is right, my lord duke." Brice's calm and cocky baritone. "Are we to be prisoners in your palace? Will you secure the city before the Longest Night Masquerade?"

Luca stopped out of sight behind the hedge and held her hand up for her guards to stop, too. She listened for her uncle's response.

"Are you insinuating something, de Moyenne?"

"No, Your Grace. Only observing that a lord of the Middle Court was murdered here and Her Highness was attacked in La Chaise in broad daylight. Have you caught the culprits?"

"I have not, but rest assured that I have the gendarmerie working as if their lives depend upon it." Threat sharpened Nicolas's words, and Luca did not doubt that the gendarmes' lives did depend upon it. Which supported Perrot's certainty that Nicolas hadn't attempted to kill Luca. Luca raised a quizzical eyebrow at Gil, but the old guard only frowned.

"The boy makes a point, Nicolas. If you intend to court the lower houses on Longest Night, you'll need to make them feel safe. Has Lady Bel-Jadot even returned from her estate? If one of the High Court is too frightened to make an appearance, why should they? I say this as a friend, Nicolas."

Luca gripped her cane tightly. So much for asking Evrard to pick her side. Their footsteps came closer, so Luca straightened.

"Good morning, gentlemen. What a lovely day to take your morning exercise all at the exact same time." She smiled with distaste, letting her gaze linger on each of them.

"My dear niece." Duke Ancier's face turned an unfortunate shade of beet. Luca smiled more genuinely at that; she wasn't above the satisfaction of catching him off guard. "What brings you here?"

"The same thing that brings you, I expect. I wanted a word with the comte. Lord Castide, do you have a moment?"

Evrard looked from Luca to Nicolas, whose face had gone murderously still.

"Your Highness, Your Grace. Forgive me, but I am too old to meddle in politics. I will ever serve Balladaire in the best way I can."

A politician's nonanswer. Luca turned to Brice. "And you, Lord LaVasse? Don't tell me you're too afraid to make a choice."

Luca gave him credit: faced with her and her uncle, Brice didn't waver. "I'll do whatever keeps Balladaire and her interests safe. With unrest in Qazāl and Masridān..." He bowed to the duke, and then to Luca, shallowly, before striding away. Gil scoffed as the younger man passed.

*That leaves only Evrard.*

"My dear uncle. Would you excuse us? I need to speak to the comte. Not about politics, but about trade."

"As you will. I need to speak with the captain of the gendarmerie. It's a pity about the young Qazāli girl. Do tell the ambassador that my people are searching as well. Many eyes, as they say."

Luca watched Nicolas walk back to the palace, his own coterie of guards trailing.

"What else do we have to talk about, Your Highness? I meant what I said. I'm too old to play this game between the two of you."

"It didn't sound like you were too old a moment ago." Luca led him farther into the maze. "Are you too old for trade, too?"

The old comte shivered beneath his heavy cloak and pulled it tighter over his shoulders. In the week since Luca had returned from Champs d'Or, autumn had sped onward and winter chased it down from the north. Cold wind bit at Luca's nose and chapped her cheeks.

"I am not. This was a lovely gift." Evrard tapped the clasp holding his black cloak tight over his shoulders. Normally his cloak was clasped with the Travers boar. It would have been better if it were a set of scales, people joked, or stacks of coins. The new clasp was made of a gem called inkstone by some, but the traders Luca had bought it from in Qazāl called it onyx. It came from farther away even than the Southern Mountains. She had had the stone fitted into a silver setting that reflected light onto the stone. This particular stone gleamed like Evrard's dark eyes when he looked from the stone to Luca. He wanted more. He could sell it. He could sell a lot of it.

"You could have that and more, my lord. The Shālan magic—"

The comte flipped his palm in a shrug. "I don't want anything to do with their superstitions."

"Would five years of exclusive shipping rights intrigue you?"

Evrard turned back to Luca slowly, his eyes narrowed.

"If your fleet is the only Balladairan fleet allowed to legally transport goods from Qazāl, you'd stand to make a substantial amount of money from our alliance."

"Not as much as I earned when they were a colony."

"Perhaps. But how long until they rebel again, damaging your goods, your ships, your profits?"

Evrard watched carefully, waiting for the catch. He frowned, stroking his white beard like Gil stroked his mustache. Luca wondered if her father would have followed these old men's fashion, these same mannerisms.

"What did you offer Ghislaine?" Evrard asked. "How did you get her interested in this alliance after they killed her daughter?"

"The Qazāli didn't kill her daughter."

Evrard scoffed. "Gil. You'd better keep a close eye on your charge. Nicolas doesn't know what he's up against, but neither do you, Your Highness." He shook his head and clucked his teeth. "Now if you'll excuse me. The cold does get into my hip."

"Think on it, my lord," Luca called after him.

Though the cold was also digging numb fingers into her own bad leg, Luca lingered in the garden, making her way to the heart of the maze where she had found Bastien.

The Royal Oak bore no sign of that night's violence. It had shed most of its leaves by now, and those that remained were dull and brown. Its own death, but not so painful, nor so permanent. The leaves upon the hedges had also begun to brown and fall, but all of the detritus was raked away by the groundskeepers before it could accumulate. The path was bare, the mud that had been made from his blood and the dirt was long dried, but there was no discoloration. Perhaps his blood had simply soaked into the earth. Perhaps there was magic, there.

Her uncle had done this. *I do know him*, she thought. *Better than any of you.*

"Luca." Gil put his calloused hand on hers.

Luca started. She was gripping the cane so hard that it was shaking. "What?" he asked.

Luca closed her eyes. She had done this before, in Qazāl. She had made hard choices, cruel choices. She had sent people to die and for reasons she regretted now. In the darkness of her memory, though, it was Touraine she saw. Touraine's face torn with anguish, barely holding herself back from killing the Droitist schoolmistress. Touraine stopping at the children's frightened cries.

"Sky above," Luca swore, furious all over again.

"What?" Gil said, growing even more alarmed.

Touraine had held herself back, but Luca didn't have to. Luca didn't *want* to.

"I need to send a runner to Madame Béryl. Tell her to be ready to take over an orphanage."

"Nicolas's school?"

"Not anymore."

Gil took a slow breath at the dangerous tone in Luca's voice. "Luca. His people are there. What are you going to do?"

"The same thing he's done to mine," Luca snarled. Then, in a whisper: "You didn't see her, Gil. You didn't see her."

Touraine, shaking as she sobbed in Luca's arms.

Gil held her gaze in silence, and Luca tilted her chin up, daring him to chastise her.

"I'll take care of it," he said.


*Keep her safe.*

Ghadin's grandmother at the pier, waving them both off, scowling and suspicious. Jaghotai, certain Touraine wouldn't dare let her down again.

Touraine dragged herself from the stables to her couch and dropped onto it like a cannonball, hiding her eyes with her hand.

A week of riding out into La Chaise with Perrot, and feeling overwhelmed by the sheer size of the city. Even breaking the city up by its quartiers—Beaux Arts with its fine crafts and artisans, all leather and wood and paintings and the theater; Le Tordu, the twisting and knotted streets with the textile workshops and their dozen workers weaving cheap clothes for the commoners or coveted rarities for people who could afford to imitate the marquise de Durfort; Le Four, where the markets and the bakeries were—they even rode back through La Gouttière, asking the captains to check their holds for stowaways and the dames to check their brothels. There was too much ground to cover, and who in this wide city would give a shit about a Qazāli teen?

Ghadin was clever. She would have gotten back to the palace if she could have.

Touraine flipped her hand over to stare at the two grief rings on her fingers. She didn't want to add another one.

She jumped at a knock on the door.

"I'm coming in," Aranen said.

Touraine grunted but remained boneless on the couch.

The priestess came in with a tray of tea. The aroma of sweet mint filled the air. Qazāli style.

"From young Mounir down in the kitchens. He's taking well to his new position."

"Good," Touraine grunted. She didn't reach for the tea even though her mouth watered for it.

Aranen handed Touraine the parcel she'd been carrying. "This came while you were out."

Touraine dropped the parcel into her lap without opening it and scrubbed her hands over her face. Aranen joined her on the couch and poured them both small glasses of tea.

"Drink. It'll help."

The glass was warm in Touraine's hands. She turned it around and around against her palm but couldn't bring herself to drink.

"It's not your fault, Touraine." Aranen blew softly over her tea. She looked into her glass with weary eyes. "You know you can't save everyone. Sometimes no matter how hard you try."

The priestess's throat worked as she swallowed—not tea but something else. Guilt or sorrow or the same failure that Touraine had been choking down all week. Maybe she was thinking about her wife. Djasha had been ill—dying—and with all of her magic, Aranen hadn't been able to stop it.

"I'm not going to stop looking for her."

"Then don't. But she's not the reason you're here. It's from Jagho-tai." Aranen gestured to the parcel.

Touraine sat up, rigid. "Is something wrong?"

Aranen pursed her lips in a frown. "I'm sure she thinks she has it under control."

Untying the package released a smell that immediately made some-thing inside Touraine ring like a bell, loud and clear. Orange blossom and mint and coffee and dry, hot dust and smoke from the water pipes.

She pulled the folded paper out and flipped it open to see the untidy scrawl that was her mother's handwriting. Between Jaghotai's halting penmanship and Touraine's only moderate grasp of Shālan script, she struggled to parse the short letter.

*I hear it gets cold there now. I got this from the Abdelnour women. Wool from the mountains. Weird sheep there. Sent your friend east to help. We'll be all right. We always are. —Jackal*

Thick rolls of fabric tumbled out of the wrapping. The soft scarf faded seamlessly from blue so deep it was almost black to a burgundy the color of spilled wine.

She closed her eyes and buried her face in the scarf. Home.

Pruett wouldn't be there, though. East. Masridān. Both of them off running errands for their new country. The stormy-eyed woman had never been complimentary about Masridān and its people before. Things were different now, though. She and Touraine were different. Pruett might find something worth keeping there. A selfish part of her hoped that it wouldn't hold her too tightly.

"What did she tell you that she didn't tell me?" Touraine asked, voice muffled by wool. "Other than everything."

"People are hungry. Istam is getting louder and louder about taking what we're owed. You and I are taking too long, apparently." Aranen fiddled with a new gold chain hanging down from her neck. It ended in a pendant that Touraine couldn't see.

"They know we're at a standstill?"

"Yes—if we're not careful, Qazāl will split between Istam and Basim. He thinks we should just take the duke's demands."

The Jackal definitely wouldn't like that. The Jackal also wouldn't like watching her people starve.

"Basim is right."

"What?" Aranen's hand stilled on the chain.

"Nicolas's version of the treaty isn't good, but—he has control here, and the Droitist schools—I could get him to surrender them."

How cold, how certain the schoolmistress had been. Like Cantic.

"What happened to helping Luca?"

Touraine stared into the weave of her scarf, thumbing the tight knit absently. "I don't know if she can win. If we take his terms, we can strike back when we're stronger."

"If we take his terms, we may never be strong enough to strike back again. Talk to her again. You owe it to your people and your allies to stop making one-sided decisions. You're not as clever alone as you think you are."

"Ouch." Touraine blinked. "That was...direct."

Aranen cocked an eyebrow. "The Third Tenet, remember?"

*The truth at the heart.*

"Besides. Since when do you fight for the winning side?"

# CHAPTER 27

# OF MIRRORS

Touraine took to meeting with Durfort at night, when she had exhausted the city's topside and its underbelly searching for Ghadin, but hadn't exhausted her mind enough to stop its spinning.

"No luck yet, El-Qazāli?" Durfort cocked a dark eyebrow when Touraine arrived that evening.

"No," she growled. "Let's go."

Durfort bowed and handed Touraine a practice blade. The weight of the sword had grown familiar, if not natural. Drills turned to sparring, and sparring kept her from careening from fear for Ghadin to fear for Qazāl to fear of asking for what she needed from Luca.

Help. Touraine needed help.

"Oh. Oh. I see. She is something, isn't she?" Durfort pressed teasingly, engaging Touraine's blade before backing away. "All that potential. I can't wait to see what kind of queen she becomes. And she's just as exciting elsewhere." She winked.

"Durfort. What under the sky above are you talking about?"

"I'm talking about the way you and Luca have both been this close"—the taller woman pressed her index finger and thumb together—"to biting my head off since you got back from Champs d'Or. I know Ghadin is gone, and that Luca is trying to steal a sky-falling throne, but I also know women—"

"Durfort," Touraine warned, but the marquise spoke over her.

"—and I know that both of you are complicated beings capable of holding both the deepest despair and unbridled lust in your hearts at once, and—"

"Your Grace!"

Durfort stepped back, blinking innocently while Touraine's face burned with embarrassment. "Respectfully, you don't know shit."

Touraine dipped the point of her blade in a feint before aiming to strike the hand. Durfort parried, and Touraine whipped the blade around. Another feint toward the hand before arcing the blade toward Durfort's head instead.

The attack met Durfort's blade, the marquise's eyes wide in surprise.

"Well, now. You're something, too. No wonder she's half-mad over you."

Each sentence a light thrust that Touraine parried to one side or the other as she backed away.

"So why are you both so frustrated?" Durfort's blade moved so fast that Touraine couldn't follow it and was jabbed in the sternum by the leather safety padding, hard enough to bruise.

Touraine rubbed her chest and scowled.

Durfort let her blade tip fall to the floor, let her muscled forearms go slack in her rolled shirtsleeves. When she saw Touraine looking, though, she flexed them again. A rivulet of sweat trickled across the ridges and down across the bones of her wrist. She flicked it away before it could reach her hand and muddy her grip.

"I'm not saying that what's going on or not between you two is my business, but I am saying—" Durfort stepped closer, lazily, and the flat of Durfort's blade caressed Touraine's inner calf. It inched upward. Durfort's eyes were dark and intent. "I'm more than willing to be an outlet."

If the immediate response of Touraine's body was any judge, she was more than willing for Durfort to be that outlet, too. What harm would it be, to forget everything for a night? Touraine tilted her chin up as Durfort closed in.

"Am I interrupting something?"

Touraine jumped at the sound of Luca's voice, half-sure she'd conjured it from her own frustration. But no—Touraine had asked Luca
to meet her here. The sparring session had run long.

"Not at all!" Durfort didn't move away, didn't take her eyes off
Touraine, but one side of her mouth tugged into a wry smile. "Things
were just getting interesting. Would you care to join, Your Highness? I
know you don't mind sharing."

Luca cocked her head, considering the two of them, though she
held Touraine's gaze longer. *I will if you will*, the look said.

A flood of heat started in Touraine's face and worked its way down.

When Touraine didn't answer the unspoken question, however,
Luca said, "Perhaps another time."

"A pity. If not to pleasure, to what do we owe the pleasure of your
presence?"

Luca pursed her lips and shrugged out of her outercoat. "I just came
to use the salle. I had a feeling there would be good company."

"That is always true. You're just in time to see..." Durfort strode
away to the corner of the room where her own jacket and the rest of her
effects lay.

She returned carrying a sword in a sheath. The handle was thin,
but it was surrounded by a gaudy cage of a basket hilt, all delicate wire
with the occasional jewel. She thrust it, handle first, at Touraine.

"A gift," Durfort said, smiling in that self-assured way she had.

Touraine unsheathed it and took a few practice swings. Its sharp
blade caught the candlelight in a stripe of silver. Despite its gaudiness,
the balance felt true.

"Thank you, Your Grace."

Durfort snorted at the title. "You're welcome, Your Excellency.
Wear it on Longest Night. You'll be very dashing, I'm sure. You can
draw it on this one here"—she nodded at Luca—"and I'll draw on you
drawing on her."

Longest Night. Throughout the palace, people spoke of it in hushed
excitement. It was the Balladairan festival celebrating the final death of
the year and the turn to life and growth as the days began to lengthen.

From the sheer number of wagons she'd seen unloading on the palace grounds, it was bound to be a spectacle. In the barracks, as children, the Sands had celebrated by making masks of scrap cloth and twine and chasing each other with their miniature batons.

"Thank you," she said again.

Luca cleared her throat. "You and Aranen will have a selection of clothing for your costumes, and your servants will see to your masks or paint."

The three of them stood awkwardly in a triangle of silence before Durfort pursed her lips. "I've just remembered, I need to taste the wine my people sent in for the festivities." She ducked her head at Touraine and then lower toward Luca, then gathered her things and left.

Luca grimaced as she watched Durfort go.

"What?" Touraine asked.

The princess shook her head. "Nothing."

"I'm sorry I asked you here so late." Touraine held Durfort's gift awkwardly at her side.

Luca offered a small smile. "Is this an assignation? Have you been spending too much time with Sabine?"

Touraine couldn't muster the levity. Her purpose bore her down. Luca sighed and picked a thin rapier from the rack. Gil trailed her in and made a show of picking out his own practice weapons.

"What, then?" Luca asked.

Touraine ran her thumbnail along the ridge of the basket hilt. "I need your help."

"What do you need? What's happened?" Luca searched her face, as if for a wound.

Which wound, exactly, would she find?

"If—when I find Ghadin, can you get us a ship? Can you send us home with food for the winter?"

"A ship?" Luca repeated. She faced Touraine, blade in hand.

"Jaghotai wrote. Qazāl is in trouble. If we don't get aid, the country will splinter before it can stand."

"Has someone challenged her?"

Touraine barked a laugh that was more of a frustrated sob. Without Durfort to distract her, Touraine's obligations charged full tilt.

"Not yet, but one faction wants revenge on Balladaire and the other thinks I'm an abomination and wants us to surrender to the duke."

"What about me? You said you would help me take the crown."

Touraine's lip curled.

"I don't want to sign his treaty, Luca." Touraine bit off each word. "That's why I'm here, asking you for your help now. You can find a way to get us out."

Luca was in her duelist's stance, advancing on Touraine as if *she* were the enemy. Touraine shifted one leg back, her hand tight around her new scabbard.

"Nicolas won't let you leave. Your chaperones, Captain Pissant. Not unless you sign his treaty."

"Captain Perrot will help me."

"The masquerade is soon. Your absence will be noted."

Touraine stepped forward, but Luca turned away. In the great mirror that Durfort was so proud of, Touraine watched Luca's jaw clench and unclench.

"It's a masquerade. No one would know. We could be long gone."

"My Trial of Competence is right after."

"You don't need us here for that."

Luca didn't answer.

"What else?" Touraine pressed. "You were willing to cross a river of crocodiles to steal magic from a cursed city. What are you so afraid of now?"

Touraine's own face in the mirror was half-desperate, and half-angry to be so desperate. Luca stared at the point of her blade. It hovered just above the floor, unwavering. *Give her what she wants*, Jaghotai said in the back of Touraine's mind. Durfort had said as much, giving away Luca's desires. It wouldn't be bad, would it? That closeness?

*Not if it helps Qazāl.*

Touraine swallowed, then stepped closer still, her boots echoing on the wooden floor.

"Is it me? Is it that you don't want me to leave?" She found Luca's gaze in the mirror and held it. "Because if that's it, I'll stay. With you."

Closer. Her breath felt too fast in her own chest, and thin. She tried to melt into the words.

"If I stay, you have to find a way to help them."

Touraine reached for Luca's shoulder.

Luca flicked the tip of her rapier up so quickly that Touraine had to jump back. She narrowed her eyes suspiciously at Touraine through the mirror. "What are you doing?"

Touraine clamped her lips tight, hot with humiliation. "I'm asking you for help."

"By insinuating that I would keep you here against your will? As my bed warmer?" Luca's stare froze Touraine, even through the mirror.

Reacting to the cold fury in Luca's voice was like dodging a blow— as easy, as thoughtless as instinct.

"Is that not what you want?" Touraine countered. "I read your letters. You asked for me to come here. You eye-fucked me five minutes ago. Why do you think the council sent *me*?"

Thoughtless as instinct. Protection and attack. Survival.

A mistake.

Luca gasped a dying person's gasp: that last little inhale when you've stabbed them, a small *ah* of pain and surprise. Such a small sound, to mean the end of something as full as a life. Her face went slack and flushed, as if Touraine had slapped her.

And Touraine felt like she had. Her whole body rang with the impact of her words. She hadn't just read Luca's letters. She had memorized them. She was just as guilty.

"Luca, I'm sor—"

Luca wheeled around, raising her blade between them. This was not the wounded Luca from the mirror. Though her eyes shone wet, she held her chin high, glaring down her nose at Touraine.

"If I have been anything less than appropriate with you since you arrived, I apologize. And if you think—" Luca blinked hard, exhaling sharply. "If I made you think you had to whore yourself out to me in the name of this alliance, I apologize again."

"That's not what I meant—"

"It's what you said, Your Excellency."

Touraine held her breath, watching the rigid coil of Luca's body as her chest rose and fell. She waited.

Luca turned away, refusing to look at either Touraine or her reflection. "If I sneak you out of Balladaire, my uncle will not appreciate being made a fool. There will be repercussions. He will want someone to take it out on, and though I've dealt with the woman at the Droitist school we visited, there are other schools. Other children to make more biddable than you."

"Shit," Touraine breathed. "What do you mean 'dealt with'?"

A grimace curled Luca's lips in profile. "It doesn't matter. Madame Béryl will treat the children well. I'll see to the rest as soon as I can, but it will take resources I don't have yet and—argh!"

She slammed her rapier back into the rack with a clatter of steel against steel. The weapons tilted and swung under the contagious force of Luca's anger.

"I'll stay. For you and for the duke, I'll stay."

Luca shook her head sharply and limped to Touraine. "I don't want you. Make your own choice. It will take time to source provisions, but you have my word. As your ally. When you're able, send a new ambassador."

The blade of Luca's anger pressed into the soft part of Touraine's chest. She grabbed Luca's arm as the princess turned to leave. Looked up into cold blue eyes. Candlelight reflected off the watery sheen and flickered against the planes of her face.

"Luca."

Touraine didn't have the words yet, for this sudden awareness: when Touraine snapped at Luca, something between them ripped, too. A tether, holding them together. Touraine didn't know how tightly she'd been holding on to it until the cord was broken and she was left plummeting to the rocks with nothing to catch her.

"I'll stay until the masquerade," Touraine whispered.

"Ambassador," Luca said, her voice frosted like glass.

"Yes?"

"Let go of me."

Touraine let go.

# CHAPTER 28

# BLOODY KNUCKLES

Fili's master did not appreciate her bringing a wounded Qazāli back to the shop, but as she'd hoped, he wasn't so cruel as to send her out. Not immediately. *It'll come out of your wages,* he'd said when he brought a doctor in. And when the doctor turned up her nose at the foreign patient, Fili had to beg her to stay.

"Why?" The doctor kept her hands close to her chest, unwilling to touch the patient. "They bring disease. Look, she's feverish."

Fili scowled, then looked back at the girl. Ghadin was her name, but Fili still didn't know where she'd come from, or why she'd been shot—the doctor had declared the wound a gunshot almost immediately, and with distaste.

Fili wasn't an expert, but she knew a little about infections. She'd done her best to clean the girl's wound, but she was shit at stitching. Then Ghadin took a bad turn, growing dizzy and fainting at Maître Gaspard's table. Heat radiated from her side.

"It's just infected! What would you give if it were me?"

The doctor frowned down her nose through round spectacles. Fili's master studiously ignored all of them while he worked on a new piece of cabinet.

"Your master won't pay—"

"I'll pay," Fili said sharply. She looked back at Ghadin. The girl's brown skin was pallid. Her eyelashes fluttered through fever dreams.

Fili wished she'd taken Ghadin to her mam instead. With the princess's money, Ghadin would have been taken care of. At least then the princess would have been good for something.

The doctor reached into her satchel. "This is what I would suggest for you, but don't expect it to work on someone like her. Our bodies are different." She held out two small pouches. "Ten sovereigns."

"Ten—!"

But Fili felt responsible. She went to the back of the shop where her cot was and dug out the small lockbox where she kept her earnings. Ten sovereigns were all she'd made in the last three months. She plucked the silver and gold coins out of the box and went back to the front. She snatched the pouches from the doctor's hand and dropped the coins in their stead. She didn't need the princess's blood money.

"Wait! What do I do with it?" she yelled after the woman, who was already leaving.

"The paste goes on the wound. The loose leaves make a tisane. She should drink it three times a day." She shrugged. "As I said, don't expect it to work."

The girl got better. The wound lost its heat, and the scab stopped oozing and smelling. It hardened into a dark, solid crust. Ghadin woke up more, and she woke lucid.

Unfortunately, she woke when Brother Michel and several of the Fingers came to visit Maître Gaspard and discuss some of the Fingers' future plans.

Fili was sitting in the back room with Ghadin, the door closed. Mostly closed. Her master had vouched for her and was glad that she wanted to be involved, but Fili suspected that bringing Ghadin in had shocked him. Not to mention that someone needed to keep an eye on her. That left Fili to hide back here instead of planning the revolution.

*Revolution is not a game*, Ghadin had said. The Qazāli girl slept on Fili's cot while Fili worked at her bench. The men's voices filtered in through the crack.

She listened while her hands moved over her latest project.

Fili had modeled the invention on the peg legs that many of Balladaire's veterans and injured workers limped on—only hers would be better. The entire device was a hollow, cylindrical wooden frame that an amputee could put their upper leg in. Beneath the cupping frame was an articulated joint that hinged like a knee. Below that, the lower "leg" was wood, but instead of a thick stick for a peg, Fili had... *changed* the wood to offer it more springiness. The sturdy responsiveness of real bone and muscle. It was a matter of reminding the core of the wood of its youthful green stage while maintaining the strength and endurance of mature wood.

She'd done something like it with Princess Luca's cane. Not that she'd wanted to gift the princess something like this. It was only her mam who insisted Fili make it *special*. Her mam didn't understand exactly what Fili did with wood, but she understood enough.

Fili glanced again at Ghadin to make sure she was asleep. She took her whittling knife and pricked her thumb, enough for a thick drop of blood to well up. She pressed the blood against the wood, then sank into the inner space where she'd felt the most comfortable ever since she was a child.

She pictured the forests and the open fields where she had grown up with her pa. Beneath her hands, the wood warmed, responding to her touch.

"Are you...healing the wood? Are you praying?"

Fili's eyes snapped open.

Ghadin sat up on the cot, mouth hanging open as she stared at Fili's hands, which were clenched hard around the leg.

"No," Fili said. She held the wood in front of her, bewildered and ashamed, as if she'd been caught naked. "Prayer's only for the uncivilized."

"You were talking to yourself and your eyes were closed. Not that different from when we pray."

*I talk to myself?*

"Balladairans don't pray," Fili said again. "Gods are for those who don't know enough to help themselves. For people who make up giants to blame because they're too weak to take responsibility themselves."

"That's not true," Ghadin said with heat. "We got rid of you lot with our god's gifts." She stood unsteadily. She came to the workbench and examined the prosthetic. A hesitant whimper escaped Fili's throat as Ghadin reached for it, but Ghadin's hand was gentle, exploratory. She might as well have been caressing Fili's own bare skin.

"This is beautiful," Ghadin whispered. "It's not like those." She nodded toward the lifeless shelves she'd been helping Maître Gaspard with. They were attractive, well made, and functional, but Fili didn't *sink* into them like she did her special pieces.

She refused to call what she did praying. Magic, maybe, but it didn't come from a god.

"No." Fili put her hand protectively over it, and Ghadin withdrew hers. "It's not. It's for my mam. She lost her leg to the princess."

Ghadin raised a curious eyebrow. "To the princess?"

"She was her royal guard."

"Oh." The other girl studied the wood some more, eyes tracing the curves of the cup where Fili's mam's thigh would rest.

"It is like healing," Ghadin said. Fili could tell she still wanted to reach out and touch it again, but she refrained. "Except you do it with wood."

"No, it isn't," Fili said sharply. "I didn't *do* anything."

The heat of panic flooded to her face, through her whole body.

Luckily, the men's voices rose loud enough for them to hear, and it arrested both of their attention.

"These Shālans are like rats," one of the men said.

Fili winced. She glanced at Ghadin from the corner of her eye. The other girl was frowning, fists clenched.

Then Fili's master said, in his pipe-smoke voice, "It's the princess's doing. We get rid of her, we send them back."

"Aren't you keeping one here, Gaspard? Ought to be more careful, hein?"

"My 'prentice brought her on. She was hurt, and Fili wanted to help her so…" Fili could practically hear him shrugging. "Not gonna turn out a gut-shot girl, am I?"

"Should have let her die in the street. That soft spot for that girl of yours seems more like a blind spot. You sure she's trustworthy? Her mam so close to the princess and all?"

Fili near swallowed her tongue. Of course she was trustworthy. She gripped the table tighter. She raised her eyes to meet Ghadin's.

"The girl hates the princess. She'll do anything to help us. I think the Shālans aren't too keen on the royals, either; I bet some of them would join us. They got the same problems we do—"

"No," Brother Michel said with finality. "We're not bringing desert rats into the Fingers."

Maître Gaspard sighed. "She'll be gone soon."

"How long has she been here, Gaspard?"

"Couple of weeks? She's been recovering."

There was a pause in the other room, then—

"A couple of weeks?" Michel swore. "You sky-falling idiot. What if she was hurt in the attack?"

"How would she have been? She's a Qazāli, for the stars' sake."

"The princess loves the sand rats, she's got a whole charity for them. Besides, it doesn't matter if she was with the princess. If she saw anything, if she can lead them to us—" He cut off with a frustrated growl, as if realizing what he was saying and who might hear him.

Wood scraped harshly across wood. Brother Michel's chair, scooting away from the table.

"Where is she, Gaspard?"

"Michel, don't—"

Heavy boots stomped toward the workshop.

"You said I'd be safe," Ghadin hissed, her mouth a flat, angry line.

"You are!" Fili whispered back, knowing full well how hollow the words sounded. "You'll see—"

Ghadin tugged Fili's favorite overshirt on.

The workshop door opened. Brother Michel, tall and looming in his too-loose coat, his heavy butcher's hands used to the easy snap of bone. He filled the doorway, and Ghadin, half his size, and favoring her wounded side, glowered right back at him. It didn't matter that her balled fists together were barely the size of one of his.

"Ghadin, don't," Fili whimpered. "Brother Michel, please don't. I swear, she won't tell anyone."

"You know her so well, girl? Hein? Why don't you earn our trust and stay out of the way? Got to protect all the Fingers. Good people out there'll hang if this girl bleats. You don't want that, do you?"

*Why do you care so much about this one Qazāli anylight?* a voice in the back of her mind asked. If Ghadin left, and she did tell someone about the Fingers, she could lead the gendarmerie right back here, to Maître Gaspard.

Ghadin wouldn't do that. She and Fili spent half of Ghadin's waking hours talking about revolution and what happened in Qazāl. Ghadin understood more than any of them what they were up against.

Fili screwed up her courage and moved between the two of them.

"Brother Michel," she tried again, the same time as he stepped forward.

Then Ghadin shoved Fili into the man. With her face muffled in his coat, she was smothered in the smell of sweat, of the lingering metallic odor of blood and earthy offal. Michel threw Fili off, grasping for Ghadin as she staggered past.

"Get her!" Michel shouted to the men in the other room. He charged after Ghadin.

There was an adze on the ground. A carving knife, a hammer. She could help Ghadin get free.

Fili lunged for a length of wood. The front door opened. The other men were shouting.

She raced out of the workshop and speared the wood at Michel's feet. It snarled up his legs and he fell. Fili didn't stop. She vaulted over him, tripped, slammed to her hands and knees. She ignored the pain that lanced through her joints, and scrambled after Ghadin.

"This way!" Fili caught up to Ghadin and dragged her off the main road as fast as she could, weaving through alleys and side roads and down a stairway that led to a walking path along the river. If you followed it far enough, you'd reach different parts of La Gouttière. It was an easy place to disappear. No one above ever looked down, unless to spit.

Ghadin leaned against the damp stone wall. Her skin was all gray, and her breathing shallow. She opened one eye and caught Fili staring at her.

"What are you doing here?" she asked.

"Was he right?" Fili chased her own breath. She hadn't even grappled with what she'd just done. "Were you really with the princess? Are you one of her Qazāli?"

"I'm no one's Qazāli," Ghadin spat.

"You were with her, though. Are you a royal? Some kind of princess?"

Ghadin snorted, then grimaced. "I'm the ambassador's page."

Fili felt like she'd stepped on an uneven stair. "You talked like you hate the princess."

"It's all of you. It's Balladaire. You're so... you're hypocrites." Ghadin shook her head. "I need to go back anyway. Touraine will be looking for me."

*Touraine.* Fili recognized the name from her mam.

"What, to the palace?"

"Yes. The palace," Ghadin enunciated with irritation.

Fili huffed defensively. The world wasn't a simple place. Fili knew that. People were complicated and had complicated reasons for doing what they did. Like her mam had complicated reasons for staying away from Fili to serve Princess sky-falling Luca. The complicated reality didn't stop Fili from feeling betrayed. She'd thought of herself and Ghadin like coconspirators, a smaller arm of her own personal Fingers. Like they could change things. To go back to the palace—! Where else, though? Not to Maître Gaspard. Not to Brother Michel.

Before Fili could get her head fit right, Ghadin walked off without her, clutching the wall for support.

"Wait—where are you going?"

Ghadin gave her an incredulous look.

"I mean—the palace guard isn't going to trust some random Qazāli girl walking up to the gates. If they don't haul you off to Le Fontinard, they'll shoot you on the spot!"

"Then what, my brilliant savior?"

"Don't be an ass. Can you walk a little longer?"

Ghadin lifted her shirt to check on the wound. The scab hadn't broken. "Yes." She wagged a bare foot.

"It's not too far. My mam lives near the upper side, farther upriver. She can get you in."

"See? Hypocrite."

"I'm not proud of it."

"Doesn't mean you get to judge me." Ghadin huffed. "Or your mother for that matter."

Fili wedged herself under Ghadin's armpit and guided her down the cobbled path. Small passenger boats floated by, but Fili didn't have the money to flag them down. Plus, boatmen were nosy and talked too much as a rule.

At the next bridge, Fili helped Ghadin up the stairs. The other girl's breath grew more and more labored.

"You okay?"

"I'm fine."

"Make sure she gets you a good doctor."

Ghadin smiled as she winced. "I came with the best healer in Qazāl."

Fili's belly gave an uncomfortable flip. Ghadin sensed the sudden tension in Fili and gave her a sidelong glance.

"It's all right to keep a god," she said softly. "There can be a strength to it. Not just magic, but peace."

They climbed the last steps and started across the bridge separating the low city from the upper city. The sky was graying and the cold settling in.

"It's not a god I believe in," Fili said. "It's the earth and the sky and the rain and the life all of that brings." She'd never tried to explain this aloud to anyone.

Ghadin smirked. "What's a god, if not life?"

She smiled self-consciously. "Maybe I just really like trees."

Ghadin stumbled, and Fili tightened her grip. The other girl gasped in pain.

"Sorry, sorry," Fili said. "Here, rest."

"I..." Ghadin looked like she was going to rebel but gave up when she couldn't even get the words out. She swore in breathy Shālan. "Just for a minute. How far away is your mother's place?"

"Um. I might have underestimated a little. It doesn't normally feel this long, but—"

Fili broke off at the sound of heavy-heeled boots marching in step. Ghadin was alert as a hare, ready to dart away.

This time, though, the instinct was wrong. Fili snared Ghadin's sleeve.

"Let me go," Ghadin growled. "You just said if they caught me—"

"If they catch you trying to get *into* the palace. We can try to explain—"

Ghadin looked like she wanted to carve Fili a new face. Fili let her go and held up her hands.

"Look, just sit with me and pretend we're friends."

Fili expected Ghadin to run. Instead, she leaned over the bridge. If she weren't Qazāli, she would have looked like any other Gouttière native, spitting into the river for luck.

Fili wasn't a Gouttière native, but she leaned over the edge and spat anyway.

"Your turn."

Ghadin managed to look disgusted and fascinated at the same time.

The boots turned onto the bridge instead of passing.

"Sometimes," Fili said, her voice coming out pitchy and rushed, "I think about hiring out as a shipwright after my apprenticeship. Sealing the wood against the water with—you know."

The footsteps stopped behind them, and Fili's trail of thought stopped, too. She forced herself to keep breathing.

"You there! You two!"

*Shit, shit, shit.* Fili whispered, "Please do not do anything stupid."

Ghadin hawked an impressive gob of her own over the edge.

"We're looking for a young Qazāli girl, by order of the princess." The gendarme spoke to Fili, but her eyes were narrowed suspiciously on Ghadin. "Your friend matches the description."

Ghadin gripped the stone railing, knuckles white.

"What's your name, girl?" the gendarme said curtly.

"It'll be okay," Fili murmured. "They'll take you back."

Ghadin shot Fili a dirty look.

"Don't waste my time, girl. What's your name?"

"Ghadin," Ghadin said softly, tossing her name like a wish over the bridge.

"Goddin?" the gendarme said, butchering the pronunciation. Her companion nodded. "Right, come with us."

The gendarme grabbed Ghadin roughly by the arm, and Ghadin yelped.

"Careful," Fili cried. "She's hurt!"

"Who are you?" the other gendarme asked.

Fili quailed under his stare. "No one." She backed up against the railing and held her breath, wishing she could disappear.

Ghadin looked back at Fili over her shoulder. The gendarme's hands were too tight on Ghadin's arms. They were just taking her to the palace. *She'll be where she belongs.*

Then why did Ghadin look so frightened? Why was Fili's stomach caught up in knots?


Fili didn't make it back to the workshop until after the stars were out and the night's carousing had begun. She hadn't been sure she wanted to go back. She'd even considered finishing the trip to her mother's. The thought of explaining everything to her turned Fili back the way she'd come.

"Fili!" Maître Gaspard stood up from the table when she came in. His arms opened to gather her in a hug, but he stopped himself. Glanced anxiously at the other man at the table.

Brother Michel sat nursing a beer from up the road. It wasn't his first. He looked up at her, expression livid.

"Where's your little desert rat, girl?"

Fili stammered. "The gendarmerie took her."

"Oh? Why'd they see fit to do that?"

Fili glanced to her master for help, but he just swiveled his head between her and Michel, silently pleading for her to give the right answer. She looked down at the floor. Someone had pulled her mam's leg from the workshop and slammed it on the ground. The spring foot had been cracked, but not all the way through. Fili could mend that.

"They said the princess was looking for her," she said in a voice smaller than she liked.

Brother Michel slammed his palm on the table. "Sky above!" he swore. "You see, Gaspard, you see? What did I say?" He slammed the table again, and Fili jumped. Then Michel took a deep breath and ran a giant hand under his cap and over his gray-brown hair. "Doesn't matter. We'll go ahead. Girl. Fili, is it?"

Fili nodded.

"You fucked us good, letting her go. You know that, right?"

"She won't tell," Fili said quickly. She was certain. Ghadin couldn't.

"You don't know that. You make it up to us, though. You want to be part of the cause, then you'll prove it."

"Michel, she's too young, it's too dangerous—"

"I'll do it," Fili said immediately over her master's protests. She wanted to help change Balladaire. She wanted to know the truth about revolution the way Ghadin did. "Whatever it is, I'll do it."

Brother Michel smiled at Maître Gaspard. "You see?" He winked at Fili.

# CHAPTER 29

# THE LONGEST NIGHT

Luca saw Touraine before Touraine saw her.

As Touraine descended the palace's marble staircase to the garden, squinting as her eyes adjusted, Luca felt as if she were watching the night itself fall. Touraine was dressed in black trousers and a black coat with a deep-purple lining. A blue cape so dark that it looked black clasped around her throat with a golden button, like the lone star in the sky.

Except it wasn't the lone star.

Touraine's golden eyes glowed in the face of her white and black skull paint. She'd cut her hair again, close to the scalp. Luca made a very undignified and very involuntary sound in the back of her throat. Cursed herself for it.

When those eyes landed on Luca, she felt the jolt all the way to her core.

Belatedly, she noticed Aranen just behind Touraine. She beckoned the ambassadors, then stared intently in the direction of the festivities to cool the blush creeping up the lower half of her face. The rest was hidden by her own mask.

*Is that not what you want?*

"Your Highness," Aranen said, approaching. "You look nice."

Luca bowed, flaring her gold cloak behind her. She was dressed as the dawn, in bleeding rose and bruised lavender, with her silver half mask for the setting moon.

"Your Excellencies. Welcome to the longest night of the year." Luca gestured to the open garden. Her gaze skittered over Touraine to steady on Aranen instead. "Stay awake with me."

The traditional greeting of the night, meant to sound inviting, suggestive. The acrid aftertaste of Luca's last conversation with Touraine lingered at the back of Luca's tongue, though, and the words came out dull.

Luca led them into the garden, urgently filling the silence that hadn't had time to form: "No paint, Aranen din?"

The priestess wore neither paint nor mask with her outfit. "I'm a physician. My face is death mask enough."

"Ah. I see." Luca cleared her throat. In a low voice, low enough for the words to dissipate beyond the three of them, she said, "Your ship is ready. It can be underway as soon as you are."

In a lower voice meant for one, she added, "And you didn't even have to fuck me for it."

It hadn't been easy to arrange. Her own ships would be watched, obviously; too many merchant ships had Nicolas's or Evrard's interests on them; and a military ship wouldn't sail without Nicolas's approval. An unmarked ship full of grain wouldn't go unnoticed for long, though.

"Thank you, Your Highness," Aranen said, inclining her head just enough. "Jaghotai and the rest of the council will be grateful. We appreciate your aid."

"Yes. Thank you."

At the roughness in her voice, Luca looked at Touraine full on.

"I take it that there's been no sign of Ghadin?" Luca asked.

"No," Touraine said. She sounded defeated and empty, but didn't elaborate. It had been three weeks now since they'd come home from Champs d'Or. Three weeks since Ghadin had run away and been lost. If she hadn't been taken in by Madame Béryl or pressed into any of the illegal work gangs or turned into a serving girl, she was either dead or worse. In the two weeks since Luca and Touraine had talked, Touraine had probably realized all of that. It hadn't stopped her searching, though.

"Do you want to wait?" Luca asked. She couldn't help it; the anger in her dulled at the sorrow in Touraine's skull-hollow eyes. Luca reconsidered how much of the dark circles were paint and how much was something else.

"No," Touraine said again. "If you don't mind, I'd rather not think about it tonight."

Luca led the two ambassadors through the gardens, pointing out the different entertainments with distant courtesy: a man conjuring multihued sparks from his hands in chemical sleight of hand; a woman who made objects disappear in smoke shaped like nightmares. The gardens smelled of sulfur and saltpeter and burning wood.

"Light and shadow," the priestess murmured.

"That's what Longest Night is about," Luca agreed. "The exchange between light and darkness, sunlight and shadow. Life and death." She gestured to the dead grass underfoot. "It's my favorite time of year."

"Is it?" Touraine said.

Luca almost misread the expression on Touraine's face as tenderness.

"You don't have to pretend to be interested," she said coldly, for Touraine's ears only. Then, louder: "Are you hungry, Aranen din?"

Behind her, as Luca led them to the buffet table, she thought she heard Touraine's frustrated sigh. Luca felt justified. Smug, even. But at the table, where Touraine snuck the small finger foods as if no one would notice, her cheeks puffing with pastry, eyes lighting up for the first time all night in delight over the flavors, Luca had to try very hard not to watch.

Across from the table, on the lawn turned into a makeshift stage, Qazāli dancers performed impossible acrobatic feats while Balladairans laughed and clapped with delicate glee. Luca might've been back in the desert on that Shālan holy night. Dancing, locked over Touraine's shoulders, with Touraine's arm around her waist.

It was a mistake to want her then, too.

*Why do you think they sent me?*

The dancers' bodies were lithe and strong, and Luca tried to lose herself in them as they piled themselves into a tower, standing on each other's shoulders, the smallest dancers vaulting to the top. The last one stood on one foot on the hands of the pair beneath them. Beside Luca, Touraine held her breath in anticipation.

*Sky above, Luca, you fool.*

Then the tower collapsed. A woman screamed. Luca's hand leapt in front of her mouth to stifle her own yelp. While the dancer at the top hurtled through the air, the dancers below jumped and flipped from each other's shoulders just in time to create a basket of their arms to catch the falling acrobat. The burst of applause and amazed laughter were nothing like the usual genteel clapping of the theaters.

Touraine's face was unreadable, but firelight shone on tears clinging to Aranen's eyelashes.

"Is something wrong?" Luca asked.

"Nothing," Touraine said, though she looked conflicted as the acrobats bowed to their audience. "They're amazing."

She looked like she wanted to say more, but a body barreled into them.

Sabine. The marquise draped one arm over Touraine and one over Luca, then grinned between them. "If it isn't my two favorite people in all of Balladaire. Stay awake with me tonight?"

The marquise smelled like a wine spill, and the slurring in her voice explained how she'd not only lost her mask but also managed to forget that they weren't supposed to look like conspirators. Luca ducked out from beneath Sabine's arm.

"Was that not the most amazing thing you've ever seen?" Sabine crowed, gesturing with the hand still draped over Touraine's shoulder.

"Sabine, how much have you had to drink?" Luca growled through her teeth. Her bad mood, it seemed, was large enough to encompass everyone this evening. It was going to be a long Longest Night.

"Not enough, my love, not nearly enough." She steadied and looked

Luca dead in the eyes. "I really will make it up to you, I swear." Then she ducked close to Luca, dragging Touraine along with her and casting a wary look around her. "In secret."

Did Sabine mean signing the Trial of Competence summons, her drunkenness, or something else entirely that Luca was better off not knowing?

"What you are *making* is a nuisance of yourself, embarrassing me and the entire Durfort line. What would your mother say?"

"Oh, sky above, is that bollock-shriveling cow not dead already?" Sabine gagged.

Sabine had made her mark in court as the roguishly charming noble pretending at coarseness, but she knew how to stick just within the boundaries of propriety. That self-awareness was gone.

"Lanquette, could you please help the *marquise* find her feet," Luca said.

"I am on my feet, Your Highness." Sabine unhooked her arm from Touraine's shoulders and frowned at Lanquette. "Come fetch yourselves a drink with me, and we'll watch these fine acrobats some more. An excellent choice of entertainment." She eyed Touraine up and down in a way that made Luca want to stand between them. "Can *you* do that?"

Touraine raised her eyebrows. "Wouldn't you like to know? Let's have that drink."

"Excellent, Your Excellency!"

"I don't think the marquise needs another drink," Luca said tightly as she trailed behind them.

A pyramid of glasses balanced delicately on the table, calling to mind the dancers. Several glasses on the table had already been filled with a deep-red wine, the scent heavy and spiced, perfect for winter. A servant handed a glass to Sabine, and Luca took it instead.

"Of course, Your Highness." Sabine reached for another. "You keep that one."

With both of her hands full, Luca couldn't do anything else without attracting even more attention, so she sipped her stolen wine coolly.

Only Aranen declined a glass, still watching the Qazāli performers from over her shoulder.

"You don't have to stay," Luca muttered to the older woman. "The company has taken a turn for the boisterous."

The priestess hid her amusement—or annoyance—graciously and left with a bow, her assigned guard stomping behind her.

Luca turned to the mess she was left with. Sabine's cup was already half-empty. Luca couldn't help but notice the overly casual way Sabine brushed against Touraine's arm or nudged her in one direction or the other. She also hadn't failed to notice that Touraine was wearing that hideous sword Sabine had given her.

*Walk away. Leave them to it*, the voice of dignity and self-preservation whispered in the back of her mind. But it stung that Touraine would let herself fall for the marquise's charms while accusing Luca of wanting too much.

Perhaps that was *why* Touraine held Luca at arm's length. She felt like Luca had staked some claim on her and resented it.

Luca stopped, ready to let them walk back to the acrobats by themselves, when Touraine met her eyes. Touraine's mouth parted in surprise, her skull-brow furrowed. Luca realized her own neutral mask must have slipped, the twist of her lips or the set of her jaw had given her thoughts away—she even reached up to make sure her physical mask was still in place.

The ambassador slipped Sabine's arm, and her mouth began to form Luca's name.

Then, in her too-loud, too-much way, Sabine jostled Touraine so hard that Touraine stumbled forward and into Brice de Moyenne, who was strutting toward them.

The marquis had taken the pale side of death and was dressed in shades of gray and white, with white face paint daubed over his freckled cheeks. Now the front of his gray doublet and his death-pale chemise were stained in claret wine.

"Watch yourself," Brice snarled. He glared down his nose at Touraine while the dark wine spread across his white cravat like blood.

Then he saw Touraine and Luca properly. He took in Sabine's drunken grin. "Lord LeMarchal, I am surprised at you."

"And I'm surprised not to see him with his horse," Sabine said in a mock whisper. She was about to make a lewd gesture with her hands, and Luca grabbed them.

Touraine had locked up again—her face blank, her hands clenched in fists at her sides, eyes cast down. "I'm sorry, Your Grace." She bowed.

Brice's fellow soldiers hovered behind him in black masks or with black paint around their eyes and mouths to make their own death's heads. In their black and gold clothing, redolent of a soldier's uniform, they almost blended into the night.

"You're lucky it's the fête," Brice said down his nose to Touraine. "Anyone else and I'd challenge you. Your Highness, if you please—" He began to turn away.

"To the contrary, dear marquis." Duke Nicolas approached, smiling from beneath his own dark blue mask painted with pale stars. He saluted them with his own wine glass. Anyone else might mistake it for his joy at the evening, but Luca wasn't fooled. "A duel sounds like just the right activity for the evening. What is a duel if not a celebration of life and death?"

"Absolutely not." Luca stepped between Touraine and the two men. "I won't risk the ambassador's life on a game."

Nearby nobles pulled their attention away from the food and games and even the acrobats to follow the confrontation between the princess and the duke. The heir and the usurper. It sounded straight out of a chevalier's tale.

Nicolas tsked and smiled indulgently. "Of course not. Just to the touch. Let us see what Qazāl has to offer us as allies. You'll fight, my lord?" The duke looked expectantly at the marquis, and the younger man nodded slowly.

"As you wish, Your Grace." Brice snapped and his body servant appeared, undoing the stained silk at his throat and taking away the stained coat. He should have looked unkempt. Instead, he just seemed even more the heroic soldier, gallantly disheveled—and already mortally wounded. A strip of pale chest and red-gold hair was bright in the light above the wine stain. He drew his sword.

"You don't have to do this, Brice," Luca said.

Brice ignored her. "To the touch, then, Your Excellency. Draw your weapon."

Fili held her breath as she trailed through the palace kitchens behind Sister Maxime, one of the palace chefs—and a Finger.

The Longest Night celebrations would be underway soon in the palace gardens, and the kitchen was busy with preparations. Fili tried not to think about what she was doing here tonight. She fingered the small pouch in her pocket that Brother Michel had given her. To prove that she was ready to commit herself to the Fingers. Her master had tried to convince her it was no shame to turn it down; no shame not to be ready.

Maxime dragged Fili close, one thick hand heavy on Fili's shoulder. The older woman's strength was reassuring. Fili straightened, eager to be worthy of the woman's regard. "Yes, madame?"

"Do you have the powder or the herbs?" Sister Maxime murmured.

"Uh, the powder," she stammered, hand drifting back to the pouch in her skirts. She didn't often wear skirts. That was part of the disguise.

Maxime slapped Fili's hand away. "Right, then. You'll be with the drinks." She handed Fili two flagons of deep-red wine. "Come back here for refills. Powder does not go in the flagons themselves, only the glasses. Pick your targets careful like."

A sharp excitement expanded in Fili's chest. "Like the princess?"

Maxime's eyes bugged as she held back a guffaw. "Only if you want every servant in the palace dead."

"Oh. Right." Fili looked down again at the wine in her hands.

Maxime took pity on her. "The duke will make a good show of hunting down a poisoner if it's just a few nobles, then he'll pick a scapegoat, hang them, and we'll all move along just like he did last week. We got to build up, you see."

Maxime scowled and Fili felt guilty, thinking of Ghadin. Last week, the duke had hanged a random pair of dockworkers in the Traitor's Corner, blaming them for the attack on the princess's carriage. They hadn't even been guilty. The point was the fear. Enough fear might drive other Chaisiens to turn on the Fingers.

"The duke or the princess," the chef continued, clicking her tongue. "You can't shake that off. One day, though, when the Fingers are strong enough."

"I understand." One day, the Fingers would be strong enough to overthrow the cruelty, and this was a step. Fili was a step. She tightened her grip on the flagons of wine.

"Good girl," Sister Maxime said. "Nice paint."

Fili half reached up, forgetting already the cheap paint she'd caked on to shape a skull on her pale skin.

Sister Maxime clenched her fingers into a tight fist, and Fili mimicked the gesture.

*The Fingers form the fist.*


The palace guests drew away from them, leaving Luca alone with Brice, Touraine, and the duke. Healthy room for the spectacle. Their eyes glinted cruel when they looked at Touraine. The covert—and sometimes overt—way they looked her up and down, lips curled. Did they crave the symbolism of a savage Shālan falling to Balladaire? Did they know Touraine as the rebel conscript, the traitor responsible for the fall of the colony? Or did they just want to see Touraine bleed? Nicolas's polite, eager smile didn't hide the hunger in his eyes.

Sky above, Luca could *see* the effort it took Touraine to raise her chin and face the two men down. Fear for her caught in Luca's throat.

"I'm sorry, Your Graces. I'm not going to duel." Touraine rested her hand on that gaudy hilt as if she were trying to force the blade to stay in its sheath.

"Just for the fête, Your Excellency. I travel south tomorrow to deal with some other barbarians' rebellion. A man deserves some fun first, does he not?" Brice grinned. "And some satisfaction after you ruined my favorite cravat?" He turned to his friends, all of them broad shouldered and bowlegged from a life of training in the saddle. They laughed on command.

Touraine focused on the duke. Something had shifted, and Luca wasn't sure what it was or when it had happened, but Touraine stood taller, her broad shoulders pulled back. Quiet anger simmered in her eyes, in the set of her lips.

"I have nothing to prove to you, my lord duke."

A different kind of ache spread through Luca's chest, hot and tender and terrifying.

She found herself taking her place beside Touraine.

The marquis de Moyenne's face faltered. His glance toward the duke was the only evidence of nervousness, but the duke was studying Luca.

He wanted to play this game, had chosen their pieces—a pawn against a chevalier? Two chevaliers? Luca suspected she knew how he saw it. Even Touraine had sensed it and tried to extricate herself from the trap. It was never so simple with Nicolas, though.

Luca had promised Touraine she would protect her.

Luca took off her cloak and tossed it at Sabine, followed by her coat and mask. Miraculously, the drunk woman caught them; apparently not all of her reflexes were soaked in wine.

Comprehension broke over Brice's face. "Your Highness. There's no need—"

"On the contrary, my lord marquis. You've challenged my guest." Luca smiled coldly. She turned the smile onto her uncle. "And while she has nothing to prove, I'm offended at how she's been treated and am in need of my own satisfaction." She pushed her sleeves up her forearms and turned to Touraine, holding a hand out. "Your Excellency, could I borrow your sword?"

Touraine's eyes flicked between Luca and Brice as she clutched the hilt of her sword. Then she glanced over her shoulder, to Sabine. The marquise seemed to have sobered marginally, but only enough to properly understand the situation. Sabine put a hand on Touraine's shoulder and nodded.

"She knows what she's doing," Sabine whispered loudly. Given the swordswoman's current state, it was not the vote of confidence Luca would have preferred.

Luca crooked her fingers impatiently. "Please, Your Excellency. I find my cane alone is not up to the task."

She gestured with the cane that Guérin had gifted her for her birthday. Her usual one—with the rapier hidden inside it—was back in her quarters.

The monstrosity that Touraine unsheathed and put in her hands was heavy. Luca grimaced at Sabine. *This isn't a weapon, it's a confection.*

Sabine shrugged, a sly smile playing on her lips.

Luca gave it a few test swings. It was a standard sidesword, heavier and with a longer reach than Luca was used to. It left her slightly off-balance. Not ideal. Her right leg felt strong tonight, though. She settled into her stance, cane in her right hand, sword in her left. She found Gil, in the near edge of the circle formed around them. He nodded subtly in approval. It was enough.

Excitement crept into her blood, a slow trickle that pooled, spilled over. The excitement of no longer hiding behind books, behind words. Of decisiveness.

"To the first touch, then. Will the esteemed marquise de Durfort serve as judge?" Luca said pointedly. Not that she expected Sabine to manage the calls; they just needed someone to make a show of it, and Sabine was good for nothing if not making a show of things.

Let them see Luca as her own champion against her uncle's proxy.

"Of course, Your Highness." Sabine dumped Luca's coat into Touraine's arms and planted herself between Luca and Brice.

Luca didn't look back at Touraine. She took calming breaths as Sabine called the terms again.

Brice attacked quickly. He thought that speed would outmaneuver Luca's bad leg, that he could put her on her off-foot and force her to yield. It was what Sabine had tried to do, too, back when they first started training together. It was the wrong idea.

Luca shifted her weight to her cane and her bad leg and pivoted away from his lunge, opening her body position while his blade passed harmlessly. She held up her own blade in the fence post guard to keep him away. She hopped to re-establish their distance. He smiled.

"Only to the touch, now, my lord," Luca teased, though she wondered if he did indeed need the reminder. The first tendril of worry curled through the excitement in her stomach.

He saluted her with his sword.

This time, he attacked conventionally, testing her with strikes that she parried easily even though the gilded cage of her hilt made her feel slow and inflexible.

Her first slash at Brice caught his shirt. The hole in the fabric showed a strip of pale skin and hairy belly. The crowd held its breath.

Brice looked down at his stomach. "Your Highness. To the touch, was it?" He smiled and bowed, slightly mocking in the way of an older child humoring the younger one who wants to play. That had ever been their dynamic.

"I saw no touch," Nicolas said.

Brice and Luca both turned to the duke, Brice in surprise.

"No." Luca straightened and pushed back the damp strands of hair that had fallen from her queue. "Nor did I."

Brice wiped his sweating forehead with his forearm. His pale shirt showed dark patches of sweat despite the cool evening. "My mistake, Your Highness."

They resumed. The circle of nobles watching them vanished from Luca's mind. Even Touraine was gone. Her mind didn't supply her with Gil's steady stream of instruction the way it did in sparring matches. There was only angle and space. After several terse minutes, she and Brice both bore shredded clothing but no blood. Luca's heavy breath fogged the cold air.

"This will be indecent soon." Sabine's voice broke the silence, and Luca couldn't help but smile even though it disrupted the spell keeping her alert.

Her hip was killing her, and unused to the heavier blade, her shoulder was burning. She was slowing down. Brice, on the other hand, looked as if he'd just warmed up to the fight.

Luca needed to end this before she couldn't.

She lunged again.

A scream from the crowd. Luca twisted to look over her shoulder.

Brice didn't have that reflex. He was trained for battle, where screams of pain were normal and distractions could cost your life, not just your honor.

Luca turned back just in time to see his blade streak toward her right shoulder. She abandoned the lunge, spinning away from the blow, opening up her right side. Her leg buckled under the strain of the quick movement. Her center of weight went left, and the lawn rushed up to meet her.

*Better this than losing.* She was nowhere near certain that was true.

In front of half of Balladaire's nobles, the would-be heir crashed onto her ass in the middle of a duel.

However, her opponent was still overstretched in his own attack position. From the ground, Luca lunged to one knee and jabbed the point of Touraine's sword into the marquis de Moyenne's left ass cheek. A red dot of blood spread like a peony on the seat of his pale trousers.

Flushed with victory, Luca pushed herself gingerly back to her feet, trying not to look as if it were a struggle even as her right leg screamed and threatened to collapse beneath her again. She looked smugly at Brice, who clutched a hand over his buttock. Beyond him, she expected to see the Qazāli dancers executing another death-defying stunt, but the acrobats were all grounded.

Another shout, unmistakably a cry for help, not one of excitement.

"Touraine?" Luca limped in a circle, trying to make sure the ambassador was all right.

She found Touraine over Sabine's convulsing body, spit foaming at the marquise's lips.

# CHAPTER 30

# A CLENCHED FIST

L uca dropped to her knees at Sabine's side.
"What's happening?" Her voice spiked shrill in her panic.

Sabine's eyes had rolled up in the back of her head. Touraine muttered under her breath, her eyes closed. Like she had over Ghadin in Ghislaine's menagerie. Touraine was trying to heal Sabine and she was failing.

Luca wiped sweaty tendrils of hair out of her face. *Calm.* To Lanquette, she said, "Get her to the infirmary. Brice, help him!"

Surprisingly, the marquis obeyed with no retort.

"Wait!" Aranen.

Luca sagged in relief. "Aranen din. Please!"

Without asking, the priestess tore off her scarf and shoved the balled-up fabric into Sabine's mouth. Then she flicked up Sabine's eyelids, revealing overblown pupils. She pulled a finger through the pink-tinged spittle at the corner of the marquise's mouth. She sniffed it, then touched it delicately with the tip of her tongue. She spat immediately.

"Poison. Infirmary, run."

"You can heal her, though?" Luca pleaded.

"She needs to vomit, and—" Aranen shook her head and ran after Lanquette and Brice, her own guard bringing up the rear.

Only then did the rest of the garden come into focus. The palace bells were ringing, and beneath that din, her uncle was shouting.

"Attack!" he bellowed. He spun wildly about him, grasping for control. "Assassins in the garden! Arrest the Qazāli immediately!"

A cordon of palace soldiers in their white-edged cloaks surrounded the acrobats. Some even came for Touraine while others looked after Aranen.

Touraine half stood, a furious shout on her lips and the abandoned sword in her hand, but Luca shoved her back to the ground. Touraine glared at her in outrage. Luca didn't care. If Touraine stood with that blade bared at the duke, the duke's personal guard wouldn't hesitate to shoot her.

"No!" Luca screamed from her knees, one hand outstretched to the guards as if she could halt them with the force of her will. "No! Stand down, in the name of the princess!"

"Arrest them!" Nicolas countermanded.

The soldiers slowed in confusion, like ants scuttling through honey.

Luca pushed herself from the ground and planted herself beside her uncle. "I said no! The Qazāli are under my protection. Search the grounds for the culprits. We'll question the staff. The Qazāli are not to be touched."

"You've risked the lives of our entire court, inviting your pet Qazāli into the safety of the palace," Nicolas said. His voice carried across the garden. "They were here the last time a noble died, too."

The remaining guests fell into two positions: huddling fearfully among each other, searching the pockets of darkness over their shoulders and trying to stay as close to the guards as possible; or otherwise blustering and drawing their own ornamental blades and trying to look as if they knew what to do with them.

Those close enough to hear Nicolas's accusation gasped.

"Don't you dare use Bastien like this," Luca growled. Then, raising her voice: "Guards, see to the safety of our guests. *All* of our guests. Get anyone who can't walk to the infirmary. Everyone, if you can walk, go to your rooms immediately and keep your own guards close."

Everyone who wasn't performing immediate aid stared at the contest of wills before them. The silence in the garden was taut and oppressive. The otherworldly magic of the night had transformed. The joyful smoke and sparks had blown away, leaving guttering candles and deep shadows.

"Guards, arrest them." Nicolas's eyes narrowed almost imperceptibly behind his blue star-speckled mask. Still loud enough to carry, he said, "Princess, your Qazāli have made no attempt to hide their disdain for us. If you truly care about your people's well-being, stand aside. We'll release them if they prove innocent after investigation."

Luca scoffed. "If they prove innocent?" She held her hand up to stop the approach of soldiers. "There's no evidence to prove them guilty."

Every moment Luca spent here was a moment she wasn't with Sabine. Sabine, who could be dying right now.

It was that fact and the way her uncle stood with the certainty that he had this well in hand—that he had *her* well in hand—that made Luca stand up taller. With his height and his bulk, he definitely appeared more powerful. His clothing hadn't been sliced to tatters in a duel, either.

Everyone had watched her win that duel, though. Brice had limped away with red spreading on the seat of his trousers to prove it. That counted for something.

"You." Luca jerked her head to a few soldiers standing by. Not the ones who had jumped to Nicolas's order to arrest the Qazāli. "Escort my guests to the suite of rooms prepared for them. Stay nearby for their protection."

The soldiers hesitated. Luca held her breath. Nicolas stepped closer to the acrobats, using his size and proximity to intimidate. It worked: as a group, the acrobats leaned away. The soldiers looked to each other. Then they looked to their lieutenant, who turned to Gil.

The king's old champion nodded.

The soldiers led the acrobats into the palace.

The look Nicolas sent Gil was murderous, but when he turned back to Luca, his own mask was back: unworried condescension, the indulgence of a precocious child. Her own chest heaved with adrenaline.

*I'll show you precocious.*

"Ambassador, accompany your Qazāli," she told Touraine. "I need to see to the safety of my people if the duke will not."

Luca didn't think Nicolas was guilty of this attack—there were too many other nobles being carried to the palace or attended to on the lawn, some of whom were certainly on his side. The truth didn't matter right now. What mattered was planting the seed of suspicion in their minds. The duke they supported was no longer protecting them.

Would it make them afraid enough to support her, or too afraid to abandon him? Luca couldn't know. Likely would not know until the Trial of Competence. The soldiers had followed her orders, though, and the nobles present had seen that.

"The rest of you!" Luca yelled into her uncle's face. He didn't flinch. His face was utterly calm, and later, Luca might worry about what he was thinking, but not right now. "The rest of you, tear this garden apart," she ordered. "Find the poisoners."

Fili ran.

She'd watched the princess's duel, awestruck—the way she used the cane to support her as she fought! For a second, she'd even wondered if she could make a better cane to suit this kind of fighting.

Then the dark-haired noblewoman with the tight trousers had collapsed. A noble Qazāli caught her, and then Fili knew only one thing—she needed to get out of there. If the guards caught her—if the princess recognized her somehow—*if this got back to her mother*—!

*Shit, shit, shit.* She didn't know it would happen like this. So quick.

Fili wove through the frightened crowd toward the back of the garden. She could hide back there if she had to. She couldn't help looking back. The serving boy who'd been at the table with her—he was innocent. The palace guard couldn't torture the whole kitchen staff, could they?

*This is the price for change*, Brother Michel had said.

"You there! Stop!" A woman's command followed Fili. It spurred her faster.

Into the maze of the garden paths, away from the light and panic and the crash of soldiers. The solace of the hedges. She wasn't supposed to leave like this; she was supposed to report back to Sister Maxime. Sister Maxime would understand.

Except Fili couldn't find a gate. Thick, high walls made of rose-bushes with wicked thorns closed the garden in. The roses were dead, some of the leaves and petals littering the ground beneath her boots. She reached into the wall and let the thorns prick her finger. Scratch her arm. She bled a little. She bled enough. In the quiet dark, she let herself become still. Her mind, her body, all still. The branches around her arm rustled and creaked as they grew into a new shape. They became supple again, and as the hole widened enough for her to squeeze through, new roses began to blossom.

She broke through the hole the hedge made for her and escaped back to the city.

# CHAPTER 31

# OF WALLS

The bells went quiet.

After seeing the acrobats to their rooms, Touraine found Luca slumped in a seat in the anteroom of the infirmary, resting her head on her hands, which rested on her cane. Her cloak and coat hadn't been retrieved after the duel, so she sat with her shirtsleeves sliding down her forearms to her elbows. Everything about her looked dull and exhausted, from the gold of her hair to the slump of her proud shoulders.

Luca raised her head at the sound of Touraine's steps. Through the doorway, Touraine saw Aranen leaning over a bed.

"How is she?" Touraine asked Luca in a low voice.

The chilly aloofness Luca had worn all night and for the last two weeks was gone. Luca sat back in the cushioned chair and let her head fall back for a second. Were those . . . tears glistening on her eyelashes?

"No," Touraine breathed. Her grief rings dug hard into her fingers.

She sat on the seat next to Luca, and in the silence of hope and fear, Touraine put a hand on Luca's knee. Luca took it in her own, and they waited.

Luca's hand was warm, the long, pale fingers still spattered with faded ink. They laced tight into Touraine's. The cord between them was there again, and Touraine felt Luca might drown if she let her go.

Aranen came out, head bowed and mouth drawn tight. When she saw them sitting there, hands clasped, her mouth pressed even tighter.

Too late, Touraine jumped to her feet. Luca followed more slowly but just as anxiously.

"Is she—"

"She's alive," Aranen said quickly. "And will probably stay alive, but I can't promise anything."

"Thank you, Aranen din," Luca said. "Thank you." She limped past Aranen and into the infirmary proper.

"What was it?" Touraine asked.

"Poison in the wine, I think. And I—" Aranen cut off abruptly, then shook her head and continued, "Romanie, the palace physician, helped me. I recognized the herb—the poison one, but she knew the antidote." Aranen chuckled darkly. "Apparently the poison was common enough for assassinations in the past that they keep its antidote stocked. But the marquise wasn't the only one, and the others..."

"Dead?"

"Some. Romanie tried to get as many into the infirmary as she could. We both thought it would be best if I waited here. The nobles don't trust me."

Touraine's heart sank into her stomach, not for the nobles but for Aranen.

"How do you do it?" Touraine whispered, giving voice to the secret tumult in her own heart. The pull of Luca and her cold rebuff. Ghadin's aching absence and the growing certainty that she was gone forever.

"This is all I have, remember?" Aranen said, looking down at her hands. "This...duty Shāl has given me." She sounded disgusted, and Touraine wondered if it was disgust for the Balladairans or if Aranen fought the same self-hatred that she did.

Aranen had said this very thing one day long ago in Qazāl, when Touraine asked her why she kept working so hard at the temple even though her wife was dying. Aranen had lost so much, and yet, here she was, still giving to those who had taken it away.

"I'll be all right." Aranen took Touraine's hand and gave it a squeeze. Then she gave the infirmary room—Luca and Durfort—a meaningful glance. "Be careful with them. And wipe that paint off as soon as you get a chance. It's toxic, too, you know."

She chuckled wearily at Touraine's alarm, then left.

Touraine joined Luca at Durfort's bedside. Sabine LeMarchal de Durfort lay in her shirtsleeves, blanket pulled up to her armpits against the chill. Normally, the woman seemed to take up all the air in any room as she pranced about like a warhorse on parade. Now she looked deflated, all that muscle too soft in repose.

Luca stood beside her, one hand brushing Durfort's fingers gently. Luca's eyes flicked over to Touraine. "She's asleep." Luca sounded as if she didn't believe the words.

"Take some time with her." Touraine had seen for herself. That was enough.

She wet a cloth in the washing area and scrubbed her face as she returned to the anteroom. She turned at Luca's footfall.

The princess's blue-green eyes were damp and her lips trembled even though she'd taken the bottom one in her teeth. She held her hands in fists by her sides, the slight length of her nails digging into her palms. She looked brittle. Not fragile. She wasn't breakable because she was precious or delicate; she was hard and rigid by necessity. Touraine could see already, with lightning clarity, that that rigidity would be Luca's doom.

She wanted so badly for that not to be true. She never wanted to see Luca shatter, but she knew she would never see Luca bend.

As they stood there, staring at each other, lips parted, Touraine's mind went utterly empty.

The silence stretched long enough for Luca's expression to start to thaw and then freeze over again. "Do you need another favor, Your Excellency? Because I'd rather you just ask."

Luca's voice wavered, and Touraine feared that Luca would shatter right now, right here.

Touraine took a half step toward her, tugged forward by the expressions flickering on Luca's face. Blank coldness, then something fiery, then back again. A wall was crumbling and Luca was trying desperately to hold it up.

The tug pulled Luca forward, too, until they were close enough for Touraine to put her hand on Luca's cheek. Luca's silver mask had been lost after the duel, too. Her cheek was warm against Touraine's palm.

"Don't toy with me, Touraine."

The anger coupled with need in Luca's voice sent a sharp twist through Touraine's stomach.

Luca held Touraine's gaze, waiting.

Like an army. Watch the enemy march into range. Hold your breath. Finger on the trigger. Wait for the command to fire.

Touraine's eyelids fluttered shut, her pulse jumping. "Luca." Her voice hoarse. Her fingers curled against Luca's cheek.

In the silence that followed, the warmth against her hand disappeared. Touraine opened her eyes. The princess had retreated, was trying and failing to regain her composure.

Touraine wanted that heat again.

*Fuck.*

"Your Excellency," Luca started, voice just as hoarse. "You should g—"

Touraine closed the distance between them and brought her hand to Luca's neck. Ran her own thumb against Luca's pink lips, parted mid-speech.

She pressed her mouth onto Luca's, and the princess opened for her. Touraine whimpered with hunger. Tongues slid against each other. Wine on Luca's breath. Rose perfume in her hair. Both hands holding Luca's face to hers as Luca—*oh sweet sky above, finally*—gripped the lapels of Touraine's coat and yanked her close, moaning softly into her mouth.

"Fuck," Touraine thought again, aloud this time, as they broke apart. They looked at each other, frozen. As one, they assessed the room, empty except for the infirmary where Durfort slept off the poison. The rest of the infirmary's anteroom was furnished like any personal sitting room—cushioned chairs, a small table for the tea tray.

They locked eyes again.

"Back," Touraine breathed.

Luca looked over her shoulder at the bare bit of wall behind her. She nodded.

They went—Luca knocked over the small table; Touraine kicked aside a footstool—and when Touraine pinned her up against the wall, Luca pulled her close again. Her hand cupped Touraine's neck and Touraine shuddered against her. Luca's kisses were insistent, as demanding as Luca herself, claiming her with teeth and nails. She hissed into Luca's mouth as the pain sent pleasure surging through her. She pulled away to see Luca staring, lips swollen. For a second, there was nothing but the heat of their panting breaths. Then a slow smirk spread across that mouth.

It was infuriating. It was intoxicating.

Touraine shoved Luca back into the wall, digging her nails into Luca's waist, knotting her hand in Luca's hair. She jerked Luca's head back, tilting her chin up, exposing her bare throat. Luca gasped in surprise, her other hand splayed against the wall. Slowly, Touraine exhaled, skimming her lips along Luca's chin, letting her breath tickle the princess's jaw. She shivered, went slack, and Touraine tightened her grip. Luca tensed rigid again, pressing her body flush against her.

"Is this what you want, Your Highness?" Touraine hissed into Luca's ear. Because Touraine wanted. Sky above and earth below, she *wanted*.

Luca's voice came strained, barely a whisper. "Yes."

"Louder."

Luca struggled to swallow, her throat moving against Touraine's wrist. This time, Luca's voice was deep and commanding and *so hungry*.

"I said, *yes*."

Touraine stifled her groan with her teeth in the other woman's neck, thrilled by the princess's gasp. She twisted open the buttons on Luca's chemise. Slid her hand inside and over the soft give of Luca's chest.

Luca caught her hand. Kissed her fingers. Moved them to the buttons of her trousers. She raised an eyebrow, wary again. Her grip tightened on Touraine's wrist, enough to hurt. Touraine's other hand was still tangled in her hair. "Do you want this?"

Touraine took a deep, shaking breath. "Please."

Luca snaked her arm around Touraine's shoulders while her other hand fumbled past Touraine's belt and inside her trousers. Touraine let go of Luca's hair, digging her nails into Luca's back instead, bracing them both against the wall while she—

"Hold on to me," Touraine said against Luca's lips.

"I—" Luca moaned as Touraine slipped inside her. The rest was quiet breaths hitching and Luca's hand slick on her and the gentle knock of their bodies against the wall until—*oh, fuck, oh, fuck, oh*— Luca's hips strained violently toward Touraine's wrist, her nails digging into Touraine's shoulders, her soft cry in Touraine's ear. They collapsed against each other, Touraine holding them steady until Luca's grip eased and she got her own feet under her again.

They smiled, then, damp foreheads pressed together. Luca laughed deep in her throat as she caught her breath. "Sky a-fucking-bove."

"I'll say." Slow, sardonic applause from the other side of the room yanked their attention.

Durfort leaned against the lintel of the infirmary door.

"Oh, for fuck's sake," Touraine muttered.


The warmth flooding Luca's body turned to ice water.

"Sabine." Luca straightened and pulled her trousers up from around her hips while Touraine surreptitiously wiped her hand inside her own pocket.

"Your Highness. Your *Excellency*." Sabine gave Touraine a wry salute.

"Durfort."

Touraine looked to Luca for her cue. For once, Luca couldn't read the other woman's expression. Luca forced herself to act as if she hadn't just been caught fucking a foreign dignitary.

"You're awake. I'm so relieved you're feeling better."

"You could say that." Sabine pushed herself upright, still steadying herself on the doorframe. Her shirt was barely half-buttoned, showing a deep V of her own bare chest; apparently voyeurism was more important than dressing properly.

"Touraine, could you please leave us? The marquise and I need to talk."

Luca's irritation at Sabine sharpened her words, and she wished she could take them back as soon as they'd left her lips. Too late. Touraine's eyes widened with hurt, and it was worse than if she'd shuttered herself off. Luca took her hand—that perfect hand—and tried to make herself soft again, but the sweet luster of Touraine's eyes had gone hard and metallic.

"As you wish, Your Highness." She bowed and left without another word, slamming the door behind her. Luca winced.

"What was *that*, Your Highness?"

Luca couldn't tell how much of Sabine's lean was exhaustion and poison and how much her insouciance.

"Did you enjoy it?" Luca asked through clenched teeth.

"Oh, very much. A little lonely over here, though."

"Next time, we'll invite you."

"I live in hope."

They stared at each other from across the room, each waiting for a signal from the other.

"What, then?" Luca said. "You have something to say. Say it."

"You're not going to like it."

"So get it over with."

Sabine sighed and limped over to the nearest chair, where she sagged, curling in on herself. Her face did look drawn, and her hair was mussed where she'd fallen and seized and then lay in the infirmary bed.

"Luca...El-Qazāli is...handsome. Beautiful. Fierce. Clever. And so fucking charmingly naive about power that it's going to be the death of her. The death of you. The death of your ambitions to the throne. Even if the way she walks around scowling with that pretty mouth of hers wasn't a political disaster waiting to happen, there's everyone else. No one wants to embrace the Qazāli. Not in a treaty.

Not in the city. They want the colonies back, as colonies. As far as they can tell, you and her—you're the ones who lost that for them. I know you think it's the best way in the long run—alliances, magic, all of that—but no one else does, and you'll get nowhere without more of them on your side."

Luca gaped at Sabine incredulously. "You've been needling me about her since before she arrived. You were practically begging to take us both to bed!"

"Discreetly! The way you moon after her—I've been dying for you to get it out of your system! Now that you have, let it go."

Luca looked slowly from her hands to Sabine's face. The disgust in Luca's expression must've been so sharp—Sabine flinched. Luca was splintering, leaving jagged edges for the two of them to impale themselves on.

She held Sabine's eyes in heavy silence before saying, "You're worried about what they'll say about me?"

"Already saying." Sabine looked away guiltily. "I'd rather not repeat it."

"I saw the broadsides last year. The Qazāli's whore. I've heard that and worse. What does that make you?"

"Not even that, I suppose," Sabine said with a rueful chuckle, trying to shrug away from Luca's building attack.

"No, tell me. What's the difference? You and her in the maze the day Bastien died?"

"I know—"

"You and her in the salle? How many times?"

"None!" Sabine yelled. "But I don't have a throne to win back! I don't have an entire empire watching my every move!"

The sting of Sabine's words was oddly satisfying. It felt good to have a reason to bite back. To lash out and protect—something.

"Of course not," Luca riposted. "What use do they have for a debt-ridden marquise whose sharpest asset is her sword? You're a liability."

"Better that than a queen who can't put her kingdom before her cunt."

The cruel words fell to the ground between them slowly, like the falling feathers of a shot bird. Sabine's bare chest heaved, flushed as pink as her face.

Luca realized what she was protecting with a sudden expansion in her chest, as if the hollow places inside of her were filling up.

"I love her." The words came out sounding astonished, and so Luca repeated them again, this time accepting the words as true, imbuing them with this certainty that filled her when she thought of Touraine. "I love her, Sabine."

And with that certainty came another: that fact alone would make taking her throne more difficult. Sabine was right. The nobles she tried to gather to her cause would think Luca weak; a foreigner's puppet. They would think this was the reason she lost their colonies, and she would continue to lose the rest. The Qazāli Council thought the same thing. This single truth would disrupt the one thing Luca had been striving for, and in fact, probably already had before Luca had even realized it. If she wanted her throne, if she believed the crown was the best way to do everything that she wanted—including help the Qazāli—she needed to put this feeling aside.

Luca let out a laughing sob, and Sabine startled.

"Luca, I'm sorr—"

"Don't apologize. You've had a difficult evening. I'll leave you to your rest. I'm sorry we woke you." Her voice was as bright as fool's gold. "Since you're so concerned with the fate of the empire, though, rest assured—no one is worth more than my crown. Not a rebel soldier. Not even a spoiled marquise."

And if she could will herself cold enough, hard enough to convince Sabine, perhaps she could convince her own trembling heart. She could will it so.

Touraine felt like she was watching her guts spill to the ground as she stood on the other side of the door, listening to Luca and Durfort. A sudden hollowness inside, where there used to be something vital, but also something she'd taken for granted. She was falling through the air all over again.

*No one is worth more than my crown.*

"This is your own fault," Touraine grumbled to herself as she strode through the palace corridors. "You idiot. You stupid fucking—" Her voice broke, and she bit her knuckle to stifle the sob in her chest. *You should have kept your distance. She already told you who she is. She showed you over and over again.*

Everyone had warned her.

She let her feet take her back to the gardens, to where she could distract herself with utility. The way she'd distracted herself for the last few weeks. Anything to keep her from feeling helpless over Ghadin or guilty over Luca.

*I love her*, Luca said.

The gardens were full of palace soldiers with white piping on their uniforms. How many of them were Luca's now, and how many were the duke's?

The festivity had been abandoned as it lay. Fallen masks on the ground, food half-eaten dropped among them. It might not even be cleaned until all the servants had been questioned.

"Your Excellency!"

Touraine whirled around at Captain Perrot's voice. "Perrot." Touraine cleared her throat and surreptitiously wiped her hand on her trousers again. "Anything?"

"Actually," he said, "yes." He looked shiftily around them, then led her deeper into the garden.

Touraine followed him toward the outer hedge wall. All of the candles had blown out or guttered into wax puddles.

"Look, Ambassador. I know I'm not supposed to know what you and the princess get up to—"

Touraine missed a step.

"—all that talk of magic and uncivilized shit—"

"Watch it," Touraine growled, relieved and irritated at the same time.

"—but some of the other blackcoats saw something. Said they chased someone down this way."

A feeling of foreboding prickled up her back. She kept her hand on the hilt of her sword, ready to draw it if Perrot turned on her in the dark corners. She thought of Bastien, throat slit and sprawled in the heart of the maze. The cracked masks on the ground turned sinister. The path was lined with the work of some famed sculptor or another, the shapes hulking in the shadows. Only sprinkled starlight lit the path. The longest night of the year. How much more darkness until the sun rose?

The outside of the hedge maze stretched overhead to the right. The hedge to the left was thicker, but winter had stripped it just as dead. Through the gaps in the branches, she could just make out a stretch of empty land that would probably lead into the city.

"What are we looking for?" Touraine asked.

Perrot halted so abruptly that she collided into the solid wall of his back.

Then Touraine saw what had stopped Perrot in his tracks.

Everywhere in the garden, winter had taken its toll on the plants: leaves littered the ground or clung singly to branches, their colorless petals blew along the paths, and bare twigs and their thorns were all that was left of the magnificent hedge walls that would bloom in the spring. Except this small section of the outer hedge wall was already blooming. A thicket of roses blossomed, the flowers as big as Touraine's hands. And, as if pruned and shaped by an expert gardener, the new roses had grown so that they left a gap in the hedge—enough for a person to squeeze through.

To the left and right of this spot, though, the hedge was dead—as it should be in early winter. Yet here, in this one spot, summer was unconquered.

Touraine stepped closer to the bush. She closed her eyes and inhaled. It smelled like Luca, being pressed against her, breathing in her ear. Touraine's stomach tugged with remembered pleasure, and she shot her eyes open.

"What is it?" Perrot asked behind her.

"I'm . . . not sure."

Touraine snapped a blossom from the hedge, gouging herself on the thorns.

Thing was, she did know what. Balladaire's magic. Balladaire's god. The question was *how*. The question was *who*.

# CHAPTER 32

# OF AGONY

Touraine found Aranen in the infirmary first thing in the morning. Her gaze skirted over the wall she had fucked Luca against. She closed her eyes as a shiver ran through her at the memory, and clenched them tight at the kick of pain when the rest of the memory caught up. She had *not* spent the night replaying any of it.

She cleared her throat. "Aranen?" She knocked on the edge of the door before entering.

She brushed the petals of the rose she'd taken from the unnatural section of the hedge wall. The flower was white and as large as her two hands cupped together, the petals as thin and soft as down. Its thorns, though, had left scratches on her hands and one surprisingly deep puncture wound, but she hadn't been able to strip them off the stem. They were strong as steel. Touraine would never have imagined she'd be frightened of flowers, and yet, here she was, trembling as she brought the evidence to Aranen.

The priestess and the Balladairan physician, Romanie, were tidying the room. They both looked haggard, and Touraine wondered if, like her, they had kept their own all-night vigils over the longest night of the year. Luckily, there was no sign of Durfort.

Aranen's eyebrows rose in surprise as Touraine entered, taking in the rose. "Touraine. I'm afraid I'm in no state to entertain suitors."

A day before and Touraine would have met the older woman's joke with a riposte of her own, but she couldn't muster more than a flat look. The worry lines around Aranen's eyes deepened. She shared a silent exchange with Romanie, who nodded and slipped out with a basket of linens and empty glass bottles. She gave Touraine a probing look as she passed by her.

When the door had closed behind the Balladairan, Aranen asked, "What now, in Shāl's name?"

Touraine held out the rose. "Perrot showed me this last night."

Her chaperone hadn't followed her back to her rooms, nor had he been there when she woke. Touraine had a feeling that his absence meant nothing good for her, but she had still felt a thrill at the small freedom.

"It's a rose."

"It is."

"A large one."

"A very large one."

Aranen shook her head, waiting for Touraine to explain.

"In winter."

"Ah. I see." Aranen examined the rose with new suspicion. When Touraine held it out for her to inspect, the priestess shook her head. "What am I supposed to do with this? Go tell the princess."

Touraine touched the tip of her thumb to a thorn, flirting with the pain.

"What did you do, Touraine?"

"Nothing," she shot back, hating the way her voice cracked when she spoke.

Something of the heartache leaked out, though, because the tight lines of suspicion in Aranen's face eased just a little.

"It was her, then? I told you to be careful—"

"I know," Touraine snapped. "I know what you told me and you were right. It's done now. This"—she held up the rose—"is not. And I don't know... I don't know if we should go to her with it or not."

Aranen backed off slightly, folding her arms across her chest and ducking her head. "You want to tell her, though, don't you?"

Touraine shrugged helplessly. "It's their magic. What good does it do us?"

"And yet, you brought it to me instead. What do you want from me? A better idea, something that hurts her back? Withhold it and sabotage her? Or is it that you want me to give you permission to give it to her?"

Touraine's face flared hot. She had spent the night full of angst and adrenaline, spinning between finding Luca immediately and trying to think of the most painful way she could throw the knowledge in the other woman's face.

"The Taargens made me—made Qazāl an offer. We could leave her to sort her own shit out. Join them." Betray Luca. Betray all of Balladaire.

"You'd make an enemy of her, as well?"

"It wouldn't be the first time."

Aranen pressed her lips tight. "It will be much harder to come back from if you do it again."

Aranen, the healer, the mediator. The one who had been right about Luca. The one person Touraine still had on her side.

She looked up at Aranen pitifully. "Then what?"

"Oh, my dear," Aranen whispered in Shālan.

Touraine was not expecting to be gathered up into the other woman's arms, not expecting the softness of the other woman's neck. She smelled of sandalwood and lavender and herbs and pungent spirits. The willowy woman's flowing garments hid surprising strength. If Touraine held on any longer, she would break into tears. It would be a rout. She didn't let go.

Aranen broke the embrace first, pushing Touraine to arm's length. Her golden eyes were shining.

"When I met Djasha, I hated her a little. More than a little. We studied together at the university, and she was the most conceited, most arrogant, must insufferable person I knew."

Touraine almost asked, *What about Jaghotai?* Aranen had a far-off look in her eyes, though, like she had a story to tell, not a quip.

"Obviously," the priestess continued, "we fell madly in bed. Even I had to admit that she was the most talented healer anyone had ever seen. Her faith was that strong. My own faith grew because of hers. She was also curious. A brilliant researcher, a theorist of Shāl's gifts. And her own people's history followed her."

"Djaya's Folly," Touraine murmured to herself. Djasha had told her the story. Djaya, the last Brigāni emperor of the old Shālan Empire, whose use of Shāl's killing gift for conquest instead of peace and protection cursed her city and her lineage.

Aranen heard her and nodded. "Djaya's Folly." She let her hands slide off Touraine's shoulders and hugged her arms around her own body, angling away from Touraine. "Djasha didn't like not knowing the whole of her power. She wanted it all. She searched and searched, all the way back into the First Library in the Cursed City."

Where Luca had tried to go in her own arrogant quest for something better left alone.

"She found it, though."

"She did. But I didn't know. I left her when she wouldn't leave her research. I wasn't—Qazāl has a long, unpleasant history with the Brigāni and the ākilīn. So when she found what she was looking for, and then when she left to find her family, I didn't know. I didn't want to know."

Aranen closed her eyes, and this time tears spilled over her lids, tracking streaks of kohl.

"Later, years later, she told me she was trying to find oblivion." Aranen looked to the royal soldier sitting in the corner of the anteroom. For once, he wasn't feigning disinterest. His eyes were bright and intent as he listened. Aranen didn't seem to care. "She came back cold and detached. I thought that the fire that had burned so bright in her had finally gone out in grief."

Aranen smiled self-deprecatingly. "She'd lost her magic, lost her faith, but she was still brilliant. We were happy. For a while. Until the Blood General came and took you children away. I wasn't paying attention, though. I didn't see the flame kindle again, burning up the blanket of contentment I thought we'd smothered it with."

The priestess thumbed her tears away, smearing the dark streaks. More tears came and she wiped them away, too. When she spoke again, it was in a tired whisper that was at once exasperated and devastated.

"I thought that I would be enough."

"But—you were. She loved you," Touraine said quickly, stupidly. "She almost killed me when I let you get taken."

Aranen laughed and took a shuddering breath. "Oh, I know. She adored me. She would have moved the earth and sky for me. That's what was so frightening. As much as she loved me, she wanted to bend the world even more. All I ever wanted was her and the life we'd built, teaching and healing. Even without her magic, Djasha wanted to remake the world."

"She saved Qazāl."

"She's dead," Aranen barked.

Touraine jerked back.

"She got herself killed and I broke an oath of peace I swore to my god when I murdered the woman who killed her. I haven't been able to touch my own magic since." Aranen leaned in close, grabbing Touraine's arms again and squeezing tight. "When I say *be careful*, I mean that fire consumes all that it touches."

"Not everything," Touraine countered.

"No, not everything. What will you have to become to withstand her flames?"

Touraine straightened into the digging of Aranen's nails. Touraine had a feeling that she knew the answer, that it lay in depths that she didn't care to excavate.

She seized on the other, easier thing Aranen said. "You haven't been able to touch your magic?"

Three heavy but ordered knocks on the door interrupted them. *Soldier*, Touraine's brain supplied just before Perrot opened the door.

"Your Excellencies," he said in a rush.

"What happened?" Touraine and Aranen said at the same time.

Perrot closed the door behind him, secretive in a way Touraine had

never known the guard to be. She put her hand on her long knife—
she'd replaced the gaudy sword Durfort had given her; if she had to
have a weapon from one of those women, better the one she knew how
to use—but Perrot didn't move on them.

"The duke has arrested the Qazāli. From last night. They're being
taken to Le Fontinard right now."

"What?" Touraine asked. "How do you know?"

"I have friends, Your Excellency. I thought you might want to be
kept updated, so I asked." He shrugged as if it were nothing, his face
pink.

"That sky-falling jackalfucker," Touraine swore across both languages. She swore again as the rose's thorns pricked her hand in her
too-tight grip. "Take me to them. Or take me to the duke."

"Aye," he said. "But there's something else."

"Sky above, what, man?"

"They said there's a Qazāli girl there, too. She's been there for a
couple of weeks."

Touraine's mouth opened—closed. Opened again. There was no
breath in her.

Aranen found the words first. "The duke has Ghadin."

The duke's man nodded. "Probably. It could be any girl, but—
probably."

"How long have you known about this?" Touraine's knife appeared
in her hand, naked blade pointing at the soldier's throat. "Have you
been pretending to look for her with me, to keep me in the dark?"

Perrot didn't flinch. "I only found out this morning."

Touraine roared in frustration. "Take me to him. Now."

Perrot had the nerve to look to Aranen for direction first.

"Talk to Princess Luca first—" Aranen said.

"The duke. Now."

She yelled outside of the duke's library, pounding on the door for him
to let her in. When he didn't answer and she'd raised enough of a fury

for Perrot to assure her that the duke probably really wasn't inside because who would willingly sit and listen to her shouting like a madwoman, Touraine pressed her forehead against the locked door.

"How much of every move we made has gotten back to the duke?" she said to the door. The request for a grain ship. To escape. The hunt for Ghadin. Luca's hunt for Balladairan magic and what they'd found in Champs d'Or. Any of it could have given Nicolas the leverage he needed.

She had taken for granted that Perrot wasn't really *her* guard, not like Lanquette and Deniaud were to Luca. It was another trapping of the nobility that Touraine had stepped into, as she'd stepped into the waistcoats, into Durfort's salle, into the stables. Perrot owed Touraine no loyalty at all.

"You know as well as I do that you can't choose your job," Perrot said stiffly.

Touraine sighed. She had blown out most of her fury. Only things left were fatigue and a deep, belly-rooted fear for Ghadin. She turned her head, still leaning against the wooden door. She met his eyes, baleful glare against baleful glare.

"Did you fight in the war?" she asked him abruptly.

"Aye. I was at Birne during the second year. Vauteur's Field."

Touraine turned, incredulous. Perrot, though, sounded carefully blank and emotionless.

The battle of Vauteur's Field had been one of the darkest days for Balladaire in the second Taargen War. A company of Balladairan soldiers had been sandwiched between Taargen cavalry and Taargen infantry, and when the two Taargen cohorts came together, the Balladairan soldiers in between had been all but massacred.

"You survived."

"Aye. One of a handful."

She appraised him with new eyes. When she spoke again, she kept her voice just as carefully empty. "That's when they brought us out. The conscripts. After Vauteur's Field." She turned and dug her fingertips into the wood. She focused on the little half moons her nails made. "They were afraid too many more Balladairan-blooded casualties would lessen support for the war effort. I wasn't even twenty."

Perrot grunted softly as if he'd been punched in the paunch. "I'm sorry."

Touraine shrugged. "Orders are orders."

They turned at the sound of heavy footsteps. The duke strode down the corridor toward them, a broad smile on his face.

"I hoped to see you here. Are you ready to sign the treaty?"

"Where did you take her, you bearfucker? Are you going to hold her hostage for your rape of a treaty?"

Touraine lunged for the man, knife drawn. She'd tear him apart with her bare fucking hands if she had to—

Perrot's thick arm made a bar around her chest, pulling her against him and arresting her in place. Half of Duke Ancier's guards aimed their bayoneted rifles at her; the other half drew swords.

"Fuck you, Perrot," she growled.

"Don't get yourself killed," he whispered, beard scratching against her cheek.

It took everything in Touraine to let the half-sprung desire to kill ebb from her body. If the duke's guards skewered her, she'd have to trust Luca to get Ghadin free. Shāl damn her eyes if she would die leaving Luca as Ghadin's best hope. Slowly, Perrot released his restraint.

Duke Ancier tsked. "Your language... Well, it's as befits you, I suppose. Would you like to come inside? We can discuss this over wine, like civilized people."

"Fuck your wine, Ancier. Where's Ghadin? Where are the rest of the Qazāli? Luca said they weren't to be harmed."

"Ah, ah. I'm sure you can understand that when several Balladairan nobles are poisoned and some of them tragically succumbed, I must take every allegation seriously. My niece brought in a score of unknown performers from a land with plenty of reasons to do us harm. Rest assured, I have my best people questioning them thoroughly as we speak."

Touraine's stomach turned at the thought of them torturing Ghadin. She clenched her fists, powerless, as she looked up into his eyes. "You know Ghadin had nothing to do with this. None of them had anything to do with it, and if you actually cared, you'd see that it was a Qazāli who helped care for your precious nobles."

"And yet, no Qazāli succumbed to the illness. Curious." The duke stepped closer, not afraid to use his bulk to take up space and reposition his opponent.

Touraine sneered. "You don't believe that."

"Who's to say what I believe? Especially since neither you nor the priestess used your miraculous healing magic to save any of my people."

"I told you, I can't do it. It doesn't work like that."

"Oh? Then how does it work, Your Excellency? Because the comtesse des Champs d'Or seems to believe otherwise. I never gave the stories credence, but she told me of a miraculous thing you did."

The blood drained from Touraine's face. While the back of her mind replayed the charade with Ghadin and Luca in Lady Bel-Jadot's menagerie, the rest of her held taut as a half-pulled trigger while the duke spoke.

"Imagine my surprise when she told me how you healed your little protégée's broken leg!" He narrowed his eyes. "I should very much like to see that."


Le Fontinard was an old fortress turned prison. It held all sorts of prisoners—political adversaries, nobles guilty of murder, and apparently, acrobats and girls the duke thought made useful bargaining chits.

Duke Ancier's soldiers had also picked up Aranen, and now she and Touraine followed the duke through the stone halls of the prison flanked by palace guards that Touraine didn't recognize.

The duke led them up a spiral staircase in one corner of the prison, and Touraine counted one, two landings before they stopped. The duke unlocked the first door they came to and ushered in a tall, thin woman in an unmarked soldier's uniform. There were no rank sheaves, no gold buttons, no piping to designate where she was stationed. She was just shy of middle age, her face creased and tendrils of pale hair falling loose from her military cap. She wore gloves as black as the rest of her uniform.

The duke's other soldiers pressed Touraine and Aranen into the room. Touraine's eyes shot immediately to the ragged heap in the corner, ankles chained to the wall.

"Ghadin!" Touraine cried. She surged forward only to be clamped back by a guard on either side.

"Mulāzim!" Ghadin sobbed, tears cutting tracks through the dirt on her face.

"Now," the duke said, pulling a knife from his belt. "Let's try this again."

A pair of guards restrained Aranen, too. The duke smiled and gestured to the unmarked soldier, who unbuttoned the cuffs of her coat and folded them back, revealing pale forearms in the dimly lit room. Her skin seemed to glow in the light filtering in from the corridor's tapers. The green fan of veins stood out starkly.

Then, without comment or hesitation, the woman held her arm out, and the duke gave her a short, perfunctory slash across the meatiest part. The woman didn't make a sound, only turned her gaze to Touraine and Aranen, arm still proffered.

"Well?" Duke Ancier raised his eyebrows.

He reminded Touraine of Cantic when she would come to observe her and the other Sands as they practiced fighting, or when she was waiting for a recitation of Balladairan history, to make sure they were learning. Becoming more civilized.

"I can't," Touraine gritted through her teeth.

"Am I to disbelieve the Lady Bel-Jadot? She's hardly a woman to be taken by fancies like my dear niece. Eminently practical is the comtesse. So show me what had her so convinced. Convince me, too, and I might consider a different arrangement of the treaty. Surely you wouldn't hold back your most valuable playing piece? Not when you're about to lose?"

Touraine looked desperately toward Aranen, but the priestess had blanched, her lips pressed tight together. Ghadin huddled in the corner, trying to keep as much space between herself and the duke's woman.

"Aranen, please, do something."

When Aranen met her eyes, Touraine knew. A part of her had hoped that Aranen was exaggerating, that she could still do *some* healing.

The priestess closed her eyes and sagged, shrinking in on herself. When she opened her eyes again, tears dripped down her cheeks. "Have mercy, Your Grace. I no longer have the gift. And Touraine is young, her faith uncertain. Neither of us has managed any aspect of Shāl's gift since that day in Qazāl."

"Hmm." Duke Ancier folded his hands behind his back and strolled across the small cell to stand above Ghadin. The knife dripped his own soldier's blood. Ghadin pressed herself against the wall, shrugging herself into as tight a ball as she could.

"I swear, if you hurt her—" Touraine strained against the guards holding her back. She wouldn't rest until she did figure out how to use Shāl's magic. The power to unknit a man's flesh. That potential had coursed through her before.

"Unfortunately, I don't believe you. More motivation, perhaps?" He turned to his soldier and nodded.

The woman took two steps toward Ghadin and snatched the girl's arm. A loud crack split the air, followed by a heart-wrenching wail of pain. Ghadin's arm dangled at an unnatural angle, bone jutting grotesque against fabric, and the girl screamed over and over as she cradled the limb close to her.

Touraine yelled wordlessly, but the guards on either side only held her tighter, locking her so her shoulders ached with every pull.

"Let her go," Duke Ancier said calmly.

The soldiers released her and Touraine fell forward. She turned that forward momentum to her advantage, stumbling toward Nicolas. His

utter calm drew her up short, though. She had no weapon, and by
the time she could kill Nicolas, what could his guards do to her? To
Ghadin?

Yes, she decided then. If she were given the chance, no matter what she had to do, she would tear this man apart. Lifeblood or
otherwise.

She turned from him and threw a fist into the unmarked soldier's
face. The blow twisted the woman's head round sharply. She staggered,
tripping, blood from her cut spattering them all, before she crashed
into the wall and lay still.

Touraine knelt by Ghadin's side while the Balladairans looked on.
"Aranen, help me," she said raggedly. To Ghadin, she murmured, "It'll
be okay, I promise, it'll be okay."

She was growing too used to telling that lie.

Ghadin's screams quelled to whimpers. When she looked at
Touraine, it was clear she knew just how much of a lie it was.

So Touraine told the truth, instead. "I'm sorry," she whispered in
Shālan. "This should never have happened. I'll make him pay."

Aranen knelt beside them. "I haven't eaten any meat in months,"
she said. "I can't even try."

"Does last night count?" Even though Touraine hadn't eaten anything this morning, she'd gorged herself on those stupid little meat
pies in the garden.

"It could—it should be enough."

"Take me through it again?"

It was as they had practiced in Qazāl, on days after Touraine's anatomy lessons when Aranen would guide Touraine through an attempt
at healing a small cut. Each of those times had ended fruitless, though,
and eventually, Touraine grew tired of inflicting the small wounds on
herself, or facing the expectant glances of the fighters with their petty
bruises.

This time, it would be different.

"Breathe," Aranen said. Touraine and Ghadin both obeyed, Ghadin's breath hitching and moaning while Touraine tried to pull her

breath from somewhere deep inside. She reached for the steadiest part of herself but found nothing.

The priestess guided Touraine's hand over to Ghadin's shoulder. The girl cried out, and Aranen murmured soothing nothings. Touraine tried not to let the girl's tears shake her.

"Now what?" Touraine's voice cracked. The duke's eyes bored into her back, and her skin crawled as the Balladairans all looked down on them, the three Qazāli on the ground. She felt sick.

"I…" Aranen hesitated. "I usually think about the way Shāl has made me strong, without fail." She gave a bitter laugh. "I think about the tenets. I believe in them, I believe in Shāl, and…" She let her hands fall open on her lap and looked beseechingly at her empty, inert palms.

She covered Touraine's hand with hers. Beneath her own hand, Touraine felt the hot flush in Ghadin's shoulder as blood flooded the injury. Once, Aranen told her that when the body was hurt, blood would pool into the area in an attempt to repair the damage. To knit. Touraine closed her eyes and focused on that. The heat.

Shāl had made her strong, once. When she'd been kneeling on the ground at Rogan's feet, Shāl had given her that power. It could be there again. It could be there now.

She imagined the pieces inside like they were Aranen's anatomy texts, careful drawings of blood and bone. Shoulder to upper arm, upper arm to elbow, to forearm, to wrist and delicate finger bones. The muscle and ligature that held it all together.

Shāl's tenets…peace over all. Touraine snorted that away in her mind. She didn't want peace. She wanted to rip Ancier's spine out by his throat. That was a means to peace, though, wasn't it? Luca on the throne and peace between Balladaire and Qazāl—

The broken bone. She had seen enough of those to picture the pale splinters clearly. Gently, so gently, she skimmed her hands down Ghadin's shirt and toward the break. The girl flinched beneath her fingers. The shirt was wet with blood where the bone had broken through.

"Balance heals the wound," Aranen murmured softly. As if she knew that Touraine was struggling to anchor herself in the god's teachings. "Truth is at the heart."

Touraine tried to sink deeper. Peace. Balance. Truth. She willed something to happen. Anything.

She didn't know how long she'd been kneeling and breathing and begging before Aranen placed a hand on her shoulder. Touraine looked up and the older woman shook her head. Ghadin had passed out.

"It didn't work, Your Grace." Aranen pushed herself to her feet. "The girl needs medical care now. I can see to her in the normal way, but if not, she'll lose the arm, if she doesn't die."

The duke's expression was dark, his face twisted in disgust and disappointment.

"Clean up this mess," he told his soldiers. "Find room for the ambassadors somewhere here."

"Wait." Touraine pushed herself to one knee and then, with the last bit of strength she had, to both feet. "If we sign the treaty, your version—"

Aranen grabbed her. "Touraine, don't—"

"If we sign it, you'll let us go? Let us take the girl to the infirmary, let us get passage home on a ship?"

The duke pursed his lips, a flicker of excitement crossing his face. "I am a reasonable man."

Touraine held out her arm for a clasp, and the duke's lip curled.

"I'll see this deal signed in ink, like civilized people, with witnesses." His mood had shifted, though. It showed in the bounce in his step as he left the cell. "Escort the ambassadors back to the palace."

Perrot went to take a set of keys off the soldier Touraine had knocked out.

"Not the girl," Duke Ancier threw over his shoulder.

"But you said—" Touraine objected.

"She'll stay here pending your good behavior. I'm not a fool."

"I'll stay in her stead," Aranen said quickly.

"No."

Then the duke was gone.

Touraine glared at Perrot, who still knelt over the unconscious soldier. Even if he did decide to find his balls all of a sudden, they were still outnumbered. They wouldn't get out with Ghadin, not alive.

She clenched her fist so tightly that it shook. She hated this impotence. This helplessness. The only thing Touraine had ever had was her body, that was the one thing she had faith in—not some god. Now even that was failing her. The duke was a tangible enemy, but his strength wasn't. It glided around her like water but kept her trapped like the ocean.

*I'll make this right, Ghadin. I promise.*

# A HEALER'S INTERLUDE 3

Aranen wishes she were alone.

She wishes she could scream. She is burning from the inside with rage.

But she is not alone. The monk who trained with her wife in the mountains, the monk who killed her wife's family, stands against the door of her chambers, protecting her and hers from this treacherous tangle of cobras.

Yet he had not stopped Duke Nicolas Ancier from hurting Ghadin.

"Why didn't you kill him?" Aranen hisses at the monk who is also an assassin who did nothing to help.

Who did nothing, as she had done nothing.

She is rage and she is rage and she is rage, and peace is something she does not believe in.

"I could not."

"You could have. You *can*."

"I will not forswear my god."

"Your god?" Aranen grimaces. Her god feels impossibly far from her, and she feels an urge deep in her fingernails to tear his god from him, too. "Your god is bought by coin paid to your abbots. The same duke who bought the death of that young noble threatens *our* lives now. Us. *Your* debt to *my* wife."

"I will not forswear my god."

Aranen flexes her fingers into claws. There was power in them once. Power to rend, to tear, to *unknit*. To break apart others as she is breaking apart. She wills it to return. It does not. There has been no sacrifice. She tells herself that she has not forsworn her god, either, and yet, she wants to rip her beads off and scatter them like sand in the wind.

"Who is your abbot to decide who should live and who should die?"

"Who are you to decide?" The monk's stare is so neutral that it is judgment as condemning as a curled lip.

"Save your sanctimony," she spits.

Roland Tessaud of the Southern Mountains approaches her as if she is a beast with her teeth bared and jaws slavering. He takes her clawed hands and folds them into his own. His palms are calloused and dry.

He holds her hands and he holds her gaze until her hackles lower and their breath flows in tandem, in and out, in and out.

His eyes are deep and dark, like Djasha's were before they turned. The pulse of his heart ticks below the stubble on his neck.

In.

Out.

"I will not forswear my god," he says, "but I will help however I can."

# PART 4

## QUEENS AND KINGS

# CHAPTER 33

# THE BEGINNING OF THE ENDGAME

Luca read the report for the fifth time. The words were clear, but she couldn't make herself understand.

Brice was taking his company to the south. He'd mentioned that yesterday, goading Touraine. The King's Own cavalry. Luca had panicked at first, seeing the report in full: to think that her uncle was sending troops back to capture Qazāl from the council. To make Luca a liar. But Brice's orders were to Masridān, the one colony without loyalty problems. Why? General Cantic had seen to the loyalty there decades ago.

It wasn't her uncle's only order. The ship Luca had loaded with aid for Qazāl had been raided by the La Chaise harbormaster "under suspicion of smuggling."

Moves on the board.

Luca folded the report in half. Tapped its edge against the desk.

She had to warn Touraine to make other arrangements. They needed to talk. About everything. But Touraine wasn't in her rooms.

The Trial of Competence was in two weeks. With Brice in the south, one of his siblings would come to make the Moyenne vote. Luca barely knew them; she doubted she'd have a chance to sway them.

With Evrard and Ghislaine, though, she might still have a chance. And Sabine...

Luca exhaled slowly and unfolded the report, flattened it, and stacked it with her other notes under Bastien's gold medallion.

Missing, notably, was any report on who had poisoned last night's guests. Though Sabine had survived, enough had not. The hunt through the gardens had turned up nothing and no one. The palace guard had spent the night questioning the kitchens, but she would have to wait longer still for confirmation or confession—

"Luca!"

Luca startled at the shout, already half standing. Her stomach dropped.

"Adile, is that—"

The body servant poked her head into the study, eyes frantic. "Your Highness, it's the ambassador."

Heavy pounding on the door to Luca's chambers punctuated the woman's sentence.

"Sky above." If last night had upset Touraine this much... Luca straightened her collar, her sleeves, the lapels of her coat. "I'll get the door."

When Luca swung the door open, Touraine's face was a rictus of fury. Luca skipped back so fast that her bad leg went soft on her. Touraine's reflexes were quick but not gentle. A tight grip kept Luca from falling.

"Sorry." Touraine released Luca as soon as Luca regained her balance. Touraine's expression softened briefly before the rage returned. She pushed in, slamming the door shut behind her. Luca thought of the tiger in Ghislaine's menagerie. All of that strength, all of that restrained violence with nowhere to turn it.

"Nicolas," Touraine growled. "He has—" She looked away.

Luca limped carefully closer, a hand outstretched. Touraine sidestepped her.

In that movement, Luca saw the bedraggled white rose in Touraine's off hand. The kind that normally bloomed in her mother's garden in the spring. It hadn't been carried gently, and Touraine's hands were smeared with blood.

"Touraine, what—"

"He has Ghadin." Touraine squeezed the rose in her fist.

"Ghadin? You found her?"

"He did," she choked out. "Weeks ago. And he arrested the acrobats."

"I don't understand." Luca gingerly plucked the rose from Touraine's hand. "Explain, from the beginning."

Touraine told it all, from the arrests to Ghadin's broken arm and the failed healing. Her agreement to the new treaty.

Another move. Now repositioning Brice looked less like a distraction and more like a safeguard for Nicolas's victory. With Brice in Masridān, he would be ready to reclaim Qazāl as soon as this new treaty was inked.

"What about this?" Luca turned the rose over in her hand, gentle around the thorns.

"Balladairan magic. Help me get Ghadin back and I'll tell you what I know."

"You...what?" Luca scoffed, baffled. "Wait. Are you trying to manipulate me again? Is this a game to you?"

"It's a game to you, isn't it? Why shouldn't I play, too? Everything is a move, everyone is a piece."

"Because I'm your..." *Friend* seemed too presumptuous. Too much. Not enough.

"Because you're my what, Luca?" Touraine's voice was even and sharp, like a good blade. The anger that she usually stuffed away was as readable as a book.

The outrage Luca had felt in the salle resurfaced to meet it.

"You should tell me because I'm your ally, Touraine. The same reason I'm going to help you get Ghadin back. It's what allies do."

"Allies. Huh. I've learned a lot more about politics since our échecs games in Qazāl." Touraine circled Luca, her sneer predatory. "For example. The best way to secure an ally is to keep them reliant on you. Then you don't even have to care about them. Use them while it's convenient, then, when a better offer comes along, you abandon them in the middle of the desert with a cup of piss and wish them good luck getting home. You did that in Qazāl, too, when you turned on the rebels just to get your hands on Shālan magic."

White-hot anger flared across Luca's vision. "You—! How—!" Touraine, who had betrayed Luca and the rebels alike—Luca pulled herself back out with a long, slow breath.

"A better offer?" she asked calmly, spinning on the spot to keep Touraine in her sights. Lanquette and Deniaud were outside. Adile had gone, giving them privacy.

*She wouldn't hurt me.*

"I haven't gotten a better offer," Luca said.

Touraine stopped circling and stepped closer. "Because you're still sucking me dry. Taking and taking and taking."

"Don't confuse me with Balladaire. I'm trying to help you. That's all."

Touraine's nostrils flared. "That's not all, that's never been all. Tell me one thing you have done for me. That was for *me* because *I* needed it, because I needed *you*. You are Balladaire, Luca, you have been and you will be. And I have broken myself for you, I have knelt for you, I left my people for you!" Her voice went shrill. She took a shuddering breath and her next words were calmer. "The only reason I'm still here is because I am an idiot and because, thanks to your uncle, my fate is chained to yours."

"The only reason?" Luca gripped her cane so tightly her hand shook. "Sky above, you're a hypocrite. Your council sent you to seduce me to get help for Qazāl! That's politics. That's *people*, for the stars' sake. Giving. Taking. This is what we do."

She advanced, pointing the rose at Touraine's chest.

"What you are not going to do is hide things from me like I haven't done everything in my power to help you and the Qazāli. Because of me, the Qazāli who come here don't starve. I had a woman killed to keep the children safe until I find a better home for them. I've stood by you, by Qazāl, by your fucking god while the court laughs at me behind my back for 'uncivilized liaisons.' "

Sabine and the other nobles were right. It had all been because of Touraine. Luca had changed the shape of an entire empire. And Touraine didn't even realize it.

"That's it?" Touraine fired into the silence between Luca's breaths. "Give us the full accounting. Does it feel good? Don't forget the ship home, or your generous donation of food to your old colony."

Luca dropped her hand and looked away. She couldn't lie.

"The ship was raided. The harbormaster confiscated the food. I'm going to fix it."

Touraine closed her eyes and dropped her head, chuckling. "I'm sure you will. In the meantime, my people will starve."

"I'm trying, Touraine! What else do you want from me? The Trial of Competence is in two weeks. Qazāl isn't my only concern, believe it or not. But don't worry! I'm keenly aware of the cost of my failure."

"And when you do lose?" Touraine snapped.

The venom of the words forced Luca back.

"Who's going to save you then? Your loyal soldiers?" Touraine held her arms wide and looked around, a cruel smile spreading across her face. "Or the savage witches from the south?"

"I won't lose," Luca growled. "I have Evrard, Sabine, and Ghislaine—"

"Ghislaine?" Touraine cackled. "And you think *I'm* naive! You don't have Ghislaine. Why do you think Nicolas tried to make me heal Ghadin?" She leaned close, baring her teeth in Luca's face. *"Ghislaine told."*

"She didn't. She said—"

"Of course she did. If you think your hold on the High Court is tight enough, check again. Your marionettes are cutting their strings, Princess."

Luca's anger flared, pushing back the hurt. She let it. Anything felt better than entertaining the small voice in the back of her head saying, *She's right, she's right, she's right.*

"You forget yourself, Touraine."

"No, I don't think I do. I know exactly who I am to you now. I know exactly what I'm worth."

"Oh? And what's that?"

Touraine's chest rose and fell quickly. Though she was the shorter by an inch or so, the heat of her golden eyes made Luca feel small.

"Nothing," Touraine said quietly. "Not compared to your crown."

Luca recoiled. Oh. *Oh*. Her face burned. Touraine had *heard*.

"Yeah."

"I'm sorry you heard that."

"Yep."

"I would have liked to tell you myself."

Touraine gave Luca a sad, crooked smile. "Which part?"

Luca couldn't help the way her eyes dropped to Touraine's lips. Couldn't help the way their proximity tuned her like a string. Left her ringing. "All of it."

Touraine pressed a palm to Luca's chest. Luca's breath caught.

"I know the score of this game, Luca." Touraine rapped her knuckles on Luca's breastbone. "Let's just play our parts. Get Ghadin back. When we've both gotten what we need from each other, I'll be out of your palace and out of your way."


Luca made one stop before she went to see her uncle. Her parents' room was as she left it from her last visit. When Touraine had come with her.

"Are you sure you're all right?" Gil asked, following inside.

"I could use a moment alone, Gil."

Gil hesitated. He turned to go and then turned back, stroking his mustache. He opened his mouth to speak—then sighed, said nothing, and left her alone with Touraine's words.

*You're trying. If that's not something they would be proud of, why are you so intent on pleasing their memory?*

Luca sat again in her mother's chair with the queen's violoncelle, restrung and tuned, resting between her legs. She held the new bow loosely in her fingers.

Luca played slowly, picking out the notes half by memory, half by the sheet music on the stand. It took time to relearn exactly how to place her fingers in the same places her mother had once put hers. Decades ago.

Just like she was trying desperately to follow in her parents' footsteps. To rule as they had. Only, where they had expanded Balladaire, Luca was cutting off its edges, curtailing its growth. She had a vision, though. She just needed time and she needed someone to give her the benefit of the doubt.

She had neither time nor the trust of her people. She didn't have the trust of the Qazāli, either.

Luca slid down the fingerboard, elbow over the body of the violoncelle, wrist arching over the strings. Their rich tremble vibrated in her chest.

If Luca lost, if Luca gave in, her uncle would claim the throne and all of its power. It was easy to see that future rolled out before her like a tapestry:

The Droitist schools and their terrified children conditioned to obedience.

Qazāl, under an even stricter regime than before, punished for daring to reclaim independence.

Touraine and Aranen and the Jackal dead, fighting against Nicolas's new regime.

Touraine, who was hiding information that Luca could use. Touraine, who was infuriating. Touraine, who was—

Touraine, who might never understand the ways Luca could help Qazāl.

Touraine, whose lips and hands she still felt when she closed her eyes.

Luca fumbled over the fingerboard at the thought. Recovered. The strings squeaked beneath her intensity as she swayed to regain her rhythm.

If Touraine was right, though, Luca had no more pieces to play. Her uncle had her cornered.

Except, that wasn't entirely true.

Her father had hunted Shālan healing magic and tried to take it by force. He'd never found the closely kept secrets—Luca had. She'd built relationships—however fragile, however temperamental—with the guardians of that magic. She had made friends with the people her father had tried to subdue. She was rebuilding what he had broken. She believed in that work, even if her parents wouldn't understand it.

Would it be so bad if history remembered her like that? Would it make up for everything *she* had done in Qazāl? For what she, and her father and her uncle and all of her forebears, did in the name of the Balladairan Empire?

Would it be enough for Touraine to forgive her? Enough to see Luca in any other way? The last time Luca had failed Touraine so badly, Luca had held Touraine's dying body in her arms. She could not— *would not*—do that again.

*You know who you are. Be true to that instead.*

Could Luca face herself if she didn't at least try?

She finished softly, slowly, breathing heavily into the echo of the high, searching notes as they died.

Luca found Nicolas in his library, contemplating a map hanging on the wall. Little Tiro sat reading at the small table, his feet kicking in the air beneath. He smiled at her and waved. Luca kissed the boy atop his tawny hair.

Then she joined Nicolas at the map.

"Nicolas, you are a monster."

"My dear niece. To what do I owe the pleasure?"

"Let the girl go. The acrobats, too. They are not your pieces to play."

"Oh? I suppose they are yours."

"They're no one's, Uncle."

"Everyone is someone's piece. Isn't that what Yverte says?"

"If you're so eager for pieces to play, then why won't you play our own?"

"Our own?" Nicolas raised an eyebrow. "Oh, like Madame Béryl. That was a clever stunt you pulled with my school."

Luca's breath caught. "I don't know what you mean."

Nicolas noticed and smiled. "The schoolmistress at my school. Replacing her with Madame Béryl. Clever. I didn't notice at first. However, Madame Tomier failed to send me her monthly report. Imagine my surprise when I investigated and found she had...disappeared. I must say, I didn't think you had it in you."

Another reminder that the pieces she lost in this game were a living, breathing weight upon her shoulders. Another reason Luca couldn't fail now.

She said, "Ambassador El-Qazāli said you tried to force her to heal for you."

"I wanted to know if it was true. Ghislaine said so, you said so. No one has yet shown me proof, though." He pinched his fingers together for emphasis, as if he should have been holding that proof.

"The god's gift isn't so simple."

"So I've been told. Ghislaine also told me you unearthed some of our own dark past."

"Balladaire's magic," Luca said warily. "Balladaire's god."

"Mm. There is a reason we banished it, but I take it you know better than the generations who came before you?"

"I know about the sacrifices. I'm surprised that stopped you, though. If everyone is just a piece to play."

"You think so little of me, dear niece. I'm no more eager for bloodshed than you. Less than you, I would estimate." He went to the table and pulled out a chair for Luca. "I recognize when it's necessary, but even dogs do not shit where they sleep. Sit."

He brought the échecs board to the end of the table opposite Tiro. Luca helped him reset the pieces by reflex.

"One thing we pass on from ruler to ruler, down the line—truth, my dear niece. We all interpret the truth differently. Other Anciers—my brother, for example—might have believed Balladaire claimed some holy magic along with our belief in a god. I don't. I think we scraped for meaning in the dirt, just like other unenlightened peoples. We attributed the things we didn't understand to magic, just like the Shālans and the Taargens. Unlike them, we learned better—it's what sets us apart. The good that we do, as humans, belongs to us. We fought for it, we strived and suffered. In a good crop season, the credit goes to our innovative sowing and harvesting, the hardy breeds of seed we've developed over time, our backs that till the land. Full bellies are because of that, not a god."

Though the words were new, everything about this moment felt familiar. He spoke, she listened. This was how they had always been. She finished setting up her rows and propped her elbow on the arm of her chair, rested her chin on her fist. Nicolas picked up his king and held it in his hand, running his thumb along the small figure's crown.

"Roland didn't play échecs. He hated it."

"He did?"

"Mm. A man of action, your father. He told me I'd never learn anything from it."

"He was wrong."

"He was. That's why I taught you."

Nicolas put the king in its place with a sharp click. He made his first move. Luca made hers.

"He thought I was wasting your time, but you enjoyed it." He looked up at her expectantly, even though she'd already taken her turn.

"And here we are," Luca said.

"Here we are." Nicolas chuckled. His eyes went distant. "I told him to leave the Shālan magic alone. He wouldn't. He swore that the magic was real and that it would save us the next time the Withering came. When the Withering came, though, we were overextended. We couldn't care for our own people. He refused to call the armies back to help. Then he died, and I was left to pick up the pieces and put them back together. I was left with a little girl, bright and curious. A little girl I saw myself in."

Luca froze, hand outstretched for her next piece. A tremor shook it, and she clenched it into a fist. A small inhalation behind her made Luca turn. Gil's lips were pressed firmly together. He stared straight past her to Nicolas.

"Your father was stubborn and obsessive, utterly myopic in his perspective." Nicolas gestured to the board between them. "I thought that I had taught you better."

The duke leaned back in his seat and folded his arms across his chest. He held Gil's gaze, daring the dead king's lover to challenge him. Gil did not.

Luca looked over her shoulder again at Gil, silently asking for any kind of reassurance. He looked away.

Luca's father had not been a good king.

King Roland had made choices—like all of them had, like each of them would have to—for the sake of Balladaire. Not every decision could be right. Luca knew that, just as she knew she would also make mistakes on the throne. Had already made mistakes.

It was the steely anger in her uncle's voice when Nicolas spoke of King Roland, though, and Gil's shame, that made Luca realize how little she actually knew the man her father had been. She knew the shape of him in her memories: The shadow of his hand on her shoulder, the oiled leather and metal smell of him behind her as she shared his saddle. His rough hand over hers on her first sword.

Only—it had been Gil's hand on hers, rough and calloused and twice as big, encircling both her hand and the handle, correcting the angle of her wrists. The smells she remembered most from her childhood were her uncle's wine and the layered honey pastries they shared while he taught her échecs. The click of stone pieces on stone squares.

Her father was just a shadow, an outline she had filled in with her own imagination, or the stories other people told. Some of it was based in truth, but—she had been a child. How much could she really see of a man, looking up from waist height?

Not much at all.

Luca picked up her queen. She was free now, at liberty to move around the board. The game was too new, though. There were few meaningful moves Luca could make without putting her in danger.

"What will it take for you to release the girl?" she asked.

"You know what I want."

Luca took a breath. Held it. Let it stream out slowly. She couldn't know what King Roland Ancier would have wanted. Whether or not he'd be disappointed in her for abandoning his legacy, or proud that she'd found answers where he had not.

She could try to live up to Nicolas's vision of her, or Gil's. The woman—the princess, the queen—they wanted her to be. The woman they would be proud of. They would die one day, too, though, and leave her with their own dim shadows. She couldn't chase shadows forever.

"I want more than that."

Nicolas's eyes turned up to hers, surprise turning to cautious interest. "Go on."

Luca tapped her queen against the board.

"When you..." Luca ground her teeth. "If I abdicate willingly, make me your minister of Shālan affairs."

"Luca, don't—" Gil barked.

Luca raised a hand—the hand with the queen—to stop him, and he bit off his words in a growl. "I will oversee it all, make all decisions, foreign and domestic—education, labor, religion. All of it."

Tiro's pages stopped turning.

"She matters that much to you?" Nicolas leaned in.

"Yes or no, dear Uncle."

Nicolas looked from the board to Luca, from Luca to Gil. Gil's face was red with fury. In other circumstances, Luca was certain Nicolas would be dead right now. But Nicolas's guards stood silently glowering in the corners, and more waited outside. And Tiro was there, his eyes wide in witness. This lesson would stick with him for the rest of his life.

"A public abdication. Signed by each of the High Court."

"As you wish. I want the girl and the acrobats released into my custody immediately. A sign of good faith. Give me time to arrange my affairs." A snarl threatened to curl Luca's lips, so she frowned instead.

"I'll give you the girl." Nicolas gestured to one of his guards, and the woman left.

Luca pushed herself up from the table. Her legs almost gave out beneath her, but she steadied herself with her cane.

The gleam of a familiar knife caught her eye from her uncle's desk. It lay unsheathed, as if her uncle had been toying with it. She went over and took it.

As she passed by the échecs board, she flicked her king over. It bounced once before rolling into the rows of white stone pieces. She pocketed the queen.

"What under the sky above was that, Luca?" Gil shouted when they were behind the closed door of her chambers.

Luca didn't answer. She reached her washbasin just in time to vomit into it.

"Why did you do it, Luca?" Gil stood beside her, one hand on his brow, his teeth bared.

Luca stared into the basin of sick, repulsed. She spat and wiped her mouth with a handkerchief. "Was he really like that?"

"Eh?"

"My father. Why didn't you tell me?"

He looked away, guilty. "I've told you before. My memory—"

"Paints him in rose. That's bearshit, Gil." Luca's stomach heaved again, but she clamped down. "I wanted to know him. As much as I could. You should have just told me."

Gil sighed, and the bed creaked beneath his weight. "Roland wanted better for the empire. Like you do."

Luca turned at the tenderness in Gil's voice. "You don't hate me?"

"Oh, Luca. Luca. No." Gil shook his head slowly and sighed. "Why didn't you wait? I said I could get you soldiers. You said the Taargens and the Qazāli would support you."

"I don't want war, Gil. Not if I can help it. The cost is too high. I knew he would be more amenable if I surrendered."

"You can't trust him."

"I know. He can't trust me, either."

Gil looked up sharply. "What are you planning?"

"I won't kill half a nation in a civil war, Gil. But I'm not above killing one man. First, though, I need to make sure Ghadin is safely delivered to her patron."

# CHAPTER 34

# THE QUEEN'S GAMBIT

Luca pushed her shoulders back, took a deep breath, and knocked twice on the door to Touraine's chambers.

No response.

Given how things ended the last time they spoke, Luca wasn't surprised, but another fear occurred to her. What if Touraine had gone? Snuck away, like she'd threatened to?

Not without Ghadin. Luca checked over her shoulder, making sure the soldiers carrying the girl's litter were still there. The doctors had given Ghadin a sedative; the girl had been too frightened and in too much pain, no matter how Luca had reassured her. It might have been better to have Touraine accompany them, but Luca hadn't wanted to wait. A selfishness she recognized too late—she wanted to be the one to bring Ghadin to Touraine.

"Your Excellency?" Luca knocked again. "Ambassador El-Qazāli?"

A door down the corridor opened. Touraine stuck her head out of the priestess's door.

"What do you want, Princess?"

Luca bit back the sharp surge of anger, curling her tongue around a cruel retort. Especially because she did need something. Now more than ever.

"Here. This is yours." Luca thrust Touraine's long knife at her, handle first. "Will you let us in? We should get Ghadin in bed."

Touraine's face went slack. "Ghadin?"

Her face went from confusion to wary hope as she took in the group clustered behind Luca. She ran out of the room in her bare feet to see the girl on her litter. The relief on her face made a lump in Luca's throat.

"Aranen! They brought Ghadin!" Touraine's voice cracked as she shouted for the priestess. Then she opened the door to the suite she shared with the girl and guided them to Ghadin's room.

Luca hung back. She stepped aside when Aranen came through, wrapping a scarf around her narrow shoulders as she went.

This, at least, was a good thing done.

Touraine finally noticed her knife in Luca's hand and took it, gingerly.

"How did you do it?" The acid in her voice was gone, leaving ragged weariness.

Luca shrugged. "Give and take."

Touraine stared at Luca suspiciously. "What did you give him?"

Luca tried to smile crookedly, to put on Sabine's insouciant mask. The half smile died, twitching. Luca dropped her gaze to the ground.

"Will you meet me and Sabine in the salle? I could use your help one more time. Only if you want. This—" Luca jerked her head to the room where the physicians, Balladairan and Qazāli, murmured to each other. "There's no debt here."

Touraine followed Luca's nod. She stared into the room, her chest rising and falling steadily. The coiled tension that kept the ambassador ready to lash out, that made her look so haggard, seemed to leach away before Luca's eyes.

"I need to see how she's doing."

"Of course." Luca turned to go.

"Luca?" Touraine said to her back.

"Hmm?"

"Whatever you did...thank you."

"You're welcome, Touraine."


"Weren't you just poisoned two days ago?" Luca put a hand on her hip and scowled at Sabine, who was already in the salle when Luca arrived.

The marquise was gingerly walking through some of the simpler sword forms with a thin practice dowel. Her movements were precise, placed in the correct spots, but her arms trembled with weakness when she tried to hold the forms.

Sabine turned and smiled sheepishly.

"You look like shit," Luca told her. She went over and took the dowel from Sabine's hand, then led her to the bench. They sat, side by side.

"I know." Sabine nodded to the great mirror, the pride of the room. "Rather hard to miss. But it gives me back a piece of myself."

Sabine's surprising sobriety hit Luca hard in her belly. *Sabine* had almost died.

The winter roses were the only evidence Luca had right now to the culprit. Sitting beside Sabine, with her sallow skin and shadowed eyes, Luca wondered if the assassin she'd taken to calling the Rose was guilty of Bastien's death, too. He hadn't been poisoned, though. His throat had been slit, and no one had heard him cry out either in surprise or in pain. That meant skill, or a talent for stealth.

She had been so certain it was her uncle, but maybe she was wrong. Though the methods were different, both killings spoke of forethought. Both had invoked terror in the palace.

Then there was the attack on her carriage, not stealth but chaos, and the single attack directed at her person. That didn't feel like Bastien's murder or the poisonings.

Wolves closed around Luca from all sides, and she didn't know which danger to watch.

Luca snaked her hand into Sabine's lap to hold the marquise's larger hand. "I'm glad you're alive."

Sabine shot her a startled glance. The expression turned guarded. "Even though I'm a spoiled marquise?" She squeezed Luca's hand once.

Luca chuckled. "Better than a queen who can't put her kingdom before her cunt."

Sabine winced. "I'm sorry about that."

"You weren't wrong. Not entirely." Luca rested her forehead on Sabine's strong shoulder and then kissed it.

"What do you mean?"

"I mean, Touraine may very well cost me my crown."

"Did Nicolas say something?" Sabine said sharply. "I told you—"

"I made my own choices. I do need your help, though. Both of you, if I can. I just don't know if she'll agree. I told her to meet us? If she wants to help. If we just wait, give her a chance to show?" Luca's uncertainty turned to rambling, and she couldn't fight the flush that came with it.

It was the right choice. *No matter what happens.*

Luca was going through the forms herself to stave off that nervous energy when Touraine arrived. She was trailed not by Perrot but by the chaperone that normally followed Aranen.

Touraine followed Luca's confusion. "Perrot wanted to stay with Aranen and the girl. Roland ... is trustworthy."

Luca started at her father's name. It was a common enough name, though, especially after the king rose. Still, it felt like an omen. The guard was older than most of the others, a handful of years younger than Gil, maybe. He didn't move like the other palace soldiers, either. Luca met Gil's eyes and quirked an eyebrow at him. He nodded in understanding, or perhaps to say that he'd already noticed. Something wasn't right.

"Very well. Thank you for coming."

"I'll hear you out. I owe you that much."

Despite the gratitude she'd shown in her rooms earlier, Touraine's voice was carefully neutral. Then Luca saw the dark look Touraine shot at Sabine, and she understood.

"As you know, I spoke to my uncle yesterday."

Sabine made room for Touraine on the bench between her and Luca and smiled. "Have a seat."

Touraine glared coldly down at her. "I'll stand." To Luca she said, "Well?"

*Once the die is cast, there's no turning back.*

"In exchange for Ghadin's immediate medical release and the release of the Qazāli acrobats—"

"Wait, he arrested Ghadin? Your little protégée?" Sabine looked up at Touraine in outrage. Touraine gave her a withering look, but that didn't deter her. "That bearfucking—"

Luca held a hand up in front of Sabine's face. "And control of all Shālan interests here and abroad…" She took a deep breath. "He wants me to step down. To abdicate my right to the throne."

"Well, of course you told him no." Sabine laughed in disbelief.

It was the flicker of surprise in the twitch of Touraine's eyelids, though, the uncertain parting of her lips, that arrested Luca's attention.

"You…told him no." Horror spread across Sabine's face. "Luca, you told him no."

"I made the offer."

Silence followed, and Luca counted the beats it took for the announcement to sink in. One, two, three, four, five, six—

"What the sky-falling fuck?" Sabine roared, jumping up.

She lost her balance in her weakness and steadied herself against the sword rack.

"For someone who signed his demand for a Trial of Competence," Luca said, "you are objecting very loudly."

Sabine yanked at her dark hair. "I didn't think—I thought you would fight it! I knew you would!"

"I am. In my own way." More to Touraine than to Sabine, Luca continued. "I am fully prepared to follow this through if we don't manage anything else. However, I don't intend to leave this agreement as it stands. That's where you two come in. I need you both."

Touraine chuckled darkly. "I guess I really am going to be the… what was it? Oh, right: 'the death of your ambitions to the throne.'"

Sabine blushed deep red. "You heard that. Luca, you should have told—"

"It's all right," Touraine muttered. "I'd rather know what you're thinking. See what's behind the charm." Touraine wasn't wearing that hideous sword that Sabine had gifted her. The long knife Luca had returned to her rode at her hip.

"What, then?" Touraine crossed her arms. Her tone had thawed a little, and that gave Luca the barest hope. "What do you need?"

Touraine's incongruous guard stood by the door of the salle, inhumanly still and staring into space.

Luca lowered her voice to a whisper. "I need to do what my uncle doesn't expect. He didn't expect me to abdicate, and he won't expect me to try to kill him."

Touraine's eyebrows shot up, and Sabine's mouth dropped open.

"Apparently, neither did you two. That bodes well. You'll help?"

"Luca, he's the duke—" Sabine's gaze darted worriedly between Luca and Touraine.

"Fuck yes." Touraine's fist clenched, and a dark, beautiful eagerness spread across her face. It would have frightened Luca if she didn't need it.

On second thought, it still frightened her.

"You know I'm with you, Luca." Sabine patted the air with her hands. "Whatever you want, I'm beside you, but—is this it? If the Qazāli are important to you, fine—he's given them to you. As many of your charities as you like, but assassinating—"

"It's not about charity, Durfort," Touraine cut in. "It's about justice. You didn't grow up in a Droitist school. You weren't a Sand. You didn't see what he did to Ghadin." The satisfaction on Touraine's face, though, had nothing to do with righting the world's wrongs.

Sabine frowned. "What did he do to her?"

"He fractured her arm to force me into healing her with magic."

Sabine paled. "Did you?"

"I can't," Touraine snarled. "I told him as much and he did it anylight." She governed herself with difficulty. Through gritted teeth, she added, "So if you'll excuse me, I want to know what Her Highness has planned."

"Are you with us, Sabine? I need you."

Sabine looked from Touraine's determined face to Luca's, then hung her head. "All right. I said I'm with you. What do we need to do?"

Relief enveloped Luca, cool as a fresh breeze. There was still a niggle of doubt in the back of her mind—either Touraine or Sabine could betray her again—but she would put her faith in them. If she had to make contingency plans, well, that was only to be expected in a coup. She laughed at the thought, and the absurdity made her laugh even harder. The nonplussed look her two sometimes-lovers shared only made her laugh harder still.

"Forgive me." Luca forced her face back into her court mask, closing off the other feelings writhing in her gut. The terror that she would fail and be caught, the frightful glee she felt at her ambition, at the possibility to beat her uncle once and for all. She pushed herself to her feet to be level with her new coconspirators.

"Touraine, the rose you found in the garden. I need you to follow up on that. Find who did it and see if they'll meet with me. I want to make a bargain. Sabine—"

"What rose?" Sabine asked. "Who did what?"

"The person who tried to kill you left something behind," Touraine answered flatly. "I can do that."

Sabine raised a questioning eyebrow at Luca.

"We suspect they have Balladairan magic. If I can get them to teach me, or to use it for my benefit, it may help with my uncle. I have a different job for you, Sab."

"Balladairan...magic?" Sabine's voice came out strangled and high-pitched.

"Yes. Unfortunately, I don't have time to catch you up on everything, so just take us at our word. I'll send you a complete compendium of all my research later."

The marquise grimaced. "No need."

"Good. How well do you think my uncle still trusts you? Does he think you're still frightened of him?"

"I am still frightened of him," Sabine grumbled.

"Do you think he would accept a conciliatory gift of your wine?"

At that, Sabine snorted and said, with no small amount of pride, "He doesn't need a gift. It's all he drinks. The wine cellars are full of it."

"And if you gave him a special bottle? Another experimental vintage or something?"

Sabine's shoulders drooped beneath grim understanding. "How special should this vintage be?"

"A once-in-a-lifetime sort of experience. He shouldn't have a chance to drink it again. Can you arrange a suitable bottle?"

"What if he drinks it and someone finds him in time? Or if he has a taster? Everyone has a taster now, I have a sky-falling taster..."

"He drinks alone in his study more often than not. There's no one to share it with unless I go to play échecs with him, not that I plan on doing that again. There is still a risk, though, yes. And he wouldn't blame you alone."

Luca could see Sabine replaying her words from the other night. *Not even a spoiled marquise.* The knob of Sabine's throat bobbed up and down, and for a moment, Luca thought she was going to refuse. Instead, Sabine bowed.

"As you wish, Your Highness."

Touraine, however, was looking thoughtfully back at Aranen's guard.

"Who is he?" Luca said quietly. "Really?"

"He's a...friend of Djasha's. I think that's why Aranen sent him with me." Touraine's eyes were hooded as she put together pieces that Luca couldn't see.

"Not Nicolas's?"

Touraine shook her head and gestured for the man to come over.

"Could you poison someone without a contract?" Touraine asked him abruptly.

"Touraine!" There was no guile in the woman; Luca was going to strangle her—

"No." The man who shared her father's name stared between Luca,

Sabine, and Touraine. "It's against my god to take a life without a contract given directly from the abbess."

Luca's mouth fell open. "You're from the Southern Mountains."

"But you're Balladairan," Sabine sputtered.

Roland nodded his head once to both of them. "I have business here."

Luca flinched back, her hand going immediately for the sword in her cane that wasn't there. "A contract."

"I am under no contract now."

He had a deep voice, patient and unhurried. He stared at her, blinking slowly. Luca recognized him—he'd been part of the delegation from the Southern Mountains that came for her birthday. They'd greeted each other briefly, but she'd been more occupied with the Taargens and Touraine and the immediate threat of war and a coronation. Months later and he was still here. What business could keep him, if not a contract?

"You are an assassin, though?" Luca clarified.

"I am a monk."

"The poison, Roland," Touraine interrupted tersely. "If— hypothetically—we needed to poison someone, especially someone who drinks a lot of wine, how would you go about it? This is why Aranen sent you, isn't it?"

He fixed his clear brown eyes on Touraine. What gifts did his god grant him? What realm did the southern god govern, and what sacrifices did it demand?

"I came because Aranen din Djasha asked me to accompany you. Let me speak again with her. Wine bottles, you said?"

Sabine nodded, the corners of her mouth drooping forlornly.

"Someone can get into the bottles?"

Sabine flicked her fingers. "That would be me."

Roland scraped his well-manicured fingers across graying stubble. "Aranen din and I will come up with something."

"Good. What's our timeline?" Touraine was brusque and efficient. Luca had forgotten that before Touraine became an ambassador, killing and dying and the risk they entailed had been her business.

Luca stifled her chuckle lest she pitch herself into another laughing fit. "My uncle wants me to abdicate publicly. Probably in the next week or so. He'll follow it up with his own coronation as quickly as possible, but he won't want to sacrifice pomp. He's as vain as any noble."

"I beg your pardon?" Sabine sniffed.

Touraine snorted and rolled her eyes.

"I beg your pardon!" She glared at Touraine.

"It's to legitimize himself," Luca cut in. "We need to move before my abdication. That means now. Are we all agreed?"

Luca held out her hand palm up and looked at each woman in turn. Surprisingly, Sabine placed her hand in Luca's first. With a heavy sigh that sounded less like resignation and more like acceptance, Touraine covered Sabine's hand with her own.

"Vengeance will make strange bedfellows of us all," Luca said.

Touraine grunted. "We're not all bedfellows, yet."

Sabine's grin was strained. "You know, we could change that. In fact, it might be wise to do it sooner rather than later. Just in case."

# CHAPTER 35

# POISONS

Sabine arrived at midnight with the wine.

She carried it in a basket covered with a small blanket, as if she and Luca were bound for a picnic. In Luca's bedroom. In the middle of the night. This, apparently, was how thrones were won.

They unloaded the bottles in Luca's study, setting them on the desk. Adile had left the fire burning at Luca's request—"a long night of reading ahead"—and the candles around the room added to the red glow.

"Five?" Luca asked. "That's so many."

"Better to be safe, isn't it?" Sabine's tone was too bright, her crooked smile too forced.

"Right. Here, then." Luca opened the drawer of her desk and pulled a palm-sized paper packet from the false bottom, along with a small wooden measure. "He"—Luca couldn't call the monk Roland, it was still too strange—"said a full measure per bottle should be enough."

Sabine clenched and unclenched her hands at her sides and nodded. "Seals first, then, shall we?"

The marquise shrugged out of her long coat and loosened the cravat at her throat. She pushed her sleeves up her forearms, then pulled a knife from her belt.

"May I?" Sabine gestured to the desk.

The politesse was almost amusing, given what they were about to do.

Luca shifted over to give Sabine room.

"And the candle, please?"

Luca pushed her desk candle over, careful not to let the wax spill out of the holder. Sabine held the bare blade of her knife over the flame, and the metal blackened with soot. Her lips moved, and Luca realized she was counting.

Then, satisfied that the blade was hot enough, Sabine bent over the first squat bottle and, with a careful hand, pressed the edge of the hot blade to the edge of the wax. She squinted as she wedged the blade beneath the seal—and then, effortlessly, the knife glided below the wax and Sabine peeled the seal away.

"You've done this before, haven't you?" Luca asked as she watched Sabine work through the next few bottles with practiced ease. As if she had a system she had perfected. "Who else have you been poisoning?"

Sabine's hands stilled on the short neck of the last squat bottle.

That word. Luca hadn't meant to say it. It brought the truth of the moment into the room.

Why should Luca not say it, not even think it? She was only doing what she needed to secure her throne. So she could do everything Balladaire needed her to do. If Nicolas hadn't forced her hand by taking Ghadin, she wouldn't be in such a desperate position. She would have had more time to maneuver. Time to find other ways.

And if it turned out that *he* had arranged Bastien's death, then he deserved this all the more. Luca would have no regrets.

*And if he is not guilty?*

If he was not guilty of that particular crime, well, there were others.

"Not poisoning." Sabine chuckled softly, a far-off look in her eyes. "I used to sneak into my father's wine. Stealing some of this, and some of that. He noticed when actual bottles went missing. How do you think I developed such a refined palate?"

She smiled at Luca. "Those Durfort winters were long. I missed you." She winked, and it was like they were just sitting over Luca's échecs board again. "Anylight, here. This is for us."

She swept to the sideboard where Luca kept a pair of wine glasses. The carafe was empty, and Sabine tutted and shook her head.

"We should have a drink first. A toast. Before we—" Sabine flicked her gaze to the paper packet and its wooden scoop.

"I don't know if that's a good idea."

Sabine unstopped the bottle and stared Luca in the eye. "I need a drink, Luca."

The wine spilled dark burgundy into the glass, and Sabine gulped down what she poured. Then she poured another, and this one she held, gazed into. Her mouth worked as she tasted her handiwork.

"Fine, I'll take one."

The corner of Sabine's lips twitched up. "Of course you will. I only make the best."

Sabine was a braggart, cocky and foppish, but this, at least, was not an empty boast. The wine was glorious. The flavor was full and deep, with a pleasant dryness that curled on her tongue. Luca tasted the grapes and the oakwood of the barrel it had been stored in before it was bottled, but there were other things, too: rose petals and a hint of spice so delicate Luca almost missed it, and many more flavors Luca couldn't identify at all.

No wonder her uncle drank it exclusively.

"I suppose it will do," she deadpanned.

Sabine put a hand to her chest, wounded. "How cruel, Your Highness."

Which brought Luca back to the moment. "A toast, then, as you said."

Sabine held up her glass. "To the throne?"

Luca stared into her cup and swirled the dark liquid. It wasn't the color of blood, not really, though if it spilled upon her clothing it might be harder to tell the difference. She held up her glass, and through it, she caught sight of the little queen figure she had stolen from Nicolas's échecs board.

"To cruelty." Luca drank. Sabine hesitated before she drank, too.

They cleared the desk of the drinking cups and the open bottle of wine; Luca decided she would keep that one for herself after all.

Then there were only four bottles of wine and one packet of poison. "Wait," Luca said. "I forgot."

She went back into her bedroom and plucked two clean cravats out of the armoire, then gave one to Sabine.

"He said to keep our mouths covered while we work with it."

"Oh." Sabine held the cloth in her hands and took a deep breath, as if it were the last one she'd take. Then she tied it over her face.

Thus prepared, Luca opened the packet.

She didn't know what she had expected. It was a fine, beige, crystalline powder, and as far as Luca could tell through the cravat on her face, it had no smell. The monk said that it was undetectable and required a high concentration to react quickly when ingested. A taster's sip would go unnoticed. A full bottle, on the other hand...

She tipped it into the measure. She didn't dare breathe. She handed the scoop to Sabine, who had unstopped another bottle and brought it below the poison. The scoop was too wide to dump easily into the bottle, though. Sabine's hand shook.

"Here." Luca snatched a piece of parchment from the desk and rolled it into a tight funnel and popped it into the bottle's mouth.

Still, Sabine's hand trembled. As she moved the scoop over the open wine, Luca was afraid the poison would spill across the desk.

"Sabine. I'm sorry. Let me do this part." Luca took Sabine's hand in both of hers, carefully trying to pluck the scoop away, but Sabine didn't let go. She closed her eyes tight.

"What if it doesn't work?" she whispered.

The question made Luca's heart spasm in her chest. Her breath came hot and cloying against her face, trapped by the cloth. Their hands were clammy and damp pressed against each other.

"Then I give it all up."

*I'll have made myself a monster for nothing.* Every mistake she'd made in pursuit of this goal, for nothing. Every person she'd hurt, for nothing. Even going through this, the act of poisoning her uncle's wine—even if he never drank it, she could never go back to being the person who had never poisoned his wine, who had never tried to kill one of the men who had raised her. The sour aftertaste of her own drink clung to her tongue.

The rise and fall of Sabine's breath calmed against Luca, and with a steady hand, Sabine turned the scoop over the funnel. Powder ran down the slope and into the bottle. She replaced the cork stopper, and it was done. Luca gasped. How sudden. How complete. How irrevocable.

*It was done.*

Three bottles remained.

As they worked, Sabine never said, not once, that Luca asked for too much. She was a duelist, not a murderer. Luca did ask too much. She hoped it would be enough.

Sabine broke the silence just as Luca was preparing the final measure of powder.

"You really love her."

Luca stopped mid-pour and looked up. Sabine was examining her, and Luca grew self-conscious, hunched as she was over the small packet and smaller bowl. Sweat trickled down her back and stomach. Beads of sweat gathered at the corners of Sabine's forehead, too, and darkened the underarms of her chemise. It was only the fire; the room was too warm. It smelled like wine, and heat, and melted wax. Dizzying. Luca finished the pour and sat up.

It wasn't a question, exactly, but she said, "Yes."

The metal in her voice dared Sabine to castigate her again.

Sabine only said, "All right," and then took the last scoop and poured it into the bottle.

Then she stoppered it, and they stared at it in silence. Slowly, disbelieving, Sabine started to pull down her mask.

"Wait." Luca grabbed Sabine by the wrist. "Wash your hands first."

They took turns at the water basin, and only after did they untie the cloths. Luca took them both by the corners and threw them into the dying flames.

Sabine took care of the bottles as if they were still her finest wines, untampered. She wiped them down with a cloth. This time, her hands were steady as she held the candle flame to fresh wax, let it drip over the stoppers, and stamped her sigil ring into them.

"And last of all..." Sabine took her knife again and lightly scored the seals she'd made, two lines through the middle of the rose and rapier. "Enough that we'll know the difference but not enough that he'll notice." Her voice cracked, and she cleared her throat. "They're ready. I'm ready."

"When will you do it?"

"Tonight, I suppose."

Luca's stomach clenched. So soon.

"Are you sure you don't want me to go with you?"

Sabine shook her head. "You'd look out of place." She put the bottles gently into their basket and covered them with the folded blanket. Then she turned back to Luca, stepping close. She brushed a thumb along Luca's tight-clenched jaw. "I can do this."

"Okay." Luca pulled Sabine down to kiss her forehead, before resting her own forehead in the same spot. "Thank you."

Sabine bowed. "Your wish is ever my command, Your Highness."

After Sabine departed, bottles clinking gently against each other like chimes, Luca wondered if she should call her back. Stop what was surely a mistake. Her own uncle. Hadn't she said this was not the kind of queen she meant to be?

If she called Sabine back, though, she may never *be* queen, any type of queen. Her uncle was this kind of king; she would meet him where he stood. Anylight, the die had been cast. Even if she called Sabine back right now, she couldn't undo what she had done. It would still mark her, wouldn't it? It wouldn't even be the worst thing she had ever done. He was one man, no matter how close they had been. She had sentenced Qazāl to worse. This would atone for that.

Was she destined, then, to fall into a cycle of atoning for greater and greater crimes?

*Let this be the last.*

Luca laughed at her desperate naiveté. She'd also thought crushing the rebels would be the last horrible thing she would do, and she would take that regret to her grave.

For the rest of the night, until unquiet dreams found her, Luca heard the soft hiss of the poison sliding into the bottle: the innocuous tinkle against the glass, the hush as it dissolved into the liquid.

It sounded like sand.

# CHAPTER 36

# MANY LEGS

The first dream that Pruett had took her and her dozen survivors to an oasis. In her dream, she'd scouted it from above, just like she'd seen the soldiers before they attacked her camp outside of Masridān. When she woke, head splitting with pain and huddled up against a camel along with a couple of her fighters, sharing their body heat in the cold desert night, she saw a familiar shape sitting on the camel's back. Pruett blinked the sleep from her eyes until—aye, there was Sevroush, staring at her with his head cocked. He scratched at the camel's blanket with an impatient claw.

A sharp burn started behind Pruett's nose, and hope spread in her chest.

She'd woken everyone else, and they followed Sev's guidance, leading their two rescued camels to a watering hole. It took half a week to get there and they stayed there for a while, rehydrating and gathering sweet, dense figs and dates, while they went in shifts to hunt what they could in the desert. No one questioned why they were following the bird. It was clear that this oasis was cared for by someone, and if the Many-Legged kept this place as one of theirs, they were all of them grateful. For his part, Sev puffed up his chest whenever anyone looked at him, as if he were a proud little innkeeper and they were his guests. The innkeeper did not, unfortunately, keep something for Pruett to smoke.

Pruett didn't admit to herself that part of the reason she waited so long was that she hoped Noé would find them. Or even Kiras. Anyone remaining of their band.

By the second dream, after a week or two or maybe three, Pruett was less taken by surprise and more puzzled.

*There is a sun in the night. There is a sun in the night. A place of people near the sun in the night.* She was intelligent and soaring and she could see a blinding flash and hear the distant crash of waves upon the shore.

Then she was in a different darkness, closed. *Scrabbling on small claws, scratching, hungry, fear, fear, hide, hungry. Whiskers twitching—*

Pruett woke again with a shuddering gasp, the headache bringing tears to her eyes. This time, Sevroush was not nearby.

Over a breakfast of fruit and water, Pruett asked the remainders of her band what they knew of the coast.

"Is there anything you might call...a sun in the night?" Pruett asked hesitantly, aware she sounded mad.

"A sun in the night?" one of the Sands asked around a mouthful of sticky fruit. "Is this another of your poems?"

"Better than the last one," Armande said, rolling her eyes.

"Watch it," Pruett muttered. Her poems were fine. More than fine. "I'm serious. Is there something like that?"

The big woman from El-Tarīq—her name was Unwah—split a fig open in her large hands and stared thoughtfully at the minuscule pink chambers within. "There's a lighthouse. Ra's El-Bahr in the north." She bit into the fruit.

"You've been?"

"No. But I read poems about it." Unwah smiled, her cheeks bunched up and eyes crinkling.

"How far away do you think the coast is from here?"

"Not a fucking clue, sir."

It turned out that it was about two weeks' walking from Sev's oasis to the coast. She'd stopped in her tracks the first night they saw the lighthouse and stared. Just stared. It stretched from a rocky promontory up to the stars, just like in her dream.

"You all right, Captain?" Armande asked.

"Aye," she whispered.

When they made it to the city that had sprung up down the valley from the lighthouse, which shared the same name and the port as well, Pruett felt like she could think again. Gather supplies, find a new path back to Qazāl. After that? She'd take the Jackal up on her offer, get dismissed, and get lost. Trouble would look for her, but she'd do her sky-falling best to keep ahead of it.

The third dream took her while she was awake, just a few days after they'd arrived in Ra's El-Bahr. They'd pooled the sovereigns they had together for a crammed room in an inn, and Pruett was supposed to be scrounging up necessities for the trip back when her vision went white with pain. She collapsed to her knees in the middle of the souq, panting. The stalls of the marketplace vanished.

*coming coming coming coming*

Ships on the ocean. Perched on the crown of the lighthouse, she could see the sails as the ships approached. They were coming to Ra's El-Bahr. *Coming coming coming coming.*

Pruett woke sprawled in the dirt of the market to a pair of familiar golden eyes.

"Touraine?" she rasped.


It wasn't Touraine. It was Kiras who draped Pruett across a shoulder when Pruett came to, and it was Kiras who dragged her to an inn room a hundred times better than the glorified barn loft Pruett and the others were paying for. There, Pruett promptly passed out again.

"What are you doing here?" Pruett said when she came to again and found Kiras sitting on the bed beside her. She leaned away from the woman without thinking, but when she realized it and felt guilty, she didn't move closer. *Eaters.*

"We've been here for a couple of weeks." Kiras's voice went chilly, her expression hurt. She held Pruett's eyes defiantly, though.

Pruett swallowed and leaned back in. Not too close, but normal. "Who else?"

"Noé is here. Safe. He went to get the rest of you."

How many did Kiras save, her and the other Eaters?

"You led the survivors out? Here?"

If Kiras noticed Pruett reposition herself, she didn't drop her guard. She sat like a dog who'd been kicked before and would rather bite than let it happen again. Pruett knew the feeling.

"I knew the way, more or less. My mother's Masridāni. We have family here."

Pruett reached out tentatively until her fingers brushed the back of Kiras's hand. "Thank you."

The other woman's expression softened into a smile. Pruett's belly twisted and swooped. More naive poets might write about that feeling.

"The Balladairans are here," Pruett said quickly, to escape it. "Or they will be soon."

Kiras narrowed her eyes. "They're docking now. Soldiers. The King's Own. How do you know?"

"Soldiers?" *The King's Own.* Shit. If *Lord Governor* Yoroub had gotten his smallclothes in a knot and complained about rebels trying to infiltrate his city and spread sedition, why wouldn't the capital send their best? Especially after the absolute shit fête that was the Qazāli rebellion. There was no Touraine here to fuck it up for Balladaire this time.

"Aye."

Pruett's eyebrows rose. "And you've just been sitting here, waiting for me to wake up?"

A gentle warmth joined the twist in her stomach, spreading in her chest like it had when she woke up and saw Sevroush watching over her. She didn't hold on to it. Holding on to feelings like this didn't ever do much more than hurt.

"You're the captain," Kiras said, as if that explained it. Her brown face flushed darker, and she pushed an escaped curl back over her head. "How did you know?" she asked again, wary.

"Something is happening to me," Pruett admitted. "It's how we got here. Sevroush . . . led me here, I think."

"He warned you when the Masridāni attacked." Kiras took it all in

as a matter of course, like it was perfectly normal for your commanding officer to get visions from vultures while your head was between
her legs. But, Pruett noted as she squirmed beneath the woman's
intense golden stare and her gaze dropped to Kiras's mouth, maybe it
wasn't so strange to her after all.

"Yes."

Kiras licked her lips. "What do we do next, then, Captain?"

Pruett had been asking that question herself while she and her
handful of fighters had followed Sevroush's cryptic guidance to Ra's
El-Bahr. What did he want her to do here? It couldn't have been a
coincidence that he led her to the rest of her people, but the Balladairans? Was that a coincidence?

Good luck was as useful as a good plan. More useful, even. Pruett
splayed her fingers over the covers.

"How many of us are there, all told?" In the back of her mind,
pieces of the puzzle were starting to come together.

"Between yours and mine? Nineteen."

Sky above. Out of fifty. She balled her fists, clenching the blankets tight. The moving pieces in her head clarified. One of them, the
brightest of all, was rage. Rage that Yoroub thought he could get away
with this, at his smug sky-falling face, a mind-numbing hatred like
she'd never felt for Balladaire.

"I have a plan," Pruett said, realizing it was true as soon as she said
it. "I need to speak to the commander of the King's Own."

Kiras pulled back, face suspicious. Pruett hadn't realized they'd
been drawing closer to each other.

"A plan for what?"

"To liberate Masridān and help Qazāl, of course." Pruett smiled her
fishhook smile, but Kiras didn't pull farther away. "Jaghotai sent us on
a mission, didn't she?"


Touraine was a shit liar. She was a shit liar because she didn't know
how to commit. She had second thoughts. She let other people get

into her head. She listened to them. That was why she was a better commander, why people gravitated to her. But it was also why she was blown in the wind. Sky above, Pruett missed that woman.

Pruett, however, was not a shit liar.

First, Pruett made her way to the Balladairan camp where the King's Own was stationed outside of Ra's El-Bahr.

Her heart thumped a riot in her chest. She knew riots, now. They haunted her dreams. Was this what Tibeau felt every time he stepped out of line in Balladaire? When he dared pray the beads? Did Tour feel like this when she waltzed over to the rebels and left Pruett behind?

It took most of the walk to the Balladairan camp to put the precise feeling into words.

There was a thrill in taking your life in your own hands, come what may.

Before she reached the camp, she was hailed by a sentry.

"Put your hands up where we can see them, sand dog."

Pruett placed her hands atop her head, which was wrapped in the desert scarf. The action left her vulnerable.

"State your purpose."

"My name is Lieutenant Pruett," she announced, "late of the Balladairan Colonial Brigade, Rose Company."

"She doesn't look like a Sand," one muttered to the other.

A lazy smile crept across Pruett's face. The calm that flowed through her was out of place and yet . . . Without a waver in her voice, she called, "I have my lieutenant pins in my pocket as proof. I trained and served under General Rosen Cantic. I fought under General Dupré against the Taargens in the second Taargen War."

More muttering: "At least she doesn't butcher Balladairan like the other dogs."

"Go check."

The one who spoke trained his musket on Pruett's chest, circling around her to keep clear of his companion. She kept her hands high while the second blackcoat approached. She took him for the younger one.

"Hip pocket." She nodded down. The soldier's fingers slipped deftly in and out, emerging with two golden pins, each one a pair of entwined wheat stalks.

"Collar pins are real enough," he called to his comrade.

"She could have killed anyone for them." The soldier with the gun came closer. "Why'd you come here, then?"

Pruett turned just enough to keep his leveled gun and his companion in her sights. "I have a message for the commanding officer. Only the commanding officer."

He scoffed. "Or we could shoot you now."

"You could do. Then you wouldn't break the siege at Samra'."

"There is no siege at Samra'," the man growled.

"Not yet." Pruett shrugged. The two soldiers shared a glance. "Just take me to your commander. Let them decide. This is above your head, and you know it."

That nudged them. The older one gestured with his gun for her to move ahead of him toward the camp.

"Thank you, gentlemen."

And with that, Lieutenant Pruett marched into the Balladairan camp, leaving her Sands long behind her. She glanced up to find the tracery of Sev's wingspan against the sky. *What do you see, Many-Legged? And what will you tell them?*

The surprisingly young commander sat at a travel desk that was scattered with correspondence and a map held down on one corner with a small dagger. Pruett had been expecting some gray-haired veteran like Cantic, all sharp edges worn down to the bone. Instead, he was a barrel-chested noble with a ruddy-gold stubble he kept stroking while he spoke.

"Lieutenant. I'm General LaVasse, marquis de Moyenne, of the King's Own. My men said you have a warning for me?"

"Yes, sir." So easy to slip into these old habits. Not for long, she promised herself. Only as long as necessary. She would never live like this again. "I came from Qazāl by way of Samra'. I escaped from the rebellion in Qazāl, and the people who instigated the insurrection in El-Wast are trying to do the same in Samra'. They plan to hole themselves up and wait for the Qazāli Eaters to attack you from the flanks." Her shudder wasn't entirely false.

"I know about the rebels. The city is secure." Moyenne kicked back in his field chair and propped gleaming leather boots onto his desk and looked her over shrewdly. "All I've heard about are some Qazāli rabble-rousers led by an ex-conscript."

*Shit.* She was hoping Yoroub would be more on the circumspect side. Stupid hope. She ran over Moyenne's implications, seizing on the rest of the comment. "*Was* secure. It took you long enough to get here."

"Well…Lieutenant. Balladaire thanks you for your help and continued loyalty. I'm glad to see some of you can still be civilized. However, I'm not used to taking the word of strange Shālans for intelligence. We'll see what happens when we get to Samra'."

He was a smarter commander than Pruett had hoped. It would make the rest of her plan that much harder. Pruett kept the rigid bar in her spine that Cantic had put there twenty years ago. *It's all right. Kiras will do her part.*

"Do you know, I met the one who started all of this trouble in Qazāl?" The man spoke absently as if the words were just some vaguely interesting anecdote—like a small but not too impressive trophy kill. Pruett, on the other hand, stopped breathing. She clung to the words and tried not to show how badly she needed them.

"Did you, sir?"

"I did, indeed," he said, nodding with his lips pursed as he picked at his nails with the small knife. "Touraine El-Qazāli. I challenged her to a duel on Longest Night, right before I set sail." He smiled to himself. "All in fun, of course, all in fun. Princess Luca stood in for her, though." He smirked. "They say all sorts of things about those two. Not the kind of thing I go for, don't worry." Judging by his smirk, he didn't put it completely out of the question, though.

Longest Night. Depending on the weather and the ports, it could take anywhere from five to ten days to get to the Shālan coast from Balladaire. Winter. Two months since Pruett left Qazāl. At least Touraine was alive.

"That's—very good, sir, as you like, sir." She hesitated, trying to make herself seem uncertain—not that she was; she knew what she wanted now, she knew how to get it. She just had to find a different way to prod that arrogant Balladairan tendency to assume everyone accepted their superiority without question—anything else was simply barbaric. Better for Kiras and the others if she had more time to try and bring LaVasse around.

"I have one further request, sir."

He raised his eyebrows incredulously.

"Protection. The same protection as the Masridāni. I want a place again." Pruett swallowed at the lump that filled her throat. This was all a performance. That's all.

The marquis de Moyenne looked up from his knife and his nails and squinted at her, as if he could see her better that way.

"Why should I trust you? Give you free rein over my camp?"

Pruett shrugged. "I'm just one person, sir. What's the worst I can do? I'll stay out of the way, easy to ignore. I don't need free rein, just a place to sleep and food to eat."

He grunted. "Very well. For the sake of the information you gave and your loyalty, you can stay, but you'll be under guard. My men will take you to the quartermaster."

"Sir, thank you, sir!" Pruett snapped a crisp salute. So easy to slip into the habit of being what they wanted to see. He smiled at her benevolently, and Pruett wondered if this was how Touraine felt. It made Pruett want to be sick all over that pretty little map. How had Touraine managed it all those years, being everyone's perfect little windup soldier?

"Make sure he gets you a proper uniform," Moyenne called after her as the tent flap fell.

After the quartermaster set her up and she'd been fed, Pruett begged a little privacy—only a little, still seemed like they were practically in her lap—to go to the latrines. They were a row of digs off the side of camp. Far enough away from the cook fires and tents that it was like walking into another world. The night was inky black and the sky above studded with pinprick stars. She took a long, grateful drag on the cigarette she'd begged off a blackcoat.

Easy to look up there and feel tiny, like nothing else you could do with your small inconsequential self would ever matter. That might make some people, like Noé and Touraine, uncomfortable. Tibeau would have argued in her face. *Everything we do matters*, he would have said. He would have said something, too, like, *We're part of that*, and he would have gestured up at the sky, trying to put them up there in that vast black, but he would have been wrong. There was nothing up there for them, because they couldn't reach it, just like there was nothing down here for them unless they put their hands out and grabbed it, daring the lash, daring the sword.

Pruett laughed at herself. Since when did she give a shit about taking something for her own? It wasn't now, all of a sudden, face-to-face with Balladairans for the first time since they surrendered Qazāl.

Earlier, then.

When Yoroub and his assistants had come, with the sticks up their asses, like they had the right to look down at her? When he'd sent a company of Masridāni blackcoats to slaughter her soldiers or scatter them to every corner of the desert?

Or was it the backhanded way Yoroub offered her what she refused to admit she'd ever starved for? As if she should be grateful when he dropped fresh shit in her bowl and said, "Eat up."

She dragged on the cigarette until the heat bit her fingers, then tossed it and squatted to look like she was having a piss. The smell of the latrines did enough to bring her down from her lofty poet's thoughts and into the shit where she belonged. She closed her eyes and looked for the knot of pain she'd come to associate with her... visions.

Was it the connection with Sev that made her want more?

An answering screech from above made Pruett open her eyes. A winged shape blotted out the tiny stars before landing in front of her.

"Hello, handsome." Pruett chuffed the bird under his beak, and he made a squawking chirrup that Pruett somehow knew was agreement with the compliment. She held out a strip of dried meat she'd taken from dinner, and he gave another squawk. Disappointment.

"What? It's the best I got, so it's good enough for you." Sevroush didn't take it. "Fine. More for me."

She shoved the meat in her mouth. She hadn't gotten over the novelty of meat she didn't have to kill herself, meat that was spiced while it smoked, meat that was definitely fully cooked and actually salted, sky above. While she chewed, she took out the two tiny scrolls she had scribbled in hasty camp-pencil scrawl, one for Kiras and one for Yoroub, and tied them to Sevroush's legs.

To Kiras: *In Masridān. Wait the carrion call.*

Pruett had wanted to write something more poetic, but sometimes you had to settle for clarity, especially on a tiny scroll. Was it the Eater who made Pruett want more than the shiftless drifting from master to master? So different from Touraine, and yet. Kiras didn't seem afraid of anything. Like she'd never had a master.

To Yoroub, one last (exceedingly generous, in Pruett's opinion) chance: *If Balladaire doesn't devour you, we will.*

"Hey! You! What are you doing?" One of the soldiers rushed her as she tied the last scroll to Sev's bird-shit-covered ankle.

"Go, go!" Pruett waved the bird on just as the soldiers reached them. One lunged for Sev, but he was already in the air. The other aimed for Pruett's head with the butt of her rifle. Pruett caught the blow on her forearm, and pain echoed through the bone. She crouched protectively over it out of reflex, but the first soldier was leveling his own gun, trying to take aim at Sev's dark shape across the sky.

Pruett dived at him as the rifle report cracked through the night.

She searched the sky until she spotted Sev winging away back toward Ra's El-Bahr just as the next strike took her in the gut. The relief was enough to make her smile through the pain. Even as they beat her and dragged her back to General Marquis de Moyenne, she smiled. Sevroush would get to Noé and Kiras, and Kiras would know what to do because Kiras was an Eater. Kiras did what needed to be done.

Kiras would do her part, because Kiras was not Touraine: Kiras would not let Pruett down.

# CHAPTER 37

# PLUCKING THE ROSE

Ghadin screamed when Aranen told her she would lose her arm. The break was bad, the priestess said—very bad. The entire joint shattered, infection making it ooze. They could wait and see, or they could amputate it and be certain.

"Please?" Ghadin had asked, when she woke up from her first medically induced doze. "Can you save it?"

A frightened child, half-delirious with pain. How had she become the crux around which an empire turned?

Aranen had drugged her with something even stronger, and with Touraine and the Balladairan physician's help, Aranen spent an entire day trying to reconstruct the girl's arm and elbow.

A week after her surgery and she was finally spending more time awake than asleep, but she barely said a word to Aranen and Touraine.

"Go to her. Sit awhile," Aranen said after Touraine had sighed a little too loudly.

Touraine was keenly aware of the passing time. Two weeks on the short side, Luca had said. One week already gone and Touraine was no closer to understanding who had left the roses or tried to kill Durfort and the rest of the nobles. Nothing that would save Luca's throne.

"Who?" Touraine asked. "Luca?"

"No, girl. Ghadin. You've been avoiding her."

Touraine flushed. "I have not."

She did look in on the girl, several times a day. She looked in, asked Ghadin how she was, accepted the grunt in return, and then— retreated like a coward.

Fine. Touraine was avoiding Ghadin. More accurately, she was avoiding the baleful way the girl looked at her arm, the way she winced when she moved, or gasped when she reached for something with the wrong arm out of habit.

Everything Ghadin suffered now was Touraine's fault.

Touraine hadn't been able to heal her. Touraine hadn't known that Nicolas had taken her, kept her in that fucking dungeon. She hadn't found Ghadin before Nicolas. She'd been too frozen by her own fear during the carriage attack to keep Ghadin safe.

Touraine had brought Ghadin to this snake pit in the first place when she knew she should have left her on the banks of the Hadd.

Touraine scrubbed her damp palms on her thighs. "All right."

Ghadin was staring at the ceiling when Touraine came in.

"Ghadin. Hey."

"I'm fine."

"Aranen says you can start flexing your fingers soon."

"She said I can try. I tried. I can't."

Touraine took the seat beside the bed. "Can I keep you company?" She waved the book in her hand. The one Saïd had given Touraine before she left. "Didn't know if you could hold it yourself, and I used to like reading when I was sick back in the barracks, so—" She stopped abruptly. She was babbling.

Ghadin looked over with hooded eyes, but she didn't send Touraine away. Ghadin might not hate her after all.

Touraine sat back heavily in the chair and flipped open the volume to the first page. "*The Sultan with No Sultanate*," she read, slowly sounding out the Shālan letters.

"That's a story for children," said the scowling child.

"Is it now?" Touraine raised an eyebrow. "I don't know it."

"You wouldn't." Ghadin stared at her knees tenting the coverlets. She glanced sidelong at Touraine. "I guess you can read it."

"You're so generous."

Ghadin gifted her sarcasm with an eye roll.

Touraine read the first story, and Ghadin listened quietly. So quietly that Touraine thought Ghadin was sleeping. She wasn't. She was still staring at her knees, her thoughts elsewhere and her eyes shining.

Touraine closed the book on her finger. "Mm?"

"When are we going home?"

"I—"

A thousand lies died on Touraine's tongue at the weariness on Ghadin's young face. The tight pain at the corners of her eyes.

"I don't know when I'm going home. I made a promise to the princess. She can send you back, though, as soon as you're well enough to travel."

Ghadin gripped the coverlet with her good hand. "I don't want to go alone."

"With Aranen, then."

Did Cantic ever feel this same wrench of sympathy looking at the Sands when they were children? Did she feel responsible for every pain? Did Cantic feel it all and still choose what she chose?

Touraine made herself meet Ghadin's eyes. "I'm sorry I didn't get to you in time, Ghadin."

"Did you even look for me, or were you just 'keeping promises' to the princess?"

"Ghadin—" Touraine warned.

The girl's jaw jutted.

"I spent every day combing the city for you. For weeks. I looked for you, I looked for whoever attacked the carriage. From sunrise until the drunks passed out in the Shāl-damned gutters. You haven't even told me where you were!"

They stared each other down until Touraine closed her eyes and exhaled sharply.

"Princess Luca is the reason you're out of Le Fontinard. So I'm going to help her find out who's trying to kill her. I won't go home until that's done."

Touraine stood and tucked the book beneath her arm. Then she thought better of it and set it on Ghadin's bedside table.

"Get some rest, kid. Yell if you need me."

"What if she's just as bad as the rest of them? What if the people fighting her are just like us?"

The words hit Touraine's back like bullets, and she froze. Turned slowly.

"What people fighting her?"

Ghadin waited stubbornly for an answer.

Touraine sighed, palms up. "That's the question, isn't it? She's willing to help the Qazāli, though, and no one else in this Shāl-forsaken empire is. That counts for something, right? Sometimes you just have to trust."

Touraine didn't know if she was trying to convince Ghadin or herself.

Ghadin mulled skeptically over the words while scratching delicately around the edge of her bandages.

"We help her," she said, "then we go home?"

"Yeah." Touraine's heart twinged at the thought. Part of her would be relieved to turn her back on this court. Another part, though... just like it had over the past year, part of her would yearn to be back here. It was home, too. Every time something happened to remind her of her resentments, something else would remind her how much this place fit her body like a warm glove. *Wrong. They carved you up to fit this place.*

Ghadin bit her lip. "I know who attacked the carriage."

After Ghadin shared what she knew—"there's a girl, she's like us"— Touraine flung open the tall window in her own bedroom and stood by the sill. Thick flakes of snow floated down. They lacked the true force of a driving storm, but there was enough wind to send a few of them floating inside Touraine's room to melt in the warmth. She shivered in the cold air. Yes, she had missed this. And she had missed complaining about it with the Sands while they stamped their feet warm and told stories of supposed conquests and teased each other when those conquests were proven false. It was home. Or at least, it was half of one. She flexed her fingers and ran her thumb along the grief rings for Tibeau and Aimée. Eventually, she would run out of fingers.

She found Perrot in the corridor. The captain was leaning against the wall with that bored semi-alertness every soldier perfected as soon as they could.

"Perrot!"

He jumped out of his doze. "Sky above, woman."

She dragged him inside by the lapel. It was easy, now, to fall into physical habits she'd had with Tibeau.

"We're going hunting."

With a grunt of satisfaction, Fili slid the wooden leg onto the stump of her mother's thigh. It made a satisfying slip-sigh as it found the resting place at the thickest point. Maître Gaspard was out, so they had the back room of the workshop to themselves.

"Ah." Guérin's sigh matched the leg's.

"How does it feel?" Fili asked hopefully from her knees.

"Surprisingly comfortable. How does it stay in place?"

Fili hopped up and took the leather harness she designed with the leatherworker's apprentice. She demonstrated how the straps cinched, and she felt closer to her mam than she ever had before. When she was a kid, she could never wait for her mam to come home from the palace, but it was only ever a month of leave at a time. Fili would cling to her like wood rot until it was time for her to go back. It had never been enough.

Not this year, though. They lived in the same city now, and her mam had no duties, but Fili had gone out of her way to avoid her. They didn't have anything to talk about—they disagreed about everything important.

Now Fili found herself full of questions only her mother could understand.

With the leg secure, Fili held out her arm to help her mam stand. Guérin shifted, trembled, shook trying to find her balance—and then she let go. She stood on two feet again.

"Here." Fili handed her mam the crutch.

They both held their breath as Guérin took one tentative step onto the new leg. Then, from the new leg to her flesh leg. Then another and another, to one end of the empty workshop.

"Does it support your weight? Is it too heavy?"

Guérin nodded to one of the questions, concentrating as she walked back. Her brow was spotted with sweat, and she was breathing more heavily.

"Is it okay?"

"Yes, yes. It's going to take some getting used to is all. My brilliant, perfect child." Guérin grabbed her and held her close, pressing her nose into Fili's hair. "Thank you. This is wonderful." Fili hid her pleased smile against her mam's chest.

"You're welcome, Maman." Fili swallowed the lump in her throat. "You'll have to practice a bit, but it shouldn't hurt."

"I'll start now, then." Guérin clapped her hands together. "Keep my mind occupied. How did you come up with this?"

For the next hour, they peppered each other with simple questions while Guérin made small laps around the shop, taking breaks for tea. It was like they were getting to know each other for the first time: letting her mam peek below the surface of who she had become, learning things about her mam that she'd never had the chance to know.

"Maman...what was it actually like guarding the princess?"

Guérin went immediately on guard, gripping her crutch even tighter.

"I don't want to fight," Fili said quickly. "I just want to know."

The wrinkles in Guérin's forehead smoothed. "She is kinder than you give her credit for," she said thoughtfully, continuing her lap. "Or...at least, she's got ambitions of kindness. Also has ambitions of ambition. It's hard." She paused to breathe and met Fili's eyes. "She's worth protecting. I don't regret keeping her alive. I want you to understand that."

Fili leaned against her worktable and dug a fingernail idly into the wood. "Did you ever kill anyone for her?"

Guérin's step hitched, and she steadied herself with a grimace. "Like who?"

The question had been eating away at Fili after Longest Night. Fili had poisoned people for the Fingers. Not to make them ill, but to kill them. That noblewoman, seizing while her friends panicked around her... Fili couldn't stop seeing her.

"I don't know. Anyone."

Guérin winced her way back to her seat. She didn't answer until she'd stretched her legs back out.

"I did. Not a lot, but I did." She held Fili's gaze defiantly, waiting for Fili to condemn her again.

"Was it hard?"

Guérin looked at Fili as if she were a sudden and surprising puzzle. "No. If I didn't, Luca would have died. It wasn't even a choice. Why?"

It wasn't the answer Fili had expected. No shred of regret, just purpose. Fili could be that, if she had to.

"I wondered what it was like."

"Why?" Guérin forced a laugh. "Are you going to kill someone?"

Fili started to laugh back, just as forced, when a sharp rap-rap-rap on the heavy outer door turned the sound into a strangled yelp.

Her mam was up in an instant, all the weight on her real leg, positioning herself between Fili and the door, gripping her crutch like she would use it as a club. The gesture made Fili feel small, but in a way she'd missed. Safe.

The knock came again, more earnest.

"Wait here," Guérin said in a low voice. She limped to open the door.

Fili couldn't see the figure waiting outside, but she heard her mam's cry of delight, and then she enveloped the other person in a one-armed hug.

"Maman?" She crept out of the back workshop and into the front room, where the fire was burning low.

Guérin was smiling, and she stepped aside to gesture at Fili. The woman Guérin spoke to was darker, like Ghadin, her hair cut short beneath a tricorn. She wore a swell's clothes, but she had the same soldier's bearing that her mam had, straight backed, eyes probing corners.

"Fili, come here. Meet a…colleague of mine." She turned back to the other woman. "This is my daughter, Phillipette. She's 'prenticed to the carpenter. Look here." She pointed down to her wooden leg. "Fili, this is Ambassador Touraine El-Qazāli. We—worked together in Qazāl."

There was a world of unspoken history in that hesitation.

"Good afternoon, Phillipette," El-Qazāli said formally.

"Fili," Fili answered automatically.

"Come in." Guérin limped toward the front table, where Fili and Maître Gaspard normally seated clients. It was close to the fire and cozy, especially after the burst of cold air the woman had let in. The ambassador stomped the snow off her boots and joined them.

"Are you here to commission a piece?" Fili's mam asked. "Something happened to Her Highness's cane?"

El-Qazāli was looking at Fili quizzically. Fili hung close to the wall, keeping the space between her and the ambassador. The woman blinked as Guérin's words reached her.

"No—that is—" El-Qazāli shook her head and looked quickly between Fili and her mam. "Fili. I work closely with the princess. She thanks you for your gift. She sent me with a token of her gratitude."

The ambassador held something out. Fili had the feeling the woman was taking note of everything.

"A rose from her mother's own garden."

Thick and beautiful, pale as fresh snow, thorns long and pointed. A fresh cutting. Fili recognized the rose immediately and gasped, jerking back. Ambassador El-Qazāli's eyes flashed.

*She knows.*

What were they going to do to her?

Oblivious, her mam frowned with her forehead while she smiled with her mouth. "It's beautiful, but why?"

El-Qazāli smiled warmly at Guérin, but her eyes never left Fili. "She appreciates the work Fili did on the cane. Present her with this and she'll offer you a boon of your choice." She flicked an eyebrow up.

*RUN*, every muscle in Fili's body shouted. But if she ran, her mam would know what she'd done, and if her mam knew, all of that pride, all of that warmth between them in the workshop, it would warp like raw wood in the rain.

*Keep working with the Fingers and she'll find out eventually*, a pointed voice said in the back of her mind. Fili could delay that, though, and find a way to explain in a way her mam would understand.

So Fili tried to look relaxed. She sat on the bench across from the ambassador and said, "I-I'm glad she liked it."

"She did. She'd love to thank you in person." El-Qazāli looked to Guérin, and her mam took the hint.

"You should go. A princess's gratitude can be…lucrative." Her mam gave the ambassador a wry look, and the ambassador snorted at their joke.

"No, thank you." Fili ducked her head down, eyes on her lap.

"I know you have your opinions, but I mean it." Guérin's voice was firmer.

"Opinions?" The ambassador gave Fili a crooked smile.

"Nothing," Fili said, the same time as her mam said, ticking off her fingers, "She thinks the princess is spoiled, irresponsible, and unfair."

"Maman!" Fili cried.

This time, the ambassador's snort turned into a full laugh before she stifled it. Her look was more appraising.

"We're all entitled to our opinions," the woman said. "The princess is used to that. If you can keep them to yourself long enough, though, you'll be safe. You have my word. The princess wants to offer you a place in her service."

Fili stilled. *In her service?*

"I don't—I don't know." She tucked a lock of her hair behind her ear nervously.

"Think on it. Quickly." The ambassador stood, placing the rose on the table and rapping her knuckles against the table with casual finality. She wasn't a very tall woman, but she was well muscled and moved like a well-oiled hinge—silent, graceful, fit to its purpose.

"I'll drop by in a day or two for a response? Your mother's right. Princess Luca's gratitude can be very lucrative."

"Don't worry," Guérin answered for Fili. "I'll take care of it."


The ambassador's visit left Fili distracted, stumbling through the motions until her mam left. Then she lost herself in the simple crafts her master needed finished, things that didn't require concentration—sanding, lacquering, and the like.

What if Fili did run? Fili could shelter with another Finger, she could find work with another carpenter, she could leave the city. She'd never be able to see her mam again without telling her what she had done, why she had run away.

If Fili went to hear Luca's offer, the Fingers would think they were right about Fili all this time.

Unless she told them.

It was late when Maître Gaspard burst into the shop with a gust of cold air.

"Shut the door, Master!" Fili laughed, setting the tools on the table. Nervous laughter, a cover over what she was girding herself up for.

He made a show of shivering in the open door before kicking it shut with his heel. "Glad to see you didn't burn down the shop while I was gone."

"Got more work done than you would have," she retorted. The usual banter, the usual comfort. She tried to let it slide over her. *He'll know what to do.*

She'd decided not to confess to her mam about the poisoning. She didn't want her mam groveling to the princess on her behalf. She also didn't think she could stand for her mam to know what she'd done. She wanted to hold that pride close to her a little longer. *My brilliant, perfect child.*

"Anything new in the streets?" she asked, casually twisting to speak to him from the workbench.

"My hands are empty," he said, waving a steaming mug in one

hand while he waved the other empty one. He grinned behind thick
whiskers.

He brought the mug to the workbench, and Fili smelled chocolate.
Her mouth watered immediately. She grabbed it and sighed with the
first sip. Milk warmed with chocolate. A new treat in the city, rare and
expensive, but Maître Gaspard knew the right people, and the right
people liked him.

Behind his words, though, was a code: if your hands were empty,
there was no news from the Fingers to report.

He hovered easily over the worktable to see what she'd gotten up
to all day, humming contentedly—he was always content with Fili's
work—as he turned pieces over.

"My hands...aren't exactly empty."

Her master looked sharply over his shoulder from the cabinet he
was hunched over. "Hein?"

"The princess—"

Her master's entire demeanor changed, from perplexed to brusque.
Fili thought he was about to shake her, he turned toward her so fast.

"Has she found you out?" He looked toward the door like he could
hear the gendarmerie coming for him. For them.

"I think so," she said in a small voice. Her master didn't know Fili
could feel the wood, the plants, the earth like a part of herself if she
went quiet enough to listen. She couldn't tell him exactly all that the
princess had found out. "The princess wants to meet me. I think—she
wants me to work for her."

"Who came? Was it that girl?" Her master narrowed his eyes.

"No!" she said quickly.

If it wasn't Ghadin, though, how did the ambassador know where
to find her? A stone dropped into the pit of her stomach. With less
conviction, she said, "Not her. It was the Qazāli ambassador. Ghadin
knows the ambassador, but—"

"So she is a spy," he growled. He punched his fist into his other
hand, and Fili was glad that Ghadin had gotten away that day.

"No." Fili put her hands up placatingly. "It has to be something else."

"If she's not a spy, how does that sand flea even know the ambassador?"

Fili went still. "Don't call her that."

She watched as Maître Gaspard considered her carefully, and then his face relaxed. He nodded and said, "Sorry."

Despite the insult, the rest of his words echoed Fili's thoughts too closely for her to rest easily.

"They—she and the other Qazāli—they don't like the princess, either. She gutted their country." Fili spoke slowly, sidling back up to something she'd been thinking about since she met Ghadin. "It might not be the worst thing, working with them. Together—"

Her master was already shaking his head—ruefully, but still. "Brother Michel and the rest have already discussed it. The aims'll be too different. Won't get everyone on board if we have to spread the changes thin across us and them. Easier to hit the nobles hard and concentrate on what we want." He wiped his mouth with the back of his hand without meeting her eyes and mumbled, "After. One step at a time."

Fili let the conversation lie, content enough to have passed on the warning. She kept thinking about the idea she'd had earlier, though. After dinner, when they had both moved on to idle work—him looking over plans for a client's shelf, her carving a vine border on a desk— she asked:

"What if I go meet her? The princess, I mean."

Her master frowned and looked up. "You want to work for her now?"

"Not work for her—not really. I could be close, though. I can get you information. The Fingers don't have anyone that close to her, do we?"

Maître Gaspard's face went dark and thoughtful. It wasn't his look; it was Brother Michel's. It was the same expression they'd all worn as they planned the Longest Night attack.

"Let me speak with Brother Michel," he said. "You're right. There might be an opportunity in this."

# CHAPTER 38

# THE PRINCESS

Sabine failed to kill the duke.

After she and Luca filled the bottles, she charmed her way into the duke's private wine cellars, claiming she had a new crate of wine for the duke. What did a servant care? She was the wine-soaked marquise, handsome and harmless. Most of the wine in the cellars came from her estates; what was another crate?

She knew just how to place them: which bottles the servants would take first, which vintages Nicolas preferred.

The duke had drunk the wine; an entire bottle was gone. And yet, he breathed.

When Luca asked, Roland the monk had only shrugged and said, "Your friend probably measured the dosage wrong. Poison is an imprecise method. I do not prefer it."

They had been so careful.

"You don't have to go through with this," Sabine said in a low voice as the three of them walked through the palace corridors to Luca's abdication announcement in the Grand Hall. "I haven't signed yet."

Touraine walked on Luca's left side. She made no such reassurances.

Touraine had also failed. Not to find the person who Luca had taken to calling "the Rose." Touraine had found the likeliest suspect, and Luca wished she hadn't. Guérin's daughter. The daughter of the woman who would have given her life for Luca's. The girl had magic;

Ghadin had witnessed it with her own eyes. The girl had also tried to kill Sabine with poison.

The revelation had come too late. The girl was coming to the abdication today, but the throne was already out of reach.

Willingly surrendered.

Luca stopped before the doors of the Grand Hall, her last allies at her side and their guards at their backs. She held her head high.

"Maybe there's another way," Touraine murmured at last. It sounded like a struggle. "The girl will be here today. If we just have more time—"

"There is no more time. I promised you I would find a way, and this is the only way left. I will keep my promises to you, Touraine."

Luca heard Touraine's sharp exhalation beside her, but kept her eyes trained forward as the herald announced her as Her Royal Highness, the Crown Princess Luca Ancier, for the last time.

The hall was full and the room was bristling with palace soldiers and personal guardsmen. So many people there to watch her give up everything she had worked for, though none of them knew it yet.

*You are working for more than a single moment*, she reminded herself. *You are building more than a throne.*

Winter was well and truly in its stride. Everyone dressed in wool waistcoats and thick overcoats. The twin fireplaces burned brightly at either end of the hall, doing their best to take the edge off the wide room's chill.

The fires did not, however, stop the tremble in her hands.

Touraine cleared her throat and gave a subtle nod to the large wall clock hanging above one of the fires. There, both looking a little out of place among the nobles, stood Guérin and her daughter. The Rose. They ambled nervously around members of the High and Middle Courts, like mice trying to avoid being stepped on.

Nicolas waited at the dais, speaking with the rest of the High Court, including Ghislaine, who had returned just for this. His eyes weren't on Luca, but she knew he was as aware of her movements as a hawk.

*It seems we're all mice today.*

"Do you want me to join them or…" Sabine raised an eyebrow toward the dais.

"Yes. I'll be there in a moment. Tell my uncle I'm just greeting a friend."

Sabine smiled wryly. "He'll think you're planning a coup."

Luca bared her teeth. "Reassure him."

Together, she and Touraine met Guérin and her daughter beneath the massive clock.

"Guérin, my friend." Touraine gave the ex-guard a soldier's clasp, and then bowed to the daughter.

Touraine wore her Balladairan finery easily these days, without picking at the hems or nervously fingering the embroidery of her waistcoat. Instead of a cravat, though, she wore a Shālan scarf, tied in a complicated knot. The beautiful colors spilled from her neck, contrasting against her dark coat and trousers. She moved with a confidence Luca had only seen her display in a fight, the wolfish grace transformed to deadly elegance for the court.

As Touraine smiled warmly at Guérin, and then at Fili, Luca realized something else—Touraine, "charmingly naive," with a face more readable than a child's grammar primer, was dissembling. Not just stuffing down her angry thoughts and obeying orders, but making a completely false face and presenting it to the world. To a friend.

"Inès. Please, introduce me to your fine artisan." Luca flashed her own court smile, a touch warmer than the usual frost. She gestured with her cane, the one Guérin and Fili had gifted her.

"Your Highness," Guérin said, bowing, "This is my daughter, Phillipette—Fili."

Luca bowed her head slightly. "An honor, Fili. It seems we have a lot to talk about. Would you two excuse us?"

Touraine's new court mask slipped as she hesitated, a flash of worry crossing her face, but Luca gave her a reassuring nod. Guérin smiled proudly and squeezed Fili's shoulder, and Luca felt a throb of guilt as the two women left.

"So. You're the Rose. You used magic to escape my palace after attacking my guests." Luca didn't stop the anger from edging into her voice, but she kept her face pleasant; Guérin would be watching.

"How did you know?" Fili's hands fidgeted in her panic. She was only, what, sixteen years old, seventeen? Sky above.

"I didn't until now. I'm not going to hurt you," Luca said, soft as she could manage. "Do you know what I want?"

"The Qazāli said you have a job for me," Fili stammered.

Luca tilted her head from side to side. "Something like that, yes."

She could feel her uncle's eyes boring into her.

"Tell me about Balladaire's magic. How it works, how it's powered, what it can do."

Fili's brow furrowed. "I don't have to tell you anything."

"You murdered people in my palace." Luca took a step closer to Fili, her voice hard, her smile unwavering. "I should have you hanged in the public square, but I'm not because I'm promising you amnesty if you tell me what you know. Despite what you've already done, despite your friends and the way you feel about me, you and I can do more good if we work together."

Fili stared at her. Luca could see the cogs turning in her mind as if they were the clock above them. The pendulum measured their breaths. Fear lurked in the young woman's eyes, but anger simmered there, too. Luca wanted to admire her.

The girl sighed. "What do you want to know?"

*Everything.*

Luca couldn't have everything here, though, now. The room was slowly filling. Her uncle, waiting for everything he wanted to fall into his hands.

"Too many questions and not enough time." Luca waved her hand at the room. "After this, though, I'm at your leisure. Will you just tell me one thing?"

"All right?"

"How do you call it forth?" Luca asked, dreading the answer. "What does it cost? The roses in the garden, for example."

"How do you know about the cost?" Fili said, eyes wide.

Luca's heart sank. If there was still a cost and the cost was too great, then—Luca glanced over at Touraine, who chatted pleasantly with the old guard and Gil, who had joined them.

Fili followed Luca's eyes to Touraine. The woman with the golden eyes. There was something new in the young woman's eyes—fear? Awe?

"Is she a—a priest?" Fili asked. "That's why her eyes are funny? She's like..." *Me?* Luca heard the girl's unsaid word.

"The Qazāli priests say that their magic—their gift—is a matter of faith," Luca pondered aloud. "Is yours something similar?"

"You swear you'll give me amnesty?" Fili shot an anxious look toward her mother. "And you won't—my mam didn't know anything about—what happened."

"Of course," Luca rushed. "Full amnesty."

"Okay." Fili knit her brows as she searched for the words. "Not exactly. Not to me, anylight. When I touch a plant, I feel how we're connected. How this—this god, I guess—meant us to be connected. My blood reinforces that." She looked down at her thumb and rubbed it. She spoke like a fish finding the words to describe swimming for the first time. Like speaking to Luca made the act new and mystifying.

Blood was the cost, though, as it was in Qazāl.

"Can that connection be used to hurt people?"

Fili bristled. "I didn't use it in the palace if that's what you're asking."

"I'm not. I want to know if we can use it to defend the empire. Should need arise."

The more benefits she could show the people, the more likely they'd follow her when—if—the moment ever came that she could take her place.

Fili frowned, but this time it wasn't in distaste. "I don't know. I never tried."

The girl was stubborn as an ink stain, and Luca didn't have time to cajole more answers out of her. Around them, the guests grew restless. They were already nervous, clinging to their swords and their guards; who could blame them? Every time they gathered in the palace, a new tragedy shook them. Their voices dropped to a murmur, and more and more heads turned to her. Luca covered the lurch in her stomach with a slight bow.

"It seems I'm needed. Thank you for your help. Would you like to stand with the rest of my guests, on the dais?"

Fili looked conflicted, and no wonder. Hopefully there was just enough curiosity in her to keep her from getting even more involved with the Fingers.

When the girl nodded, Luca led her to the dais where the High Court waited. She steered Fili to Touraine and Gil, just to the side of the High Court, with the other councilors and advisors. Sabine stood between Ghislaine and Evrard. The old man bowed deeply to her but said nothing. The expression on his face, however, looked like that of a gambler waiting for dice to fall.

*That makes at least two of us.*

They weren't the only ones who had gambled on the outcome of this particular game. Who else would pay the price for her surrender?

Luca gave the comtesse her coldest glare. There was also the Moyenne representative—not Brice, who had sailed off to subdue the south for her uncle, but his younger sister, Camille.

Luca stepped into place beside her uncle. She felt a dizzying moment of déjà vu.

"You're making the right choice," he said softly. He was as nervous as she was. His brow was damp. He kept scanning the placements of his guards. "I'm proud of you."

The words were a mockery, but Nicolas was right about one thing. Luca stepped forward. *You chose this.* She clung to that thought. If she didn't, she would weep.

"My noble Balladairans." Her voice cracked. She cleared her throat and tried again, pitching her voice to carry. "As you know, my father named me heir to the throne before his death. I was meant to succeed him. Since he succumbed tragically during the Withering, my uncle has led this empire for over twenty years as regent while waiting for me to come of age. However..."

Her uncle stood rigidly beside her, waiting for some last trick in her speech that would turn this all around and spear him instead. Luca had no more tricks.

She had made Touraine a promise. The acrobats were still in Le Fontinard. There was still good that Luca could do. So she told herself when the next words refused to come out.

She swallowed and started again.

"However, my uncle and I have decided it best to divide our efforts. In my travels to the Shālan colonies and what is now again the sovereign nation of Qazāl, I developed an understanding with the Qazāli about their culture, their needs, and even their religion."

Gasps hushed across the hall.

"It has put me in a unique place to oversee Balladaire's relations with the Shālans at home and abroad. I hereby renounce my claim to the throne and will instead serve as minister of Shālan affairs for my uncle, who will take the throne as king, unless he is incapable or no longer able to fulfill his duties therein."

The entire room was silent, and every single eye and jaw-dropped mouth was turned to her.

And so, it was not a surprise that no one, not even Luca, saw the palace soldier fire until it was too late.

The report of the shot cracked through the great hall like a whip, and the audience scattered like spooked horses.

Luca turned for Touraine, as if she were a magnet and Touraine her lodestone. The ex-soldier stood, frozen, looking glassy-eyed toward the sound. Luca dived back, reaching to pull the woman close, to force her to the ground, even as the palace guards flurried to movement around the dais. Protecting the most noble. Fili, too, was frozen in fear like Touraine. Looking for her mother, perhaps.

"Get down!" Luca extended her arm to the girl, too, *she could protect them all*—

And then, just as Luca pulled Fili close, the girl's face hardened into determination.

"Luca!" Touraine had shaken off her daze. She reached for Luca, reached for Fili, pulling at the back of the girl's coat. Luca didn't see, she didn't expect—

Fili, with a sharp finger of steel, curling around Luca's torso as if in a hug.

Sharp pain in her ribs. In her stomach. Short punches, again and again. Steel poking through Fili's knuckles like a claw.

"No!" Luca pushed Fili away, but the girl got the blade in close.

Luca struggled harder and harder to draw a full breath. Her bad leg gave out, and she went down to her knee.

"Touraine?" Luca whimpered.

Fili's knife clattered to the ground beside Luca. The girl didn't stay to gloat over the body of the fallen princess. Her enemy. Luca only saw her leap from the dais and into the chaos of the terrified nobility.

Luca reached for Touraine as she fell.

# CHAPTER 39

# ON SELF-INTEREST (REPRISE)

"Touraine?"

Touraine's focus homed in on that word, that voice. Luca, reaching out as she folded to the ground. Fili, sprinting away. One part of her mind was still bewildered, trying to piece a story together. It wondered who was shot and if there were more attackers. It wondered if this was coordinated or opportunistic.

Another part cared only about one thing.

Touraine slid to Luca's side, grabbing her hand.

"Perrot!" Touraine shouted, looking frantically around for him.

He appeared at her shoulder.

"Get Aranen!"

The soldier hesitated only a second before looking at the princess on the ground. He sprinted away.

Touraine turned Luca over and pulled open her coat. She tried to catalog the wounds: one jab between the ribs, several in the belly, all narrow but deep. *Oh, Shāl. Oh, sky-falling fuck.* Touraine propped Luca on her lap to keep her from drowning in her own blood.

"Touraine?" Luca choked out. Her face was white as paste.

"You're going to be all right, Your Highness." She tried to fake a reassuring smile.

"Help me—up—"

"Shh. Stay. Perrot's gone for help." She stroked Luca's hair back from her face.

The rest of the High Court, including Durfort and the duke, remained on the dais in the protective cordon of their personal guards. They hadn't yet noticed the attack closer to hand.

Touraine shouted for the marquise. When Durfort saw Luca bleeding on the ground, she leapt over with a cry.

"Sit here, keep her tilted up—and give me your coat." Touraine slid out from beneath Luca and laid her in Durfort's lap.

As Touraine held the proffered clothes, though, she hesitated. It wasn't a bandage Luca needed—blood loss wasn't going to kill her. Aranen wouldn't get there in time to stop Luca from suffocating. Luca was still warm beneath Touraine's hands. That warmth soaking through Touraine's clothing. Every moment she didn't do something, Luca slipped further away.

Luca's eyes were too bright as they held hers. She reached for Touraine's hand with trembling fingers, catching only Touraine's sleeve. "I'm so . . . stupid."

"Shut up," Touraine said. "Aranen is coming."

"You . . . try?" Luca's eyes fluttered shut as she exhaled raggedly, then blinked slowly open again.

Touraine shook her head. "I can't." She put her bloody hand to Luca's mouth as the princess opened it to speak again. For a second, it did quiet the other woman. Her blue-green eyes went round with shock and her parted lips were still.

Her lips, turning faintly blue. Frothy blood bubbled at their corners.

"I can't breathe," Luca gasped. Her chest seized as her body panicked for air.

"El-Qazāli, please! Can't you do something?" Durfort begged.

She couldn't. She had tried. With Ghadin whimpering in her arms and Nicolas looking on, she had tried and she still hadn't been able to.

"I can't," she said again, trying not to see the fear in Luca's eyes as she coughed blood into her face—but Touraine couldn't look away.

Luca reached again for Touraine's hand, and this time, Touraine caught it. Grasped it tight in her own bloody fingers.

She had to try again.

*Please, Shāl,* Touraine prayed. *Please, I am begging you. Help me heal this arrogant woman. I know she's an asshole and this is probably completely fair in the bigger scheme of things, but please. She owes us more than death.*

Luca kept closing her eyes, then fighting to keep them open. To keep them on Touraine's.

"I love—"

"Shut up. Shut the fuck up. You don't get to say that to me. Not right now," she growled. Tears—angry tears, desperate tears—pricked at Touraine's eyelids.

*Please, Shāl. She owes us. She owes me. This is not how she will pay her debts.*

The heat in her hands grew as they slicked with Luca's blood. It was blood. Very likely Luca's lifeblood. Touraine swallowed, her entire body rebelling at the thought of Luca's coppery tang in her mouth. She didn't need to do that, though—that was only for unknitting. How had she done it to Rogan? She'd been three steps to dead herself. She'd had nothing left, she'd been nothing. Except anger. Except hatred.

What was she now?

She burned. She felt Luca's body not just as the thing she was cradling in her arms but as the individual pieces that made it up. She felt the spasming struggle of her lungs, the rupture of gut, the slashed skin and muscle aching to stitch back together.

"I deserve more than your death, Luca."

Touraine pressed her thumb to Luca's bloody skin and then to her tongue. The metallic thickness coated her entire mouth.

Luca's eyes fluttered open again at the words. Then they went wide as they landed on Touraine.

Then the heat flooded from Touraine's hands and back into Luca's body. Luca spasmed beneath Touraine's hands, jerking wildly before she went rigid, back arching away from Durfort's lap and into the hand Touraine had slipped up Luca's shirt to rest on her belly.

Was Touraine hurting her? What was she doing wrong? *Help me, Shāl. Guide me. I can do this*, Touraine thought. *I can do this. I have to do this.*

Luca's eyes rolled into the back of her head, and she went unconscious. She wasn't dead. Touraine could feel the surge of blood pumping in her chest, through her body. It moved like the River Nervure, flowing through La Chaise. But her breath was still.

"What are you—" Durfort's voice was a distant buzz, like a mosquito.

Touraine closed it out.

"You owe me, Luca," she growled. She closed her eyes and concentrated. Something was happening. Touraine imagined Luca whole, imagined her breathing, imagined her humming in her office as she worked, imagined her laughing at her own obscure jokes. "You owe me." The tears escaped Touraine's lashes.

Another burst of heat surged through Touraine's body, ripping a scream from her. Beneath her hands, Luca jerked and shuddered again. Touraine heard the rush of boots and saw Perrot's stricken face as he pulled Luca's body out of her hands. Touraine grasped for her, clutching her closer. She couldn't hold on, though. Her grip went slack.

*I'm not done.* "I'm not done," Touraine yelled, pushing herself to her knees.

She held up a bloody palm. Maybe it was the words, or the look in her eyes, or the fact that she was terrifying and covered in blood, but Perrot put Luca back down.

"Touraine. You did it." Out of nowhere, Aranen was beside Touraine, her eyes tight at the corners. She took Touraine's bloody hands and put them back on Luca's body. "Here, and here," she murmured.

"Are you—is she—can she do it again?" Durfort. Aranen hissed her quiet.

Touraine looked over at the marquise, expecting to see some sort of disgust, but Durfort's expression was hopeful and determined, not afraid. Touraine saw belief. Touraine saw faith.

Aranen put her hand on top of Touraine's, pressing something onto her—her prayer beads. Touraine turned her bloody palm to accept them.

When she touched Luca, she searched, she felt. She closed her eyes and tried to sink into Luca's body, to become aware of the other woman as she had been before. This time, the heat Touraine felt was definitely coming from within herself; Luca was so, so cold. She sensed the slow—too slow—ticking of Luca's heart.

Touraine squeezed the beads in her fist and prayed.

# CHAPTER 40

# NOT THE PRINCESS

Touraine read Luca stories from *The Sultan with No Sultanate* while she slept.

She sat on the edge of Luca's bed, her stockinged feet propped in the chair beside it, cradling the book from Saïd on her lap. Touraine rarely left, and though Durfort was almost as constant, Touraine had a lot of time alone. Luca's room, with the smell of her rose eau de parfum, the undercurrent of coffee and parchment, was as good a place as any to think about what would come next.

As a child in Balladaire, Touraine had imagined herself one of Balladaire's bright and victorious heroes, just like the stories she and Luca had grown up reading, worlds apart. The Shālan heroes were different. Humbled by their mistakes and by pain, they sacrificed for love and for Shāl. There was no clear victory, no savior, not even Shāl.

She hated what these stories asked of her.

The choice was coming to her soon—stay, or go? Qazāl or Balladaire? Embrace Shāl's magic, or push it away and hold it at a safe distance? She felt untethered, floating in a gray space of potential.

Once, she had felt too tethered. Chained by her history with Balladaire, held down by her desire for Cantic's approval—and then Luca's and even Durfort's.

On the other hand, she had a duty to right the wrongs of the past, some of which she'd caused. She wanted Jaghotai's and Aranen's approval just as badly, and Pruett's and even Ghadin's.

For the last two years, these desires had pulled her so hard that she had failed everyone, including herself. She'd cost herself the people she loved most.

She wanted to be free of it all, but she couldn't see the path to that freedom. Was it in Taargen? Was it in the mountains, where Djasha and Roland the monk had found their own oblivions? Was it in Shāl? The gray space felt like a fog, hiding her, muffling the world—its weight, its pain, its demands. She liked it.

There were no wrinkles in the coverlet, but Touraine smoothed the blanket out over Luca's stomach all the same.

Now that Nicolas would soon be king, she was in a political gray space as well. She had, in a roundabout way, achieved her goal: though Luca was not queen, Luca was still in the position to manage the Qazāli treaty. Touraine had accomplished what she'd come to do for Qazāl.

Now, Touraine would have the time to explore her own power. Another gray space within herself.

"How is she?"

The marquise de Durfort sauntered in with her usual affected carelessness, but her low voice was somber these days as they shared vigil over Luca's recovery. Instead of taking the chair at Touraine's feet, she sat on the other side of Luca's bed, so that she and Touraine were sitting side to side, with only Luca's legs between them. She smelled of horses and musk.

"The same."

The silence stretched awkwardly. Despite the overlapping vigils, she and Durfort hadn't spoken of the magic Touraine had used to heal Luca or the overheard conversation or even the failed plan to save Luca's crown. They hadn't talked about what that failure meant. What Luca had given up and for whom. In Touraine's mind, Luca was still the princess.

From the corner of her eye, though, Touraine saw Durfort glancing at her, and she knew that was about to change.

She met it head-on. It was easier to do, from this suspended gray calm.

"What do you want?" Touraine asked.

Durfort smiled ruefully to be caught out, her cheeks flushed with embarrassment that she shrugged off easily.

"I understand that I'm..." Durfort searched for the right words. "I'm not always what Luca needs. I mean, I'm charming and handsome and an excellent lay, but she'll need more than that when she wakes up."

She craned her neck to grin, but she didn't manage to joke away the pain in her eyes. Touraine wasn't the only one who had had too much to think. When Touraine didn't smile back, the marquise sobered again.

"You'll stay, won't you?" Durfort put her hand on top of Touraine's, where it rested on Luca's bedclothes.

Touraine slid her hand out from under Durfort's. "I thought being close to me was a political death?"

"Was I wrong?" Durfort raised her eyebrows pointedly. "I thought I was giving her the best advice at the time. As usual, she had other ideas."

"You were afraid."

Durfort nodded. "I was. Afraid for her, afraid for me. I still am. If she hasn't told you, I'm something of a coward."

"And?"

Durfort turned her hand up, gesturing at Luca. "Now, things are different."

"You mean she's not trying to keep a crown so she can do whatever she wants," Touraine said flatly.

Touraine expected Durfort to try and backtrack toward a different explanation, or to make the truth sound better, but the other woman only nodded.

"Exactly that."

"No."

"No?"

"Nothing's changed. If Luca had wanted to, she would have found a way to fight for me and keep her crown. She was just as scared as you."

Durfort frowned, dark brows knitting together. "You're not staying?"

A gentle knock and the delicate click of someone clearing their throat heralded Aranen's arrival.

Durfort jumped to her feet and bowed in half at the priestess, all traces of tension vanished. "My lady."

"Your Grace." Aranen returned the bow with a nod. "Would you please leave us with our patient for a moment? You can wait just outside if that's all right."

The look that Durfort threw Touraine promised another talk later, but she said, "No need. I have horses that need riding and flowers that need watering. I'll leave the—ah, I'll leave Luca in your excellent hands." She bowed again, grinning undaunted in the face of Aranen's wry skepticism.

Aranen clicked her tongue and rolled her eyes after Durfort left. "That woman is a force of nature."

"One particular aspect of nature, if we're being specific."

Aranen sniffed a delicate laugh. "It's all part of the balance. How is the patient? Or have you and the marquise been flirting over her unconscious body all this time?"

Touraine scowled. Aranen just waved her away. She checked Luca's pulse with two fingers at Luca's wrist and again at the princess's throat, just below her sharp jaw. Touraine's own fingers itched to reach out. To touch the soft skin, to make sure the pulse still fluttered beneath.

Then she pushed Touraine's feet out of the chair and sat in it. "She's doing well."

"Good."

"Good. So?" Aranen folded her hands in her lap and looked up at Touraine expectantly.

"So?"

"Will you stay?"

"Will *you* stay?"

"I find myself at a crossroads. I am drawn to a certain ambassador, and yet"—the priestess tilted her head to the side as she drew out the syllable—"I won't be disappointed to go back home."

Home. Olives and sand, or rosemary and the stretching plains? *Neither*, a voice said from that gray, untethered space.

"She gave up everything to help us," Touraine said, and believed it.

"She claimed to have our best interests at heart once before. I ended up in her jail cell. She also left you to die in one, if I recall correctly."

"I remember."

"You trust her now?"

Touraine tucked the blanket tighter around Luca's sleeping body.

"These are yours." Touraine unlooped the string of beads she had taken to wearing like Aranen did, tangled around her wrist. She hadn't managed to get all the blood out of the grooves, but she'd tried.

Aranen shook her head but didn't meet Touraine's eyes. "Keep them for now. They'll serve until you have your own."

"Would you help me study more healing?"

Aranen understood. "It seems like you're doing well enough for yourself."

There was pride on the other woman's face as well as in her voice. Touraine held out her forearm, baring a few fresh scars. Healed. Whatever was blocking her, she had found a way around it. She wondered if Shāl had anything to do with this gray detachment, this not-here-not-there feeling.

"How did you find your way?"

"I don't know." Touraine had been asking herself the same question, analyzing the heat that flowed from her fingertips. "I was thinking about it wrong, maybe? Faith, but faith in myself. Or just emptiness. Empty enough to be empty of doubt."

She didn't tell Aranen how much of her pleading had centered on not letting Luca go without making good on their bargain.

"By all rights, you could call yourself a priest, you know." Aranen gave her a small smile.

"No," Touraine said quickly. "I'm just a soldier."

Aranen raised her eyebrow. "My girl, you haven't been just a soldier in a very long time."

Touraine was about to give the other woman a wry retort, but a stirring beneath her hand drove every last thought but one from her mind.

"Luca?"

Luca blinked blearily and then—she smiled. "Touraine."

Luca's voice was hoarse and scratchy with disuse, but her name was the best thing Touraine had heard in ages.

She handed Luca a cup of water, holding it carefully to her lips, tipping it slowly. Luca didn't take her eyes off Touraine's while Aranen checked her over one more time. Then, as she so often seemed to need to, the doctor-priestess left discreetly.

"You saved me," Luca said.

Touraine nodded.

"Why?" Naked hope crinkled Luca's forehead. She was too tired for her mask.

Touraine should have said something jaunty, like *I didn't want to work with Nicolas* or *You still owe us*. The words wouldn't come. She could only stare at that mouth, the frown lines surrounding them. Luca's hair, loose and messy, falling across her shoulders. She wore a long white bed shirt that was open enough to reveal the edges of bare shoulder and collarbone and hard sternum.

"Touraine? Why?" she asked again. Her voice, usually so calm, so self-assured—it quavered.

Touraine closed her eyes. Braced herself to speak. In the long days and nights, listening to that clock tick, waiting for the princess to wake up, begging her to live, Touraine had found the courage to admit that the tether binding her to Luca wasn't their bargain for the Qazāli. In accepting that, Touraine was able to step away from it. To look at it from a distance and ask herself if it was actually what she wanted. If she would stay in Balladaire for the sake of whatever was or could be between them. If they ever could build anything worth holding on to.

"Why did you give up your throne?"

"For similar reasons, I suspect. I hope."

Luca held her gaze, and Touraine found it easy to match her, stare for stare. She didn't feel like shrinking away from her anymore. Luca looked away first. She caught sight of several baskets Touraine had stashed in a corner.

"What are those?" Luca asked sharply, sitting up in her bed.

"Honey pastries."

"From my uncle." It wasn't a question. Luca chewed on her lower lip.

"Yes?" The man hadn't brought them himself, but the basket had come with a card that Touraine had almost thrown into the fire along with the cakes themselves. She only hadn't because she didn't want to smell burning honey cakes while she sat with Luca.

"He used to send them to me when I got sick as a child. When I shattered my leg, he sent me so many I ate myself sick." Luca gave a pained smile.

"Don't eat them."

The smile faded. "He wouldn't hurt me." Luca forestalled Touraine's protest. "I know. I won't. I only...I wish things were different. Is that final, then? Has he had his coronation?" There was no energy behind her bitterness. Nothing but resignation and loss.

"Not yet. I think even he can't avoid how shitty that would look."

"And Fili?"

Touraine shook her head again. "Gone."

"How long have I been in bed?"

"Less than a week."

"Oh." Luca blinked. "It feels like so much longer. Like the whole world should have changed by now."

"It has." Touraine felt it, too.

Luca sighed and eased back against her pillows, wincing. "It seems like I'm not the only one interested in what you're doing next."

"You've been awake."

"You aren't the only one who can eavesdrop." Luca smiled, wry and tired. "I could use your help here, still. If I'm going to work with the Qazāli, I want to do it right."

Touraine felt a reflexive need to step back even as Luca reached out. Luca was threatening her delicate bubble of peace.

*You'll stay, won't you?* Durfort had said. The question was an afterthought to the demand. As if Touraine's answer were a given. Maybe that was the reason to make her choice. To step away from the clutch and grasp of empire. Before it sucked her in, devoured her like it did everyone, its poorest and its privileged.

And in Qazāl? Peace over all, the Shālans taught, but she had seen how willing plenty of them were to bend that tenet.

"You said I was done. One more thing, you asked, and I did it."

Luca opened her mouth, ready to spill out a new set of justifications. She closed her mouth. "Okay."

"I just want to be free." The words came out in a whisper. Touraine didn't even realize she'd said them out loud until Luca responded with a harsh, coughing laugh.

"If you're looking for an escape from duty, it never comes." Luca took Touraine's hand. The tenderness of the touch, her long fingers twined in Touraine's own, belied the bitterness of her words. "It will plague you, keep you up at night, make you hate yourself. You will never be good enough to satisfy it. It will make you give up the thing you want most in the world for what is necessary. You can't escape unless you stop caring. Can you do that?" Luca tilted her head, daring Touraine to lie.

With a heavy sigh, Touraine pushed herself to her feet and slid into her boots, one by one.

"Touraine?" Slight panic behind the question. "Where—"

Touraine leaned over and cupped her hand around the back of Luca's head. The princess stilled as she looked into Touraine's eyes, then down at Touraine's lips. Up again. Her eyes were blue as the ocean and shining with emotion. And when Touraine leaned down, Luca closed her eyes. Instead, Touraine pressed her lips onto Luca's forehead and held them there. Sky above, her heart was screaming at her. *Stay. Stay, stay, stay.*

Touraine rested the bridge of her nose against Luca's forehead and whispered, "You were dying, Luca. I..." To say the words she felt would be to knot another line to Luca, to Balladaire. So she said only, "Qazāl needs you alive."

She released her, then walked out of the room without meeting Luca's eyes again. If Touraine saw her face, she wouldn't be able to cut the line threatening to pull her back.

"Touraine, wait—" There was a rustle of bedclothes. A thunk as Luca's feet hit the ground.

Touraine strode through the anteroom quicker, but Luca followed, noisy as she struggled, her body still weak from the healing.

"Touraine, wait—is there anything—*anything* I can do to make you stay?"

Touraine stopped at the door, her hand outstretched on the curved handle, ready to open it. The metal was cool against her fingertips. It would have been easier not to turn around. Safer. It was the catch in Luca's voice that made her turn.

The ex-princess's face was blotchy pink. Touraine's throat tightened, but she forced her next words out.

"No. That's just it," Touraine answered softly. "You can't make me. It's my choice."

"Fine. It's your choice. Just tell me—" Luca pressed her fist to her mouth and took two shuddering breaths. "Is it because the council got everything you wanted out of me?"

Touraine's guilt was a bayonet in the gut. She *had* gotten everything she wanted out of Luca as far as Qazāl was concerned. The right promises, at least.

"No. I need something for myself."

Touraine swung the door open so quickly that Deniaud's hand was on her sword as Touraine passed her. The hiccuping sound of Luca fighting to keep her pain inside followed Touraine, and she walked faster. The calm, gray peace shattered as the sound sank into her bones. She had made her choice.

As soon as she turned the corner, she ran.

# CHAPTER 41

# THE DEATH KNELL

W e're leaving, then?" Aranen said when Touraine made it back to their rooms. The priestess was drinking Qazāli tea with Ghadin. Ghadin looked hopefully up at Touraine.

Touraine ignored Aranen—if she stopped, she would sit on the floor and never get up again. She strode into her bedchamber and closed the door. With her back flat against it, she hissed through her teeth. Here, outside of the gray space, the world hurt, and her eyes blurred.

Eventually, someone knocked. When she didn't answer, they opened the door, nudging Touraine forward until she rolled out of the way enough for Aranen to slide through. She took Touraine by the arm.

"Come. We're going to have a bath drawn for you, and you're going to sit in it and feel all of this." She led Touraine to the bathing chamber and pulled the bell to call the servants with water. Then she sat on the edge of the basin and regarded Touraine.

Touraine studied the tub, the bell pull. The perfumes and soaps on decorative shelves. What a bold extravagance. Hers now, as long as she was in the palace. As long as she was Luca's.

"I know I'm not supposed to want both," Touraine said, her voice low in her throat. "I know I'm not supposed to love the chains."

"I'm not your mother—"

"No, my mother is mean as cobra spit."

Aranen pursed her lips. "I'm not your mother, but I think you deserve better than her."

Touraine stared up at the ceiling, blinking rapidly. Inhaling through her nose, exhaling through her teeth.

"Maybe I do. Or maybe, just maybe, I deserve what *I* want for once. And…"

She trailed off, picturing Luca biting back her tears. Touraine had walked away from that in pursuit of an illusion of neutrality that crumbled as soon as she left. She hadn't wanted to choose at all. And yet, as Touraine left Luca behind, she knew.

"I think it might be her, Aranen. I may be the world's biggest idiot, but I think I want her. And for the first time, it won't hurt anybody else."

Aranen's breath caught in surprise. She waited a second, then said, "You're right. No one can ask you to martyr yourself to misery. But if you leave her now, the pain will pass. You'll make a new life. If you stay with her, it will never be easy, even at her side."

"You would know."

Touraine's laugh was biting, but Aranen only looked at her with gentle pity and squeezed Touraine's forearm.

"I *would* know."

Awkward silence filled the space between them like steam until Touraine dissipated it. "Since when did you become so invested in my relationships?"

"At this rate, my dear, all of the colonies should be invested in your relationships."

After another long silence, with her gaze focused somewhere Touraine couldn't follow, Aranen added, "Truthfully, though, if saving Princess Luca led you to—" She tapped her chest. "I am the last to stand in the way of Shāl's gifts."

When the bathing basin was full and Aranen was gone, Touraine stripped and sank into the hot water scented with lavender oil. She closed her eyes and let the water lap against her neck with each breath. The water was Luca. Aranen was right. If Touraine rested too easily, let herself be lulled by the sweet comfort, she would slip under.

The palace bells startled Touraine awake so abruptly that she swallowed a mouthful of perfumed water and choked. It took her even longer to realize what the mourning bells must mean.

*Nicolas. Dead.*

She splashed out of the tub and wrapped herself in one of the thick towels, trailing sopping footprints into the sitting room.

Aranen and Ghadin looked at each other and then to Touraine with fear in their eyes. They didn't know. For once, this was a good thing. She grinned at them.

*Luca would be queen.*

An insistent knock made them all jump, including Touraine. Roland entered and immediately took up his post beside Aranen, as Perrot poked his head in.

"Everyone all right in here, aye?" Perrot asked. "Something's happening in the halls. I'll go check with the guard." He looked to Touraine for permission, tactfully ignoring the fact that she was wearing just a towel.

"Aye," Touraine said. "Have a look." She was eager, but the soldier in her wouldn't rest easily; if Nicolas was dead, retaliation might follow.


Luca curled on her chaise, letting Sabine hold her while she wept over a sky-falling ambassador whose heart she had broken and who had broken her heart in return when the palace's sonorous bells began to ring. The heavy sound rippled through the room, not impeded by flimsy things like layers of stone and wood and bone. The peals traveled through the walls and straight to her chest.

She sat bolt upright, using Sabine as a lever.

"Nicolas," she breathed. She let herself hope. It wasn't too late.

"Is he—" Sabine breathed back.

They both looked at Gil, who was on his feet, his pistol in hand. He gestured for them to stay while he went to the door.

Luca ignored him, of course, standing up to follow him to the door. Her guards muttered together in confusion before Gil waved for

Lanquette to go. He'd barely started loping away with his long strides
when a child came sprinting down the corridor, almost colliding with
the tall guard's kneecaps. Lanquette deftly swerved and the boy shot
past, stopping in front of Luca, Gil, and Deniaud.

At first, he looked around the corridor bewildered, as if he thought
he had misplaced something. Then he seemed to realize exactly who
he was standing in front of. His eyes went round and wide as saucers,
but that didn't explain the utter fear in the child's face.

"What's happened?"

"Beg your pardon, mesdames, messieurs, but Mademoiselle Adile
wanted someone to tell if anything happened—"

"Quick, lad," Gil said with gruff impatience. He looked up the hallway where Lanquette was still waiting. The guard captain held up a
finger. *Wait.*

The boy wouldn't speak, though. He trembled in silence as his
mouth worked. All the while, the bells rang and rang and rang.

Adile coaxed it out of him, kneeling beside him, pulling a sweet
out of her pocket and urging him to *whisper in my ear, my little one,
hurry*—and then Adile's face went pale and she pressed her fingers to
her mouth.

"Sky above, what is it?" Gil growled. His breath came quick. He
was nervous—no, Gil was afraid.

The longer they waited, the more Luca's hope soured into vinegar.
"Adile?"

"It's not Nicolas," Adile whispered, her voice full of tears. "It's Tiro,
Your Highness. Little Roland is dead. It—poison."

*Roland is dead.* A distant part of Luca noted how strange it was to
hear those words again in such a different context and so long between
each other. And here, this little boy who delivered the news was probably of an age with Luca's young and now dead cousin.

*Poison.*

Luca reached out for Sabine and found the other woman just behind
her. The marquise stared, mouth open in shock.

"Sabine?" Luca grabbed Sabine by the arm and shook her. "Sabine.

You need to get to Touraine now. Tell her what happened. Tell her to run—get out of the palace, get out of the city, anything. Go with her."

Sabine blinked and shook her head, re-collecting herself. "Go with her? What about you?"

Luca swallowed hard and forced a smile. "I have Gil. Go. Take Deniaud."

Sabine took a trembling breath before crushing Luca in a hug and kissing the side of her head.

"Get her out of here safe, old man," the marquise said to Gil.

Gil grunted. "Always."

After Sabine and Deniaud sprinted away, though, Luca turned to him. "Do you think we can get out?"

The rush of booted steps gave Luca her answer.

"We can fight our way through," Lanquette said.

Gil looked at Luca, and then at Adile and the little boy. His expression wasn't optimistic.

Calm acceptance passed over Luca. She pushed Adile and the boy into her rooms.

"Go into my bedchamber and wait there until it's quiet. I don't care how long it takes." She raised her voice over Adile's protests. "I need you to be all right."

She needed Touraine and Sabine to be all right. If the people she loved were safe, it didn't matter what happened to her. *You deserve what's coming*, a dark voice in her heart whispered.

The boots grew louder, along with commands that reverberated in the halls but were too garbled to make out clearly. They were coming for her.

A fist of fear knocked on the glass calm surrounding her, threatening to break through. She grabbed Gil's hand. His calloused palm gripped hers tightly. He would not be safe. Not if anything happened to her. He would be the first to fall. But not if she—

"Don't even think about it, my girl." Gil frowned down at her, the droop of his mustache emphasizing the movement.

"He's right, Your Highness." Lanquette drew his own pistol and readied it. "We're your guard. Let us do our job."

The resolution in the tall man's voice bolstered Luca.

"Then here we go." They strode forward to meet her uncle's soldiers.
"Surrender now, by the order of the king!"
*Well. That's new.*


Touraine was wearing nothing but a silk chemise when the marquise
de Durfort burst into her chambers. Touraine reached for a towel, but
Durfort didn't even look at Touraine's bare lower half.

"It's not the duke," Durfort said, bracing herself on the doorframe
to Touraine's bedchamber with both hands.

"His supporters?"

Durfort's face crumpled in anguish. "It was Tiro. I killed Tiro.
Nicolas is out for blood."

Touraine froze. Durfort's student, the little boy she and Ghadin had
practiced swords in the salle with. The child who hadn't had a chance
to grow into his father yet.

"Sky above," Touraine swore.

"It's fucked, El-Qazāli, it's all fucked. We have to get back to Luca. I
don't know what you two said to each other, I don't care if you hate her
now, just please help me save her."

"Save her?" Touraine asked stupidly, even though her brain was
already picking up the pieces and carrying them further, faster. Nicolas would want blood. Luca's. Durfort's. Touraine's. Everyone, anyone
that Luca had ever cared for. "Oh. Oh no."

Touraine dropped the towel and grabbed her trousers. This time,
Durfort's eyes did follow, her mouth making a slight O.

"Put your cock away, Durfort, tell the rest of them it's time to go!"

Touraine jumped into her trousers, tying them at the waist as she
wriggled into her boots. She hesitated only half a second over Durfort's rapier or Luca's long knife. The rapier could poke things and
look pretty. The knife was meant to kill. She belted on the knife. At
the last minute, she added Aranen's prayer beads. *For luck.*

Touraine reached the anteroom and stuttered to a halt. Aranen was
directing Ghadin—*no, no changes of clothes, no books*—

Touraine's place was here, with them. Protecting them.

"Durfort, I can't." She slowly shook her head. She should have felt like she was being torn in two, but she didn't. She couldn't. She had already made her choice. "Take Deniaud. Take Perrot if you find him. I have to get Aranen and Ghadin out."

Durfort's expression was disbelieving. "Nicolas will kill her. She needs you."

"They need me."

"They don't." Roland, the false guard, stepped between Touraine and Aranen. "I'll get the priestess and her ward to safety. Go."

The relief his words gave Touraine was so crushing that she almost sank to her knees. Still, she hesitated. Could she look the Jackal in the face knowing that she'd left Aranen and Ghadin in the hands of a strange Balladairan?

If she survived this, she would find out.

"Ghadin, here." Touraine placed the gaudy rapier in the girl's good hand. She struggled with the weight before steadying it.

Durfort cleared her throat—with chagrin, Touraine would have said, if she didn't know the woman better. "Actually, I might be able to make better use of that blade."

Ah. She wasn't carrying one. Touraine looked at her incredulously. "What the fuck, Durfort?"

"What?" She threw her hands up. "I didn't know there was going to be a sky-falling coup!"

Ghadin huffed at the noblewoman and handed her the rapier.

Touraine turned to the priestess. "Aranen, I—"

Aranen gripped her upper arm, and as their eyes met, something like a spark passed between them.

"Shāl go with you, my girl."

"If I don't...tell Jaghotai..." Touraine didn't know what she wanted Aranen to tell her mother, only that she wished she had time to talk to that jackal of a woman again.

"Shh." Aranen put a hand on her cheek.

Touraine's throat worked around a lump, and she squeezed the older woman's hand. She clasped Ghadin on the shoulder.

"You act like you're leaving us to die." Ghadin jutted her chin out. She wasn't crying, but her chin trembled.

"The last time I did something this stupid, I did." Before Touraine could think too hard, she kissed the girl on the temple, then followed Durfort into the corridor. Deniaud was there waiting, glaring up and down the hallway, tight lipped.

"Where is she?" Touraine said.

Outside of the room, away from the little family she'd made, a miniature Qazāl, Touraine slid back into the self she had been *for* Balladaire. Soldier. Fighter. Someone who knew that death ticked always closer—it was a matter of when, not if. Someone with a single, pointed focus at the end of a rifle.

"When we left, she was in her rooms. With Gil and Lanquette."

Touraine followed Durfort's lead.

"Listen," Durfort said in a low voice as they jog-walked through the passages, looking around corners before turning. "You aren't mad at her because of what I said that night, are you? It's just, she was upset and—"

"Not the time." Touraine stopped against the wall at a corner and craned her neck around. She beckoned them with a nod.

"Oh, it's just something I wanted to get off my chest now. You should never go into battle with a heavy heart, you know."

"You've never been in a battle, and this isn't a fucking chevalier tale. Now shut up so we can find her without getting killed."

The thing about Durfort was that the woman had told the truth: she was something of a coward. She was so full of self-loathing that no matter how much she covered it with bravado and charm, it cowed her out of doing what she thought was right until it was too late.

Nearly too late.

"Fewer palace soldiers than I'd expect," Deniaud muttered.

Perrot. Somewhere, somehow, he was helping. He'd gotten some of them to stand down, or he'd gotten the soldiers loyal to Gil and Luca to fight.

Another corner check. This time, Deniaud put a finger to her lips and frantically waved them back against the wall. She made the signal for "five and five." The footsteps came next, and instead of getting farther away, they came closer, and fast.

Shit. Ten was too many unless they could take them by surprise.

Beside Touraine, Durfort inhaled slowly. "Right, then. Once they're distracted, you two go." She pushed off the wall and Touraine yanked her back by the coat.

"What are you doing?" Touraine hissed.

"They won't hurt me. Probably. I'm still the marquise de Durfort, and I'm more valuable alive than dead. I think."

She plastered her usual insouciance back onto her face. Touraine knew now that it was just as false as Luca's disinterested, icy stare. As false as Touraine's own unwavering obedience. *We're all just pretending. Keeping shields up and hiding as best as we can, from friends and enemies alike.* They were all so unbearably lonely under the masks. Durfort's mask was cracking, her smile slipping at the corners.

"Give this to her, from me." She ducked down and kissed Touraine on the corner of her mouth. She winked, and Touraine couldn't help smiling. That part, at least, was honest Sabine de Durfort.

She left before Touraine could protest again.

Though Deniaud tugged at Touraine's sleeve impatiently, Touraine listened as Durfort swaggered up to the soldiers, listened to her cajoling lilt as she pretended to ask what was going on. Then came the unmistakable sound of a fist slamming against skin, followed sharply by the unmistakable thud and groan combination of a rifle butt jammed into a stomach.

Deniaud pulled Touraine again, hard.

She followed.

# CHAPTER 42

# A FAMILY (VARIATION)

Nicolas's palace soldiers marched Luca through the corridors. At first, she thought they would take her to her uncle. Instead, they were leading her away. Le Fontinard. If she was locked up in the prison, Nicolas could take his time with her. His entertainment wouldn't be limited to a single lecture, to one killing blow.

Surrendering might have been a mistake.

She was going to die, soon or after a long and drawn-out misery.

The only positives that she could cling to were double-edged blades.

One: she was not alone; Gil was with her, the chains around his wrists clinking merrily as they walked. However, he and Lanquette would probably also be jailed and killed alongside her.

Two: Touraine and Sabine were gone, hopefully safely escaped, warned in time; and yet, she would have given anything to see them one last time. Now she never would.

Luca had lost to her uncle. The endgame of their grand game, and the victor was clear.

"Luca!"

She turned at that voice, behind her and so close. The guards at her elbows gripped her arms even tighter, but Luca dug in her heels and twisted around. "Touraine!"

Touraine spilled from the mouth of a hallway that intersected the path the guards were leading them all down, toward the stables, a coach, and Le Fontinard.

Her golden eyes glowed in the light of the tapers lining the hall. She was dressed, ironically, like a Balladairan dandy, in a silk chemise half-open at the neck and tight dun riding trousers. The corners of Luca's mouth twitched up.

The last person Luca wanted to see and the only person.

Deniaud emerged with her—but not Sabine. Luca felt a twinge between her sternum and spine. Not the only person.

The escort leveled their rifles toward Touraine and Deniaud, their bayonets fixed. The two fighters were drastically outnumbered. Touraine flinched as the barrels pointed toward her.

"Stand down in the name of the king!" cried the soldier at the front of Luca's escort.

It wasn't any less strange to hear her uncle called that a second time.

Gil cleared his throat with a gentle click, and Luca caught his eye. He flicked his glance down at the ground and then side to side, at their guards. Luca coughed her understanding.

Then she let herself fall.

Or try to fall. Her dead weight put the guards restraining her arms off-balance, and she threw herself back and forth to further stagger them. Behind her, other guards grunted as they fought with Lanquette and Gil, their no longer quiescent prisoners. Touraine and Deniaud rushed in.

The scuffle was over in what felt like mere moments. Luca, her guards, and Touraine stood over the small squad that Nicolas had sent to apprehend her.

As Deniaud unlocked Gil and Lanquette's cuffs, Touraine came to her.

"You're all right?" Touraine searched her with her eyes, holding her hands at a distance to either side of Luca's body, as if she were afraid to touch her.

"Of course. Where's Sabine?" Luca asked briskly, as if she could make Touraine's next words hurt less by sounding unbothered.

When Touraine shook her head, though, it stole her breath.

"She bought us time." Touraine took her hand. It was sticky with blood, emphasizing the messy accounting of lives that they knew all too well. "Time to get you out."

Luca took her hand away from Touraine's insistent pull. "If I run now, there's no coming back. The Qazāli in La Chaise are done, the children at the school are lost, and Nicolas will be at war with Qazāl within the year. A war you won't come back from."

Slowly, Touraine's expression hardened in determination. "Let's deal with this jackalfucker, then," she swore in Shālan.

Luca led them through deserted corridors toward the King's Library. The corridors that were her home. The walk to her uncle's library, so familiar, so often trod, was an all-new journey with heaviness in every step.

She had never marched into battle where she knew her fate would be determined when she arrived. Knowing her fate would very possibly be death. Knowing that others marching beside her might not live even if she did.

The dread made the empty halls seem too quiet, as if her ears had been stopped with cotton. They seemed foreign, as if she'd never walked them before, and every painted vase on a plinth in a shadowed nook, every tapestry hanging from the wall, every oak-leaf wrought-metal sconce was startling in its unique beauty. She might never see this painting of her great-great-grandmother again—had the slight smirk in the painted woman's face always been there?

At the same time, the corridors brought back a rush of memories she'd forgotten with devastating clarity. She had pulled Sabine into that nook, there, to kiss her, the two of them giggling like children and hiding from Sabine's mother and Brice and the rest of the whole sky-falling world, and she had scraped her wrist on the stone in her haste. And the marble floors themselves? Oh, she could have walked them with her eyes closed: they led to her parents' rooms, just as they led to her uncle.

Her uncle's library.

For now. If—*when* Luca won, she would take it back along with her crown. This was her place. This was her home. Her people marched at her side.

And if they marched to this battle and died there, at least they could not say that she did not fight.

But a dozen palace blackcoats blocked them at their next turn. Half of them leveled their rifles.

"Halt!" The speaker brandished her drawn sword. With her other hand, she signaled the rifles to hold their fire. "Surrender, and we won't fire."

"And risk hitting the new heir to the throne?" Luca laughed, the humor slicing her heart to shredded parchment. *Oh, Tiro. I'm so sorry.* "I think not."

"The king has made it clear that no one who comes through here should be spared. Heir or no."

Touraine stilled at Luca's side. Her face was grim. She didn't shrink back.

"Remember Ghislaine?" Luca muttered.

Touraine met her eyes with a sidelong glance and shook her head. "You think I'll scare them and they'll just let us pass?" She signaled silently to Deniaud. "I'm not leaving them at our backs."

"Wait—!"

Luca reached for Touraine's arm but grasped only air. Touraine was already sprinting for the soldiers, knife drawn and gleaming in the light of the corridor's tapers. Two strides in one direction, the soldiers readied their rifles. Touraine pivoted and their shots went wide, pinging against the walls. Two more steps and Touraine was airborne, body arcing and spiraling over the gunfire as she flipped through the air. Luca held her breath, her heart in her throat, until Touraine landed. Her knife was a blur in the backs of the soldiers.

With a shock, Luca realized that Deniaud and Lanquette were already cutting through the fray. Through the smoke of gunpowder, she saw the flash of their swords against rifles. Though the corridor was too small and the soldiers lacked the range to keep shooting, her people were still outnumbered. Luca hovered between racing into the fight to help—they were fighting for *her*—and pure, practical fear. She had no blade, no weapon, not even her cane.

"Gil," she said, as calm as she could. "Get me a sword."

The grim set of his mouth tightened. "Stay here," he said.

The old man moved quicker than he had any right to, ducking around a bayonet thrust, stabbing the soldier, then kicking him down. A moment later, the rifle, with its blood-spattered bayonet, skittered across the floor in Luca's direction.

It wasn't a sword, but it would do. She scooped it up and limped toward the knot of fighters, trying to find a place to be useful. The gun had already been discharged, but—there, Deniaud was backed up against the wall by two soldiers, one with a sword and one with a spent rifle. The guardswoman ducked a blow, and the sword smashed a vase into shards. Deniaud tackled the swordsman, and the second soldier went sprawling.

As the soldier picked himself up, his eyes fell on Luca. Alone and unprotected.

Luca's awareness dimmed to one pair of eyes and the way his face hardened as soon as he chose his target. She gripped the barrel of her stolen rifle, bayonet aimed at his chest. He was a bear of a man, running at her, his own rifle in both of his hands—

*I'm going to die.*

He knocked Luca's gun out of his way with his, jerking her arms to the side and twisting her off-balance. From the corner of her eyes, she saw him angling his bayonet toward her stomach.

Luca felt the hot, arterial spray of his blood as Touraine's knife sliced into his throat from behind.

"What under the sky above are you doing?" Touraine yelled. She didn't see the other soldier coming at her back, sword raised.

"Behind you!"

Luca shoved Touraine as hard as she could, out of the way, to her right. Touraine was too heavy, and too confused—she resisted Luca's urgent press, but in her confusion she twisted to look over her shoulder. It created just enough space.

The sword clipped Touraine below her raised arm, tearing along her back and ribs. Luca leaned out of the sword's path and thrust her bayonet into the opening the soldier's attack had left.

The soldier's eyes went wide with surprise and pain. She looked down at her chest. Her fingernails scraped the barrel of the gun as she tried in vain to pull it out. Luca leaned her weight into the rifle's butt, and the soldier fell to her knees, dragging Luca down, too. After a moment, Luca felt the woman's chest stop moving beneath her.

This was not the theoretical application of troop movements and provisions, done from a distance on a scrap of parchment. Yverte had neglected to describe how a woman stared at you, eyes pleading, as you stole her last breath with your blade. Their slow dulling.

It wasn't poison, slipped into a bottle and sent away in secret.

"Luca?"

Touraine's voice was far away. All Luca could see was the dead woman beneath her, and the blood pooling beneath the body. Luca's gorge rose, her mouth tingling with spit and the urge to vomit. She swallowed and swallowed again.

She took a shaky breath and then another, just to prove that she still could.

And then Touraine was beside her, giving Luca her hand, helping Luca balance on her good leg while she tested her bad one.

"I'm fine." Luca made her voice firm even though her legs were still shaking and bile still burned her throat. *This was necessary.*

Luca bent over and picked up the dead woman's sword. It trembled in her shaking hands.

"That jump," Luca said, trying to distract herself. "Where did you learn to do that?"

Touraine cracked her neck. "From my mother."

She was so nonchalant. So were Deniaud and Gil and Lanquette. They had all killed before—for years, all of them. Luca took a deep breath, and then another. She had killed, too. She had never been so close to the bodies she was responsible for, their blood drying in the cracks of her skin, but she had ordered them dead just as easily. It was good, she told herself, to become familiar with it. To know intimately what she was asking for. To bear the responsibility.

"Is everyone all right?" she asked, limping through the bodies and chunks of clay and plaster and shattered porcelain.

A chorus of "aye" and "yes, Your Highness."

Then there was just the library. Luca tried to march up to the door, but Lanquette and Deniaud pushed her back and shook their heads, swords raised. Luca understood.

Deniaud swung the door open. The gunfire was immediate. One bullet pocked into the thick wooden door. Lanquette growled as another shot took him in the leg, but he stayed on his feet, shouldering his way into the room with Deniaud.

"Hold." Her uncle's imperious voice stayed his guards. "I want to see her."

Luca followed Gil and Touraine inside.

Her crown was just one move away. Her crown, or her death.

Four of Nicolas's personal guards in their short gold cloaks waited inside: two on either side of the door, their swords pointed at Lanquette and Deniaud, and two more guards on either side of Nicolas, who leaned over the table where he and Luca played their weekly game of échecs. Where Tiro had studied beside them. Their échecs board was on the floor, the stone cracked in half and the pieces scattered underfoot. Nicolas's fingers were claws, digging into the wood with all his strength.

And Tiro's body lay atop that table, legs straightened and his little arms folded across his stomach. His lips were blue, his closed eyelids a deep bruise.

"Tiro," she moaned, her throat catching. She stepped toward him.

"Don't pretend you care, Luca," Nicolas snarled, slamming his fist on the table, making Luca flinch back. "Where were your precious ideals when you murdered my child?"

"I didn't mean—" Like the whimper, the words escaped Luca's

mouth before she could stop them. The sorrow in her chest sapped the self-righteous confidence that had buoyed her this far.

"I don't care what you meant, girl, my son is dead!" Nicolas pushed himself away from the table, making it rock. "Wasn't it you who said that people weren't playing pieces?"

Luca felt Touraine's eyes on her. So much was at stake. She shifted, trying to put Tiro out of the periphery of her vision, but that made her feel too much like her uncle was right. She owed it to Tiro to acknowledge his death, even as she fought his father for her place. Especially as she fought his father.

His death was a tragic accident—*and you won't let that stand in your way, will you?*

"He was never meant to die."

"Of course he wasn't. I was." Nicolas went behind his desk at the back of the library, his guards following to stand on either side. A simple desk: A crystal goblet of wine, full, with a half-empty bottle beside it. A stoppered inkwell, a holstered quill. A neat stack of parchment between two desk lamps, weighed down by a pistol. His instruments of power, as they were Luca's.

Gil shifted in front of Luca, his eyes on the weapon. Nicolas didn't pick up the pistol, though. He picked up the wine glass and tilted it back and forth, peering into it, examining it. He sniffed it and closed his eyes. He put the glass down and kicked something at his feet behind his desk, and a keening moan emerged. He kicked again until a bound figure toppled pathetically out from behind the desk.

Sabine.

"The delightful vintages of the north. You both know how partial I am. I'll admit that was my mistake. 'The habitual man, et cetera, et cetera,' as Yverte says."

Luca clamped down on the urge to cry out for Sabine. Her handsome face was swollen, and the dashing swoop of her hair was plastered with sweat. Tears streamed from bruise-blue eyelids that matched Tiro's.

"Durfort," Touraine cried, stepping forward.

"No, no, Your Excellency." Nicolas took the pistol from his desk and knelt beside Sabine. He pressed the barrel of the gun to her skull, and the marquise mewled in pain as he moved her. "Do stay there."

His guards closed in at the corners. They were surrounded, but evenly matched—for each of Nicolas's guards, Luca had hers, and she had Touraine. But Nicolas had the advantage, because he had someone she couldn't bear to lose.

Touraine froze in her tracks and looked to Luca for guidance. "I can kill him. Let me just fucking kill—"

Luca held up a hand and Touraine went quiet.

"If you wanted to hurt me," she said to her uncle, "she'd be dead already."

"You assume she isn't. What have I taught you about assumptions?"

Keeping the gun pressed to Sabine's head, he reached for the wine glass on the desk and brought it down to Sabine's mouth. She clamped her lips together, craning her head away.

"I don't know what you gave my son, but one glass was enough for him. If the marquise has already had one, perhaps it's just a matter of time. Two, however..." He pried open Sabine's jaw, and wine spilled into her mouth, onto her white chemise, onto his sleeves. Sabine gagged and choked, but she swallowed.

"How long will it take, do you think? Do you have an antidote, or did you not think so far ahead? Let me go and you can tend to your friend. The quicker, the better, I would surmise."

Luca thought frantically. There might be an antidote, but if there was, it was with Roland the assassin. Sabine didn't have time.

"Luca." Touraine was tightly coiled, ready to pounce if Luca just let her.

"Why do you assume I won't kill you?" Luca asked quickly.

"If you wanted to hurt me, I'd be dead already," Nicolas mocked. "It's not an assumption; it's knowledge. Observed, tested. You think you're not like me. Despite everything that you've done to get your way, you think that you are kinder than me, more just than me. You think you will rule better than me. You think you have a better vision for the future of Balladaire, of the world, than me. You are a naive and arrogant child, and if you sacrifice your marquise to get to me, then you will prove that all you want to be is a lie."

He pressed the gun into Sabine's skull.

Each accusation landed precisely where her uncle meant it to. Everything she hated about him, she was guilty of. Touraine had told her as much, and more than once. And yet, Touraine was here, by her side. So was Gil. They were here because they cared for her and believed not just in her claim but in the good she could do. A better Balladaire.

Sabine looked up at Luca, her dark eyes wide, but not with fear. Or, no—not *just* fear. The tilt of wry acceptance in the woman's mouth made Luca want to cry out. Sabine would die on this sky-falling floor because she trusted Luca to be better.

"Luca...don't. It's o—" Sabine's rasp was strangled off with a yelp as Nicolas punched the butt of the gun against her head. Blood trickled down her forehead.

If Luca let Sabine die, Nicolas would have no leverage left. She had plenty of time to deal with her uncle. He was frightened. Backed into a corner like a wild animal. Let the others take care of his guards, and she could kill him or imprison him to the end of his days.

"Do you know, dear Uncle," Luca said, taking a single step forward. "After Father died, I used to imagine that I would rule with you at my side. Advising me, guiding me." It was true. A part of her was afraid to kill him because...what if he was right? What if he was smarter than her? What if she needed him? She took another step, away from the doubt and toward her uncle. "You're desperate. There's nowhere else to turn. Let her go. We'll see to her wounds. You'll live under guard in the palace with every comfort. Would you do that? Be my advisor?"

Yet even to her own ears, the proposition rang false. The truth was, if Luca let Nicolas live, it would only be a matter of time before he manipulated her out of position. She would live the rest of her life on guard for assassins; if she fought back, civil war would wreck the lives of their people. Once Nicolas took the throne, the Qazāli would never have anything close to peace, in La Chaise or in their own country.

Nicolas tilted his head up and smiled a sad smile. "My brilliant girl. I had hoped for better." He heaved himself to his feet, leaving Sabine on the ground.

Gil kept himself between Luca and Nicolas, but the duke still didn't move toward her. He went instead to the oil lamps on the desk and picked one up by its base.

"Here are all of the things I'm going to take away from you, my dear niece. First, your fop of a lover." He pointed to Sabine with the pistol. "Second. The magic you want? The secrets we safeguard are all here, in this library, kept by me, by your father, by our parents. So many generations of House Ancier."

Before Luca could pull in the breath to scream *no*, Nicolas hurled the lamp against the far bookshelf. The left side of the room exploded in a bright bloom of light as burning oil splashed books and scrolls and dry tapestries.

Then everything happened at once.

Swords clashed behind Luca as Lanquette and Deniaud leapt at Nicolas's guards. Touraine took her advantage, too, trying to catch the guard nearest her by surprise, but her knife wasn't enough to fight a swordsman trained to protect the royal family.

"Gil, help Touraine!"

"I'm not leaving you." He kept his sword pointed at Nicolas, keeping his body as much between Luca and Nicolas's gun as he could.

Nicolas sneered. "You aren't going to touch me, Gillett. You're her dog, like you were Roland's dog."

Gil didn't rise to the bait. His focus held Nicolas and the final guard at Nicolas's side, a woman with a sword and dagger bared. Nicolas picked up the other lamp on the desk and hurled it, too. Shards of burning oil-covered glass landed on the massive map of the world, and Luca watched Balladaire burn.

Thick smoke began to fill the room.

Then Sabine's body arched up from the ground, her heels kicking on the ground as her body spasmed. Great gasps tore from her chest.

Luca lunged for her, but Gil held her back.

Touraine had seen. She roared in frustration. She was still struggling with her guard, but with Lanquette's help—Lanquette who was
wounded, who was flagging, the hair in his queue coming loose, his
breath heavy and his arms slow from blood-loss fatigue, Lanquette who
couldn't get his sword up in time, who left himself open, inviting Nicolas's guard to take advantage, who fell to his knees and collapsed silently
with the other man's sword in his gut an instant before Touraine made
the decisive blows to the back of his killer's thigh and then throat.

Luca watched Touraine take one despairing breath over Lanquette's
body before slumping to the ground at Sabine's side. The ambassador pressed one hand to Sabine's chest, one softly to Sabine's forehead,
eyes closed. Focused. It looked nothing like the show they'd put on for
Ghislaine.

Nicolas smiled.

"Oh, and her, too," Nicolas said.

He pointed his gun at Touraine.

Smoke choked Luca's throat and blinded her with stinging tears,
but she found the breath to scream, to beg, as she pushed past Gil's
protective shield and leapt at Nicolas's arm, dragging it away from its
target. "Uncle, don't!"

It was no use, though. Nicolas shook Luca off easily, and she landed
poorly on her bad leg. She fell and her head slammed into the wooden
floor. Her vision exploded in stars of pain and then—gunfire.

"No! Stop!" Luca cried out, reaching blindly from the ground, pulling herself toward Touraine while pain radiated through her skull.

When Luca's vision cleared, though, Touraine still knelt over
Sabine, alternately coughing and pressing her hands against the other
woman's chest. Gil stood above them. Between them and Nicolas. His
grim mouth and solemn eyes were open wide with shock. His empty
hand reached for the wound in his chest as he collapsed.

Luca screamed as she reached him. She pressed her hand against the
wound, but the blood had already stopped pumping from it. It flowed
steadily now, with no heartbeat to spur it. His eyes were lifeless, his
gray mustache smeared with blood.

"Oh, sky above. Oh, Shāl." Luca closed her eyes and fought the wracking coughing fit that took her. *Please.* "Oh, Shāl. Oh gods, please."

Nothing happened. There was only choking smoke and Touraine half on her feet, half on her knees, hunched over, fists in Sabine's coat. Sabine lay still.

"We have to go, Luca, now, or we're all going to burn," Touraine said frantically, dragging Sabine toward the corridor. Then she saw Gil's body. "Oh. Oh, fuck. Luca, come on. It's over, come on!"

Luca was frozen. The heat built around them. Flames licked from the shelves to the other walls, eating across the priceless rugs. She stared up at her uncle.

Nicolas stood alone. Deniaud had killed his last guard and stood with her bloody sword aimed at his throat. Smoke swirled around him. He held his shirt over his face with one hand and the spent pistol in the other. He looked at it as if it had surprised him—as if it had killed Gil of its own volition. Beneath the shock, Luca saw the faint edge of a gruesome, hateful smile. He'd hurt Luca like she'd hurt him. There was justice in this.

It was Nicolas's grim satisfaction that gave Luca the strength to release Gil from the cradle of her arms and stand to face him.

"Are you happy, then?" she asked. "You've killed my second father. The love of your brother's life. Is that enough?"

"I was as good as a father to you," Nicolas wheezed through the cloth.

"You were." Luca bowed her head. "Once."

The ache in her left no room for anything else, not even pity. She looked over to little Tiro's body. Flames climbed up the échecs table's legs. She couldn't watch him burn like this. She could get him out, grant him dignity, at least.

Touraine was right. It was over.

"It's done, Nicolas. Deniaud, get Gil." Luca limped over and lifted the small boy's body. His pale hair was soft as she pressed her cheek against his head. *Oh, Tiro.* Pain lanced from the sole of her foot all the way up her spine, but she gritted her teeth and forced her leg to hold.

"How dare you touch him?" Nicolas roared.

He started toward Luca, but Deniaud stepped between them, and Nicolas shrieked in pain as the guard disarmed him.

"How could you do this to him? To me?" The rage of Nicolas's grief was burning out as the fire closed in on them.

Luca took a burdened step backward, toward the door, and her leg buckled. Tiro's head lolled against her shoulder. Would it matter, to point out how many of her people Nicolas had killed? It wouldn't change the truth or ease her guilt.

"I didn't mean to, Uncle. I swear to you. You don't have to die here, either. Come out with us."

"Luca! Hurry!" Touraine cried from behind as the flames encroached upon the single exit.

With her sword still pointed at Nicolas, Deniaud grabbed Gil's collar with the other hand and pulled him back toward Luca, toward the corridor. His body painted a thick streak of dark blood across ornate silk geometries.

"Should I rather die later?" Nicolas scoffed, holding his bleeding hand where Deniaud had cut him.

"You *should* die," Luca said, cloaking herself in icy calm. "I should kill you for this. But for now, you'll go to Le Fontinard, if I have to walk you there myself."

She coughed as she took another step toward the door, lungs burning. Her leg buckled again and she caught herself before she dropped Tiro, biting her lip with the pain of it.

Nicolas lurched forward, his face trembling. "Give him to me," he rasped.

Deniaud kept the sword pointed at him and he stopped, his empty hands raised.

"Let me carry my son." He was unarmed and desperate. Tears leaked down his face from smoke or sorrow or pain.

What could he do if Luca gave him this one mercy?

"Here," she said.

Disbelieving, Deniaud followed him with her sword point, but

Nicolas didn't lunge at Luca or try to flee. They closed their sheltering bodies around the child, and for a moment Luca imagined she was also in her uncle's protective embrace. Then Nicolas took Tiro in his arms. His strength and size made the boy seem like a doll.

"My boy," Luca heard him whisper.

Luca covered her own tear-streaked face and ran from the library as the fire claimed it.

She gulped in the fresh air. Touraine had dragged Sabine down the hallway and Lanquette's body as well, but fire would spread soon. Deniaud still had Gil by the collar and Nicolas at sword point.

"Is she all right?" Luca shouted to Touraine.

*Please*, she begged any gods that would listen. *Let her be alive.*

"She's breathing, but—get back! Soldiers!"

Luca's stomach plummeted at the sound of rushing boots.

Captain Perrot and his soldiers sprinted into the corridor. The chaperone Nicolas had set to dog Touraine's heels and report their every move to Nicolas. Luca held her breath. Where was his loyalty now?

Perrot looked from Luca, with her bloodstained hands, to Nicolas, cradling Tiro's small frame, to the wallpaper in the hall buckling and curling as the flames licked it from the other side.

Captain Perrot saluted. "Duke Nicolas Ancier, you're under arrest for treason against the crown."

# CHAPTER 43

# VICTORY

Luca left her wheeled chair in the corridor and used her cane to walk on shaky legs through her parents' room. The fire had spread from the King's Library and down the corridor, eating away two of the walls here and leaving the room exposed to the elements. The entire palace smelled of smoke and ash; it was overwhelming, despite the open air. She had seen the damage from without, too—as if a great bear had clawed a gouge in the place.

Her breath hitched as she steadied herself.

"I thought I would find you here."

Luca spun around at Touraine's soft voice behind her. Touraine's face was somber, and she kept her hand on her knife as if someone might jump out of the ashes and attack.

"How are you?" Touraine asked, coming close beside her.

"It's all right. I'm fine."

Her mother's violoncelle was ruined, the wood soaked and warped by the pompiers. In the library, her father's journals were ash. Luca had hoped to read them one day, them and the centuries' worth of knowledge that Nicolas had kept locked away from her. Sabine clung to life in the infirmary yet again. Lanquette was dead.

Gil.

Tiro.

None of it was all right, but she had her crown, didn't she? An ashen victory.

"This isn't how I expected it to happen," Luca murmured.

The squelch of Touraine's boots on the sodden silk carpets was an incongruous sound in the gloom.

"No one gives up power for free." Touraine bent down and picked up the dead queen's bow. It had been cracked by the heat, half of the horsehair singed away. She put it delicately down on the bout of the violoncelle.

"I wasn't lying when I told him I wanted to rule with him as my advisor. I used to. If he'd said yes in that moment, I still might have."

"He's still alive."

"He killed Gil. I don't want his help."

Except that Nicolas was the only one left who knew the contents of the library. Like an army salting the earth as it retreated, he'd denied her one last prize.

"But I killed Tiro," she whispered, her voice cracking. "Nothing he did compares."

"Oh, Luca. Come here." Touraine wrapped her in an embrace, her strong arms protective and yielding at once. Her voice husky in her ear: "I'm so sorry."

Luca tensed, her whole body going rigid. She almost let herself relax into it, almost let her head rest on Touraine's shoulder. She could be safe, in the curve of this neck. She could weep here, she could put the weight down. But the memory of the last time they'd been this close intruded. She broke away.

A cold gust of air made them both shiver and brought a flurry of small white flecks. Touraine scowled at the sky, and the snowflakes landed on her cheeks like freckles before melting against her skin.

Touraine caught Luca staring.

Luca cleared her throat and turned. "How are Aranen and Ghadin?"

"They're safe. Roland brought them earlier this morning."

Another silence, and Luca pretended to ignore the heat of Touraine's gaze.

"There's a story the kids in Qazāl told me to help me with my

Shālan," Touraine started, taking a step closer. "About a scorpion and a jackal who are friends?"

"Is this about Jaghotai?" Luca asked skeptically.

Touraine waved the question away. "The scorpion is small and needs the jackal's help to travel from place to place. The jackal isn't bothered by the weight, so she lets the scorpion ride along all nestled in her fur, and the scorpion eats fleas and flies and stuff."

"Scorpions eat fleas? And flies?"

"I don't know. I guess. Shh. One day, after a few journeys, the jackal is loping along to their next destination when she feels a sharp pain in her back, and then another and another.

"'What's happening?' the jackal asks, and the scorpion says, 'I stung you,' and the jackal asks, 'Why the sky-falling fuck did you do that,' and the scorpion says, 'You carry me around all day to sting other things, why would I not sting you? I am what I am.'"

Luca squinted at Touraine. "Are you sure you remember the story right? I don't think scorpions can kill jackals. I read about them in great detail before I left for Qazāl, they don't release enough venom—"

"It's just a story, Luca." Touraine scowled playfully. She was actually standing quite close. Luca rather liked the way the ambassador had to look up a little to meet her eyes.

"And in this story," Luca asked, "am I the scorpion or the jackal?"

Touraine gave Luca a sharp-edged smile that showed her teeth. "I'm saying, we are who we are."

Luca stepped back, putting a safe arm's distance between them. "Do you remember when I wrote you and said that I don't deserve you, not—"

"'Not as a soldier, nor as a woman.' I remember." The wolf's smile was gone. Touraine watched her warily, as if wondering from which direction Luca might attack.

Luca had been rehearsing the words she would say to Touraine one day, if it ever seemed like things between them would be different. Things weren't different, though. She was still who she was. Touraine had a right to want no part of that.

So, all Luca said was "I meant it."

Luca stepped away and toward the ruin of the outer wall, tucking her hand in her pocket to hide its trembling. Cold wind blew through, and she ducked into her shoulders at the sudden gust. Outside, whether Touraine stood by her side or no, Balladaire would move. Lurching on shaky legs until it accustomed itself to her rule.

Touraine followed Luca to the opening, picking her way gingerly across charred and damp sections by turns. Luca raised her gaze from Touraine's path to her eyes. The look there was soft and warm and steady.

"Luca."

The sorrow with which Touraine spoke told Luca all she needed to know. She looked away and tried to swallow the sudden ache in her throat.

Touraine turned Luca's jaw back to her with gentle fingertips.

"We are who we are. We want what we want."

Touraine tilted Luca's chin down and captured Luca's mouth with her own. Her breath was warm against the cold, her tongue seeking.

Luca opened her mouth to the question. Everything in her body answered—the instant heat between her legs, the undignified whine in her throat, the unconscious roll of her hips toward Touraine's—a resounding *yes* that sang through her like a struck chord.

Touraine's body answered back. She sighed into Luca's mouth as Luca ran a hand up the back of her neck. Over her shorn hair. She shivered as Luca's nails trailed along her scalp, her hands large and heavy and promising on Luca's waist.

Desire pulled tight, finally snapping. Grief, grasping at warmth to fill the gaping spaces. Victory.

Luca broke the kiss and looked down at Touraine, dazed and breathing heavily.

"Come with me."

The bedchamber was warm, braziers instead of the fire to keep it so. Touraine unbuttoned the top of Luca's chemise and traced Luca's collarbone tentatively with her fingertips. Then with her lips. The other hand slid up from below, gliding over Luca's bandeau and—

"If you wanted—I could take this off for you," Luca breathed.

"Could you?" Touraine said from somewhere in the curve of Luca's neck. The murmur of Touraine's lips on her skin sent another pulse of heat between Luca's legs.

Luca yanked the shirt and the bandeau off over her head at the same time while Touraine's hands at her hips kept her steady. Touraine's thumb grazed one of the scars along Luca's ribs. The flesh wasn't puckered the same way as scars that healed normally.

"Does it hurt?" Touraine asked.

"No—"

Touraine grazed her nipple and Luca forgot the scars entirely.

"Can I?" Luca breathed into Touraine's mouth, ready to feel Touraine's skin against hers. Luca tugged the laces of Touraine's trousers undone with one hand, tugged at the hem of Touraine's shirt with the other, was tugging Touraine's lower lip between her teeth when Luca felt a pause in the other woman's breath. A momentary stillness.

Luca pulled back. "I'm sorry—"

"No. I—" Touraine hesitated, her hand on Luca's hand at the hem of her shirt.

"We don't have to—"

"I want to." Touraine shrugged out of her top, her broad shoulders flexing. A bandage wound loosely around her ribs, and she winced a little as it caught, but she smoothly slid Luca's hand down to cup her ass and Luca was suddenly very distracted. If Touraine didn't want to stop, neither did she.

Luca kissed her backward until Touraine's legs hit the back of the bed and her knees buckled into it. They toppled together with a yelp.

A smile crept across Touraine's face as she stared up at Luca, her golden eyes softening. "Huh."

Luca blushed under the sudden scrutiny. "What?"

Touraine shook her head, still smiling. She brushed Luca's cheek with her fingers, then curled the escaped wisps of hair around her finger. "Nothing."

"No." Luca pressed a forceful hand down on Touraine's chest, holding her there. She dug her nails into the firm muscle. "What?"

Touraine's eyes widened in surprise and she hissed, nostrils flaring. Luca's mouth went dry at the sudden flash of challenge. Touraine took Luca's wrist in her hand, but she didn't move Luca off her. She just laughed and glanced away, shaking her head. The softest, most perfect sound Luca had ever heard. Then she looked up at Luca through long eyelashes and said, "You're beautiful."

*Oh.*

Luca had never dared imagine how good it might feel to hear Touraine say that. It felt so good that Luca didn't move, didn't speak, didn't even blink until Touraine tried to rise beneath her.

But she looked too good there: the heavy rise and fall of her breath, the thin strip of dark hair between ridges of muscle, leading to the jut of her hips where her trousers had slipped down...Luca licked her lips and caught Touraine in a wrist lock. Careful of her bad leg, she straddled her. Touraine's eyes went wide again, then she smiled wickedly. She tried to twist out of Luca's grip but Luca twisted with her, riding her hips, just as wicked.

"You know...I could just pick you up and throw you onto your back," Touraine growled. She traced a path of shivers up Luca's ribs with the fingertips of her free hand.

The thought was not unappealing.

"You could." Luca pressed herself over Touraine, skin against skin, and squeezed her wrist again. Her other hand snaked between them, trailing down Touraine's belly, past the waxen scars the healing had made of her bullet wounds—*she didn't want me to see*—to the seam of her trousers, where Touraine radiated heat through the fabric. She pressed Touraine into the bed harder, grinding into her until she made a low, frustrated moan in her throat. "But you won't. I think you want me here, don't you?"

Maybe this was not the kind of thing that moved the borders

between hearts and changed the shape of empires. Maybe this was only a gasp of a moment, something they wouldn't even be able to recollect in twenty years, not even to remember fondly, not even to regret. In a week, in a month, it could flare and disintegrate into ash, burning them both up along with everything they cared about. Maybe it was nothing at all.

When Luca looked up from Touraine's undone trousers, the other woman's eyes were hooded, her bottom lip between her teeth. Luca scraped her nails down again, slowly, without taking her eyes off Touraine's. Down hard muscle until her fingers grazed tight curls. She stopped. "You want me here?" she asked again.

Beneath Luca's hand, Touraine's body was tight with the tension of waiting. Luca saw the calculus in her golden eyes—give in or fight back, surrender or advance. Luca would have been thrilled by either—she loved the play of Touraine's strength against hers—but when Touraine said *Yes*, slow and low, lifting her hips up to meet Luca's fingers, and *she was so*—

*Sweet sky above.*

Luca forgot how to breathe.

There were things that Luca did not know about Touraine, maybe would never know, stories that Touraine would never tell her. Stories that Luca was afraid to hear because of what they meant for them, for this, for her. Things about Touraine that she was afraid of, like those scars and the coiled strength arching up beneath her. But this, the wet heat of their bodies, the clench of Touraine around her fingers, the single voice from their throats—Luca was not afraid of this.

It was a long time before they had had their fill of each other, but when they had, Luca cradled Touraine against her chest. The other woman fell asleep first, her even breaths from powerful lungs. How perfect it was. She rested her head atop the soft waves of Touraine's hair. Then, as Luca pulled her closer, her thumb rode over a ridge of flesh on Touraine's back. She froze.

Only then did Luca feel the other scars her empire had left—etched on the back of the woman she loved.

*     *     *

It wasn't every day that Touraine woke up with her arm thrown over a warm body, naked skin damp and sticking to her cheek. That hadn't happened in a very long time, if she was honest. Too long.

It definitely wasn't every day that that person was about to become queen of the empire that had subjugated her people and tried to steal their holy magic. Though that had happened once before. That day had ended with one of her best friends dead and the other ready to kill her.

But it also wasn't every day that Touraine woke up with a curl of warm contentment in her chest. Warm enough that she could bury her face in Luca's neck and think about the pleasant aches from the night before and try to forget all of the rest. The satisfaction that she had taken something that she wanted. Something that felt good.

"You're awake." Luca shifted in Touraine's arms to face her, hissing and wincing at joints tightened by sleep. Touraine tried to school her face, but Luca had already seen the conflict there.

"Do you regret this?" Luca asked, placing a hesitant hand on Touraine's waist.

"No." Touraine brushed a thumb across a dark spot on Luca's pale shoulder. She bent to kiss it and tried to smile. "It's not that. It's just... we're in a delicate situation. I don't want to talk about it. Let's go back to sleep." Touraine tried to sink back into the pillows and pull Luca to her chest, but the other woman resisted.

"You never want to talk. We should talk."

The sun beaming in through the windows was cold, gray winter light, bright without warmth. It was impossible to tell how early it was, but Touraine's money was on not early. The light revealed a spatter of dark freckles on Luca's chest, belly, and hips. She marked them with a kiss, then drew a line with her tongue, connecting each one.

"Touraine!" Luca gasped, squirming. She grabbed Touraine by the chin and tilted her face to look up at her.

Touraine *looked*. She took Luca in, all of her, in a way she had desperately avoided for so long. The wry quirk of pleasure in Luca's mouth. Sky above, her lips, just yielding enough. The demanding cant of her dark eyebrow and the sharp edge of her jaw. Her unbound hair spilling over her shoulder in a wave of gold, dark and bright, shielding sharp collarbones and the strong cords of her neck. The surprising muscle in her shoulders and back, her wiry frame half duelist and half scholar. The strength in her long fingers, holding Touraine in place.

*She'll make a handsome queen.*

Luca shivered under Touraine's gaze and she licked her lower lip. "Talk first."

"All right," Touraine groaned, surrendering the bliss she'd been clinging to and flopping back onto the pillows. "Let's talk. I need to send a message to the council."

"Ah." Luca gave her a flat look. "To tell them you accomplished your mission." Her tone was bitter, and her glance between their bodies made it clear why.

Touraine stiffened. "They didn't tell me to fuck you. I mean I didn't—that's not why—this was just me. Only me."

The tendons in Luca's jaw stood out as she clenched her teeth. "Jaghotai isn't going to like this, is she?"

Touraine snorted. "She'll hate it. She has a right to, doesn't she? After everything you've done?"

Luca pulled back, her hand sliding off Touraine's waist as she retreated. "No. She doesn't. She's not the one I spent the night with."

"She is on the council, though."

"Does the Qazāli Council need to approve of your bedmates?"

"Does the High Court need to approve of yours?"

They stopped and looked away from each other. Touraine wasn't the only one feeling ashamed and hurt and afraid.

Touraine sighed. "We can't sweep the past to the floor and forget about it, Luca."

"I don't intend to, Touraine." Luca's fingers tightened on the bed between them, like she was keeping herself from reaching back out to touch her. "We can't change anything for the better if we pretend the worst never happened. Since we met in Qazāl, I've told you, 'When

I have my crown,' 'When I take my throne.' I know how hollow that must have sounded, but we did it. We're here now. You can have anything that you want. Anything that I can give you."

The last time they had lain like this, Luca had promised Touraine her freedom. She had written up the papers releasing her, drawn up a proper employment contract. Everything. Luca had been true to her word, and Touraine had done the equivalent of lighting it all on fire in a massive "go fuck yourself" because it wasn't enough. It had taken Touraine too long to realize that Luca couldn't *give* her freedom.

And yet, Luca had never once lied to Touraine. So Touraine asked what she was most afraid to ask.

"What if the things that I want for Qazāl and the things that you want for Balladaire don't fit together?"

The queen-to-be nodded and gave a small, sad smile. "It may happen. Does that mean we can't try?" Luca rolled onto her side and ran her fingers down Touraine's chest and belly. "Start with this one human joy?"

Touraine tracked Luca's eyes as they fell across her scars. Watched them cloud over with sadness.

"Why me?" Touraine asked the other question twisting in the back of her mind. "Am I just something you couldn't have? Did that make you want me even more?"

Luca's lips parted in surprise. "No. Well, maybe sometimes." She chuckled softly to herself, looking down at her hand between them. "You weren't—easy. To bring alongside. Your respect without obligation, I mean. I did want it. I wanted to earn it. I still do, I—I feel like I weigh everything I do through your eyes, now. Since Qazāl. You make me want to be better. Not just a queen for the histories, but to be good."

Touraine frowned. "You want to keep me around as your conscience because you can't figure out right from wrong for yourself?"

"No, that's not what I mean." Luca dug her nails a little into Touraine's skin, as if afraid Touraine might run while she stumbled after the right words. "You see me? You see everything. Everything I am. The ways I've—the mistakes I've made, yes, but also the world I want to build. I know you think that I spend all my life playing people like pieces, but everyone else sees me as a pawn. Or some other piece they need to woo, avoid, or capture. I'm a person to you."

"Oh." Touraine's mouth was too dry.

Luca swallowed and looked away. "Yes. Well."

Touraine traced a finger up Luca's forearm. "I thought you said everything is give and take? All of us, pieces in the game."

Luca smiled ruefully, watching the slow journey of Touraine's hand. "Maybe not everything."

Touraine tucked Luca's hair behind her ear and turned Luca's face back to her. "I do see you. And I..."

Her chest was too full. She recognized the power she held over Luca for what it was. Luca *had* bent. Luca had bent *for her*.

Luca's body went taut, utterly still, cheeks pink. "What?"

Touraine stroked her thumb down Luca's jaw. "I trust you to make the right choices even when I'm not here. You'll make them because you know they're right. Not just because you're afraid of disappointing me."

Luca closed her eyes and sighed into the touch. Kissed Touraine's wrist.

*This one human joy.* But for how long?

They settled into the silence.

"You know, in the old days," Luca started tentatively, "after a war, countries often sealed the peace by marrying scions together. It made both sides less likely to renege on agreements and reopen hostilities."

Touraine raised a wary eyebrow. Luca had to be teasing. "So, what you're saying is, it's in our best interests if the good of Balladaire depends on the good of Qazāl."

"Yes. And vice versa."

"Balladaire has gotten rich off us before. Strengthened its borders with our blood."

"You and I could build something new."

Touraine's breath caught in her chest. She studied Luca's face. "You're serious."

"Extremely serious."

For a moment, Touraine saw everything she could ever ask for in the solemn set of Luca's face. At Luca's side, she could restore Qazāl. Could destroy the Droitist schools. There would be no more Sands.

She would still have a duty to her people, but she would be sovereign, well and truly.

It was exactly what the Qazāli Council would want.

And yet, there was so much she would have to leave behind. Jaghotai. Her mother. They'd barely begun to know each other. Saïd's stories and poems, all meant to bring Touraine back. Pruett's feigned indifference, certain Touraine would stay in Balladaire. Friends new and old who would never join her here. To say yes to Luca was to leave it all, what she had begun to build on her own. Not forever, perhaps, but a loss nonetheless.

To wed the queen of Balladaire. It was overwhelming to imagine, especially lying naked in bed with her, the air heavy with their cologne and their sex and the faint smoke of a coup. Right now, Luca was just warmth and comfort and a sweet fading ache.

Touraine hesitated with Luca's fingers twined in hers. "Let me think about it."

"Of course."

No sign of Luca's frosty court mask, now. Only hope.

# CHAPTER 44

# WELCOME, JOLLY SOLDIER

Pruett rode on a prisoner's ass, tethered to the horse of a jumped-up lieutenant named Fougaire as they approached Samra'. It hurt to sing and it hurt to whistle because her face had been beaten most way to a pulp before Moyenne had stopped his soldiers from killing her. She hummed instead, a marching song every Sand knew because she had written it, and Sands from all of the squads had added lines until it was like a single unifying anthem.

*Welcome, soldier. Welcome, jolly soldier. How can I help you today?*
*Can I take your boots, sir, your army-issued boots, sir?*
*How can I help you today?*
*Can I take your coat, sir, your army-issued coat, sir?*
*How can I help you today?*

"Stop that," General Marquis de Moyenne said from just ahead of them. He didn't say it like a small man would, peevish about anything he couldn't control. It was more like the reflexive swatting of a fly. It didn't matter if you'd actually killed it.

She stopped anylight. For a minute. Instead, she stared up and up and up at the walls of Samra' as they came closer to the gates. They loomed higher than Pruett could have imagined, standing back at their camp a mile away, and yet they carried an unspeakable age. She wondered again how the Balladairans had gotten behind them in the first place. She wished again for a cigarette.

She smiled to herself as Moyenne announced himself at the gates and the doors were opened, as he'd expected them to be. As she had expected them to be; there was no revolt—yet. He shot her a dark look and she shrugged, raising her bound fists. *I'm the prisoner, remember? The traitor.* They rode through the gates. Moyenne wasn't the only soldier whose ears crept toward his shoulders even as he tried to ride with a Balladairan's entitlement.

Pruett didn't have the patience for the pretense. She was half sagging in the saddle from her bruises. She'd been expecting worse, if she was honest, but Moyenne wasn't Rogan.

*Can I take your legs, sir, your army-issued legs, sir?*
*How can I help you today?*
*Can I take your arms, sir, your army-issued arms, sir?*
*How can I help you today?*

A pomp of Masridāni met them well inside the gates, at some village square type of place, only this was a city as large as El-Wast. A sign nearby in the Balladairan style called it the Place du Général, and unlike the Grand Bazaar midan in El-Wast, which had featured a gallows from the moment Pruett arrived until the rebels tore it down, the Place du Général featured a sculpted fountain in the Balladairan art style: a rearing horse bearing the stylized depiction of a woman with a long queue beneath a tricorne.

Pruett knew who it was before she found the plaque at the base of the fountain.

*General Rosen Cantic.*

The statue was too old to be a memorial of the late general, and the stone woman before her was younger than the stone woman who'd died a year ago.

*Can I take your head, sir, your army-issued head, sir?*
*How can I help you today?*

In front of Cantic's statue, Yoroub waited for them. His handsome face split into outrage as he saw her. She grimaced her fishhook smile at him and fluttered her fingers in a wave.

"My lord general!" Yoroub strode up to Moyenne, just managing to keep on the good side of dignity. He bowed hurriedly. "My lord, this is the woman I wrote to you about. The seditious Qazāli!"

"I'm Masridāni, actually," Pruett piped in.

Moyenne didn't bother to acknowledge her.

"I received another note from her just the other day, attached to a filthy vulture. We tried to capture it, but it escaped."

*Sev.* Pruett could feel him soaring overhead, waiting.

Like Pruett was waiting. Like Kiras was waiting. Like Noé was waiting.

Yoroub sneered at her. "I'm glad you caught her, my lord. As you can see, the city is under control."

Moyenne scanned the square, as if he could read the hearts and minds of all assembled to pay witness to his mighty King's Own, a rare and shining gift. Then he smiled down on Yoroub, like a father smiling at a good son—not that Pruett had any idea what that might be like, just a healthy imagination—even though they had to be near about the same age, and Yoroub smiled right back at him, and Pruett thought she was going to be sick.

Pruett gagged. "Could you at least suck each other off in private?"

She rolled her eyes all the way up into the back of her skull and looked for the spot in her mind that was Sevroush.

*I am soaring. Carried by the wind. Wings open and aloft. I am hungry. Stop atop the tall stone. Eat.* Pruett looked down and saw the body of a rat. Torn partially by her claws, though it still struggled feebly in her grip. *Her grip.* She bent down and tore into its flesh with her sharp beak. *I am ready.*

"Hold your tongue," de Moyenne snapped.

*Now.*

Sevroush let out a bone-grinding call, and everyone in the square flinched. The call came again and again, and some of the blackcoats even reached their hands up to cover their ears just in time for the guns to crack and the bullets to find their flesh.

She ducked close to her donkey's neck and sought its mind like she had on the plodding journey from El-Bahr to Samra'. She found its hay-munching brain, like an extension of her own, and then she wondered, why stop there, why, when she could—

*Steady, steady,* on top of her, her rider was a steady weight and he was *shouting, shouting,* the bit in her mouth sharp, cutting, the spurs in her side as he urged her to turn, and Pruett saw herself.

The sensation was dizzying, and Pruett felt she was in two places at once. It knocked her back into her own body but not before she urged Moyenne's horse—*up.*

Moyenne's horse reared, panicking at the intrusion into its thoughts.

"Ha!" she shouted in victory just as the rope binding her wrists to Lieutenant Fougaire's horse dragged her to the ground.

Pruett scrambled to her knees only to be jerked back down in the tangle. She was going to die here, trampled into the dirt at the feet of a statue that looked like the woman who raised her. There was a poem in that, too.

She tried to get up again, and this time made it as far as her feet before getting crushed between the heaving sides of two horses. She didn't dare slide into any animal's head again. It took all her concentration just to keep enough grip on the rope to stay on her feet. Her wrists were burning raw.

An arm reached from behind her and grabbed at her rope. She twisted, biting, screaming, ready to kick at her attacker, when she realized it was Kiras with her jewel-studded knife in one hand and a rifle and ammo pouch in the other. The bayonet was already bloody. When Kiras bared her teeth in a hunter's smile, however, her teeth were not. Pruett could have kissed her.

With a few quick saws at the rope, Pruett was free from the tether and, a moment later, free from the bindings.

Kiras shoved the rifle into her hands. "Go!" Her braid was half-undone, and the curls sprang wildly about her head or were plastered with sweat. She looked positively feral, and Pruett knew she did, too. It made Pruett want to be back in a tent together, loud and wild and free. *Later, later.*

While Kiras wrestled the lieutenant from his horse, Pruett flexed her stiff fingers around the gun and ran, weaving this time between horses and battering away Balladairan blackcoats and Masridāni blackcoats, none of whom knew who to shoot at, and so they were shooting at each other. It was perfect. In her own black coat, filthy as it was from not being given a spare, she added to the confusion, jabbing her bayonet into both sides as she ran for higher ground.

*Here I am. I am hungry. Claws scratching on dirt. Claws scratching on stone. Like skittering sand across the gallows stand. My claws. I am hungry. I am hunted. I am—*

She crashed into a door, vision blurring, that led to stairs, and raced up them, her tiny heart pounding—no, *her* heart, her real heart pounding as she scattered rats, sprinting to the roof. She reached it and gulped down the air and the space. Here, she was free. Finally.

*I am soaring, I am soaring.* Sevroush landed beside her.

"Hello, handsome."

Pruett lay down on the edge of the building, stabilizing her weapon on the clay brick. This was familiar. This was like Qazāl. This was like the plains of Moyenne. A rifle in her hand, an enemy to spot. This was what she was good for.

She looked for Brice de Moyenne and found him standing on the ledge of the fountain, shouting commands to his King's Own and scanning the crowd. Looking for her.

*Can I take your dead, sir—you're dead, sir, you're dead, sir.*

*"I cannot help you today."*

She sighted down the rifle and fired.

# NOT THE PRINCESS (REPRISE)

Touraine had never seen the Grand Hall so empty.

In all the wide space, there was only a handful of servants skirting the edges of the room. It was a different place without the duke. Deflated, without his threats hanging over Qazāl. Now, it was just a too-big room with a big clock on the wall and a gilded chair. The throne sat, abandoned. Over there was the dais where Luca had abdicated, and almost died in Touraine's arms. There was where the Taargens had propositioned Touraine.

"It's so quiet," Aranen murmured.

For the High Court's safety, the coronation wouldn't be held in the lower hall. The emptiness of the hall was countered by the building noise of the crowd outside in the gardens. The new commander of the palace guard, one Commander Perrot, would keep order out there, while the public watched Princess Luca become queen.

Touraine's boots echoed on the marble stairs as they ascended to the upper level. Maybe it wasn't Nicolas's absence. Maybe Touraine had changed enough that the seat of Balladaire's power didn't frighten her anymore.

The High Court had taken their places in a half circle on the balcony overlooking the gardens, with Luca at their center. Before her was a desk with a pen and inkwell and two long pieces of parchment covered in elegant script. Beside the desk stood a small pedestal with a silk pillow, and on that pillow, a golden crown of spinning leaves studded with clear stones the same blue green of Luca's eyes.

Durfort stared soberly out at the crowd. A twitch tightened the corners of her dark eyes. She steadied herself with a hand on the desk.

Beside Durfort, the acting marquise de Moyenne, Brice de Moyenne's younger sister, pursed her lips, her hands folded behind her back. She reminded Touraine immediately of Cantic—precise and dutiful, with none of her brother's excess swagger.

De Travers stood opposite them, the gray fur collar of his cloak pulled close with a sparkling black stone clasp. His eyes shifted from the other members of the court to the crown as he occasionally licked his thin lips. Like he was waiting for something. He had been conspicuously absent during Nicolas's attempt to kill Luca. Despite his nobility and the fact that he'd never labored a day in his life, Luca told her that Travers was, above all, a merchant. Perhaps the duke had no longer been able to afford the comte's price.

Lady Bel-Jadot des Champs d'Or, however, had tried to flee the city. Only Luca's quick thinking had seen her arrested at the gates. Now, she was being held in the palace as a "guest." Better than being locked up in Le Fontinard, which was what Touraine had recommended (to be honest, Le Fontinard was Touraine's second choice). Even now, guards that Luca trusted stood close, hands on swords.

And Luca, in trousers and a coat the same pale blue as the afternoon sky, sparked with gold like summer sunlight. She turned when she heard Touraine and the others approach.

"I see you let her into your kohl," Aranen muttered under her breath.

Touraine smothered a smile. The makeup did look uncommonly good on Luca.

"Ambassador El-Qazāli. Ambassador Aranen din Djasha. Ghadin. Welcome." Luca bowed her head graciously. Her eyes were red, though her face was calm.

"Your Highness." Touraine bowed deeply. "Your Graces."

A wary nod from the younger Moyenne, and a jerky half smile from Durfort. Lady Bel-Jadot watched Touraine and her companions without even trying to veil her contempt. They had all seen Touraine heal Luca from certain death in this very hall. It would take them time to figure out how to deal with this new player in the game they'd thought they alone controlled. Touraine willed her steps steady as she joined them.

*You belong here as much as they do.*

"Your Excellencies." De Travers bowed slightly to them before handing Aranen a small envelope. "Forgive me, but this is for you. I thought it would be appropriate since we're also cementing our alliance today."

Aranen took the letter and unfolded it suspiciously—for a moment, all of them forgot about the coronation. "He got food to the Jackal," she murmured to Touraine in Shālan. "Grain, supplies, tools, lumber." She looked up, stunned, and said in Balladairan, "My lord, Qazāl thanks you for your generosity."

Travers patted the air humbly. "It was as much to aid the queen as to aid our allies. I noticed that one of Your Highness's ships came under difficulties. I simply eased them." The comte gave Luca a calculated smile that pricked at Touraine's shoulder blades.

Lady Bel-Jadot scoffed, drawing a sharp look from Moyenne and Durfort. It was against the rules to pretend these exchanges were anything less than genuine; Touraine had learned as much now. She wasn't eager to find out what de Travers would ask in return.

"A kindness, my lord," Luca said neutrally. "I'll remember it."

"Thank you, Your Highness."

"Yes." Touraine cleared her throat. She hid her unease with a small smile and bow of her head. "Thank you, my lord."

De Moyenne cleared her throat. "Is this everyone we're expecting? We should begin."

Luca gave Touraine one last look, and Touraine could see all of the fear and excitement Luca held back. The ceremony began, and Touraine stepped back with Aranen and Ghadin.

As Luca made her oaths to empire and citizen, Touraine thought back to the offer Luca had made her. She hadn't stopped thinking about it. Luca wasn't as charismatic as Durfort, but Touraine was drawn to her quiet command. To her coldness—the ability to be cold—as much as to the quiet moments of warmth she rarely showed anyone. Here, hanging just outside of the glaring light that was Luca's winter sun, Touraine admired her without wondering if she should or should not, if Luca would be a good queen or not. If Luca would be *good* or not. It was the beginning of her reign. The story was unwritten.

Touraine had not managed to put aside Ghadin's words, or what she had learned about the Fingers from Fili's evasions and Perrot's investigations. In the dark nights beside Luca, she'd seen the way the Fingers' struggle mirrored the Qazāli rebellion. She hadn't brought herself to tell Aranen, yet.

She'd questioned her own misgivings, her reluctance to go back among the Balladairan commons like Ghadin wanted to, and she hadn't liked the answers she found in the quiet, truest places in her mind. If the Fingers had their way, they'd topple the throne. Luca would lose her power. If Luca lost her power, where would that leave Qazāl? Where would that leave Touraine?

The last thing that Touraine expected was the tears clogging her throat as Luca bowed in front of de Travers and let the comte place the golden circlet atop her head.

Then Luca stepped farther out on the balcony and raised her hand to the crowd below. Though Touraine's stomach clenched tight with fear, there was only loud whooping and cheering. *May her reign be bright*, they shouted.

*May your reign be bright, Luca.*

"Ambassador." Luca stood beside the desk again, this time holding the pen out to Touraine.

"Me?" Touraine asked Aranen in a whisper.

"Who else?" Aranen smiled wryly.

"You?"

"Tch. Go."

Touraine's legs carried her stiffly into the waiting circle. She took the pen from Luca, conscious of the way their fingers brushed, of the way Luca leaned over the desk and over her, just barely not touching.

As she dipped the pen in ink to sign her name on the treaty beside Luca's, the weight of Luca's unanswered question pressed down on her. The weight of nations rested on her shoulders—not just Qazāl and Balladaire, but all of the Shālan colonies. She was so, so tired, but she could see the possibilities as they stood there. Together.

Aranen's words returned to Touraine: *That fire consumes all that it touches. What will you have to become to withstand her flames?*

The scribble of her name was such a small movement to change so much. How much they had given to get here, for the flick of her wrist to start the healing of decades of pain.

Touraine turned to Luca, conscious of the eyes of the High Court. She smiled tentatively. "We did it."

Luca grinned back, letting the court see her truly, just this once. The optimist. The idealist. "We can do more."


That night, Touraine and Luca walked in the garden, winding through the hedge maze for a modicum of privacy. Their array of guards trailed them at a polite but alert distance, and Perrot walked up ahead. Just in case. His commander's cloak gave a strut to his step.

Their breaths puffed before them in the cold air, but Touraine didn't mind. Today, she savored it. She smiled and turned to Luca only to see the other woman's eyes on her.

The new queen wasn't as celebratory as one would have expected from someone who'd gotten everything she'd ever wanted. Luca was contemplative, her steps slower than normal, her breathing deep and relaxed.

"How does it feel?" Touraine asked.

"Honestly? I feel I'm walking through a dream, and one day, I'll walk through the wrong door and it will take me back to the waking world." She took Touraine's gloved hand in hers. "I would very much like to stay here, though."

They walked like that for a time, silent, hand in hand. When they reached the center of the maze, the queen took a deep, forced breath. Touraine didn't need to look at her to follow her gaze to the place where she had found Luca cradling Paul-Sebastien LeRoche's body on her birthday. *Sky above, how time moves.* Luca fiddled with one of the newest grief rings on her finger: there were two now on her left hand beneath the glove, one for Tiro on her smallest finger and one for Bastien next to it. Another, heavier ring for Gil rested on a chain against her heart. Luca would never forget what this throne had cost her.

Touraine followed Luca to the Royal Oak. The tree was completely bare, now, but it was no less majestic for that. There was something about it, alone in this garden, that left Touraine awestruck. Or it was the way Luca's face softened around it. They fanned their cloaks to sit on the stone bench beneath it. The cold of the marble seeped through to Touraine's thighs, but it was bearable.

As she sat here with Luca, she felt again like she was in that gray peace. She didn't feel detached from everything—Luca's warm body beside her was a comfort—but she felt detached from the heaviness of her choices and the weight of her mistakes. When they went back into the noise and light, they would go to sleep, and when they woke, they would be different people. Luca would wake as the queen of Balladaire for the first time, and Touraine... The tethers that pulled them, the politics, the people, the duty—all of that would snap tighter around them than ever before.

Touraine could tell that Luca was avoiding that, too, and so she almost said nothing, and let them both enjoy the night's emptiness. But if Touraine could wake up as anything she wanted, she knew what it would be. She knew what she wanted to do with the power she had.

She pulled Luca's cold hand into her lap. "Your Majesty?" she said, teasing to cover the sudden flutter of nerves in her stomach.

"Touraine, I swear—"

"What if we did?" Touraine asked.

Luca's face went slack with surprise.

"What if we really can build something new?" Touraine continued.

Quickly, before she lost the clarity she felt. "With the gods, with the Taargens, with the people in the city? Something better."

Luca searched Touraine's face cautiously. "You want to? With me?"

"I want to."

Touraine didn't realize her hand was shaking until Luca tightened hers around it.

"Then we will."

Le Fontinard was a dreary place. La Chaise was a city of light, even in the dark of winter, and Le Fontinard sucked all that light away. The gray and black stone was like a pit without end. Once, her ancestors had ruled from this fortress. Well, for half a generation, after stealing it from the kings Fontine in a bloody coup that involved bodies thrown from the crenellations and heads on spikes. Then the palace had been built and Le Fontinard was turned into a prison, as if the family Ancier could keep its history of bloodshed in one bleak block of stone. Le Fontinard had been the center of the city once. What a nightmare that must have been.

The gendarmes opened the heavy doors to the prison with bows and murmurs of "Your Majesty," and that just made walking through feel even more like a trap. How did she imprison the man and still he managed to make her feel on the brink of losing to him? She was queen now! There was no more game to play!

Not exactly true. The paper packet was damp in her clammy hand.

Luca reconsidered her victory as she climbed the stairs to Nicolas's cell, coming up with a new curse for every click of pain in her hip. She'd exhausted Balladairan and Shālan and was moving on to her expansive Taargen repertoire when the jailer stopped in front of an iron-banded wooden door with a sliding slit near the bottom for food and drink, and a slit near the top for looking through.

Breathless, she opened her hand for the key and waved the man away with silent thanks. She waited until his steps had ceased to ring out upon the stone floors. There were no carpets here to muffle booted footfall, no tapestries to warm the cold walls. There weren't even torches. The only light was the lantern Luca carried. A lantern like the ones her uncle had thrown in their library.

Luca hadn't come here to talk about the library, though. She didn't want to ask what, in there, he was trying to hide from her or what he wanted her to need from him. He could content himself well enough with the fact that he was alive.

She'd come because...

She'd come because...

The smallest ring she wore seemed to tighten on her little finger, and tears sprang to her eyes again.

She'd come because she hadn't meant to kill Tiro. The paper in her hand crinkled, and she realized she'd clenched her fist tight around it, the small ring that matched hers inside. A twist of dark gold, like Tiro's hair in the summer sun, with a small inset sapphire like his eyes.

"Who's there?" Nicolas Ancier's voice sounded hoarse. Smoke damage, or disuse after sitting alone in prison for weeks?

Luca wasn't perfect, but she could think of a few things that her uncle did deserve for his cruelties—if Luca deserved them, too, well, then, it was good that she was on this side of the cell door—but losing Tiro like this was not one of them. So here she was, not with a peace offering but with something like an apology for a trespass that could never be forgiven.

"Luca? Have you come to visit your poor dear uncle?" Even prison couldn't stop the game. It wouldn't stop until he was dead, and sometimes, Luca wished she had let Touraine have her way. That would have been a kind of peace, wouldn't it?

All of her books certainly said so.

Yverte: *If any man could challenge you in either intellect, charisma, or military might, bind him to you with secrets or kill him; there is no other choice.*

Carlwic, the great Taargen war theorist: *Leave no enemy behind you unless you've severed his head.*

Pêcheuse, that great échecs master: *If someone's on your back row, quite frankly, you are fucked.*

She had loved Nicolas once, though, and he had loved her.

*What kind of a queen is too weak to kill her enemies?*

No matter what excuses she gave—he was still useful, she would look less legitimate—it made her rise feel incomplete, that she had not sent the order to the executioner.

An unfinished sentence.

The ring, she thought, might be a period, or, if not a full stop, some other division of a clause; some separation between her rule and his, an end of their crimes against one another.

Luca put the lantern on the hook outside of Nicolas's door and raised her hand to the slide that would allow her to look in, to speak, to push the small packet through.

"Luca? You're still there."

What would come after this punctuation, then?

Her hand shook, balled around the ring, hovering at the grate. She let it fall.

She put the ring back in her pocket, picked up the lantern again, and returned the way she had come, her footsteps and the tap of her cane echoing endlessly in the stone corridor.

Luca wasn't ready.

"Your High—Your Majesty, it's about my daughter."

Luca pressed her lips to steepled fingers while Guérin pled for her daughter's life.

They were in the small audience chamber just off the Grand Hall, and while it was less opulent than the neighboring room, it was still intended to impress. Though Inès Guérin had been in this room with Luca dozens of times before, today she looked frightfully small among the gilt decorations. Small and very afraid.

Luca wished that Guérin had not come here, like this, to plead her case. In public. With Luca sitting on the small throne-like seat and no other chairs in the room, it was designed to intimidate a petitioner or a foreign dignitary.

Luca stood and held a finger up for Guérin to wait, please. She lifted her voice to fill the room. "Clear the room. I'd like to speak with Guard Guérin alone."

In a slow trickle, the various attendants left the room, some craning their heads nosily to look between the two women, and some very pointedly looking only toward the door. Touraine also made to go, but Luca held her back with a gentle touch to the wrist.

When the room was empty save the three of them and Luca's personal guards, Luca walked down the dais and met Guérin face-to-face. Guérin was taller than Luca, and broader, and softer now around the belly. The lines in her face were deeper than they'd been on Luca's abdication—or had she just not noticed? The woman's eyes were bloodshot.

Guérin had come alone to Gil and Lanquette's funeral pyres, and she didn't approach Luca then, though she stood close enough that Luca watched the tears track down her face until the fires went cold. They were the last ones there, together. Then Guérin had bowed, once to the ashes and once to Luca, before limping into the night. Luca had been too grief-wrecked to stop her then, to find either accusation or commiseration for the grief they shared.

Luca had had time to callous herself since then.

She pointed down at Guérin's feet. Foot. Her new foot. "Did she make that for you?"

Guérin's face colored, and Luca didn't miss the pride and love shining through her face, though Guérin tried to subdue it. Guérin had been so proud in Qazāl when she'd gotten word about Fili's new apprenticeship in La Chaise.

"Aye, Your Majesty."

"It's an amazing piece of art." Amazing in every way: its ingenuity, its beauty—Luca had never seen the like. "Has it—did she use magic on it?"

Guérin's color deepened, in embarrassment this time, or perhaps offense. "I can't say, Your Majesty. I don't know if it has aught to do with—what she did."

"Inès, I—" Luca looked away and exhaled sharply.

She owed this woman her life, several times over. Guérin had devoted herself to Luca, and if it hadn't been for the accident, she might still be standing at Luca's side. She couldn't help the shudder that ran up her spine. Would she have put a knife in Luca's back?

"I need to know." Luca looked Guérin straight in the eyes. "Did you have any inkling of this?"

Guérin looked down at her feet, one booted, one curve of wood. Luca's heart fell. Touraine's face hardened.

Guérin raised her head, chin strong, like a woman on her way to the gallows but certain of every step that brought her there. "I didn't know about the attack. She's never liked you, though. She…" She looked away again, folding her lips into her mouth. "I think she resented you for taking me away. Resented me for going. I haven't been the best parent in that respect."

It was odd, to hear that many words from the woman at once. She'd usually been broody and taciturn as Luca's guard, saying as much with a silent regard as most did in speeches. Except, of course, on those few occasions when the distinctions between guard and royal diminished and Guérin spoke glowingly about the girl she'd left in Durfort with her father.

"What about your husband?"

Guérin shook her head fervently. Protectively. "He didn't know."

"And the magic? Do you keep the old god?"

The silence stretched a hair longer. "There are things we do up north that maybe we take for granted. Might be that's the same as the god."

Luca stepped back from Guérin and turned to pace before she caught herself. One of the old guard's eyelids flickered at Luca's tell—how many times had Guérin watched Luca pace over a problem she couldn't or didn't want to solve?

"Let me be the one to find her, Your Majesty. Please."

Instead of the gendarmerie Luca had sent to hunt her down and bring her in for questioning.

Luca believed Guérin would accept it if Luca demanded that Fili be brought in to face trial for assassination and sedition against the crown, and then executed. Luca might even learn to live with it herself. She was queen, was she not? It would not be the first decision that broke her heart, and it wouldn't be the last.

If Luca let her remain free, the hand of mercy might be enough to get Fili to talk to her about Balladaire's god. Without the King's Library, Luca barely knew where to start. If Luca let her remain free, though, Fili and her anti-royalists would strike at her again. *Mercy is only for the secure*, Yverte wrote, and Luca was walking a sky-falling rope bridge over the River Hadd, crocodiles and all.

From the corner of her eye, Luca saw Touraine watching her. Once, Luca and Touraine had fought over how Luca had taken Guérin for granted. How Balladaire took everyone who served it for granted. Touraine's regard sat heavily on her now. Touraine was a soldier, though. She knew how dangerous it was to bring a—a scorpion onto your back. Luca chuckled. *Who is the scorpion and who is the jackal?*

One way or another, she was going to regret this. If there was a chance that this scorpion could be useful, then so be it.

"Find her," Luca said, her voice hard. "I owe you that much. Bring her to me. If she wants amnesty—I'll need something from her, too."

Guérin's face crumpled into desperate relief, and Luca tried not to let her own face show her fear and uncertainty. As Guérin left, Touraine gave Luca a slow nod of wary approval.

Luca was still thinking about Guérin and Fili the next day in her study as she dug through a stack of incomplete missives and correspondence for the duke—things the seneschal had held in keeping, both newly arrived and old enough that the duke was meant to return to it.

She picked up another letter, this one dated just weeks before the— *the coup*. Around the time Luca had promised to surrender the crown to Nicolas.

Touraine knocked in her particular code on the door, and warmth sparked in Luca's chest despite the tone of the letter.

"Come in," Luca called.

As she continued reading, though, the spark was smothered utterly.

"Your Majesty." Touraine bowed as she entered, unwrapping the Qazāli scarf from her face. Her nose was red with the chill.

Luca looked up at the grave tone of Touraine's voice. Touraine's face was drawn with fear and ... apology?

"You've heard, then?" Touraine asked. She slouched in, leaning her backside on the desk beside Luca, careful not to sit on the wet ink of her notes.

Apparently, Luca hadn't suppressed her feelings, either. "Yes. He'd been hiding it from me." She held up the missive she'd just picked up. She ran the other hand absently along Touraine's muscled thigh.

Touraine slumped, as if relieved not to be the one to tell her. "I never expected her to do something like this. I thought ... I thought she'd moved beyond it. She never seemed to care about Balladaire."

Luca startled alert. "What? Who? What are you talking about?"

"Wait—that's not about Masridān?" Touraine nodded down at the letter in Luca's hand.

"What about Masridān? Have you heard from Brice?" Luca's hand froze on Touraine's thigh. Why would Brice write to Touraine first?

Touraine popped her knuckles and avoided Luca's eyes. "Samra' fell, and de Moyenne with it."

Luca's blood ran cold. "What under the sky above are you talking about?"

"Samra' was sacked, and de Moyenne's company was destroyed." The muscle beneath Luca's hands went rigid, as if braced for a blow, as if there was something even worse to tell than this, and frankly, Luca didn't see how that was possible.

"By whom?"

"By my ... friend. Pruett. She's taken the city for her own." When Luca said nothing, Touraine raised her gaze from the floor and asked, "What were *you* talking about?"

Lieutenant Pruett. The stormy-eyed conscript in Qazāl who had never looked at Luca with anything less than the purest hatred.

"Your lover."

"We aren't like that anymore."

Luca sagged back in her seat and threw her letter onto the desk. Incredulous laughter bubbled out of her.

"The Withering is back. It cropped up in the outskirts of the empire last month. It's only a matter of time until it's in the city."

"Oh, fuck."

"It's all right." Luca pushed herself to her feet, one hand steadying her on the desk as a wave of lightheadedness took her. The other she knotted in the shoulder of Touraine's shirt.

Touraine steadied Luca with a hand at her waist, shaking her head. "I don't think it is, Luca." Her mouth was pulled tight, and somehow, the weary hollows of her eyes conspired with her kohl to make her look hauntingly beautiful.

"It will be. We'll fix this."

Of course she would.

She was the queen.

The story continues in . . .

Book Three of Magic of the Lost

# ACKNOWLEDGMENTS

People say that the second book in a trilogy, the second book you publish, is harder, and I have to say I absolutely agree. Because of that, though, I have even more gratitude for those who helped me through it.

First, again, to the professionals in my corner: my agent, Mary C. Moore; my editors, Brit Hvide, Tiana Coven, and Jenni Hill; my amazing publicists and marketing team on both sides of the Atlantic, Angela Man, Nazia Khatun, Ellen Wright, Maddy Hall, Paola Crespo, and Natassja Haught; my copyeditor, Vivian Kirklin; the managing editor, Bryn A. McDonald; and the artists, including Lauren Panepinto on design, Tommy Arnold on the cover, and Tim Paul on the map.

Since this is a pandemic book, I would also like to acknowledge all the workers who traveled, delivering food, groceries, and other necessities during lockdown, to those of us who were able to work from home.

I started writing this book in earnest while I was in Paris, during research at l'Institut du monde arabe, so thanks to the helpful staff there, as well as to Shakespeare and Company, which gave me a bed to sleep in, a bookstore to play in, and a cat to cuddle.

For inspiration and the inspiration to keep going, thanks to Coach Bennett on Nike Run Club; Sunni Torgman, who got me as swole as Touraine; and Peter Chiykowski for the Story Engine Deck. To Dave and the rest of the swordsfolk, who inspired some sword moves—anything that makes sense is their fault, anything that doesn't we'll call creative license.

Thanks to Jess Barber, for reading early and keeping the enthusiasm coming. To the Zoom crew, the Slacks, the London Supper Club, and all the writers and publishing folks who kept me company with their books, and text messages, and mutual rants—you kept me sane even though we're all overworked and underpaid.

To everyone who came out in support of Touraine and Luca and the Jackal and the whole messy crew—for your support for this queer grappling with colonialism, for every fan artist who helped me see the characters even sharper, for every meme that made me laugh—thank you. There were days when I asked myself, *Why am I doing this?* You were and continue to be one of the loudest answers.

Thank you always and ever to S, for the love and support and, most importantly, for going through scene after scene with me, arguing over sentence structure, comma placement, and how many times I'm allowed to write *love* in this book.

And as always, thanks to you, reader. I couldn't do this without you.

# extras

orbit

# meet the author

Jovita McCleod

C. L. CLARK graduated from Indiana University's creative writing MFA program and was a 2012 Lambda Literary Fellow. She's been a personal trainer, an English teacher, and an editor, and is some combination thereof as she travels the world. When she's not writing or working, she's learning languages, doing P90something, or reading about war and (post)colonial history. Her other work has appeared in *Beneath Ceaseless Skies*, *FIYAH*, *Uncanny*, *PodCastle*, and elsewhere. You can follow her on Twitter: @C_L_Clark.

Find out more about C. L. Clark and other Orbit authors by registering for the free monthly newsletter at orbitbooks.net.

# if you enjoyed
# THE FAITHLESS

look out for

# THE LOST WAR
## The Eidyn Saga: Book One

by

# Justin Lee Anderson

*In the wake of a devastating war, an emissary for the king must gather a group of strangers and travel across a ravaged, plague-ridden, and violent land to restore an exiled queen to her throne in this debut epic fantasy novel from Justin Lee Anderson.*

*The war is over, but the beginnings of peace are delicate.*

*Demons continue to burn farmlands, violent mercenaries roam the wilds, and a plague is spreading. The country of Eidyn is on its knees.*

*In a society that fears and shuns him, Aranok is the first mage to be named king's envoy. And his latest task is to restore an exiled foreign queen to her throne.*

*The band of allies he assembles each have their own unique skills. But they are strangers to one another, and at every step across the ravaged land, a new threat emerges, lies are revealed, and distrust threatens to destroy everything they are working for. Somehow, Aranok must bring his companions together and uncover the conspiracy that threatens the kingdom—before war returns to the realms again.*

# CHAPTER 1

*Fuck.*

The boy was going to get himself killed.

"Back off!"

Aranok put down his drink, leaned back and rubbed his dusty, mottled brown hands across his face and behind his neck. He was tired and sore. He wanted to sit here with Allandria, drink beer, take a hot bath, collapse into a soft, clean bed and feel her skin against his. The last thing he wanted was a fight. Not here.

They'd made it back to Haven. This was their territory, the new capital of Eidyn, the safest place in the kingdom—for what that was worth. He'd done enough fighting, enough killing. His shoulders ached and his back was stiff. He looked up at the darkening sky, spectacularly lit with pinks and oranges.

The wooden balcony of the Chain Pier Tavern jutted out over the main door along the front length of the building. Aranok had thought it an optimistic idea by the landlord, considering Eidyn's usual weather, but there were about thirty patrons overlooking the main square with their beers, wines and whiskies.

Allandria looked at him from across the table, chin resting on her hand. He met her deep brown eyes, pleading with her to give him another option. She looked down at the boy arguing with the two thugs in front of the blacksmith's forge, then back at him. She shrugged, resigned, and tied back her hair.

Bollocks.

Aranok knocked back the last of his beer and clunked the empty tankard back on the table. As Allandria reached for her bow, he signalled to the serving girl.

"Two more." He gestured to their drinks. "I'll be back in a minute."

The girl furrowed her brow, confused.

He stood abruptly to overcome the stiffness of his muscles. The chair clattered against the wooden deck, drawing some attention. Aranok was used to being eyed with suspicion, but it still rankled. If they knew what they owed him—owed both of them...

He leaned on the bannister, feeling the splintered, weatherbeaten wood under his palms; breathing in the smoky, sweaty smell of the bar. Funny how welcome those odours were; he'd been away for so long. With a sigh, Aranok twisted and turned his hands, making the necessary gestures, vaulted over the bannister and said, "*Gaoth*." Air burst from his palms, kicking up a cloud of dirt and cushioning his landing. Drinkers who had spilled out the front of the inn coughed, spluttered and raised hands in defence. A chorus of gasps and grumbles, but nobody dared complain. Instead, they watched.

Anticipating.

Fearing.

Aranok breathed deeply, stretching his arms, steeling himself as he passed the newly constructed stone well—one of many, he assumed, since the population had probably doubled recently. A lot of eyes were on him now. Maybe that was a good thing. Maybe they needed to see this.

As he approached the forge, Aranok sized up his task. One of the men was big, carrying a large, well-used sword. A club hung from his belt, but he looked slow and cumbersome; more a butcher than a soldier. The other was sleek, though—wiry. There was something rat-like about him. He stood well-balanced on the balls of his feet, dagger twitching eagerly. A thief most likely. Released from prison and pressed into the king's service? Surely not. Hells. Were they really this short of men? Was this what they'd bought with their blood?

"You've got the count of three to drop your weapons and move," the fat one wheezed. "King's orders."

"Go to Hell!" The boy's voice cracked. He backed a few steps toward the door. He couldn't be more than fifteen, defending his father's business with a pair of swords he'd probably made himself. His stance was clumsy, but he knew how to hold them. He'd had some training, if not any actual experience. Enough to make him think he could fight, not enough to win.

The rat rocked on his feet, the fingertips of his right hand frantically rubbing together. Any town guard could resolve this without blood. If it was just the fat one, he might manage it. But this man was dangerous.

478

Now or never.

"Can I help?" Aranok asked loudly enough for the whole square to hear.

All three swung to look at him. The thief's eyes ran him up and down. Aranok watched him instinctively look for pockets, coin purses, weapons—assess how quickly Aranok would move. He trusted the rat would underestimate him.

"Back away, *draoidh*!" snarled the butcher. The runes inscribed in Aranok's leather armour made it clear to anyone with even a passing awareness of magic what he was. *Draoidh* was generally spat as an insult, rarely welcoming. He understood the fear. People weren't comfortable with someone who could do things they couldn't. He only wore the armour when he knew it might be necessary. He couldn't remember the last day he'd gone without it.

"This is king's business. We've got a warrant," grunted the big man.

"May I see it?" Aranok asked calmly.

"I said piss off." He was getting tetchy now. Aranok began to wonder if he might have made things worse. It wouldn't be the first time.

He took a gentle step toward the man, palms open in a gesture of peace.

The rat smiled a confident grin, showing him the curved blade as if it were a jewel for sale. Aranok smiled pleasantly back at him and gestured to the balcony. The thief's face confirmed he was looking at the point of Allandria's arrow.

"Shit," the rat hissed. "Cargill. Cargill!"

"What?" Cargill barked grumpily back at him. The thief mimicked Aranok's gesture and the fat man also looked up. He spun around to face Aranok, raising his sword—half in threat, half in defence. Nobody likes an arrow trained on them. The boy took another step back—probably unsure who was on his side, if anyone.

"You'll swing for this," Cargill growled. "We've got orders from the king. Confiscate the stock of any business that can't pay taxes. The boy owes!"

"Surely his father owes?" Aranok asked.

"No, sir," the boy said quietly. "Father's dead. The war."

Aranok felt the words in his chest. "Your mother?"

The boy shook his head. His lips trembled until he pressed them together.

Damn it.

Aranok had seen a lot of death. He'd held friends as they bled out, watching their eyes turn dark; he'd stumbled over their mangled bodies, fighting for his life. Sometimes they cried out, or whimpered as he passed—clinging desperately to the notion they could still see tomorrow.

Bile rose in his gullet. He turned back to Cargill. Now it was a fight.

"If you close his business, how do you propose he pays his taxes?" Aranok struggled to maintain an even tone.

"I don't know," the thug answered. "Ask the king."

Aranok looked up the rocky crag toward Greytoun Castle. Rising out of the middle of Haven, it cast a shadow over half the town. "I will."

There was a hiss of air and a thud to Aranok's right. He turned to see an arrow embedded in the ground at the thief's feet. He must have crept a little closer than Allandria liked. The rat was lucky she'd given him a warning shot. Many didn't know she was there until they were dead. Eyes wide, he sidled back under the small canopy at the front of the forge.

Cargill fired into life, brandishing his sword high. "I'll cut your fucking head off right now if you don't walk away!" His bravado was fragile, though. He didn't know what Aranok could do—what his *draoidh* skill was. Aranok enjoyed the thought that, if he did, he'd only be more scared.

"Allandria!" he called over his shoulder.

"Aranok?"

"This gentleman says he's going to cut my head off."

"Already?" She laughed. "We just got here."

All eyes were on them now. The tavern was silent, the crowd an audience. People were flooding out into the square, drinks still in hand. Others stood in shop doors, careful not to stray too far from safety. Windows filled with shadows.

Cargill's bravado disappeared in the half-light. "You...you're...we're on the same side!"

"Can't say I'm on the side of stealing from orphans." Aranok stared hard into his eyes. Fear had taken him.

"We've got a warrant." The big man pulled a crumpled mess from his belt and waved it like a flag of surrender. Now he was keen to do the paperwork.

Perhaps they'd get out of this without a fight after all. Unusually, he was grateful for the embellishments of legend. He'd once heard a story about himself, in a Leet tavern, in which he killed three demons on his own. The downside was that every braggart and mercenary in the kingdom fancied a shot at him, which was why he tended to travel quietly—and anonymously. But now and again...

"How much does he owe?" Aranok asked.

"Eight crowns." Cargill proffered the warrant in evidence. Aranok took it, glancing up to see where the rat had got to. He was too near the wall for Aranok's liking. The boy was vulnerable.

"Out here," Aranok ordered him. "Now."

"With that crazy bitch shooting at me?" he whined.

"Thül!" Cargill snapped.

Thül slunk back out into the open, watching the balcony. Sensible boy. Though if this went on much longer, Allandria might struggle to see clearly across the square. He needed to wrap it up.

The warrant was clear. The business owed eight crowns in unpaid taxes and was to be closed unless payment was made in full. Eight bloody crowns. Hardly a king's ransom—except it was.

Aranok looked up at the boy. "What can you pay?"

"I've got three..." he answered.

"You've got three or you can pay three?"

"I've got three, sir."

"And food?"

The boy shrugged.

"A bit."

"Why do you care?" Thül sneered. "Is he yours?"

Aranok closed the ground between them in two steps, grabbed the thief by the throat and squeezed—enough to hurt, not enough to suffocate him. He pulled the angular, dirty face toward his own. Rank breath escaping yellow teeth made Aranok recoil momentarily.

"Why do I care?" he growled.

The thief trembled. He'd definitely underestimated Aranok's speed.

"I care because I've spent a year fighting to protect him. I care because I've watched others die to protect him." He stabbed a finger toward the young blacksmith. "And his parents died protecting you, you piece of shit!"

There were smatterings of applause from somewhere. He released the rat, who dropped to his knees, dramatically gasping for air. Digging some coins out of his purse, Aranok turned to the boy.

"Here. Ten crowns as a deposit against future work for me. Deal?"

The boy looked at the coins, up at Aranok's face and back down again. "Really?"

"You any good?"

"Yes, sir." The boy nodded. "Did a lot of Father's work. Ran the business since he went away."

"How is business?"

"Slow," the boy answered quietly.

Aranok nodded. "So do we have a deal?" He thrust his hand toward the boy again.

Nervously, the boy put down one sword and took the coins from Aranok's hand, tentatively, as though they might burn. He put the other sword down to take two coins from the pile in his left hand, looking to Aranok for reassurance. He clearly didn't like being defenceless. Aranok nodded. The boy turned to Cargill and slowly offered the hand with the bulk of the coins. Pleasingly, the thug looked to Aranok for approval. He nodded permission gravely. Cargill took the coins and gestured to Thül. They walked quickly back toward the castle, the thief looking up at Allandria as they passed underneath. She smiled and waved him off like an old friend.

Aranok clapped the boy on the shoulder and walked back toward the tavern, now very aware of being watched. It had cost him ten crowns to avoid a fight...and probably a lecture from the king. It was worth it. He really was tired. The crowd returned to life—most likely chattering in hushed tones about what they'd just seen. One man even offered a hand to shake as Aranok walked past; quite a gesture—to a *draoidh*. Aranok smiled and nodded politely but didn't take the hand. He shouldn't have to perform a grand, charitable act before people engaged with him.

483

The man looked surprised, smiled nervously and ran his hand through his hair, as if that had always been his intention.

Aranok felt a hand on his elbow. He turned to find the boy looking up at him, eyes glistening. "Thank you," he said. "I... thank you."

"What's your name?" Aranok asked. He tried to look comforting, but he could feel the heavy dark bags under his eyes.

"Vastin," the boy answered.

Aranok shook his hand.

"Congratulations, Vastin. You're the official blacksmith to the king's envoy."

# if you enjoyed
## THE FAITHLESS

### look out for

# THE FOXGLOVE KING
## The Nightshade Crown: Book One

### by

# Hannah Whitten

*In this gilded, gothic, and romantic new epic fantasy series from* New York Times *bestselling author Hannah Whitten, a young woman's secret power to raise the dead plunges her into the dangerous world of the Sainted King's royal court.*

*When Lore was thirteen, she escaped a cult in the catacombs beneath the city of Dellaire. And in the ten years since, she's lived by one rule: Don't let them find you. Easier said than done, when her death magic ties her to the city.*

*Mortem, the magic born from death, is a high-priced and illicit commodity in Dellaire, and Lore's job running poisons keeps her in food, shelter, and relative security. But when a run goes wrong and Lore's power is revealed, she's taken by the Presque Mort, a group of warrior-monks sanctioned to use Mortem and working for the Sainted King. Lore fully expects a pyre, but King August has a different plan. Entire villages on the outskirts of the country have been dying overnight, seemingly at random. Lore can either use her magic to find out what's happening and who in the King's court is responsible, or die.*

*Lore is thrust into the Sainted King's glittering court, where no one can be believed and even fewer can be trusted. Guarded by Gabriel, a duke-turned-monk, and continually running up against Bastian, August's ne'er-do-well heir, Lore tangles in politics, religion, and forbidden romance as she attempts to navigate a debauched and opulent society.*

*But the life she left behind in the catacombs is catching up with her. And even as Lore makes her way through the Sainted court above, they might be drawing closer than she thinks.*

# CHAPTER ONE

No one is more patient than the dead.
—Auverrani proverb

Every month, Michal claimed he'd struck a deal with the landlord, and every month, Nicolas sent one of his sons to collect, anyway. The sons must've drawn straws—this month's unfortunate was Pierre, the youngest and spottiest of the bunch, and he trudged up the street of Dellaire's Harbor District with the air of one approaching a guillotine.

Lore could work with that.

A dressing gown that had seen better days dripped off one shoulder as Lore leaned against the doorframe and watched him approach. Pierre's eyes kept drifting to where the fabric gaped, and she kept having to bite the inside of her cheek so she didn't laugh. Apparently, a crosshatch of silvery scars from back-alley knife fights didn't deter the man when presented with bare skin.

She had other, more interesting scars. But she kept her palm closed tight.

A cool breeze blew off the ocean, and Lore suppressed a shiver. Pierre didn't seem to spare any thought for why she'd exited the house barely dressed while mornings near the harbor always carried a chill, even in summer. An easy mark in more ways than one.

"Pierre!" Lore shot him a dazzling grin, the same one that made Michal's eyes simultaneously go heated and then narrow before he asked what she wanted. Another twist against the doorframe, another seemingly casual pose, another bite of wind that made a curse bubble behind her teeth. "It's the end of the month already?"

Michal should be dealing with this. It was his damn row house. But the drop he'd made for Gilbert last night had been all the way in the Northwest Ward, so Lore let him sleep.

Besides, waking up early had given her time to go through Michal's pockets for the drop coordinates. She'd taken them to the tavern on the corner and left them with Frederick the bartender, who'd been on Val's payroll for as long as Lore could remember. Val would be sending someone to pick them up before the sun fully rose, and someone else to grab Gilbert's poison drop before his client could.

Lore was good at her job.

Right now, her job was making sure the man she'd been living with for a year so she could spy on his boss didn't get evicted.

"I—um—yes, yes it is." Pierre managed to fix his eyes to her own, through obviously conscious effort. "My father…um, he said this time he means it, and…"

Lore let her expression fall by careful degrees, first into confusion, then shock, then sorrow. "Oh," she murmured, wrapping her arms around herself and turning her face away to show a length of pale white neck. "This month, of all months."

She didn't elaborate. She didn't need to. If there was anything Lore had learned in twenty-three years alive, ten spent on the streets of Dellaire, it was that men generally preferred you to be a set piece in the story they made up, rather than an active player.

From the corner of her eye, she saw Pierre's pale brows draw together, a deepening blush lighting the skin beneath his freckles. They were all moon-pale, Nicolas's boys. It made their blushes look like something viral.

His gaze went past her to the depths of the dilapidated row house beyond. Sunrise shadows hid everything but the dust motes twisting in light shards. Not that there was much to see back there, anyway. Michal was still asleep upstairs, and his sister, Elle, was sprawled on the couch, a wine bottle in her hand and a slightly musical snore on her lips. It looked like any other row house on this street, coming apart at the seams and full of people who skirted just under the law to get by.

Or very far under it, as the case may be.

"Is there an illness?" Pierre kept his voice hushed, low. His face tried for sympathetic, but it looked more like he'd put bad milk in his coffee. "A child, maybe? I know Michal rents this house, not you. Is it his?"

Lore's brows shot up. In all the stories she'd let men spin about her, *that* was a first—Pierre must have sex on the brain if he jumped straight to pregnancy. But beggars couldn't be choosers. She gently laid a hand on her abdomen and let that be answer enough. It wasn't technically a lie if she let him draw his own conclusions.

She was past caring about lying, anyway. Lore was damned whether or not she kept her spiritual record spotless. Might as well lean into it.

"Oh, you poor girl." Pierre was probably younger than she was, and here he went clucking like a mother hen. Lore managed to keep her eyes from rolling, but only just. "And with a poison runner? You know he won't be able to take care of you."

Lore bit the inside of her cheek again, hard.

Her apparent distress made Pierre bold. "You could come with me," he said. "My father could help you find work, I'm sure." He raised his hand, settled it on her bare shoulder.

And every nerve in Lore's body seized.

It was abrupt and unexpected enough for her to shudder, to shake off his hand in a motion that didn't fit her soft, vulnerable narrative. She'd grown used to feeling this reaction to dead things—stone, metal, cloth. Corpses, when she couldn't avoid them. It was natural to sense Mortem in something dead, no matter how unpleasant, and at this point she could hide her reaction, keep it contained. She'd had enough practice.

But she shouldn't feel Mortem in a *living* man, not one who wasn't at death's door. Her shock was quick and sharp, and chased with something else—the scent of foxglove. So strong, he must've been dosed mere minutes before arriving.

And he wanted to disparage poison runners. Hypocrite.

Her fingers closed around his wrist, twisted, forced him to his knees. It happened quick, quick enough for him to slip on a stray pebble and send one leg out at an awkward angle, for a strangled *"Shit!"* to echo through the morning streets of Dellaire's Harbor District.

Lore crouched so they were level. Now that she knew what to look for, it was obvious in his eyes, bloodshot and glassy; in the heartbeat thumping slow and irregular beneath her palm. He'd gone to one of the cheap deathdealers, one who didn't know how to properly dose their patrons. The veins at the corners of Pierre's eyes were barely touched with gray, so he hadn't been given enough poison for any kind of life extension, and certainly not enough to possibly grasp the power waiting at death's threshold.

He probably wasn't after those things, anyway. Most people his age just wanted the high.

The dark threads of Mortem under Pierre's skin twisted against Lore's grip, stirred to life by the poison in his system. Mortem was dormant in everyone—the essence of death, the power born of entropy, just waiting to flood your body on the day it failed—but the only way to use it, to wake it up and bend it to your will, was to nearly die.

If you weren't after the power or the euphoric feeling poison could give you, then you were after the extra years. Properly dosed, poison could balance your body on the cusp of life and death, and that momentary concession to Mortem could, paradoxically, extend your life. Not that the life you got in exchange was one of great quality—half-stone, your veins clotted with rock, making your blood rub through them like a cobblestone skinning a knee.

Whatever Pierre had been after when he visited a deathdealer this morning, he hadn't paid enough to get it. If he'd gotten a true poison high, he'd be slumped in an alley somewhere, not asking her for rent. Rent that was higher than she remembered it being, now that she thought of it.

"Here's what's going to happen," Lore murmured. "You are going to tell Nicolas that we've paid up for the next six months, or I am going to tell him you've been spending his coin on deathdealers."

Fuck Michal's ineffectual bargains with the landlord. She'd just make one of her own.

Pierre's eyes widened, his lids poison-heavy. "How—"

"You stink of foxglove and your eyes look more like windows." Not exactly true, since she hadn't noticed until she'd sensed the Mortem, but by the time he could examine himself, the effect would've worn off anyway. "Anyone can take one look at you and know, Pierre, even though your deathdealer barely gave you enough to make you tingle. I'd be surprised if you got five extra minutes tacked onto the end of your life for *that*, so I hope the high was worth it."

The boy gaped, the open mouth under his window-glass eyes making his face look fishlike. He'd undoubtedly paid a handsome sum for the pinch of foxglove he'd taken. If she wasn't so good at spying for Val, Lore might've become a deathdealer herself. They made a whole lot of money for doing a whole lot of jack shit.

Pierre's unfortunate blush spread down his neck. "I can't—He'll ask where the money is—"

"I'm confident an industrious young man like yourself can come up with it somewhere." A flick of her fingers, and Lore let him go.

Pierre stumbled up on shaky legs and straightened his mussed shirt. The gray veins at the corners of his eyes were already fading back to blue-green. "I'll try," he said, voice just as tremulous as the rest of him. "I can't promise he'll believe me."

Lore gave him a winning smile. Standing, she yanked up the shoulder of her dressing gown. "He better."

Pierre didn't run down the street, but he walked very fast.

As the sun rose higher, the Harbor District slowly woke up—bundles of cloth stirred in dark corners, drunks coaxed awake by light and sea breeze. In the row house across the street, Lore heard the telltale sighs of Madam Brochfort's girls starting their daily squabbles over who got the washtub first, and any minute now at least two straggling patrons would be politely but firmly escorted outside.

"Pierre?" she called when he was halfway down the street. He turned, lips pressed together, clearly considering what other things she might blackmail him with.

"A word of advice." She turned toward Michal's row house in a flutter of faded dressing gown. "The real deathdealers have morgues in the back. Death's scales are easy to tip."

✤

Elle was awake, but only just. She squinted from beneath a pile of gold curls through the light-laden dust, paint still smeared across her lips. "Whassat?"

"As if you don't know." Lore shook out the hand that had touched Pierre's shoulder, trying to banish pins and needles. It'd grown easier for her to sense Mortem, recently, and she wasn't fond of the development. She gave her hand one more firm shake before heading into the kitchen. "End of the month, Elle-Flower."

There was barely enough coffee in the chipped ceramic pot for one cup. Lore poured all of it into the stained cloth she used as a strainer and balled it in her fingers as she put the kettle over the fire. If there was only one cup of coffee in this house, she'd be the one drinking it.

"Don't call me that." Elle groaned as she shifted to sit up. She'd fallen asleep in her dancer's tights, and a long run traced up each calf. It'd piss her off once she noticed, but the patrons of the Foghorn and Fiddle down the street wouldn't care. One squinting look into the wine bottle to make sure it was empty and Elle shoved off the couch to stand. "Michal isn't awake, we don't have to pretend we like each other."

Lore snorted. In the year she'd been living with Michal, it'd become very obvious that she'd never get along with his sister. It didn't bother Lore. Her relationship with Michal was built on a lie, a sand foundation with no hope of holding, so why try to make friends? As soon as Val gave the word, she'd be gone.

Elle pushed past her into the kitchen, the spiderweb cracks on the windows refracting veined light on the tattered edges of her tulle skirt. She peered into the pot. "No coffee?"

Lore tightened her hand around the cloth knotted in her fist. "Afraid not."

"Bleeding *God.*" Elle flopped onto one of the chairs by the pockmarked kitchen table. For a dancer, she was surprisingly ungraceful when sober. "I'll take tea, then."

"*Surely* you don't expect me to get it for you."

A grumble and a roll of bright-blue eyes as Elle slinked her way toward the cupboard. While her back was turned, Lore tucked the straining cloth into the lip of her mug and poured hot water over it, hoping Elle was too residually drunk to recognize the scent.

Still grumbling, Elle scooped tea that was little more than dust into another mug. "Well?" She took the kettle from Lore without looking at her and apparently without smelling her coffee. "How'd it go? Is Michal finally going to have to spend money on something other than alcohol and betting at the boxing ring?"

"Not on rent, at least." Lore kept her back turned as she tugged the straining cloth and the tiny knot of coffee grounds from her cup and stuffed it in her pocket. "We're paid up for six months."

"Is that why you look so disheveled?" Elle's mouth pulled into a self-satisfied moue. "He could get it cheaper across the street."

"The dishevelment is the fault of your brother, actually." Lore turned and leaned against the counter. "And barbs about Madam's girls don't suit you, Elle-Flower. It's work like any other. To think otherwise just proves you dull."

Another eye roll. Elle made a face when she sipped her weak tea, and sharp satisfaction hitched Lore's smile higher. She took a long, luxurious swallow of coffee and drifted toward the stairs. There'd been a message waiting for her at the tavern—Val needed her help with a drop today. It was risky business, having her work while she was deep undercover with another operation, but hands were low. People kept getting hired out from under them on the docks.

And Lore had skills that no one else did.

She'd have to come up with an excuse for why she'd be gone all day, but if she woke Michal up with some kissing, he wouldn't question her further. She found herself smiling at the idea. She liked kissing Michal. That was dangerous.

The smile dropped.

The stairs of the row house were rickety, like pretty much everything else in the structure, and the fourth one squeaked something awful. Lore winced when her heel ground into it, sloshing coffee over the side of her mug and burning her fingers.

Michal was sitting up when Lore pushed aside the ratty curtain closing off their room, sheets tangled around his waist and dripping off the mattress to pool on the floor. It was unclear whether it was the squeaking stair or her loud curse when she burned herself that had woken him.

He pushed his dark hair out of his eyes, squinted. "Coffee?"

"Last cup, but I'll share if you come get it."

"That's generous, since I assume you need it." He grumbled as he levered himself up from the floor-bound mattress, holding the sheet around his naked hips. "You had another nightmare last night. Thrashed around like the Night Witch herself was after you."

Her cheeks colored, but Lore just shrugged. The nightmares were a recent development, and random. She could never remember much about them, only vague impressions that didn't quite match with the terrified feeling they left behind. Blue, open sky, a churning sea. Some dark shape twisting through the air, like smoke but thicker.

Lore held out the coffee. "Sorry if I kept you awake."

"At least you didn't scream this time." Michal took a long drink from her proffered mug, though his face twisted up when he swallowed. "No milk?"

"Elle used the last of it." Lore shrugged and took the cup back, draining the rest.

Michal ran a hand through his hair to tame it into submission while he bent to pull clothes from the piles on the floor. The sheet fell, and Lore allowed herself a moment to ogle.

"I have another drop today," he said as he got dressed. "So I'll probably be gone until the evening."

That made her life much easier. Lore propped her hips on the windowsill and watched him dress, hoping her relief didn't show on her face. "Gilbert is working you hard."

"Demand has gone up, and the team is dwindling. People keep getting hired on the docks to move cargo, getting paid more than Gilbert can afford to match." Michal gave the room a narrow-eyed survey before spotting his boot beneath a pile of sheets in the corner. "The Presque Mort and the bloodcoats have all been busy getting ready for the Sun Prince's Consecration tomorrow, and everyone is taking advantage of them having their proverbial backs turned."

It seemed like Gilbert was doing far more business during the security lull than was wise, but that wasn't Lore's problem. That's what she told herself, at least, when worry for Michal squeezed a fist around her insides. "Must be some deeply holy Consecration they're planning, if the Presque Mort are invited. They aren't known for being the best party guests."

Michal huffed a laugh as he pulled his boots on. "Especially not if your party includes poison." He rolled his neck, working out stiffness from their rock-hard mattress, and stood.

"Be careful tonight," Lore said, then immediately clenched her teeth. She hadn't meant to say it. She hadn't meant to *mean* it.

A lazy smile lifted his mouth. Michal sauntered over, cupped her face in his hands. "Are you *worried* about me, Lore?"

She scowled but didn't shake him off. "Don't get used to it."

A laugh rumbled through his chest, pressed against her own, and then his lips were on hers. Lore sighed and kissed him back, her hands wrapping around his shoulders, tugging him close.

It'd be over soon, so she might as well enjoy it while it lasted.

Despite Michal's warmth, Lore still felt like shivering. She could feel Mortem everywhere—the cloth of Michal's shirt, the stones in the street outside, the chipped ceramic of the mug on the windowsill. Even as her awareness of it grew, a steady climb over the last few months, she was usually able to ignore it, but Pierre's unexpected foxglove had thrown her off balance. Mortem wasn't as thick here on the outskirts of Dellaire as it was closer to the Citadel—closer to the Buried Goddess's body far beneath it, leaking the magic of death—but it was still enough to make her skin crawl.

The Harbor District, on the southern edge of Dellaire, was as far as Mortem would let her go. She could try to hop a ship, try to trek out on the winding roads that led into the rest of Auverraine, but it'd be pointless. The threads of Mortem would just wind her back, woven into her very marrow. She was tied into this damn city as surely as death was tied into life, as surely as the crescent moon burned into the bottom curve of her palm.

Michal's mouth found her throat, and she arched into him, closing her eyes tight. Her fingers clawed into his hair, and his arm cinched around her waist like he might lift her up, carry her to their mattress on the floor, make her forget that this was something finite.

The fact that she *wanted* to forget was enough to make her push him away, masking it as playful. "You don't want to be late."

He lingered at her lips a moment before stepping back. "I'll see you tonight, then."

She just smiled, though the stretch of her lips felt unnatural.

Michal left, that same step squeaking on his way down, the windows rattling when he closed the door. Lore heard Elle heave a sigh, as if her brother's job were a personal affront, the thin walls making it sound like she was right next to Lore instead of all the way on the first floor.

Lore stood there a moment, the light of the slow-rising sun gleaming on her hair, the worn silk of her gown. Then she dressed in a flowing shirt and tight breeches, made her own way down the stairs. She had a meeting with Val to attend.

Elle was curled up on the couch again, a ragged paperback novel in one hand and another mug of tepid tea in the other. She eyed Lore the way you might look at something unpleasant you'd tracked in from the street. "And where are you going?"

## extras

"Oh, you didn't hear? I received an invitation to the Sun Prince's Consecration. I wasn't going to go, but rumor has it there might be an orgy afterward, and I can't very well turn that down."

Elle rolled her eyes so hard Lore was surprised she didn't strain something. "There is something deeply *off* about you."

"You have no idea." Lore opened the door. "Bye, Elle-Flower."

"Rot in your own hell, Lore-dear."

Lore twiddled her fingers in an exaggerated wave as the door closed. Part of her would miss Elle when the spying gig was up, when Val had a different running outfit she wanted watched instead of Gilbert's.

But not as much as she'd miss Michal.

She couldn't miss either of them for long. People came and went; her only constants were her mothers—Val and Mari—and the streets of Dellaire she could never leave.

That, and the memories of a childhood she was always, always trying to forget.

With one last glance at the row house, Lore started down the street.